Also By the Author

The Menmenet Mysteries
The Jackal of Inpu
The Lion of Bastet
The Bull of Mentju

The Founding Fathers Mysteries
Murder at Mount Vernon

The Pirates of Khonoë Series
Hyperkill

THE BULL OF MENTJU

A Menmenet Alternate History Mystery

Robert J. Muller

Poesys Associates

San Francisco

To the Nations: you know who you are.

And I should like to be able to love my country and still love justice. I don't want
any greatness for it, particularly a greatness born of blood and falsehood. I want
to keep it alive by keeping justice alive.
Albert Camus, Resistance, Rebellion and Death: Essays

People will not look forward to posterity who never look backward to their
ancestors.
Edmund Burke, Reflections on the Revolution in France

Behold, Seteh the wretched returns.
He has returned in order to rob with his hand.
He thinks of seizing violently
as if he were as he used to be.
When destroying the sites,
when tearing down their temples,
when uttering screams in the sanctuaries,
He has inflicted grief, he has repeated hurt,
he has caused isft to come into being again.
The Rite of Overthrowing Seteh and His Confederates
The Ritual Books of Pawerem

Reality is that which, when you stop believing in it, doesn't go away.
Philip K. Dick

North America

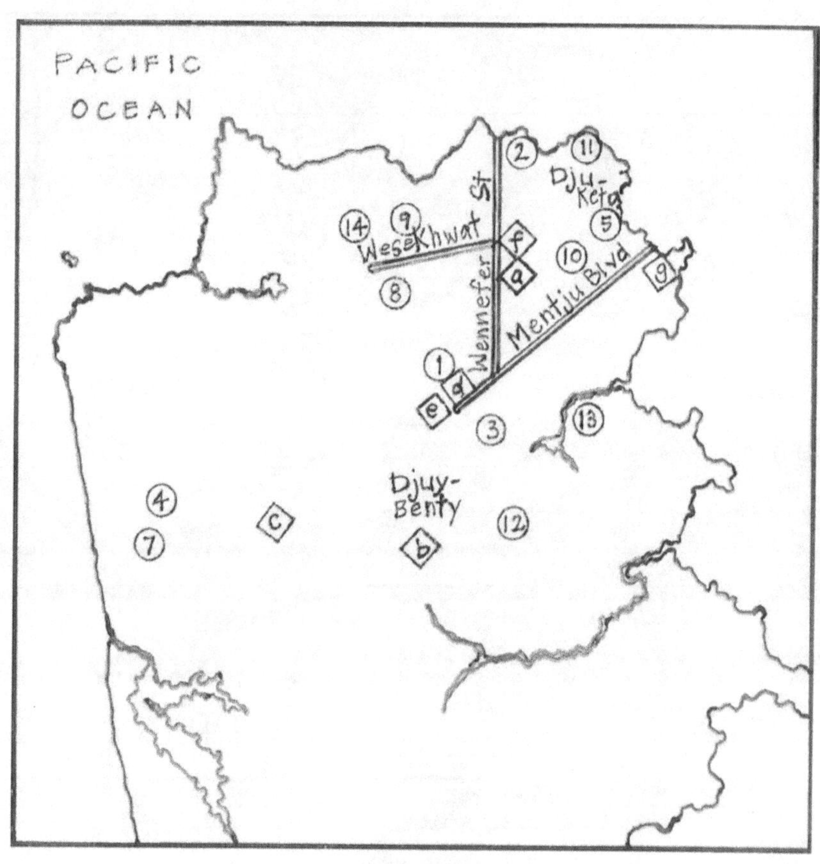

Menmenet

Key

Temples

a Bastet
b Imen-R'a
c Inpu
d Ma'at
e Mentju
f Sekhmet-Hut-Her
g Seteh

Locations

1 City Palace
2 Ferry Terminal
3 MacIntyre's Apartment
4 Necropolis
5 Neferti Restaurant
6 Nekhen's House
7 Nekhen's Tomb
8 Nesimen's House
9 Palace of the Republic
10 Per'ankh Restaurant
11 Shesmu's House
12 U. S. Embassy
13 Wenmyt Restaurant
14 Yaotl's Palace

CHAPTER ONE

MacIntyre Falls Off a Cliff

CHERYL MACINTYRE MOVED FROM HAPPY to pissed off to a state of incandescent rage, all in the space of an hour of her working afternoon.

MacIntyre had hunted and pecked her way through the case report on a nasty pair of murders. "Dispute" was the accepted police-report term for the wholesale butchery when the Aztec and Russian gangs threw bullets at each other. Both Aztecs and Russians excelled at disputation. She felt she had done a fine piece of work there, and she even took pleasure in writing the report about it for once. Many bad people were going away for a long time. A hard-working hutyt-er-semetyu could take strong satisfaction in a case like this.

"MacIntyre! In the office, now!" Her boss, Idnu Djehutymes, must want to congratulate her.

Her smile was genuine as she put the computer into secure mode, got up, and headed for the idnu's office. She walked past vacant cubicles; the other semetyu were out doing actual work. She stepped into Mes's office. Mes sat at his desk, and another man sat in one of the office chairs, an American from the look of him.

"Shut the door."

This was not a good sign. In MacIntyre's experience with him, Mes liked the noise of his admonitions to be audible to the team, management theory be damned. Usually he waited to deliver his speech until everyone was back in the office, writing up their day of toil. That way, they could all get the full benefit of the lecture he delivered to the chosen sacrifice of the day. She was it today. But he must have something more on his mind than the usual lecture, since there was no one around to hear it. She thought back over the case and found nothing that was likely to have gotten his ire up. Well, there was that incident with the Russian slug and the Taser. That could be it. She had gone a bit outside the rules on that one.

"MacIntyre, this is the United States Consul General, John Smith." Mes's voice was flat and noncommittal.

She smiled and said in English, "Seriously? John Smith?"

John Smith frowned, but said, "Sergeant."

"It's hutyt, Mr. Brown, hutyt-er-semetyu. Sorry, Smith." She smiled. MacIntyre hated the guy on sight. She felt disgust just looking at his sour American face behind his little, round glasses. She could tell from the lines on his face he spent much of his time frowning.

Mes frowned too, but then that was his natural expression.

"MacIntyre. You're fired," he said.

She blinked. "I'm sorry?"

"Sit down."

"Why, if I'm fired? I'm going to dinner, I'm hungry." The queasiness in her stomach wasn't hunger, though.

"Sit down, now!"

His eyes weren't meeting hers. This was another bad sign. Mes always confronted things. He looked you in the eye while berating your stupidity or lack of discipline.

"MacIntyre. Cheryl. This is hard." Now, Djehutymes was the crustiest, least-tolerant supervisor in the whole department. "Touchy-feely" was a swear word to him. MacIntyre knew this was not good; this was a bright red flag.

She sank into the straight-backed chair in front of his desk. He had his hands folded, eyes staring down at them. He raised his eyes to hers.

"I have been instructed," he began, then stopped. He tried again. "Mr. Smith is here because you're American, with a United States passport."

"So what?"

He shrugged irritably. "You're fired because you're American."

MacIntyre stared, uncomprehending.

"American? So what?"

"Don't you read the papers?"

"No, I only read the online conspiracy sites. You can't believe anything you read in the paper. Come on, the president had a bad dinner and blamed it on the hekasepat? Now you're firing all Americans?" The papers obsessed over the details of the incident involving Our Glorious Leader, the democratically elected head of state of the Ta'an-Imenty Republic. John Smith regarded her with unblinking eyes behind his gold wire-rim glasses.

"MacIntyre. He didn't just blame the hekasepat, he threw him out the back door of the White House like garbage. No offense, Mr. Smith."

The unblinking eyes didn't blink as Smith stared at them.

"Do you know what NATO is, MacIntyre?"

"Sure, the North American Treaty Organization. The Numunuu Empire, the Plains Federation, and the U. S. playing war games with tanks and toy soldiers in the desert."

"The government doesn't think they're games anymore, MacIntyre. The Temple of Mentju worries about isfet and going to war. So the hekasepat mentioned it over wine and steak and the President threw him out."

"How does that have anything to do with catching murderers, Mes?"

"It doesn't, except that Remetjet are getting irrational, which you know is like blood in the water. The politicians—and in particular the haty'a—are getting even more irrational than the people that voted for them. So you're fired. Isfet."

The American Consul General didn't know what that meant. "What is 'isfet'?"

Mes explained. "Isfet is the chaos, irrationality, and criminality that the god Seteh brings into the world. It's our primary job to fight it as w'abu of Ma'at."

MacIntyre brought the conversation back to the point. "Americans can be irrational too, trust me on this one. And my being American means what, I'm undermining the Republic? I'm meat to the sharks? Anyway, I'm a citizen of the Republic too."

Mr. Smith stirred. "Your being American means we can help you, Sergeant. The United States commits to helping its citizens wherever they might be in the world."

Djehutymes glared at him. "Don't interrupt! MacIntyre, it all trickles down."

"Until it pisses on me?" MacIntyre was tapping her foot with impatience. "That's not irrational, that's stupid. Power." She laughed without humor. "All the power I wield wouldn't light up a light bulb."

"No doubt." He straightened up. "You're still fired. Gun and badge, please."

She stood and eased the requested objects from her holster and pocket and deposited them on his desk, squaring them up in front of him. The feeling in the pit of her stomach enlarged, and her rage grew.

Mr. Smith said, "If you need any kind of help, I'm here."

MacIntyre scorned this offer. "The last help I got from an American was a ticket out of the place. I don't need any more, thanks." She turned back to her ex-boss. "Thanks for everything, Mes, you know how much I appreciate this special attention."

"Cheryl, please." The idnu's voice was gentle, but his eyes were as cold as ever.

"I know, you're doing what you're told. I don't think that always works out all that well, Mes. Doing what you're told leads to isfet, not ma'at."

"Could be you're right, could be not. You can complain to the haty'a, but I don't think it will do any good." He shrugged.

She mirrored his shrug and put some extra into it as the rage took hold. She didn't trust herself to speak and walked out, leaving Mes and Mr. Smith to console one another.

The window of MacIntyre's small third-floor apartment opened onto a quiet street in the middle of the city of Menmenet. It was quiet the same way many of the streets were quiet in Menmenet. They meandered around or dead-ended in blank walls of Remetjy houses. Her apartment building on the edge of the American district catered to American tastes. Its windows looked onto the street, the exact reverse of the typical Remetjy house. And yet, the mix of different facades made for a quiet ambience. She'd learned to love those streets in the last ten years. She'd even explored several interesting places to see outside of Menmenet, the capital city of the Ta'an-Imenty Republic on the West Coast of North America.

She'd learned to love the fog, natural air conditioning. She'd learned to love the people with their relaxed attitudes, loose clothes, and sandals. She'd learned to love the not-American ways of thinking.

MacIntyre gazed out her window at the quiet street, late in the afternoon of the day Djehutymes had fired her. The rage grew. She turned away from the quiet of the street to the quiet of her empty apartment and sat at her kitchen table, trying not to cry from the rage.

She hated the murderers in Menmenet. But that was—had been—her job: tracking them down and putting them in prison for life. She was a hutyt-er-semetyu on the homicide squad of the Menmenet medjau. It was that sense of ma'at, balance in the universe, that had made her join the medjau in the first place. A scum Aztec lowlife had raped and murdered her wonderful lover R'aia, the most exquisite woman she had ever loved. It was why she had taken the oath of Ma'at, the goddess of justice, to become a priestess, a w'abet of Ma'at, even though she didn't believe in the religion. And she'd become a citizen of the Ta'an-Imenty Republic. Any person with a serious intent to rise in the medjau hierarchy had to be a priest and a citizen.

And she had that serious intent. She had impulsively run from her controlling parents in Boston. Her lover was raped and murdered. Then she took three bullets from a bank robber while on patrol. She needed to be in charge, not a victim. She'd worked her way off patrol, out of the desk job they put her in after the shooting, and up to the rank of hutyt-r-semetyu. She had been looking forward to taking the idnu's exam soon.

Now, the future was bleak. They had fired her. She felt as though they had thrown her off a cliff she didn't even know was there. American. Fired for being an American, even though she was now a citizen of the Republic. Fired for being an American.

Nothing she could imagine came close to this, and her rage knew few bounds as she fell off the mind-cliff.

MacIntyre drummed her fingers on her kitchen table, rage flowing. She hadn't pounded a table in years, ever since leaving her Boston home. This was partly because of self-control gained over years of medjat training and partly because of the memory of the broken hand she took onto the plane out of Boston. Table-pounding had its merits, but mostly it was a waste of energy with too long a recovery time.

MacIntyre saw herself as a strong, autonomous woman. After years of working as a medjat, she'd polished her emotional armor to where nothing got under her skin. But this was like a snakebite. She needed help.

She picked up her phone and called Shesmu, the man she depended on for emotional support, food, and sex. Shesmu would come and comfort her, help her past her rage, feed her, make love to her, and make her feel good about herself again.

This romantic haze lasted less than two seconds after he picked up.

CHAPTER TWO

Shesmu Loses a Friend

I LOOKED AROUND ME, THE restaurant kitchen coming together nicely as we started the night's work. The *opening* night's work. If you haven't started a new restaurant and lived in the kitchen for weeks, you have no idea what was going on with me. Opening night! The Wenmyt was going live!

There were no guests yet, but the kitchen blasted with action and noise, everyone straining to get things just right even though it was the first time for everything. These were all experienced line cooks, and my sous chef, Khay, had worked with me and my best friend Sebek for several years at the Neferti, my other restaurant. I'd asked him to join me here, pissing off Sebek a little by stealing his sous chef, because I knew I needed somebody I could trust. And I could trust Khay.

I stood by approvingly while he took one of the new line cooks through proper grilling technique. The man had worked in American restaurants but never in a Remetjy kitchen and didn't quite get the subtle shifts in heat required on the grill, which had wood and coals distributed in specific areas to get specific heats for different purposes. I knew the cook would get it, he just needed experience. I'd spent the last few weeks training everyone and working with them to get the kitchen into shape. I'd probably been too harsh with some; we'd soon see who would last and who would quit and who would be shown the door.

My restaurant manager, Webkhet, rushed around the front of the house, occasionally bringing her wait staff into the kitchen to show them how to do something. I had finally progressed to the point in my career where I could hire the top professionals in Menmenet. Webkhet had jumped at the chance to manage the restaurant when I first started looking around for staff. The name of the restaurant, the Wenmyt, came from an epithet for the Kemet delta cobra goddess Wadjet—the devouring flame that consumed the enemies of the empire. We specialized in the delta foods that used a grill and other flame cooking techniques. I was already feeling as though the name were prophetic: the flame was devouring me.

A true firestorm of work, hard work, not all of which got done over the last two weeks. But we were opening, so all that was behind, and now the real work began. Some of my friends, MacIntyre included, had urged me to take a break after leaving my previous restaurant, the Per'ankh, in the hands of my sous chef, but I couldn't help myself—I needed to be running a restaurant, tired as I was. I still owned the Neferti and the Per'ankh, I just didn't want to run them, I wanted —needed—something new. Sebek and Henutsenu, good friends, had told me I was easily bored, but I felt the pull of new things coming from a deeper place than boredom.

I always found the energy when I needed it, but having a great safety net felt good. Webkhet and Khay were my insurance that it would all get done, and done well. But I still had the urge to dive in and do everything, to get the details just right. I had to force myself to step back and look on as the team came together. That's actually harder work than doing the work itself, at least for me.

My phone beeped with a text message. I didn't need any bad news about non-deliveries tonight. What I got was worse. The text from Tuy was short and horrifying: "hi shesmu - khenmes missing and feared dead - sorry." I stepped to the back of the kitchen, reading the message again. The kitchen noise disappeared as my heart absorbed the message. Khenmes dead?

Tuy was Khenmes's wife, and Khenmes was a very old friend of my family's. When my father died, Khenmes stepped in as a surrogate father. Last I'd heard, he was living in Washeshu and doing quite well. I called Tuy rather than texting her back. I stood in a corner of the loud kitchen, finger plugging my other ear.

"Hello? Shes?" Her voice sounded as though she were right next door.

"Yes. I just got your text. What in the world has happened?"

"We don't know, Shes." She was sounding very sad. "I've started getting in touch with all his friends, anybody that might know something."

"What happened?"

"He didn't come home a couple of days ago, and nobody's heard from or seen him since. The police here haven't found anything at all. Have you heard from him?"

"No, nothing, not for weeks."

"Oh."

"Are you OK?"

"Not really. You know? Not really." She gulped. Waashiw people had the reputation of being stoic and reserved, but in my experience they warmed up pretty quickly once you got to know them. I'd known Khenmes and Tuy most of my life.

Khenmes was a friend of my father's, younger than him but a good deal older than me. He was a Waashiw, the First Peoples tribe that occupied the little country called Washeshu to the east of the Republic. He was in his late fifties and enjoying being back in his own country after years spent fooling around with us Remetjy in Menmenet. He'd moved back to his great Washeshu lake, Da'owaga'a, after my mother died. His Waashiw wife Tuy would have made a great surrogate mother if I hadn't had a perfectly good one of my own. But then my mother died, and Tuy took that on too for a little while before she moved back to her country with her husband.

Now Khenmes was gone. His disappearance hit me just like with my father dying, so many years ago. *Just* like my father, who vanished and was presumed dead. And my mother, who died of grief—at least, that's what my 10-year-old heart thought. I'd felt abandoned then, I felt it more now with Khenmes going missing and possibly dead. Too much death, and I couldn't even revere my father's mummy to compensate for it all: there wasn't one.

I stumbled over my response. "Is there, can I, what can I do to help?" My voice was shaking.

"Well…if it's not too much to ask, we're getting together a death ceremony, at the lake. Can you come? Do you have a passport? The more friends, the more power, at least that's what the demomili says."

"What's a demomili?"

"Oh, sorry—he's the shaman, the medicine man."

Shamans weren't really my pot of beer. I'm a restaurateur. I had incredible amounts of work to do to open my new restaurant, but I had no choice but to help. Khenmes and Tuy were family. No choice at all.

"Yes, I'll come and add my power."

"Oh, good." Tuy sounded pleased. "It's scheduled for two days from now, here at the lake."

"I'll be there tomorrow, we can talk then and see what's what." I was rapidly recalculating the four-hundred-and-thirty-six tasks I needed to do between now and tomorrow, knowing it would all get done somehow. I had to be there.

"Thank you, Shes, thanks." Then she was gone.

The time I'd had with Khenmes was intense. It was Khenmes who taught me how to handle bullies, Khenmes who showed up for my ball games with my mom, Khenmes who taught me how to act, how to be a good man. After he went back to his lake, I missed him for years while I grew into manhood without him. I'd heard from him occasionally, visited him at the lake a few times, but we'd both grown away from each other; yet here I was, feeling like I'd been hit by a collapsing building. I stood there, stunned, holding my phone. Losing Khenmes, this couldn't be happening. It felt like my father dying all over again. I looked at the same kitchen, the same line cooks, but I saw none of it, I only saw Khenmes.

My phone rang. I let it ring awhile, then, exasperated, I answered without rational thought: "What!?"

"What the fuck is wrong with you, you jerk!"

MacIntyre. My heart unfroze and thought began again, but it was a little late. I read her mind over the phone: explosive anger at my completely insensitive and hopelessly unromantic greeting.

"Sorry, Cheryl, sorry. There's, it's, a lot going on here."

A little silence, then she said, "Humph. Well, I called because I need your help."

"No!" This came out involuntarily despite my heart working again.

"What do you mean no." Her tone was dangerous again, the short phrase an anger-charged statement, not a question.

"I mean…Do you not realize it's opening night? At the Wenmyt? You know, the place you decided you didn't want to be tonight because you hate foodies and didn't want to be surrounded by them for a whole evening?"

More silence. "I forgot."

Khay was signaling me from the cold station, something going wrong. I held up a finger, rigid, not looking at him.

"You forgot. OK, you forgot. Why are you calling?"

"I need to talk with you, it's bad, it's personal. I know it's a lot to ask but can you come?"

"Now is not the time. No, I can't come. Why would you even *think* that I could come?" I could hear the words punching their way out of my mouth, and I regretted them, but I couldn't stop them.

"Can I come there? I really need help, the kind of help you can give. *Only you.*" She was pleading. OK, that was not MacIntyre, somebody had taken over her body and heart and was talking to me on the phone.

"OK, come here, yes. Maybe I can get some time, I'll make the time somehow." I used what little power of rational thought I had left and said, "I love you."

"I'll be there in ten minutes. I love you too, sort of." Her anger hovered in the air over my phone after she disconnected. More anger than usual. This should be interesting, I thought to myself. Then my heart went back to Khenmes and Tuy, but Khay's frantic signals trumped even that—I'd deal with Khenmes and Tuy tomorrow, in Washeshu, but not here, not tonight. Opening night!

Webkhet had an intuition that reached into every corner of the restaurants she managed. It was why she was at the top of her profession in Menmenet. If there was something wrong, Webkhet was there dealing with it. She kept her hands off the kitchen workers, but everything else was fair game.

Within two minutes of MacIntyre's call, Webkhet was in the kitchen heading straight for me. I'd dealt with the recalcitrant cold station cook, and Khay had moved along the line to the next problem. I was standing leaning against the cold table, again thinking about Khenmes but wondering what I would say to MacIntyre when she got here.

"What's up, chef?"

I looked at my restaurant manager. Her large brown eyes in her middle-aged mother's face showed a depth and sympathy that nearly made me tear up.

"Webkhet. I need…some time. Time with my girlfriend."

"Now's not the time, chef." She smiled without meaning it.

"I didn't mean that, I meant she's coming here to talk to me about some personal thing she's got going."

"On opening night? I'll take care of it." Her eyes got a little fierce.

"No, I think I've got to talk to her. Can you keep things going for a few minutes? And—I just heard that an old friend has gone missing, maybe died, and I'll need to go to Washeshu tomorrow."

"Wa—" Her voice locked up. "You can't be serious."

"Very serious."

Her intuition kicked in again. "You're really hurting, aren't you?"

"Yeah. This old friend, he was—is—like a father to me."

She stared at me for a minute, then said, "We'll deal. But you've gotta get back here as soon as you can, ready to work, OK?"

"Guaranteed." One says these things so easily.

It was some little time later that I saw MacIntyre's face at the door to the prep room and I beckoned her over. We kissed, and I held her a little longer that might strictly have been necessary. There was a lot of very deliberate non-looking from the line.

I said, "I love you. What's wrong?"

"You can take the time?" She nodded sideways to indicate the loud kitchen.

"I have to, don't I?"

"Can we, is there…somewhere more private?"

I smiled. "No. Well, sort of." I led her over to the walk-in refrigerator, and we went in. I figured that not only would this be private enough, it would also have the ironically beneficial effects of cooling MacIntyre down and shortening up the time she needed from me. It was the only place in the restaurant that wasn't filled with people rushing around. She looked around and didn't see any of it, didn't even notice the cold; she was focused entirely on what was going on inside her.

"I was fired today."

"Fired?"

"They took my badge and gun." She was gripping my hands with hers, tightly, as she faced me and looked up into my eyes. "Mes told me I was dismissed because…."

Whatever it was, she couldn't get it out. A tear started trickling down her cheek, whether of pain or frustration or anger I didn't know.

"Cheryl…."

"Because I'm American." She rubbed away the tear with a furious wipe of the hand.

"That can't be right."

"It isn't right, it's totally wrong!" Her voice got louder as her anger took over from her pain.

I hugged her again while I thought about this development. American? What the fuck did being American have to do with getting fired from the medjau? My heart decided right then and there that I couldn't deal with this in addition to opening night and Khenmes missing or dead. And tomorrow I wouldn't even be here.

"Cheryl, something's come up, I have to go to Washeshu tomorrow."

"No, you don't. You have to help me through this." Her face nestled in my neck.

"I really have to, Cheryl. I have to go."

She stretched her neck back to look me in the eye. "Why?"

I let her go and stepped back. "An old family friend, he's gone missing and his wife is afraid he's dead. I need to go to help her."

"Why?" I could sense outrage in her question, and I wasn't sure I could convey what it all meant to me. I'd never really told her about my parents. I explained in some detail about Khenmes and my father dying and my mother dying. I told her how Khenmes missing and maybe dead affected me. I think she got it at some level, but she was hurting so much from being fired from her dream job that it didn't matter. I had to try something else.

"Maybe I can help," I said. "I know the idnuhaty'a, 'Aapehty, and he might be able to put in a good word with his boss the haty'a. They're in charge of every-thing about the city government, they ought to be able to intervene with the medjau and get you back in there. I'll get in touch with him the first thing tomorrow, before I leave, OK? He's pretty slimy, but he's my in to the city government."

"It's a start, I guess. OK. But being American, what can I do about that? I need to find out what's going on with that."

"I might be able to help with that too. You remember Karkin?"

She smiled for the first time, a small smile. "The mysterious Ramaytush?" She'd met him briefly after he'd killed some Russians who had her tied up and were ready to kill her. Karkin was a local, really local, a member of the tribelet that populated the Menmenet peninsula for hundreds of years before my people showed up and ruined the local oyster beds. He was also an international police-man with a secret portfolio that he kept very much to himself. But if there was something going on with Americans in Menmenet, he'd know all about it.

"Yes. He's plugged into everything, he can help you understand what's going on. Here's his number, give him a call." I dug out a dog-eared business card that Karkin had given me last year and gave it to her.

"Thanks," she said. "It's a start."

We embraced again, then I mumbled into her neck, "I need to go."

"Tomorrow. Come home with me, come to bed. Now. I need you. I need to be warm."

I rubbed her back and imagined a night of bliss and knew I couldn't do it. I needed to be warm too, but it would be from the grills, not from her body.

I said, "Stay, have dinner at the chef's table, we can talk some more, but I've got to work, it's opening night, and I'm leaving for Washeshu tomorrow. I'll be here most of the night. You can stay."

I tried. It wasn't good enough, I could see that. She needed more than I could give.

MacIntyre pushed me away, glared at me briefly, then turned and walked out into the kitchen. She looked around and found the chef's table over at the side of the room in a little niche we'd constructed for it. She marched over to the table, grabbed a pot and spoon from a rack nearby, then climbed up on the table and started banging. The kitchen fell silent. Webkhet dashed in through the kitchen doors and skidded to a halt.

"Hey, everyone," said MacIntyre in a loud medjat voice. "You don't know me, I'm Shesmu's girlfriend. I just wanted to say, before I go, that I think Shesmu is the best damn chef in the world, and he deserves to have you make this the best damn opening night he's ever had. Am I right?"

The line cooks—line cooks tend not to be very inhibited—the line cooks shouted "Fucking right" in four different languages.

"So give him everything he wants. He likes this place better than sex! I'll check in later to make sure you've given him the best orgasm of his career! If not, I'll come back and lock the doors and burn this place to the ground! OK?"

She tossed the pot and spoon to the floor, jumped down from the table, stalked out of the kitchen past Webkhet, and didn't look back. The kitchen erupted in sound as the line cooks chattered and got back to work.

Webkhet walked over to me, put her hand on my shoulder, looked at me with compassion in her eyes, and said, "I think she's pissed."

CHAPTER THREE

The System Humiliates MacIntyre

THE NEXT MORNING, MACINTYRE SAT at her kitchen table, naked, sipping a cup of very hot instant coffee, looking out at the grey blanket of fog that filled the space of her window. The coffee tasted terrible, but it was the only stimulant in the apartment. The sleepless night following her speech to the line cooks at the Wenmyt required stimulation to relieve her depression. She finished the coffee and got dressed, then puttered around her apartment cleaning things that she had never cleaned since she acquired them. She wasn't really much of a housekeeper. Then she sat at the big bay window and looked out at the busy street below, cultivating her anger at her plight, picking out probable criminals from the passers-by, and speculating on what crimes they had committed in the last day or two.

At about 11 am, just after she'd convinced herself that the little old lady with the walker crossing the street against the light was a serial murderer, Shes texted her that he had made an appointment for her at 1 pm with the idnuhaty'a, who would be overjoyed to meet her and take on her problems as a favor to his favorite chef. Life was looking up! Maybe it really was just an old lady with a walker and a death wish, not a serial murderer.

She reconsidered the Muse t-shirt and the raggedy short-shorts she had put on. Not quite right for the idnuhaty'a. So she picked out some reasonable Remetjy business clothes. Remetjy businesswomen dressed pretty well, unlike the American businesswomen MacIntyre had known in her short stints in the Boston financial district. She put together a combo with a form-fitting white top with a crossover strip between her breasts and a mid-calf white sheath skirt with a rose edge diagonally across the fold in front. She wore her dress sandals, the ones she kept in the back of her closet for special occasions so they'd look like she had purchased them recently.

She headed out to the City Palace for her appointment. As she was leaving her apartment, she felt something missing and realized that in the process of creating her new look she had forgotten her pin: a single silver feather, representing her status as a w'abet of Ma'at. Even fired, she couldn't go out without that; Ma'at wouldn't approve. She nearly laughed; maybe she was more religious than she thought she was. They could fire you from the medjau, but the oath of Ma'at was permanent. She went back and pinned it over her right breast.

Her apartment was within walking distance from the Temple of Ma'at and her ex-office, which was within walking distance of the City Palace. It was a fine day for Menmenet, not too foggy and not at all hot, so she walked. All this finery plus her blonde hair and blue eyes generated quite a few second glances from passersby as she walked over to the Palace.

The City Palace was as grandiose a building as any palace in Kemet. A lot of tax money and disaster relief funding had changed hands to build it after the big earthquake in 1906 knocked down the previous, much more restrained palace. The new palace had about 200 lotus columns and large brass metal doors all over the place. These days most of the doors stayed locked and barred for security reasons after the incident 10 years ago when a Numunuu separatist group had entered in force and shot the place up pretty good before the medjau showed up. Now you couldn't park in front of the Palace because of the blast barriers to prevent car bombings. MacIntyre eyed all this with professional interest as she walked in the front door and went through the security checkpoint. Slack, but not so slack that they'd miss a gun or a knife. She looked for the traces of the bullets that had pocked up the murals, but found none: evidence of the true diligence of the Menmenet government.

She took the elevator up to the third floor and walked down the massive hallway (100 more columns) to the idnuhaty'a's office. The secretary looked her up and down and said, in English, "You must be Ms. MacIntyre. The idnuhaty'a is expecting you, go right in." It was the first time in a long time she'd heard the title "Ms." It felt kind of odd, not having the authority granted by her job title, hutyt-er-semetyu, and being addressed with the American title in English. Now, she was just another immigrant looking for a favor.

Idnuhaty'a 'Aapehty stood near a chair looking expectant. He smiled and said, "Ah, Ms. MacIntyre, a pleasure. You are truly as beautiful as the sun itself!" He indicated the chair across from his, and they both took seats.

'Aapehty was a large man. His largeness occupied the broad direction, not the tall direction. He had puffy, fleshy features and thick lips, and his skin had a slightly unhealthy looking pallor to it, as though he had mistakenly spent too much time under fluorescent lights thinking they were tanning lights. His sharp and predatory eyes looked out under thick eyebrows, and his bald head gleamed in the office lighting, fat wrinkles cascading down his neck.

MacIntyre knew she wasn't beautiful. She knew some beautiful women. She liked to think on a good day she had some nice-looking qualities; perhaps some might think her "striking;" but her nose was too prominent and her smile was too wide to be called beautiful, at least according to Remetjy standards. This man radiated good will, behind which lurked any number of lubricious demons. This fanciful metaphor had her smiling despite herself. She imagined the goddess Ma'at nudging her from within; judgment made but withheld.

"I'm very grateful you agreed to hear me out, sir," she said.

"Yes, yes. But first, would you care for a libation?" He waved a hand at what looked like a full bar over in the corner. The only thing missing was a pool table.

"Um, sure." She thought a moment, then pushed a pawn. "Do you have any bourbon?"

"Ah, good American whiskey. Certainly, certainly." He rose and waddled over to the bar. "Ice?" he asked.

"No thanks, straight up." He smiled and poured out double measures of the golden liquid into two glasses.

She tasted, remembering similar tastings courtesy of her father: barrel-aged and small-batch, not the blended stuff. Very nice. It meant he was a connoisseur. It was one of her father's more annoying qualities. And it meant that 'Aapehty didn't disapprove of American things on principle.

"To Menmenet," she toasted. He joined her with a big gulp of bourbon and smiled, swallowing.

"Shes said you were having some problems and asked me to see what I could do for you. May I call you Cheryl?"

A smooth operator, definitely. He'd found out about her before she arrived, and probably not from Shes. "Certainly, sir." Put him in his place.

"Cheryl, what a beautiful name. American women's names are so much smoother on the tongue than Remetjet names, just like this wonderful distillation." He licked his lips and sipped bourbon.

Geez, this was heavy going. Better get to the point.

"Well, sir, yesterday the medjau fired me. I understand that it has something to do with my being American, even though I'm a citizen of the Republic. They really didn't give me a chance to understand the situation and respond."

He grimaced. "I see. How terrible! You would think the medjau commanders would have more common sense. And I understand you are quite a valuable asset to your department." He swirled the bourbon in his glass and looked at it with a smile. "It would appear that the political environment is not the best right now for Americans here."

"No, I understand that, sir, but Ma'at must be respected, and firing me is not going to help with that."

"You must understand, Cheryl, that sometimes things have to happen that don't appear on the surface to be fair."

The rage rolled over inside her at this patronizing statement. She stamped it down. "Sir, I was thinking that if you could just put in a good word for me with the haty'a, and if I could meet with him and explain that I'm completely loyal to the Republic, we could all go home and do our jobs."

"Yes, yes, I see." He pondered and took another swig of bourbon. "I *could* do that, of course, but I would be expending some *precious* political capital to do it, you know, my dear. More than just a little, too, the political situation with America being what it is." He looked at her, expectantly.

"I could probably afford a few hundred debenu, if that would help out." She smiled knowingly, or at least tried her best. She imagined her wallet filled with debenu, another fantasy that would soon be dispelled when called upon to supply them to this cretan. Without a job, debenu were going to be rare beasts in her wallet. But no, he had something else in mind.

"No, no, no, nothing like that, you misunderstand me." He smiled rather greasily in return. "I could never accept a monetary gift from a city employee and w'abet of Ma'at, it wouldn't be, well, ma'at." He wriggled, that was the only word for it. "No. No, I just thought, perhaps, that you might consider having dinner with me and spending a wonderful evening talking and enjoying ourselves. It is vital, after all, for the higher ups in our city to understand and appreciate—" Here he looked her up and down. "—appreciate *fully* the true worth and quality of those who uphold our laws."

MacIntyre realized the sad truth. Sleep with him and she'd be on her way back to her job. Maybe, maybe she'd be on her way. Maybe. She wasn't worth anything to him beyond what any common prostitute could give him. She looked at him without expression. She considered chopping his balls off then cutting his tongue out, but neither action would get her job back. She noticed she was tapping a finger on the arm of her chair and folded her hands in her lap. She wasn't really very good at handling frustration. Violating the human rights of this cretan wouldn't help. She was a little disturbed that she had even thought about it. Too angry, she thought.

But this was, after all, a delicate situation. It called for diplomacy rather than military action. Yes. Control. Yes. She knocked back the rest of the bourbon in her glass, then said, "Oh, I wouldn't want you to do that much for me, sir, certainly not. Political capital is precious, and to spend it so freely for someone with no power or influence such as myself would be both unwise and imprudent. Don't you think?"

He looked at her and grinned. "No, I think it would be extremely pleasurable to give you everything you want, Cheryl. *Everything.* And of course nothing would get back to Shesmu, a truly wonderful chef, but not a terribly perceptive man. Would you care for another drink?"

She considered upping her bid to a few thousand debenu, or going to look for a knife at the bar, but looking at his hungry eyes, she knew no amount of money would divert him, and she didn't need a knife. What she needed was dignity and respect, and she wasn't going to get it from this humiliating lecher or from the bar. The extremity of this thinking made her pause; should she reconsider and just do it? She needed that job. She looked at him and saw impossibility.

"No, thank you, sir. I'm sorry, sir, I just don't think an evening as you imagine it would work out well." She shook her head and smiled at him, as warmly as she could. She crossed her legs and her arms, a little body language never hurt. The bourbon warmed her nicely, diffusing her anger into what remained of her hope.

He smiled back, though not as warmly. "I see. Well, I truly wish I could help, Ms. MacIntyre, I truly do, but I don't see how. The haty'a is very busy, very busy indeed, Ms. MacIntyre, and a matter, a *settled* matter like this, you know—we really can't interfere with internal medjau operations. No, we certainly can't do that, Ms. MacIntyre." He pouted a little, then rose. "So, if there's nothing else?"

Though her inclination still ran toward a swift front-kick to a vulnerable spot, she restrained herself, rose and bowed, and said, "Thank you for seeing me, sir." After all, there were bridges here. Important bridges, bridges that should not burn down to the water line. Control. Yes. Control. She curled her fingers, fingernails digging into her palm, the mild pain deflecting her from the possibility of inflicting major pain out of humiliation and rage.

'Aapehty bowed graciously and replied, "Please—feel free to come see me anytime, should you have more to offer me. It has truly been a pleasure seeing you. A true pleasure indeed."

As she walked out of the idnuhaty'a's office, she considered several alternate wordings for the text she was going to send to Shes, telling him how well his suggested in to the City Palace had worked out and how much the idnuhaty'a really respected him as a man. She settled on no text at all; she was too humiliated. She tasted the excellent bourbon at the back of her throat and swallowed the last of her hope.

MacIntyre stood in the long hallway for a few minutes, stewing about 'Aapehty's attempt to get her into bed or worse and thinking about how else she might get to the haty'a. Her phone rang, and she saw it was Shesmu. She ignored it. Later.

Getting to the haty'a turned out to be easy. The haty'a came to her, or at least passed right by. A bustle arose at the elevators down the hall, and Haty'a Kh'abekhnet emerged, striding forward with his entourage of aides beside him, heading for his office. MacIntyre stood against one wall while this group passed by, ignoring her. She stepped out into the hallway and followed the group down the hall.

The aides split off to their desks in the haty'a's outer office, and the haty'a stood for a moment talking with his secretary. MacIntyre stood in the doorway a moment, then as the haty'a went into his inner office, she strode quickly across and went in right after him and closed the door.

"Who the fuck are you?" said the startled Kh'abekhnet, swinging around at the noise of the door closing.

"If I could just grab you for a couple of minutes, honored lord," said MacIntyre, walking up to him and laying it on thick, "I'd like to tell you my story and see if you can help."

He looked over her shoulder at the closed door, then blurted, "You're American."

"Yep, that's right. That appears to be a problem right now." She reached in her pocket, and Kh'abekhnet flinched involuntarily and stepped back. She took out her card case and flipped it open. She didn't have a badge, but she did have her w'abet identification. She gave it to him.

He read it over. "MacIntyre, w'abet of Ma'at, hutyt in the medjau. Ah. I know who you are. Why the fuck are you in my office? You should be out looking for a new job, preferably in New York or someplace out there in America-land."

He strode over to his desk, tossed the card case on it, and sat down, swiveling to look at her with a stern expression. At this point, MacIntyre's diplomatic instincts, fragile and broken as they were, simply disappeared. She marched over to the desk and leaned on it, pushing her face toward his.

"Lookit, I've had about all I can take of authority figures today. I've just been propositioned by your idnu after being kicked out of my job by *my* idnu, and I'm not having any more."

Kh'abekhnet eyes twitched a little and his head pulled back into his neck. MacIntyre inferred that he wasn't confronted by angry American women much.

"What is it exactly that you want?" he asked.

"I want back into the medjau. You can't kick me out just like that, just for being American. Why did you, anyway? I'd really like to know." She leaned over and picked up her card case and put it back in her pocket, mainly so she wouldn't start pounding the desk.

"Who said I did that?"

"Me, I just did."

He stared at her angry face, moving his chair back slightly from the force of it. "Well, yes, I suppose I channeled the orders, but…" He caught himself up. "I won't put up with this from you, a fucking American! You can't bully us anymore, we won't stand for it." He stood up. "We can't afford to have people like you stirring up trouble in the bureaucracy and aiding and abetting the enemy." He backed away from the desk.

"I'm not the enemy, I'm a goddam citizen! Don't think you can bully me either, because you can't."

But she was wrong about that. The door behind her burst open and six rather burly security guards stumbled into the room, guns drawn.

MacIntyre faced them, put her hands up, and said, "OK, you got me, I surrender."

The haty'a put up a hand and said, "It's OK, boys, she's only a threat to herself. Get her out of here!" The guards warily moved toward her.

"I won't leave until I get an answer. Why did you have me fired?"

Kh'abekhnet screamed, "Get her out of here!"

"Come on, miss, you don't want us to get rough, now," said the gray-haired leader of the guards. His tone was fatherly. This, of course, was precisely what got

MacIntyre into trouble at home; she did not react well to fatherly advice to sit down and shut up like a good little girl. But restraint won out over rage and humiliation.

"OK," she said. "I'll leave. But before I do, I just want to say something." She turned back to the haty'a.

"What?" said the haty'a, looking gracious now that he thought she wasn't a threat.

"Fuck you and whatever god you worship. If any." There; that bridge quite satisfactorily burst into flames.

She turned and marched through the guards, who jostled each other as they comically tried to get through the door after her. She walked out through the anteroom and back to the big hallway. The older guard caught up and gripped her elbow.

"Let go." She looked at him and smiled with what she hoped was a disarming smile.

"Sorry, miss, I have to make sure you leave the building."

"Let go now or I'll rip your arm off and paint this nice wall with your blood." Her feelings welled up into a surge of humiliation that she had never before experienced. She restrained herself from assuming the Tae Kwon Do stance.

"Now, is that ladylike?" But he let go and calmly waved a hand at the elevator. "In my day, w'abut were a little more reasonable."

"Yeah, those ladies are all dead now of old age." She smiled, tension diminishing, aware that he was at least a little bit on her side. "Do you, personally, have any problems with Americans? Just curious."

He grinned and replied, "Just the one. Now, are you getting on the elevator with me?"

Her dislike of being in closed spaces under duress from father figures held her motionless until the gentle self-assurance of the older guard won through to her better self. She walked into the elevator with him. He showed her to the front of the building and waved goodbye as she went out. She stood on the street behind one of the concrete blast barriers, pondering the downward spiral of her life, telling the haty'a who could get her her job back to go fuck himself. She didn't even have the man she loved available to berate for it all. She got out her card case and extracted the card Shes had given her. Maybe Karkin would be some help. Or maybe she could just give *him* hell and relieve her feelings. Either way, it couldn't hurt.

CHAPTER FOUR

Shesmu Meets a Demomili

I STEPPED OFF THE PLANE at the Da'owaga'a airport with about 50 people of a certain age. I had come for information; they had come to throw their money away at the casinos, hotspots, and brothels that littered the streets of the three main towns in Washeshu. Recreational tourism was the main industry there, that and pine nuts. The silver and gold mines that funded the Waashiw government were farther east, out in the mountains and deserts. The Waashiw had found the casinos and the ski runs markedly more lucrative than the pine nuts or even the silver and gold. As it was summer, people were coming for the gambling rather than the skiing.

Da'owaga'a was a mountain city that actually circled the center of Waashiw life: the large lake of the same name. The ski areas surrounded the lake, but the Waashiw made sure the more disreputable industries stayed over the snowy mountains that ringed the lake. Despite the frenetic activities around the casinos and other recreation spots, the lake itself was sacred and quiet, and so were the Waashiw that lived around it.

The airport was to the north of the lake. It took about 30 minutes for the cab I snagged to get me down to the west side of the lake where Tuy and Khenmes had built their little house. During the long ride, I thought hazily back to the accolades heaped on our restaurant opening and fought to stay awake, having had no sleep at all during the evening, night, and day that followed. Then MacIntyre's exit from the kitchen popped up into my consciousness, and my eyes snapped open and my toes clenched as I considered the potential end of our relationship. I didn't want that to happen.

I took out my phone and called her, no answer. I left a voicemail telling her that I was sorry I couldn't be there and how much I cared what happened to her. I'd already texted her with an appointment to see 'Aapehty, and I hoped that would put her in a better mood about things. The text, that is; I didn't hold out much hope for 'Aapehty. Worth a try, though. MacIntyre, MacIntyre.... Since I'd set foot in Washeshu, my chest had been tight with anxiety, and my thoughts about MacIntyre didn't help.

The Waashiw taxi driver pulled up to the curb on the little street and looked dubiously at the tiny house. "You sure you want this address, bud? We're pretty far away from the action." He was speaking colloquial Remetjy, as many Waashiw did.

I smiled and said, "All the action is here. Just visiting friends. A death ceremony. Could you wait? I'll be continuing on to my hotel. Here's enough to cover everything." I handed him a 25-debenu note—in a town full of Remetjy tourists, the locals didn't hesitate to take the foreign currency.

"OK, it's your funeral." He grinned at his own joke, turned off his engine, put away the money, and settled back to wait for me.

It used to be that there were a few hundred Waashiw at the lake. Once civilization descended upon them and the pine nut business industrialized, the Waashiw population grew, and now you could actually find people who didn't know everybody around the lake. I'd visited several times, mostly for food service conventions held at various hotels, and Khenmes had kept me up on Washeshu doings and perspectives.

I walked up the little path to the door. Before I could knock, the door opened, and Tuy peered out at me. We hugged, a lingering, sad hug. Tuy was a small woman in her early fifties, the grey streaking her black hair. She had never been beautiful, at least by Remetjy standards, with her round face with the light tattoos on the chin and cheeks. She'd been crying.

She said, "I'm some glad you could come, Shesmu." She reached out and touched my face.

"I should go to my hotel and get settled, then come back for a talk."

"Hotel? I got your room all ready, you're staying here."

"I don't want to impose, you must be—"

"I need to have somebody around the house." The taxi driver was glad to take the money and run, and I put my suitcase on the bed in the small room I usually occupied on my infrequent visits.

"When is the ceremony?" I asked.

"5 p.m. at the dance hall."

In Washeshu, the "dance hall" didn't host wild disco or line dancing. The dance hall served as the religious center for the community, the place where Waashiw joined together in dances and ceremonies. I visited once in a droughty winter when the ski lodges worked with the local shamans to perform a snow dance. There was no snow on the slopes, and they hoped to engage the interest of the gods to help patch the holes in their revenue streams. I would bet that they had a dance to help the house win in the casinos too—they loved their dancing.

We walked out to the living area and sat on the couch. I asked, "How does the ceremony work?"

Tuy said, "It's kind of unusual because we don't actually know that he's dead, you know. But better to be safe than sorry when spirits might be involved."

I asked, "Did Khen—"

Tuy frantically interrupted me, her hands suddenly gripping my arm. "Don't say his name!"

"What?"

"His name, his name. Don't say it!"

"I don't—"

"Shes, I thought you knew. If you speak the name of the dead person, you call the spirit. Never a good thing, never, to call a spirit. All kinds of bad things can happen. Just say 'he' and we'll know who you mean."

"Huh. With us it's the reverse: A Remetjy speaks the name of the dead to make the dead person come alive in the afterlife. If the name disappears, so does the ka."

Tuy closed her eyes and teared up. To give her time, I stood up from the couch and walked over to the window and looked out at the peaceful lake shimmering in the summer sun. Washeshu, Da'owaga'a. Nothing bad ought to happen in a place this beautiful. But something had.

"What happened? To 'him.'"

Tuy looked miserable. "I don't know. He just vanished."

"No trips scheduled? No week-long drinking binges?" The idea almost made me laugh, remembering Khenmes's legendary sobriety.

"You know my old man, steady and reliable as an old pine tree."

My own eyes were prickly, and my chest was tight. I said, "He was always there for me as a kid, so were you."

Tuy smiled. "Who wouldn't be, you were so cute."

There is nothing a grown man dislikes more than being reminded of his cuteness when very small, but I guess she had a right to remember me that way. But those memories stirred the feelings of that cute five-year-old boy with a father gone missing.

"How did he know my dad?"

Lips pressed tight, she shook her head.

"Tuy?" I'd never asked her about my father, and my tight heart prompted me to ask more. "Why can't anyone tell me about my dad?"

"Don't press me, Shes. Please don't. I got reasons, good ones. It ain't up to me. I promised your mom. I can't talk about your dad." She changed the subject back to Khenmes. "I think he pissed off the we'muhu—the water babies."

I may not have known about names and spirits, but I did know about water babies. For a Waashiw to invoke the water babies was a serious thing indeed. They are creatures that live in the great lake, malignant spirits that when offended can destroy you. I think of them as the very embodiment of isfet, Seteh's creatures that spread evil and chaos in the world.

Khenmes once told me the Waashiw often attribute an early death to the influence of the water babies. He was warning me about not swimming in a certain part of the lake. I didn't think they were real, but the Waashiw knew they were, those water babies. That beautiful lake, just outside, frothed with evil and chaos ready to take you in a minute if you didn't watch your step.

I asked, "How would he have made the water babies mad at him, Tuy?"

"I don't *know*, Shes! But it must be that for him to just disappear!" She burst into tears. "He's gone, and it's gotta be the water babies!"

I tried a joke. "Water babies didn't get my dad, did they?"

She smiled, wiping her tears away with her palm. "That's all you know. I bet they got all the way down the mountain to the bay through the rivers and got him there. But I promised your mom. It's a promise I got to keep."

Her pain and worry needed relief. "Let's talk about something else, this is making you upset, and the ceremony is coming up." I'd have to follow up later, when things had settled down a bit, to find out more about what Khenmes was doing and what might have happened to him.

"Sorry, sorry. I'm just overwhelmed by it all."

I looked at the clock on the wall. "Time for the ceremony." But my mind was back in Menmenet with my mother, a little kid again wondering where Dad was, why he had never come back to us, why she wouldn't talk about him. This whole situation was like stumbling through a cave with no light at all.

* * *

We walked down to the lake, taking the long trail down to Tzlatlee Tosh, the beautiful little bay where the dance hall nestled among a massive grove of old pine trees. From the top of the slope, you could see the lake beyond stretched out to touch the snowy mountains that rimmed the lake to the East, and the little island in the middle of the bay beckoned with mysterious power. If there were water babies, I was pretty sure they were swimming near that island.

The dance hall was a large building decorated with the plants and symbols of power that represented the gods of nature that the Waashiw worshipped. I felt very far from the ancient gods of Kemet, though I knew they shared their powers with the gods of Washeshu. Nature is nature, gods are gods, and what you call them is just a matter of culture. Water babies aside, that is.

People began to arrive, and we went into the hall. The interior was illuminated only by a vented fire pit in the middle of the floor and by light coming in through clerestory windows along the sides of the building. Once you were inside, you could see nothing of the Sacred Pine Grove or Da'owaga'a, the lake, but you could feel their power surrounding us. You could smell the pine smoke and herbs burned there over the many years of its existence.

Tuy greeted various friends and relations, introducing me as she went. I tried to remember names, but as they were Waashiw names, I quickly lost track. Tuy translated for me.

The ceremonial dancers were a combination of friends of the family and dancers hired for the occasion. They straggled in and changed to their dancing clothes in the dressing rooms behind the main hall, then gathered around the fire pit. About half an hour before the scheduled start of the ceremony, the demomili arrived and changed into his regalia, then set up his tools around the fire. He was a very old man with long white hair, short and stout but still very powerful, with well-muscled arms and legs from long years of dancing. His face was a mass of tattoos and wrinkles.

I asked Tuy, "What happens in the ceremony?"

"It's kinda complicated, Shes, too much for right now, but it's got two main things going on: getting the water babies to leave him alone, and quieting his spirit so it leaves *us* alone." Tuy stared intently at the demomili, then looked at me. "I won't be able to translate once things get going, you'll just have to go with the flow. You know, clap when everybody claps, that kinda thing. It don't really matter, there's a lot of people here to pray."

"Do I need to do anything?"

"Pray for the spirit. I'm sure you have a helpful god or two you can call on?" She smiled.

"I can probably persuade a couple." Yep: Aset and Nebethut, the two Kites, the Remetjy gods that protected the dead on the way to judgment. Maybe they'd scare off the water babies along with all the other demons and nasty things one faced.

At 5 p.m. exactly, the demomili called the ceremony to order and got everybody arranged in the right place. The rest of us sat in a large circle around the pit, with the dancers in the middle. The demomili said something in Waashiw to the crowd, tossed an aromatic bundle of green into the fire pit, and the dance began with shamanistic chanting and drums.

It was really quite odd. Khenmes and I had gone to dance ceremonies here before, and it was interesting but I wasn't overwhelmed with religious ecstasy or anything. And yet…this one was different. As the minutes went by, I watched, clapped when other people did, and muttered the ritual invocations for Aset and Nebethut. Praying for me was an exercise in meditation, I didn't expect any result other than quieting my own anxious heart. And yet…there was something there. My chest, already tight, got tighter, crowded to bursting, as though I had eaten too much rich food. That actually happened fairly often, especially when I worked in the Per'ankh's very French kitchen in Menmenet, tasting everything that went out to the dining room. But this crowding just grew and grew. Sweat poured off me, it felt like the fire was right next to me. I guess I twitched or moaned, because Tuy put her hand on my arm.

"Shes? What's wrong?" she whispered.

"I…don't know. It's, it's very strange." I shut my eyes, it didn't help.

"Shes?"

I stood up, I had to get out and get some air. Something was very wrong here.

The demomili saw me. He shouted something in Waashiw, and the whole dance and ceremony went suddenly silent. He beckoned to me. I shook my head and pointed at the door. He beckoned again and took a couple of steps toward me, his face imperious and urgent.

Tuy stood up and pushed me toward him, then followed behind me. I stumbled up to the demomili, who stopped me by extending a hand to my chest. He jumped back and shook his hand as though he'd burned it. He said something.

Tuy said, "He wants to listen to your heart."

"How will he do that?"

"I don't know. Never happened before. Never."

"I … need air, I need to get out of here." I gasped with the heat.

Tuy spoke to the demomili, but he shook his head and pointed at my chest, and barked a word.

"Heart!" said Tuy. "Let him listen, Shes. Please!"

I was really past responding, but the demomili stepped up to me and carefully unbuttoned my shirt, then put an ear to my chest without quite touching it. The eagle feather in his headdress brushed my forehead, tickling. After about ten seconds, he jumped back with a look of alarm. He spoke.

Tuy just stood there, transfixed.

"Tuy? What did he say? Help me out here," I gasped.

"He…he said, Shes, he said he's alive, he's alive."

"Khenmes?" My hope jumped within me. I had to find him—if I could get out of this room alive.

A stir in the crowd, some of whom started looking around nervously.

"Don't say his name, Shes!" Tuy gripped me from behind. The demomili shook his head and spoke again.

Tuy was shocked. "He says the god in you told him he's alive, and it don't matter if we speak his names anymore. He says the god within you wants you to find him. He says—"

"I don't have any god within me!" Except the idea of Ma'at, but she was a special goddess and wouldn't be talking to Waashiw shamans through my heart. Guaranteed. Ma'at never gave anyone information, just instructions to fix things. I looked around and saw only silent Waashiw faces, blank with shock, staring back at me, the one foreigner in the room.

"He says it's a foreign god, Shes." The demomili spoke again. "It spoke to him in Miwuk." Tuy's face filled with fear. "Shes, I can't understand…. He says foreigners are holding Khenmes, somewhere to the south…. Miwuks…. I don't understand!"

The demomili extended his hand again and pressed it against my chest. This time, he did not withdraw it, though he gritted his teeth, his face a study in concentration. The crowded feeling diminished and disappeared. He took his hand away, and I sank to my knees in relief, but I will admit to a certain amount of terror. The crowd's voices swelled around us in excited chatter, and Tuy helped me up. And that's when I threw up.

CHAPTER FIVE

MacIntyre Does Lunch with Karkin

KARKIN MET MACINTYRE THE NEXT day at the Neferti, Shesmu's restaurant overlooking the bay. MacIntyre hadn't seen him since the night he showed up to help Shes clean up the Russian mess last year.

MacIntyre walked into the Neferti fifteen minutes ahead of her reservation. She asked to see Henutsenu, the house manager and an old friend, and waited for her in the bar.

"Cheryl, so good to see you again!" The elegant Remetjet walked up and embraced the American with genuine affection and an air kiss. She stepped back and looked her American friend over. Then she hugged her again. MacIntyre felt the tug of sexual attraction she always felt when seeing Henutsenu.

"We've been neglecting our wardrobe again, haven't we?" Henutsenu wore a stunning white sheath dress with golden trim, her black hair braided with gold beads, a modern version of an ancient temptress from a wall painting.

MacIntyre laughed. "You know me too well, Henutsenu. This is the best I've got."

"And you've come for fashion advice?"

"No, lunch."

"With a gentleman? Or a lady." The probe was gentle but definite.

"A local, name of Karkin. He's some kind of international cop, friend of Shes."

"Oh, that one. Yes." She shuddered delicately and smiled. "Business."

"Very personal. The medjau fired me. For being American."

Henutsenu looked a little nonplused but said, "Well, I suppose it could be good for you to explore to get a sense of the real opportunities out there."

MacIntyre responded, "That's why I'm meeting Karkin, to get him to help me get back on the job."

"Ah. Well, good luck with that."

"And I want to talk with you later. Has Shes filled you in on Washeshu?"

Henutsenu raised questioning eyebrows. "He mentioned he'd be away for a little while, but no details."

"He called me yesterday with a nice apology for being a jerk, but I'm thinking I need somebody to talk to right now, and not a man or a medja." She looked Henutsenu in the eye, and Henutsenu looked right back, and smiled.

Henutsenu put a hand on MacIntyre's arm. "Girl talk. All right, I'll be around when you're done with lunch and that Karkin."

As always, Henutsenu's touch sent that little thrill of pleasure through MacIntyre. She used to think it was the natural attraction you get from someone sexy. After last year's adventures at the Temple of Bastet, Henutsenu became the Hemet-Netjer-en-Bastet by surviving a religious ritual involving lions. MacIntyre detected the power of the gods of Kemet in her. Not that she believed in them, but there was this emanation from the woman that she couldn't explain any other way.

Karkin delivered a dash of cold water to her Henutsenu afterglow.

He was a small, disheveled Ramaytush, a member of the indigenous sub-tribelet resident on the Menmenet peninsula as far back as anyone could remember. Karkin looked out of place in the elegant setting of the Neferti when he walked in through the front door in his green army jacket. Not so much under-dressed as dressed wrong and looking for trouble. Karkin had a morose face set off by a rather large, flat nose. He wore his hair long—too long. The hostess looked like she'd sat on a bee. MacIntyre observed this with humor, but got to him first before he said anything to the hostess.

"This is the gentleman I'm meeting. Is our table ready?" MacIntyre tried for suave, businesslike, and cheerful. The hostess, still looking bee-stung, said nothing and checked off MacIntyre's reservation and took them to their table. Henutsenu had made sure they sat in view of all the VIPs that frequented the restaurant at lunch.

"I hope you don't mind visibility." MacIntyre looked around.

"No."

"Would you like a drink?"

"No."

"Would you care if I had one?"

"No."

"Do you actually speak Renkemet, or just the one word?"

"Yes."

"Heartwarming, that's what it is. Heartwarming."

"You called me."

"I did. True. Well, I've been—"

"I know all about it."

"You do. How?"

"I'm in the business."

"What business is that?"

"Knowing things."

"I never thanked you for your help in rescuing me last year."

"You're welcome. You called me."

"I did."

At this low point in the conversation, the waiter approached and took their orders. MacIntyre had the smoked eggplant and the saffron-infused oxtail; Karkin had oysters and the rockfish in seaweed.

"All right, now we've gotten reacquainted, what can you do for me?" asked MacIntyre.

"Not much."

"Boy, you are a true mine of good will."

"Yes." The oysters came and went. MacIntyre forked eggplant to keep up.

"Is there anything you can tell me? Anything at all?"

"Like what?" he parried.

"Well, stuff like why being American is enough to get me fired."

"You're American?"

She opened her mouth for a savage retort, then realized he'd made an actual joke, for the first time since she'd known him. She acknowledged the joke with a smile, then said, "So, where is this pressure to fire Americans coming from?"

He shook his head but came through. "From the top."

"The top of what?"

"Your government. Ta'an-Imenty government, that is."

"Like, the haty'a?" The head of the Menmenet civic government.

"Higher."

"The Temples?" The Temples were the several temples that made up the working government of the sepat, much like the federal departments in the United States.

"Higher."

"Are you claiming that the hekasepat, Our Glorious Leader, is the source of this?"

"Trying my best not to say so."

"I see." She paused for thought. "Why would the hekasepat be down on Americans? Aside from being insulted by the American president?"

"Military stuff."

MacIntyre swallowed oxtail and cleared her throat. "Would you," she asked, "care to expand on that?"

"Secret."

Another bite of oxtail calmed MacIntyre's impulse to find an oyster knife to open him up. Oysters had nothing on him, she decided. But maybe there was a pearl to be found by persuasion.

"Look, Karkin. I need to know enough to know how to get my job back. I've alienated the Menmenet city government officials; who should I alienate in the sepat government? Other than the hekasepat, who I'm pretty sure I can't ambush."

He looked at her. "Mentju."

"Mentju. Temple of? The god of war? The army?"

"You could check into Hem-Netjer-Tepy Setehnekhet."

Setehnekhet, the dynamic leader of the Temple of Mentju, had appeared multiple times in the papers in the last few weeks as military affairs became interesting.

"Why might Setehnekhet might be down on Americans?" she asked.

Karkin was silent.

"Any idea why me in particular?"

"No."

MacIntyre addressed her oxtail. She remembered the dinner at which Shes had introduced her to the dish, despite her imagined dislike for the tails of oxen. Shes; where was Shes? He could make sense out of this idiot. He could make sense out of nonsense.

"Any advice?" she asked.

"Would it help?"

"Have you ever heard the word 'proactive'?"

"No."

Exasperated, MacIntyre chewed another bite of oxtail, swallowed, then expostulated, "I'm unemployed and won't be able to buy food soon. I need some help here."

"Especially after humiliating yourself in the Haty'a's office, right?"

"How…never mind. I don't want to know."

"My advice is to keep your head down and ride this out."

"What about food?"

Karkin smiled and said nothing while he enjoyed some rockfish.

"OK, so I sleep with a chef. Look, Karkin. If I investigate a little, can you get me some information?"

"Dangerous."

MacIntyre smiled. "Danger is my business."

"You're unemployed."

"Will you rescue me again when I get in too deep?" She smiled without hope.

"No."

"Well, thanks for the help." She raised her glass of wine to toast him.

"You're welcome."

"Is there such a thing as a Powerless Lunch?"

Karkin finished his rockfish, wiped his mouth, then said, "Right. Is that all?"

"No, that's not fucking all. Lookit, Karkin. I know you're on the right side. Shes knows you're on the right side. I owe you for my life. I'm in bad shape here. Why not help me through this?"

"Can't." He looked at her with stony black eyes.

"Is it you think I can't play this game with you men?"

"Nope."

"What, then?"

He was silent, considering his response. "I have a job too. I like it. Helping you would get me fired. No sense in both of us being fired. There are things you don't know. Keep your head down, things will be different."

"I notice you're not saying things will be better."

"Is that all?" He put his napkin on the table.

She shook her head. "Unless you want dessert."

"Nope."

"Well, this lunch has been a real revelation to me. I hope we can do it again sometime, say in 20 years."

"Sorry. Got to go." He arose and went.

MacIntyre finished her wine, sat in her chair for a while, ignoring the humiliating stares from the surrounding tables, then walked out to the bar, asking the hostess to let Henutsenu know she was waiting there. But she had already decided that she needed to do something about the Temple of Mentju. She just hadn't figured out what. Perhaps a cocktail would help.

CHAPTER SIX

MacIntyre Thinks Different

HENUTSENU TOOK CARE OF A few minor items requiring her personal attention in the kitchen and dining room as the restaurant swung into dinner prep mode, then turned the restaurant over to her assistant for the day. Cheryl was a piece of work, but she was a good friend, one you could depend on, and that blonde hair and those blue eyes were something. She thought back to the day years before when Cheryl had introduced herself as Hutyt-er-Semetyu MacIntyre, showed her badge, then shut down the restaurant to question everybody about a murder. And then the thing in the Temple of Bastet. My, how things had progressed since then. But she was Sebek's woman now, really, though she had to admit to temptation. To take the edge off that, she said a warm goodbye to Sebek in the kitchen, to the amusement of the line cooks. Her eyes checked the table settings automatically as she walked back through the restaurant to the front of the house.

She went into the bar and found her friend leaning heavily on it, talking very familiarly to the bartender. He glanced at Henutsenu and rolled his eyes.

"Hello there!" Cheryl got up from her bar stool, staggered a little, then messily hugged the elegant Remetjet, who eyed the bartender with disfavor and patted her friend on the back. The hug lasted a little longer than Henutsenu was accustomed to from Cheryl, and she wondered if the sexy American was finally ready to acknowledge the attraction between them. Her experience told her that it was more likely the drinks.

"How many?" Henutsenu asked the man behind the bar.

"Lost count," replied the bartender. "Sorry."

Henutsenu said, "Cheryl, let's sit down over here at a table for a minute and talk, then we'll decide what to do."

"I'm not going dancing with you! I hate cats, 'specially dancing cats. Let's have another cocktail."

"No cats tonight, then. And I think no more cocktails." She raised a finger to the bartender and mouthed the word, "Taxi." He scurried off to do her bidding. Cheryl's thoughts appeared to have turned to the Myu-Myu Club, Henutsenu's favorite Bastet-themed nightclub. Henutsenu grinned as she remembered the scantily-clad Bastet dancers screaming and dashing every which way as Cheryl and Shesmu intervened forcefully in the fight between those two European crooks. No, no dancing cats tonight.

"Cats, 'shpecially black cats. Can't abide 'em." Cheryl had not noticed that she had switched to English. Henutsenu, who did not speak English but got the gist, patted her hand.

"We'll head over to my place. No cats there." Sebek was allergic to her favorite animal, so she had to keep her kitty at the Temple of Bastet.

A tear welled up in Cheryl's eye, which she furiously wiped away. "Won't cry about this, isn't worth it." She had switched back to the Renkemet language. "Your place. Good thought, private place to talk and conspire to overthrow the state." She looked at Henutsenu with tight lips, then another tear dripped and she said, "I'm sorry, I'm so humiliated that I'm like this with you, you especially, I hate this, this, this…humiliation." She wiped the tear away with a floppy hand.

Seeing that things were spiraling out of control, Henutsenu maneuvered Cheryl out of the bar and out to the street, where the taxi was just pulling up. She got Cheryl in the back seat of the taxi, then got in the other side. By that time, Cheryl was resting her eyes in a corner of the cab's back seat.

"375 Mentju Street, please," Henutsenu said to the driver. "It's the big highrise."

"Got it. She going to be ma'at?" The man looked worried about his seat upholstery. Henutsenu just nodded and waved him onward. The driver shook his head and muttered, "Americans. Fucking drunks."

They drove off. Cheryl rested peacefully enough and didn't say anything more about fomenting revolution. They arrived at the apartment building, and Henutsenu persuaded Cheryl out of the taxi and over to the front door. Once her eyes were partially open, Cheryl was still ambulatory, just a little inwardly focused. The two women took the elevator to the 23rd floor and Henutsenu got Cheryl into her apartment and onto the couch in the living room. The big windows looking out over the Bay were showing flashes of light off the water and ferries appearing and disappearing through the swirling fog.

Cheryl was crying again, so Henutsenu got some tissues and helped her clean herself up.

"Sorry, I don't do this," said Cheryl helplessly. "It's just...."

"I know, I know," soothed Henutsenu. "Just take it easy and we'll see what we can do about it all." She thought for a minute, then picked up her phone and punched in a number. Sebek would just be getting ready for the dinner rush.

"Hi Sebek, it's me. Yes, I left with Cheryl about fifteen minutes ago, we're at my apartment. I think you shouldn't come over tonight, sorry. Girl talk. Lots of girl talk. At least when she wakes up." She looked over at her friend, who had slumped over on the couch and had apparently gone to sleep, more tears glistening on her cheeks. No, she felt this was definitely not something Sebek should see. "Yes, she's pretty much at her wit's end. No, I can handle it. She's just overwhelmed. Sebek! No jealousy, please. And Bastet can help her. I'll let you know what happens. I wish Shes were here! Love you!"

She found a pillow and a blanket, then arranged Cheryl in a semblance of a normal sleeping person on the couch and covered her up with the blanket. Her friend's blonde hair splayed out over the lotus-patterned pillowcase, and her face was peaceful. Henutsenu smoothed away a couple of stray strands of hair that lay across the sleeping woman's face and wiped away the wetness on her cheeks with a tissue. She stroked the sleeping woman's cheek and sighed.

She took care of chores around her apartment as the daylight lengthened and went away, changed to her nightclothes, made herself a light supper, then streamed a film highly recommended by a friend. It was from Sweden and featured two women who lived by themselves in a bleak stone house by a dark, bleak lake. They pretty much did nothing for two hours, then died, separately, over another hour. Henutsenu watched this epic to the end, curious to see whether anything would actually happen and depressed that it didn't. She sat next to the sleeping woman, who didn't move the entire time, despite all the excitement.

Henutsenu stroked Cheryl's face again, thought some about dark bleak lakes and blonde American friends and black cats and Bastet and Sebek, then made her obeisance to the small black cat statue in a niche and took herself off to her own rest, as Cheryl was clearly going to be asleep for a long time.

"Cheryl, wake up now. Time to wake up, Cheryl. Cheryl, it's time."

"Henutsenu?" Her friend shook her gently awake. The sun streamed in through the big windows.

"Yes. We're at my apartment."

"Ow." The pain actually managed to surpass the pain a rubber truncheon wielded by a Russian gang boss had inflicted on her last year. "Who the fuck hit me and with what?"

"You had a few too many cocktails, I'm afraid."

"Can't remember. Concussion?"

"No, vodka. Up we go." Henutsenu helped MacIntyre to her feet, took her into the bathroom, ruthlessly undressed her despite her protests, gently pushed her into the shower stall, then turned on the cold water full force, shut the stall door, and left the room.

When her involuntary screams had died down, MacIntyre, shivering, came out of the shower and dried herself off, then got dressed. She looked at herself in the mirror, poked at her wet hair, and decided that nothing was going to help. She considered making a run for it but in the end just ran her fingers through her hair and went to face her friend and tormentor.

"Thanks, I guess." She made an attempt at a smile, which Henutsenu returned with warmth.

"Are you awake now?"

"Yep, though I wish I weren't."

"Breakfast."

"Pass, at least for now. Maybe later."

"We need to talk, then. Let me get something together for myself and we can make a plan." She made some Remetjy tea along with a couple of eggs and sat at the breakfast table, where MacIntyre joined her. They stared at each other in silence.

"Tea?" Henutsenu asked.

MacIntyre thought she'd prefer about a gallon of strong coffee, but she said, "Yes, thanks." Henutsenu poured a cup and set it in front of her along with a bottle of pain relief pills. MacIntyre took some pills, washed them down with the lightly stimulating herbal tea, then stared at the cup silently for a good long time. She looked up at the beautiful Remetjet and said, "I am totally humiliated."

Henutsenu reached and took her hand. "Sometimes it happens to the best of us."

"But I'm supposed to be tougher than this." MacIntyre squeezed her friend's hand.

"Give tough the day off and tell me about it. Tell me about your history, why you came to Menmenet."

MacIntyre nodded, winced at the resulting pain in her head. Where to start?

"My dear old dad. He's a big-time lawyer in Boston, and he wanted me to get the best law school education and join the firm and take it over and be a big-time lawyer there."

"Did you have any brothers?"

MacIntyre smiled. "No. I've always figured that's why Dad put so much energy into me. He treated me like a goddess, when he wasn't treating me like a prisoner. Then I smarted up and took charge."

"So, what happened?"

"I got into Harvard Law School."

Henutsenu looked confused. "That's a bad thing?"

"It would have been a bad thing for *me,* anyway. I grew up in the higher reaches of the American legal and corporate world. I'd met the movers and shakers, and I'd been allowed to look under a few rocks to see what was underneath. I didn't like it."

"Why did you do it? Why did you apply?"

"To please my dad. Actually he insisted, I think he had strings to pull. Then I got the acceptance letter and knew I had to do something."

Henutsenu, fascinated, raised her eyebrows. "What?"

"Told him I was going to Nepal to bum around for a few years."

"Why Nepal?"

MacIntyre smiled again. "Stupidest, most distant destination I could think of on short notice."

"You wanted to upset him."

"I wanted him to be furious and hate me and tell me that he wouldn't pay for anything, so I could do what I wanted."

"And what was that?"

"Not go to Harvard Law School."

"This logic seems…circular."

"Actually, it was pretty much of a downward spiral from there. I set the acceptance letter on fire with a candle on the dining table. He was furious and hated me and refused to pay for anything. I think the favors he had called in, those strings I mentioned, he was seriously pissed at the possibility of wasting them. Then he said he'd lock me in my room until I got some common sense." MacIntyre's voice faded away, and her eyes shut as she remembered.

"And did he?" Henutsenu smiled.

"He tried. He laid hands on me. My mom was sitting there, screaming about the fire on the tablecloth. Dad was shouting."

"Quite a scene."

"Yeah. So, I grew up as a spoiled rich kid in Boston private schools. They didn't teach you much but had a lot of activities. I took up Tae Kwon Do, a martial art. I had black belts of various designations as I cruised through four years at Boston College. Gave me something to do when I wasn't busy skipping classes." MacIntyre rubbed her aching head.

"Um. So…"

"My dad would get out of breath getting out of his easy chair. Things developed. When Dad regained consciousness, and Mom had put out the fire on the table, we all sat down to discuss things."

"You knocked your father unconscious?" Henutsenu was incredulous.

"I'm not proud of it. The situation just…developed. I lost control. I'm impulsive, you know that."

Henutsenu just grinned. She'd been around for several impulsive events in MacIntyre's recent life. It was actually an attractive quality at times.

MacIntyre rubbed her aching head some more, unsuccessfully trying to rub out the memories. "Anyway, we talked. Dad wouldn't listen to reason, but he didn't try locking me in my room again. He started shouting, I shouted back, and there was some table pounding. At that point, I got up and stole all the money I could lay hands on in the house, got my things together in a suitcase, and took a cab to the airport. The first thing I saw was a sign advertising vacations in Menmenet, so I bought a ticket and here I am."

"And you don't want to go back."

"Fuck no. Certainly not to my parents."

"But to America? Why not New York or Miami or someplace like that?"

"I hate the place. The country is corrupt as hell and getting worse. Useless politicians. War, war, war. They've been fighting wars with everybody since 1917. Shit, since 1776. Remember the war against the Remetjy Empire in 1805? North Africa. The fucking Shores of Wy'at, as the Marines remember it." She shook her head in disgust.

"I've always wondered why you decided to become a citizen here. Why you joined the medjau."

"Long story." She stopped, then went on, more slowly. "A lover. A woman. She…somebody raped and murdered her." MacIntyre's throat closed up at the remembrance of her dear R'aia.

Henutsenu took the American's hand in both of hers. "I'm so sorry."

"I wanted to do something about the murder. The medjau solved the murder and put the guy away for life with my help as a witness. So I joined up. Somebody told me that there wouldn't be any chance of getting onto the homicide squad unless I became a citizen and a w'abet too. The funny thing was, the minute I took the oath to Ma'at, I felt this funny feeling come over me. I've never felt anything like it. It was *right*. Ma'at was exactly right for me."

Henutsenu nodded. "I had the same feeling when I started worshipping at the Temple of Bastet during dance school. I didn't take the oath to become a w'abet, but I felt the pull."

MacIntyre nodded. "I was raised a Congregationalist in Boston. By the time I got to college, I was an atheist, didn't believe in anything. I came here, went through hell, and took the oath of Ma'at. I still don't believe in it as a religion, though. I feel kind of bad about that. Maybe a little faith would help me out of my hole."

Henutsenu pursed her lips. "I'm very religious, Bastet is a demanding goddess. But a lot of Remetjet don't really believe any more. All our institutions are religious, the temples are the government, so you can't really separate things. A lot of people that work in the temples just work there, they don't worship anything but their government paychecks. I don't think you need to feel bad about it. But now you're out of the Temple of Ma'at?"

"I guess I'm still a w'abet, they haven't thrown me out of the temple yet, I'm still wearing the feather. But I can't stand it. They took away my badge. They took away my badge for being *American*. For having blue eyes." Her voice rose and she gritted her teeth.

Henutsenu calmed her down. "Easy, I can see the pain. Relax." She reached over the small breakfast table and put her hand on MacIntyre's cheek and stroked it, exactly the way you'd stroke a cat. This damped down the fire in MacIntyre's heart, and she slumped in her chair and rubbed her forehead.

"I'm so humiliated. You know Shes is away?" she asked.

"Yes, he came by yesterday to tell Sebek and me that he was going and what had happened to you."

"So I was humiliated before I even got to the restaurant?"

"Cheryl, you are not humiliated, just upset. Find ma'at." Henutsenu's voice was sharp.

"You don't find ma'at, it finds you." MacIntyre closed her eyes and discovered that indeed, the goddess had found her. She no longer felt furious or humiliated, just driven. Ma'at wanted all her medjau focused on bringing order to the universe. She needed to get a grip and get on with it.

Henutsenu asked, "What do you need to do?"

MacIntyre opened her eyes and said, "I need to get my job back."

"Do you know anyone in the government?"

"Nobody that will talk to me and a few that would just throw me out of their offices." She related her adventures at the City Palace. Henutsenu laughed, and MacIntyre laughed along until the pain made her quit.

Henutsenu said, "Why not go undercover?" MacIntyre thought she'd been watching a few too many American crime shows. She smiled and fluffed her drying, very blonde hair.

"My chances of being undercover in Menmenet are between slim and none. Unless you have in mind a complete makeover with a dye job and colored contact lenses."

Disappointed, Henutsenu said, "There must be some way to investigate."

"What would Bastet do?"

Henutsenu's face lit up with her most cat-like smile, and she said, "Ma'at is sometimes too straightforward for one's health. Let's see. Maybe...why not cuddle up to the people behind this and make them think you like them? That's what a kitty would do." She paused, holding her tea in both hands, and looked at the blonde American.

"What?" asked MacIntyre, a little disconcerted by the concentrated stare.

"You know what," said Henutsenu.

Shes was away, he'd never know. But she would know.

"I...Henutsenu, I just can't."

"But you want to, I can feel it." She gazed into MacIntyre's eyes.

"What about Sebek? What about Shes?"

"What about them? This is us, not them."

MacIntyre sighed. "I want to, but I don't. I can't. It's...too soon, for me, a woman, after R'aia and her murder. And there's Shes." MacIntyre thought about R'aia and the good times they'd had before the murder and felt pretty bad. She thought about Shes. Her head hurt and her heart hurt worse. There was that tug, though. "I'm sorry."

The series of personal failures that had brought her to this state rolled out before her. They all clamored at her: Mes, John Smith the American Consul General, Shes, 'Aapehty, Kh'abekhnet, Karkin, the bartender, and worst of all Henutsenu. And maybe a taxi driver, though she didn't remember much about that part.

She had thought she could climb back up the mountain after falling and falling again due to her own stupid, strong-willed, misguided actions, and she just fell again at the Neferti bar. And yet this woman wanted her, this beautiful friend to whom she had shown the humiliated face of total failure. But that would be falling again, she knew it in her bones. The feather pin over her breast could crush her with its weight, and it got heavier every time she opened her mouth.

Henutsenu shook her head with disappointment. "All right, but if ever..." Her voice was soft.

MacIntyre smiled a little sadly.

"I was just thinking, you know," said Henutsenu, changing the subject, her smile deepening and voice strengthening, "this might be a real opportunity for you. A medjat is worthy and all, but really, *so* many opportunities in the world. You should think beyond getting your job back. Bastet encourages ambition. You deserve more. You'd rise to the top. You're wasting yourself running around investigating tiny crimes. The American thing will pass, you need to be ready to ride the next wave. Find a job that puts you in a better position and gets you more money and higher status. No more humiliation. That's what Bastet would say." She glanced at the black statue in its niche and saw nothing but feline approval.

MacIntyre's brain rearranged itself into a new way of thinking and devised alternatives. She absolutely had to ferret out why being American limited her horizons here in Menmenet, why every level of local government saw her as a threat or liability. There was really only one place to do that, and it wasn't in the medjau. Karkin had mentioned two people: the hem-netjer-tepy of the Temple of Mentju and the Hekasepat of the Ta'an Imenty Republic. A new job could get her into a better place to investigate, and a side benefit might be that she liked the new work, you never knew.

She replied, "Maybe you're right. Maybe I've been too complacent, too backward looking. I'll look for a new job today. And I'll aim for the top." MacIntyre reckoned that once she'd sussed everything out and worked herself into a position where she could do something about it, she'd have a choice. And she didn't really care what she had to do to get to that position—as long as it didn't involve sleeping with fat, slimy male slugs. There, she drew the red line. She definitely wasn't into slug sex, male or otherwise.

"Where are you going to start?" asked Henutsenu, eyes alight at the change for the better in MacIntyre's attitude. MacIntyre flipped a mental coin and decided the hekasepat was out of her reach.

"Mentju, the god of war, who hates Americans. The Temple of Mentju. I'm going to war. My way."

CHAPTER SEVEN

Shesmu Falls Off a Cliff

I COULD NOT TELL YOU which was worse, the bouncing or the rattling.

The bouncing came from the road, although calling it that was overly optimistic, as roads are mostly smooth and flat. This thing was a long, winding pile of boulders wrapped around massive mountains up to the Serqu pass, the most northerly pass in the Shen'aserqu mountains. OK, they weren't really boulders, but flat is definitely not a word I would use for that road.

The rattling was coming from the shaking parts and pieces of the trucks we were traveling in, which to my estimate had to be older than time. The Waashiw squaddies in the back seat slept through it all.

"Couldn't we have gotten more reasonable trucks for this?" I asked in between boulders.

The Waashiw sergeant driving the truck grinned. "Place we're going, you want to look like somebody that nobody would worry about. The truck is camouflage. The four-wheel-drive transmission and the engine are new and ready for anything."

If my trip to Washeshu had taught me anything to this point, it was that I certainly needed to be ready for anything, so the sergeant's calm reassurance put my doubts to rest. Of *course* it did.

The sergeant was one of a squad of ten Washeshu special forces soldiers assigned to get me to where I needed to go. Once the demomili and Tuy had got me back to her house and everybody had calmed down a little, it turned out the demomili had a lot of influence with the local military leadership. His frantic phone call, which I didn't bother to have Tuy translate because at the time I was still pretty punchy, resulted in these guys showing up before my stomach had a chance to settle. Fortunately, I had managed to avoid throwing up on the demomili; he probably would have tossed me to the water babies instead of helping me on in my quest.

I lay on the couch, still recovering from my attack of heart or whatever it was. Tuy puttered around in the kitchen getting tea for everyone. The demomili conferred with the head of the military squad over the dining room table and wrote out something on a piece of paper. He handed it to the soldier, who pursed his lips in thought, then came over and smiled at me and introduced himself as the sergeant. He spoke very good Renkemet.

"Looks like you're gonna take a nice little hunting trip, sir. Get some of that wonderful Waashiw mountain air." He held up the paper. "These are directions that the boss doc here says he got from you, or what's inside your heart. I don't know about that, but it takes us down the back of the mountains and across a pass." He pulled out a phone and scrolled around. "Looks like about 90 miles, but shitty roads for the last part. Should take most of the day tomorrow. You all packed?"

"Slow down. Sergeant of what?" I sat up.

"Washeshu National Rangers, sir, and that's all you get to know."

"All day. South. 90 miles. That puts us back in Ta'an-Imenty."

"Not quite, sir, but close to the border."

"And why exactly are we going there?"

The demomili spoke sharply from the table. Tuy turned and looked at me with big eyes.

The sergeant said, "Boss doc says your Miwuk spirit god needs you to go there to get your friend."

Another burst of talk from the demomili. Tuy translated rapidly. "He says there are some bad people at this location and that they are holding Khenmes and he does not know why or how, but he says the spirit is saying you must go. Shes, if he's really alive, you have to go get him!"

"Let's all just calm down a little now." I rubbed my head. "This…spirit god. What the fuck, excuse my language, Tuy, am I supposed to believe about this?"

She said, not a trace of smile, "Don't ignore the spirit, Shes. Just don't. When a spirit talks, you listen and do what you're told. Even a Miwuk spirit. *Especially* a Miwuk spirit." She shut her lips tight, her chin tattoos quivering.

"I've never been very good at that, you know, Tuy. Doing what I'm told, I mean."

"I know, but this isn't Menmenet anymore, Shes, it's my country, and here it's water babies and spirit gods and animals that guide us, and doing what we're told. Please, Shes!" An irrational hope for Khenmes somehow took root in my heart at Tuy's plea.

The demomili spoke sharply again. The sergeant spoke up. "He says it's a matter of national security, sir. He don't exactly know what the matter is, but he sounds damn sure that if we don't get you there pretty damn quick there's gonna be bad things happening here. Did she say water babies?" He looked concerned. "Can't have that."

I practically screamed. "No, please, no more water babies! I don't believe this stuff. And I don't know if I'm up to a military adventure." I felt like I'd been roasted slowly from the inside.

"Don't really matter what you believe, sir. Got to go, boss doc says so. National security; we got to check the situation out and report back, then get you to Miwuk territory in the Republic. You packed?"

"Please, Shes!" cried Tuy, frantic tears in her eyes, abandoning her Waashiw stoicism once again. "Just find out if the old man's alive and get him back to me."

Well, all I had to do was run three restaurants and take care of a crazed girlfriend and recover from some kind of spiritual heart attack, so I had a little time on my hands anyway. Why not?

"It's the spice of life, that's what it is," I mumbled. Then I told the sergeant, "I'm packed."

I laid myself back down on the couch doubting I could make it to the door, much less to some crazy spiritual test in the Washeshu mountains. The sergeant grinned and Tuy came over and leaned over and hugged me in relief. I felt her hope but I also saw myself on a trip to the Duat, overcoming all the challenges and tests that Inpu and Wesir place in the way of the dead. I felt sure that the reward at the end would be worth it, if Inpu didn't feed me to the crocodiles for my sins.

The soldiers camped in Tuy's back yard that night, and in the morning more soldiers showed up with the two rattletrap trucks and a bunch of old, well-worn camo hunting suits and fancy hunting bows. They packed away some vicious looking automatic rifles in chests in the back of the truck.

My body was functioning again in the morning, though I still felt pretty roasted on the inside. I put on a hunting suit and admired myself in the mirror. I almost looked like a mountain warrior instead of a celebrity chef. The sergeant put me in the front cab of one of the trucks with himself driving and four squaddies in the back, and we set off for the mountains.

We reached the turnoff for the Serqu Pass about five hours later. The sergeant pulled us over, the other truck coming to a stop behind us. He turned to me.

"You any good with a bow?"

"You could say so." I'd been shooting since I was a kid and still got out to the archery range in Menmenet every couple of weeks. It was a good way to center myself. I didn't think the sergeant cared whether I would center myself with the bow he was pointing at, which was a miracle of technology. One of the soldiers in the back seat handed me the bow and five razor-sharp hunting arrows.

"Let's see." He got out of the truck, and I got out too. "See that tree? The skinny pine next to the big rock there." He pointed to a small tree slightly set apart from the others, about 50 meters away.

"Sure."

"Hit it."

"Sorry?"

He tapped my bow with a finger. "Take the bow and an arrow...."

"OK, sure!" I looked the bow over to make sure I understood everything going on with it.

"What's all that stuff?" I asked, pointing to a smallish gadget mounted on the bow.

"Infrared, for night shooting."

"One doesn't hunt at night."

"*We* do."

I was silent. I hefted the bow. Nice weight, good grip, nice size for my hand. New bowstring, no fraying.

"Practice shots?"

"Need 'em?"

"Guess not."

"Go."

I racked the arrows in the rack on the side of the bow, keeping one out. I leveled the bow and pulled back to see what the weight was, then eased off again. It was a little on the light side for me, but that was OK. I nocked the arrow, took an oblique stance, and apologized to the little tree as I centered my attention on a small knot about half way up the tree, head height. I drew back under my chin, held it until the bow stopped moving, adjusted a little, and loosed. The tree shook with the impact. The sergeant walked over and pulled out the arrow and brought it back to me.

"Have any military experience?"

"Couple of years in the army."

"Ever seen action?"

"You could say so." Being around MacIntyre seemed to bring on action.

"Ever killed anyone?"

"You could say so." Last year, to rescue MacIntyre, I'd shot two men, a Russian gangster and a corrupt medja. It didn't worry me much.

"Why and how?"

"Can't tell you."

"Gimme a hint."

"I was rescuing my girlfriend and there were Russian guards, that's all I'll say."

"Armed?"

"Assault rifles."

"Did they shoot?"

"They didn't get the chance, we got the drop on them. The two inside tried but we were too fast for them and the shots went wild."

"Hmm. Good enough!" He slapped me on the back. "Welcome to the squad, you're an honorary Waashiw Ranger today." He paused before getting back in the truck. "Unless you don't like to eat deer or pine nuts?"

"Like 'em fine, I serve them at my restaurant."

"Well, then." He got into the truck, and I joined him. I held the bow between my legs.

The sergeant looked at a fancy-looking GPS device mounted on the dashboard. We crested the Serqu Pass, according to the map, and started down the mountain.

"We'll drive by, just a group of hunters, see what's what."

We wound down the dirt road. The terrain was like nothing I'd ever seen, massive walls of eroded granite spires looking like towers out of a fantasy world. Below the cliffs, pine forest ruled. The lower we got into the valley, the more trees.

"A lot of old growth here," said the sergeant. "Not too many people around burning things, I think. Probably good hunting. Maybe we'll take a day and..." His voice petered out.

Stretched across the road were two tanks. Well, not tanks, but close—kind of big humpy things with a largish turret machine gun, pointed right at us. The sergeant slowed to a stop, and the other truck stopped behind us.

"Um. Keep quiet and let me talk," said the sergeant.

A man walked toward us carrying a rifle at port. He, like us, wore a hunting suit with no insignia, but his rifle was not a hunting rifle. He had a scarf covering much of his face, but his skin color said First Peoples. His eyes, though, were not Waashiw eyes, their ferocity was not the calm of the eyes I'd been looking at for the last couple of days.

"What's up, guy?" asked the sergeant, affably, when the man approached his window. "Why the armor? There bears around?"

The man didn't smile. "ID?"

The sergeant handed over a card.

"You Miwuk?" asked the man, speaking Renkemet.

"Naw, Waashiw. Come down to hunt us some deer, great hunting around here. Deer is waitin' for us, I can feel it."

"Area's closed to hunting. Government business."

"Aw, man, really? We just drove a hundred miles, do the trip every year. How can it be closed? Bastards are waitin' for us."

"Sorry, special operation."

"Shit. How about down lower."

"Can't let you through, sorry. Orders. You can hunt up by the pass but don't hike down this way." I couldn't quite place his accented Renkemet, but he wasn't a native speaker.

"See, there's this little creek, comes down the mountain…great deer country there. Bastards are waitin'!"

"You got bugs in your ears, bud? Turn around."

"OK, OK, don't get any of 'em up your butt, son. Let me go talk to my buds." He got out of the truck and walked back, conferred with the driver, and came back. "OK, we're good. We'll go north from the pass, how's that?"

"Fine. Just turn 'em around and get gone." He shifted the rifle suggestively.

"OK, we're outta here." The man stepped away from the truck, and we backed and turned and drove up the road. We drove a couple of miles and pulled out into a little bulge in the road. I looked out the window down a sheer drop of about 100 meters to a creek.

The sergeant unhooked his phone and swiped a few times, then said, "It looks like they were blocking a road that goes down along a river, the river must source up in the hills above. Looks like a little valley along there, a nice place to hide something."

"Satellite maps?"

"You bet." He smiled. "Scary thing is, Deer *is* calling me. Must be a good sized herd around here, real close. Well, another time."

I guessed we wouldn't starve to death. I opened the door and damn near fell off the cliff, but somehow got myself and my bow around to the back of the truck. The squad assembled in the road, half carrying bows, the other half assault rifles.

"We're gonna follow this little creek here down to the middle of this little valley, come up from the side," said the sergeant. "We'll see what we can see and do what we have to do."

It took us a couple of hours to navigate down the creek. It wrapped around a huge granite escarpment that looked to me like it would fall on us at any minute. As we got closer, the sergeant told me, "We're going to go in real quiet, no talking, no sound if we can avoid it. You good with that?"

"Yes."

He nodded, and we moved silently down the creek. At some point he held up a hand and pointed, and I saw a road through the trees. We headed off through the trees parallel to the road, careful not to make any noise. One of the big vehicles we had seen earlier rumbled down the road, and we followed it for about a mile or so, or followed its dust trail. The walls started to close in on us, and the sergeant looked like he was pretty unhappy about that. Then we came around a corner and there it was in a large meadow that opened out in front of us.

The military vehicle parked in front of an intimidating array of wire fence and razor wire. There were two rectangular perimeters with about 10 meters in between them, both heavily topped with razor wire. Inside was what looked like a set of open-air cages covered with a fancy roof held up by lightweight braces, but I couldn't really see much through the fence.

The sergeant stopped dead and looked around carefully, then whispered. "What the fuck is that?" He then answered his own question. "It's a prison compound." He looked at me with renewed respect. "Looks like the boss doc heard pretty good from whatever's inside you, son. Your friend—what's his name?"

"Khenmes, don't know his Waashiw name."

"Well, good bet your pal Khenmes is in there and not happy about it."

"Sarge, looks like 6 guards, two in the towers, 4 patrolling," whispered one of the Washeshu soldiers. "Probably more troops down the road, too."

"Shit. OK, let's take a break and think some." He sat back against the rock wall, out of sight of the compound.

I said, "I can get a better look at it from up there," pointing at a ledge up the cliff face. "I think I can see in but they won't be able to see me around the cliff."

The sergeant was dubious. He looked at the cliff.

"Kind of a climb, son."

I grinned. "I majored in cliffs in boot camp."

"Ten years ago, maybe. One of us might be better."

"Any of you know Khenmes?" I asked. None of the squad said anything.

I said, "I want to see if I can spot Khenmes, none of you can do that." I could sense Khenmes in there, caged, wanting out; but there was also something that told me to verify before jumping off the cliff. That was probably Ma'at, she was always kind of a look-before-you-leap goddess. I'd never felt so confused in my life, there was way too much going on inside of me.

The sergeant considered, then said, "Boss doc was pretty clear what happens is up to you, so go ahead. We're here if you need us, son. Here, take this radio, you can use it to tell us what you see." He gave me a hand-held radio, then turned and hunkered down to look at the compound from behind the rocks.

I gave one of the soldiers my pack and bow. I climbed and climbed, looking at the compound every so often and the little group of men below me less often, as they got farther and farther away. Reached the ledge. Still not enough height, I couldn't see past the razor wire. I got the radio out and told it, "I can't see enough, going higher."

"Roger. Careful, son."

I could see another ledge ten feet or so up. The direct route was too smooth, so I inched diagonally to a crack, then reached for a small ledge above my head. I hauled myself up and turned to look. I reached for the radio—but as I twisted one hand down, the other slipped and scrabbled on some loose gravel. I hung suspended for a few brief seconds, fingers trying to find a purchase on the rock and failing. The last thing I remember was the cliff face falling away as I lost my grip and fell backwards.

CHAPTER EIGHT

MacIntyre Finds a New Job

CHERYL MACINTYRE SAT AND WAITED at the bottom of her new career ladder, a chair in the reception area of the Temple of Mentju. She had filled the day before with phone calls to anyone she thought might have an in to that temple. After following up a few dead ends, she finally spoke with a woman sehyt who had worked with clients at the temple. The lawyer called back late in the endless day with a name: Pashed.

"So, Cheryl, be prepared for this guy. I worked with him on a couple of cases of discriminatory hiring practices, guess which side he was on? He's a huty-netjer, one of the hiring managers for the w'abut in the Temple of Mentju. I managed to keep his hands off me using creative seating arrangements, you get my drift? He's a sucker for anything in a dress. So I gave him a call, reminded him of old times, and gave him your name. I did make a few suggestive remarks about you, just to soften him up; you can take it from there. He's *so* anxious to meet you." The woman cackled. "So you owe me a big one."

MacIntyre wore a sexy red dress with gold trimming. She did not wear her feather pin. During her 30-minute wait for the huty-netjer, Pashed, MacIntyre called Shesmu three times, going to voicemail three times. The first time, she just told him to call her. The second time, she told him about her new career plans. The third time, at the 25-minute mark, she thought very dark thoughts and left no message at all for fear of going overboard on him.

Five minutes later, as she was for the twentieth time rearranging her skirt, MacIntyre saw a man emerge from a side door and look around until his beady little eyes settled on her.

The huty-netjer was on the wrong side of 50 and weighed at least 100 kilos on the hoof. He didn't need to worry about his chin, because he had three of them. The small, bristly mustache set off his large, rubbery lips. He was, like all priests, bald, and baldness did not suit him. He smiled, showing a lot of very bad teeth.

MacIntyre was of two minds. She wanted to check his priors and run him in just for standing the way he did. But she needed a way into this temple, and this guy was almost certainly her only shot other than breaking in at 3 in the morning.

Pashed greeted her with a bow and led her back through a maze of hallways to his office, which was just big enough for a desk, two chairs, and a large couch along one wall that looked like it had sustained a lot of use. MacIntyre sat in a chair on one side of the desk, and Pashed sat on the other side. She handed across her identification and her résumé, then waited while he tried to make sense of it all. He finally looked up and examined her with two beady eyes.

In a surprisingly high and nasal voice, he complained, "You're already a w'abu, of Ma'at according to this. And a hutyt-semetyu. And American."

"Not any more, on all three counts. I think it's time for a change. I really want to help the Republic and prove my loyalty as a citizen, you know? They won't let me do that in the medjau now, and I think I'd be more valuable here anyway given my knowledge of America."

"You'd be taking a good-sized pay cut, you wouldn't have the rank anymore."

"That's OK. Something is better than nothing, which is what I'm bringing in right now. I'll learn the business and work my way up."

He smiled, again showing the teeth under the little mustache. "There's plenty of room for advancement for somebody who plays the game, my dear. Plenty. But the problem is, you're American."

"I think that's actually an advantage, Huty."

"Pashed, just call me Pashed, my dear."

"Pashed. My being American can only bring insight to the team on our enemies. I can help people see how Americans think."

"And what are you willing to do to get the job?"

"Whatever I need to do, Pashed." She smiled at him. "I really need a job." She crossed her legs and adjusted her skirt.

"Well, that's just fine, Cheryl, just fine. We should be able to reach an accommodation. Yes. Oh, yes. I'll need to clear it with the hem-netjer-tepy, can't possibly hire an American without his OK. He's the high priest of the temple and has to approve this."

"Will I need to interview with him too?"

Pashed examined her closely, still smiling. "I don't think so, he's pretty busy most of the time with figuring out how to defend the Republic, doesn't have a lot of time for the w'abu. I'll keep you mostly to myself."

"Well that's just fine, Pashed, it would be great working for you. What would I be doing, job-wise?" MacIntyre knew already what she'd be working at not doing on the side. She glanced again at the couch. A challenge, but not insuperable. There are so many excuses, and she wasn't going to be around that long.

"I could start you out on hetepu, the altars. Pay is 5 debenu an hour."

"Hetepu? Making sacrifices to the god?"

"Well, no, that requires a lot of training. Cleaning them. If that works for you, Cheryl."

"Sure does. I've always been really strong at cleaning up bloodstained furniture, being in homicide!"

"And a great sense of humor about it, too! I can see we will work well together." He licked his lips in anticipation. "You know, I don't think we need to bother the Hem-Netjer-Tepy with this, he'll be fine with it. I'll just go get an application form." Pashed heaved himself to his feet and went out. MacIntyre took the opportunity to rifle his desk drawers. She closely examined the contents of the lower left drawer, which included a pair of pink, fur-lined handcuffs and other implements of romantic adventure. She was back in her seat with a better knowledge of the depths of human nature by the time Pashed returned with a form.

He said, sitting down and handing her the form, "Here, fill out this application, and I'll put it through. When do you want to start?"

"The sooner the better, gotta eat you know. How about now, Pashed? And I'll need 10 debenu, I'm worth it."

Pashed looked a little taken aback but recovered quickly. "Certainly, though I'll need to make…arrangements…" He thought. "I can go up to 8 debenu, final, with a six-month salary review if things…work out. Over time."

MacIntyre shrugged. "I can live with that. Deal!"

He smiled, showing his bad teeth. "Well, Cheryl, I would love to show you the ropes right now, yes I would. Yes. But I have a meeting." He licked his fat lips. "Let me give you over to one of the w'abu. And we can get together later to, erm, see how you're doing. Once I've made my arrangements. Yes."

"Sure. Lead the way." She handed him back the form, which she had filled out with what little detail was required. Being a w'abet of Mentju did not seem to require a lot of background or skills, at least for cleaning hetepu. She was in!

The day after her interview, the newest w'abet of Mentju felt that she had seen just about as much blood as she was willing to see in her life—in the past twenty minutes.

Mentju, being all about power and sexual potency and who knew what other excessively masculine aspects of the universe, sacrificed bulls. Apparently—and this was new to MacIntyre—they sacrificed a bull a week.

The problem was, she was on the cleaning detail, and that day was sacrifice day. The main job of the cleaning detail was to clean the hetep on which the priests of Mentju had sacrificed the latest bull. MacIntyre had not been aware of the amount of blood contained by the average bull, nor had she been aware of the implications of the sacrifice during the ceremony of Mentju with respect to the poor, lower-level w'abu that cleaned up after it all. It was, in fact, a fucking mess.

So. The supervising w'ab gave her a set of coveralls and a pair of rubber boots. The coveralls had a nice little bull embroidered on the sleeve. A nice Chinese w'abet showed her how to use the appropriate tools and receptacles to deal with it all, then left her to it. Two hours later, MacIntyre wearily changed back to her street clothes at her locker and tried to concentrate on how to avoid meeting up with the huty-netjer for drinks and an evening of sexual bliss. As it turned out, not a problem: the huty sent a message that he was busy with the latest crisis in management and, disappointingly, had to defer their "meeting" until the next day. This may have had something to do with MacIntyre's way of keeping her job, which she had put into effect immediately.

The Chinese w'abet, being a stand-up kind of person, had advised her strongly to avoid coming to the notice of the hem-netjer-tepy during the ceremony of Mentju, over which he presided. The w'abet said that Setehnekhet, the hem-netjer-tepy, while he was a "just and judicious" leader of the w'abu, harbored unfortunate beliefs and attitudes toward foreigners. The Chinese w'abet said that being Chinese was bad enough, but being a blonde, blue-eyed American was probably enough to cause him to look for a local volcano suitable for human sacrifice. MacIntyre, despite the warning hisses of her comrades on the cleaning team, made very sure the hem-netjer-tepy saw her at every opportunity.

On her way out of the locker room, the receptionist called her over and gave her a note: the hem-netjer-tepy expected her in his office at 6 a.m. the following morning. The man smiled, primly, after handing her the note.

"How about that, a promotion already!" exclaimed MacIntyre. The receptionist rolled his eyes.

MacIntyre got up at 4 a.m. after a restless night. She couldn't get the smell of blood out of her nose. If MacIntyre had had bad dreams, they would have been of bellowing bulls and oceans of blood; fortunately, she had few dreams and didn't remember the ones she did have.

She showered and chose her clothes carefully. No slinky Remetjy sheath dresses like the red one she had worn to her interview with Pashed. No miniskirts, no carefully draped tops with figure-enhancing decorations. Nope; this time, she would go as an American businesswoman. A challenge, as she had never been an American businesswoman. She had once had to do a presentation in college before an audience of American businesspeople, however, and the ensemble she'd scrabbled together for that occasion still existed in the back of her closet. And the medium heels, of course. That outfit ought to make the hem-netjer-tepy sit up and take notice.

This exotic presentation excited quite a few stares as she rode up the elevator to the fifth floor of the temple. She arrived at 5:55 a.m. to find the hem-netjer-tepy's assistant already waiting for her. At 6:00 precisely, the assistant answered his phone, then showed her into the inner sanctum.

Setehnekhet looked the part. Mentju appears as a man with a falcon's head or as a large bull with an attitude, according to the temple's manual for w'abut that MacIntyre had gone through the previous evening. MacIntyre saw both aspects of Mentju in Setehnekhet. He had the beaked nose and piercing eyes of the raptor and the stocky, heavily muscled, hard body of the bull. An imposing man, nearly two meters tall. And he definitely had attitude.

Setehnekhet's office, on the fifth floor of the temple, was dark and imposing in itself, with a large statue of the god in a corner and lots of scenes of the many wars of the empire, all showing the generals looking fierce and accepting khepesh swords from the god. Ma'at did not regard time spent bashing other people or being glorified for bashing other people as a particularly useful way to spend one's time and energy. Ordinarily, the medjau did not have many dealings with the Temple of Mentju.

"Hutyt-er-Semetyu MacIntyre. I will not say it is a pleasure to meet you. Please sit there." He pointed to an uncomfortable-looking chair across from a couch. MacIntyre walked over and sat and looked at him alertly. He remained standing near his desk, the statue of Mentju looming over him. He smiled, a smile that changed the angles of his face into a malicious, raptor-like formation.

"I summoned you, our latest w'abet, because I saw you yesterday at the bull sacrifice ceremony and was not well pleased by the sight." He looked her over. "And this morning, you have deliberately dressed to offend me with your American clothes."

"Sorry about that, boss." Time to let a little air out of his puffed-up language. But this familiarity did not go over well with him.

"You will address me as Neb-Waset Setehnekhet, w'abet." His voice was smooth and commanding. His tone did not invite argument.

"Certainly, Neb-Waset Setehnekhet. I'm a little new at all this, you know," she apologized.

"I did know. Entirely too new. I would assume that Pashed was thinking with his balls again."

MacIntyre smiled. "I didn't sense anything much higher than that, no. But it did give me the opportunity to get to your office very quickly." She waved a hand around. "Charming, really."

Setehnekhet's falcon eyes fixed on her. "So you admit you have come under false pretenses."

"Certainly not. I was right out there. I just knew I would not get past the first floor if I tried to see you directly. Hence the cleaning detail. And I'm not exactly in disguise here."

"Just what is it that you want, hutyt?"

"Make up your mind, sir. Hutyt or w'abet?"

"Let's make do with hutyt for now, until I fully understand what is happening here. Why, under the current circumstances, is an American medjat trying to gain access to the Temple of Mentju?"

"It's just those circumstances I'm concerned about, Neb-Waset Setehnekhet. I'm no longer a medjat. I may have an American passport, but I'm now a citizen of the Ta'an-Imenty Republic. My oaths to Ma'at, and the one I gave yesterday to Mentju, bind me to the gods of Kemet. I am no longer American. Seriously—I am on your side in this."

"Mentju may have your oath, but only he knows whether you will keep to that oath. I certainly don't. But say I accept your profession of loyalty to the Republic. Why are you here?"

"You know that the medjau have fired me?"

"Yes, I gave the order to terminate Americans in critical security positions throughout the Republic at the request of the hekasepat. I have a copy of your notice of dismissal here." He pointed to his desk, which was bare except for the single sheet of paper. She looked around and realized the office had nothing, no details, that revealed anything about the man to her—other than the oppressive, dominating presence of the god Mentju.

MacIntyre resisted her natural urge to confront this man as the true source of her problems. This man was not a lecherous, indolent idnuhaty'a or an elderly security guard, he was a charismatic, well-built killer. She wasn't going to dominate him with martial arts expertise or sexual wiles. But he hadn't had her summarily ejected from the temple, he'd brought her to his office. Why? The only possible answer: he thought she might be useful in some way. And his clear falcon eyes were not fooled by her evasions and pretenses.

She said, "Neb-Waset Setehnekhet. You had me dismissed, yet here I am. You saw me at the ceremony of Mentju in all my Americanness, yet here I am. You know everything about me, yet here I am. What can I do for you?"

He smiled again, the falcon eyeing the prey. "Very good, hutyt. Excellent reasoning. If you had not come to us, we would have come to you. We think you may be able to help us with some of our internal projects, ones that will allow us to use you without necessarily trusting you. You come highly recommended for your medjat skills, but you have a simple quality most medjau lack: you are American, and we must now understand Americans and American thinking. Tell me why we should consider you for such a role."

Highly recommended. MacIntyre, intrigued, wondered by whom? She hadn't given any references, Pashed didn't need any. "Try me. Anything to get off the cleaning detail. But here's the big reason: I need money. I need to make a living, and I need to do that here, not in America. I have no loyalty to America. I certainly understand what it means to be American and to think American, and I can help you with that. You've taken away my job, give me one I can do, so I can eat."

Setehnekhet leaned against his desk and folded his arms. "Why should we put any trust in you at all?"

"Why worry? I'm right under your eye," said MacIntyre, pointing at a very nice rendering of the wedjat eye on the wall behind Setehnekhet. "And under Mentju's eye as well as the Eye of Heru, and I've given my oath to Mentju. And if," she said, looking him directly in the eye, "that means departing from the way of Ma'at, so be it."

There, she'd said it; she was willing to abandon her goddess for the falcon god of just war. She didn't mean it, though. MacIntyre knew, down deep, that her goddess Ma'at didn't really care about lies and deceit, or even fucking with the other gods, as long as the path to ma'at was clear. Not that she believed in the goddess, but she did believe in ma'at and knew how to get there. Her path was very clear: she needed to find out what Setehnekhet was doing and how Mentju was playing into it all. And the real reason why they fired her. Why was being American so dangerous to the state?

The raptor's stare nailed her to her chair. She didn't move but narrowed her eyes and stared back, challenging the falcon. Few rabbits did that. MacIntyre felt that it would not serve her well to make Setehnekhet think she was a rabbit.

Abruptly, he made his decision. "Very well. Subject to review, you are promoted to hutyt-netjer in the Security Department with C-level access. That means, in practice, that all you can do when you come in is to read the newspapers, but you have to tell us everything we want to know."

"Pay?" MacIntyre wanted to reinforce the impression that she was in it for the money. She didn't have a lot of trouble producing that impression as she thought about life without a job.

"The salary is 30,000 debenu per year for the provisional rank. Is that sufficient to ensure your loyalty? With a bonus for excellent results, of course. And special perquisites as a member of our elite, of course."

"Loyalty…to Mentju?"

"And to me." Setehnekhet's tone was emphatic. "No conditions, no exceptions, no equivocations. Absolute loyalty, to me, and to Mentju—and to the Republic."

"I agree. Absolute loyalty to the Republic." But not to him, he'd gotten her fired. Let him think she was committed, at least until she figured out what was really going on here. She'd fought men like this most of her life and wasn't going to stop now. And breaking oaths to gods had few consequences in the real world, at least until the priests caught up with you, and she didn't intend to let them.

"Welcome to the temple, hutyt." Setehnekhet smiled, his eyes now veiled. "Third Floor, Room 52. See Atchet-Netjer Sheritr'a, who is in charge of the

Security Department. I will advise her of your promotion and appointment. And please be aware that she and the Security Department will watch everything you do very closely. They will keep you on a very short leash for now."

MacIntyre arose and bowed. "Yes, Neb-Waset Setehnekhet. Thank you for your confidence in me. You won't regret it. And I'm looking forward to that bonus."

"Let us hope we will both have no regrets," said Setehnekhet with a pleasant smile, hooded eyes, and a dismissing wave of his hand.

CHAPTER NINE

Shesmu Has a Vision

THE SOUNDS AROUND ME WERE muted and confusing as I stirred, consciousness returning slowly. My dreams had me running after coyotes and climbing mountains and hunting deer. Had I gone native? Had the gods finally gathered me in and sent me to the Duat, or somewhere worse? And who the fuck *was* I?

The mists in my brain gradually cleared, and I opened my eyes. I was in a bedroom, lying on my back on a small bed. I twitched my fingers over the covers and discovered wool blankets, thin and rough. I was looking up at a ceiling of white plaster with cracks running across it. My heart, which does most of my thinking, navigated the cracks and saw ships and mountains and coyotes walking across the ceiling. I gradually resolved my feelings into a very painful left ankle and a dull throbbing in my head.

I said, "Ow."

"Hey! You're awake." A largish man with a broad, dark, coppery face with long, white hair and heavy, white eyebrows sat in a chair against one wall. The wall was white plaster and had cracks too. The man had cracks in his face, it was a lived-in face that had seen many years of trouble, it seemed to me.

"Feel like some water?"

I was suddenly ravenously, dangerously hungry. "Yes." I cleared my throat. "Yes, please. And food."

"I don't have any Remetjy food, just acorn mush. Daughter is out getting some supplies, she'll be back soon."

"'S-OK, OK. Mush would be great." I rolled my head back and forth and began to move my arms and legs. "Ow."

"Hurt your ankle, son."

"Yeah. Who am I?"

"Got me. They just dumped you here and said you could take it from here."

"They?"

"Bunch of Waashiw guys. Looked like hunters, talked like soldiers."

My memory suddenly washed over me.

"The sergeant."

"The big one with the huge hands?"

"Yeah. That's him."

"He did all the talking. Seemed pretty sure you knew what you were doing."

"Where am I?"

"My house."

I thought about that for a minute, processing it and considering ways and means.

"And where is your house as a matter of geographical location relative to some fixed point?"

"Sounds like you're starting to think again, son!"

I closed my eyes, imagined my restaurant kitchen in Menmenet and wished myself there. I opened my eyes. Didn't work.

The man said, "You're in Kikyapaply, little village in the mountains, up from the Central Valley. Over the hill from Washeshu, I guess that's where you came from, right?"

"Right. There was a dirt road, I remember that, and a big wire compound, and a cliff. Yeah, I remember the cliff, that's the last thing I saw."

"Damn lucky to fall the way you did. I guess you weren't up all that high."

"High enough." I looked at him again. He hadn't moved. "Didn't you mention water and mush?"

"Sure, sure." He got up and went out of the room. I heard some rustling around, and then he came back in holding a clay cup and a small, tightly woven basket. He put them down on a little table next to the bed. I scrunched my body up and leaned my back against the wall behind the bed. I drank the water from the cup, and wonderful it was, too.

"More, please," I said, holding out the cup. He took it and went out.

I looked at the basket, it was full of a steaming white mess. I took it up and slurped a little. Acorn. Tastes about as good as it sounds, too. I slurped again. I thought that it might be awhile before I was in my own restaurant eating the kind of food I was used to. I slurped the rest of it down.

The man came back in with the cup. I washed down the acorn mush with more wonderful water.

"Wonderful water, where is it from?"

"The river. Runs right down the middle of the valley, a little walk away."

Mountain river water. I could bottle and sell this stuff in my restaurant. I drank some more.

I put down the cup and asked, "Did the sergeant say anything else?"

"Just that he had to get back to his own country before anybody found out he was here. He said he had strict instructions from his shaman to deliver you here, to me, so when you got knocked unconscious, they just gathered you up and came here. That was last night. He said what you need to do starts here."

I asked, "Did he say anything about my friend Khenmes?"

"Nope."

"What I need to do is find my friend."

"I don't think you're going anywhere right now, son, not with that ankle the way it is."

I remembered more and more about my adventure. I should have let one of the Rangers climb that cliff. I should have worked with them like the cooks at my restaurant—a team, each one doing what he was best at. Why did they bring me here? Why did they leave? Kikyapapli? What do I do next? Work with whoever these people were. I looked at the white-haired man. I had no idea who he was.

"Do you have a name?"

"Yep. Do you?"

I smiled, remembering Khenmes's lessons on how First People hated to give names. Remetjy didn't, names were vital to us. I gave him mine. "Shesmu, Shesmu za-Akhen."

His eyes sharpened. "Akhen?"

"My father's name."

The old man didn't say anything, just sat and looked at me.

"Does that name mean something to you?" I was curious because his look was intense.

"Maybe, long time ago. Maybe not. Have to see."

"Name? Please?" I asked.

He considered, then said, "Heh."

"Are you laughing at me or is that the name?" Heh means "wind" in Renkemet.

"Name."

"OK, Heh. Well, I'm going to try to get out of bed now." I threw back the blanket and inched my legs out of bed and to the floor.

"Can you stand?" Heh got up and came over and extended a hand. I carefully put my foot on the floor and grimaced with the pain, then grabbed his hand and pulled myself up. The pain was pretty bad, but I didn't collapse. He helped me limp around a little, then let go. I stood in one place until the worst of the pain subsided, then shuffled around a little.

"I think you need a healing ceremony," said Heh.

"I think I need a psychiatrist." I replied.

"We'll wait until daughter gets back, she'll set everything up." He went back out through the doorway. I followed, slowly, out into a bigger room with a table and chairs and a sofa and a little kitchen in a niche.

I hobbled over to a window and looked out. The sun was bright, shining over a grassy meadow. The air coming in through the open window was hot in the late-morning summer sun. You could see the river; it was about 10 meters wide, and I could see whitewater and big pools in its curves going up the valley. What you couldn't miss, though, were the cliffs and the waterfall, spectacular against the blue sky. The waterfall cascaded down a cliff, and another huge cliff jutted out beyond it, granite upon granite going up to the sky.

"I've died and gone to the Field of Reeds," I said in awe.

Heh looked over at me and grinned. "It hits most people like that the first time you see it. Guess it hits you like that even after you've lived here 60 years. We call the valley Hetchetci, the name of the grass that grows here."

"Why have I never heard of this place?"

"Lots of reasons. Especially in your case."

"What do you mean?"

He just shook his head. "Let's just say we prefer to be a little out of the way, here. Off the grid. We like the old ways, you know? But with modern conveniences like toilets."

This worried me. "Exactly what kind of ceremony will this be?"

"I'm a bear shaman, so I'll call on Bear to give you his strength, that ought to fix up your ankle pretty quick." He looked at my leg. "Yeah, pretty quick."

"So you're the shaman here?"

"One of the shamans, yes. Bear shaman, like I said."

"Why do you think Bear will help?"

"He always has. Powerful medicine in the Bear, and Bear is generous with it." He looked at me without smiling. "Bear will help you, Shesmu. You'll understand when he does."

A healing ceremony. A waste of time. I needed to find Khenmes. And I needed to talk to MacIntyre, to let her know I'd just fallen off a cliff, not off the end of the Earth. And I didn't believe in magic ceremonies, I believed in modern medicine. I took my phone out of my pocket. No service. I did believe in the magic of wireless phone technology, but apparently everything has its limits.

"Heh? No cell service here? Is there a land line?"

"No, we don't use any of that modern technology stuff. Much. Got electricity. Got a truck if we need to go somewhere, there it is now."

So I wasn't going to be explaining to MacIntyre, and I wasn't going to be finding out how the Wenmyt was doing, and I wasn't going to keep my promise to Webkhet. Strangely, all this made me resolute about finding Khenmes; it seemed like the only thing in my power.

The door to the little house swung open and hit the wall with a crash, and a small woman in jeans and a t-shirt backed in, carrying two bags in her arms. She'd opened the door with her butt.

"Hi, Dad. Hey, mystery-man: you're awake! Who the fuck *are* you?"

I said, "Shesmu. And before you ask, I have no idea at all why I'm here."

"Great, 'cause neither do we. But I got food, so you won't starve eating just acorn mush. I'm Tahefnu." Tahefnu, which meant in Renkemet "belonging to the hundred thousand." Interesting.

Tahefnu chattered while she put things away. "I had to drive all the way down to the foothills to get your food. Can't hunt cans with a bow. Dad, I got gas. Stopped at that shitty little place with—"

"He needs a healing ceremony," Heh broke into the flow.

"Right away? Or can I shower first?"

"Well, soon as we can. I get the feeling he's gotta be moving on soon." Heh studied me. His daughter turned and studied me.

"Well, shit; better get to it then," she said. She turned back to her work and put away the last few groceries.

Heh spoke with pride. "Daughter, she's training up to be a shaman too. She'll be a good one once she lets go of her heat. Hummingbird shaman, though, not bear."

I desperately wanted to ask what her heat was, but thought better of it. Tahefnu was a little over one-and-a-half meters tall. She looked like she was about

30 years old, with long, smooth, dark black hair, a flat nose, beautiful brown eyes, and a straight, full-lipped mouth. Except for being diminutive and Miwuk, she reminded me of Henutsenu, my business manager at the Neferti, the most beautiful woman I knew aside from MacIntyre. MacIntyre had ruined me for dark-haired beauties, though. So had Neferaset, the dark-haired love of my life who never really loved me back and was long, long gone. I found myself warming to the father-daughter team despite their magical thinking.

Tahefnu gave me the eye. "Thinking about another woman, aren't you?" she said with her dimples flashing. "Where's she at?"

"Menmenet."

"And you look like you're a pretty upscale individual when you're at home."

"I used to be until I started falling off mountain cliffs and hiding out in Miwuk villages. I own some high-end restaurants in Menmenet. I cook."

"A chef! You can help in the kitchen, then. After. Can't do a healing ceremony on a full stomach. Let's get things together and get over to the roundhouse and get to it."

"Unless," said Heh, "you just want to hurt for a week or two."

Father and daughter studied me again with expressionless faces. I asked myself how bad could a magical ceremony be, and what could it hurt that wasn't hurt already? There were no cliffs involved, so I decided to trust them, at least as far as doing magic was concerned. Maybe the power of positive thinking was what I needed most at this point in my life.

I committed myself. "All right, let's do it." The shamans smiled.

Tahefnu went out to get the chain of communication started that would bring in everyone in the valley. Heh negotiated his doctor's fee with me: a feast, cooked by yours truly, that would feed everyone in the valley. When she came back and heard about this, Tahefnu's eyes got dreamy about what she called a "fire feast." I suspected my health insurance wasn't going to reimburse any of this.

I asked, "Can I get a stick or something? I can walk but it hurts."

Tahefnu grabbed a stick by the door. "Use this, it's Dad's hiking stick." She walked over and handed it to me. It was some kind of light-colored wood, heavy, worn smooth, and with a lovely gnarled top that twisted around into a little handle. It had a small fork at the bottom, which ought to make it more stable. I looked at Heh, who waved a hand to take it.

He said, "Let's get going, a lot to do."

The roundhouse was a little ways up the valley from Heh's small house. Partly underground, it was covered by bark rising up to a smoke-hole in the middle. The entrance was a big, square awning with tree-trunk poles holding up a bark covering. It was easily large enough to hold 25 people.

We went in and I sat on a log, my leg stretched out in front of me. Heh and Tahefnu started setting up for my ceremony. Tahefnu built a small fire in the middle of the floor using kindling and wood stacked against the side of the room. Heh went over to a trunk by the side of the roundhouse and drew out several pieces of feathered regalia and gave them to Tahefnu. She then shook it out and performed some kind of ritual with it, dancing around the roundhouse. Once she'd finished the ritual passes, Heh put everything on, including a large head-band of small feathers that stretched across his forehead and a feather apron around his waist.

Over the next half hour, two dozen Miwuks showed up and took places in a circle around the fire. Tahefnu introduced me to them, one by one, as they came in. The flames illuminated their coppery faces, the dim light producing an eerie atmosphere that only grew with the mutterings in a language I did not understand. Heh sat me down in a spot between the circle of people and the fire.

Tahefnu, satisfied that the fire was good enough for the ceremony, did a head count and said, "OK, Dad, everyone is here." She came over and reached out a hand and caressed my cheek. "And you, just go with the flow. Bear will take care of you, and I'll take care of you after. Relax, you're all tight." She tapped my cheek lightly with her hand and turned away.

Heh grinned and said, "Let's get it done, then." He then spoke some words in Miwuk and everyone quieted down and looked at him. He turned to me and said, "I'm gonna dance around you and activate the healing energy through Bear. You don't need to do anything, just sit and absorb the healing energy, all right?"

I nodded. I had an odd feeling that mixed anticipation with a little fear. I dismissed it as an unwarranted fear of the unknown, just a little flutter in my stomach. I touched my cheek where Tahefnu had caressed it and felt very strange.

"How long will it take?" I asked.

Heh replied, "Oh, usually half an hour or so to get through the ritual, then I check to see how you're doing and we take it from there. Things heal at their own rate, can't rush it. Nothing's broken, so it won't take a long time for the spirit to heal you." He grinned. "A nicely broken leg can take days of dancing. Big fee too!" He turned away to start the ceremony. I tried to relax.

A man started a drum beat, and some of the people nodded in time to the beat, then began softly chanting in Miwuk. Heh started up his ritual dance, and Tahefnu threw some herbs on the fire. I smelled pine and sage as the sounds of the ceremony built around me. Tahefnu threw a mixture of seeds from a small basket into the fire. She kept doing that as the ceremony progressed.

For the first 10 minutes or so, all I felt was the continued pain in my head and ankle and the little flutter in my stomach. The heat grew, and I started to sweat. I guess I nodded off at some point, because I awoke suddenly, feeling a punch in my stomach. I'd been dreaming a little, something to do with MacIntyre. I moved uncomfortably on my log and looked around to see what had happened, but nobody was near me. Heh was dancing about three feet away, shaking some feathers in his hands. Maybe this stomach thing was part of the ceremony; it sure made me forget about the pain in my ankle for a minute or two.

I felt another lurch in my stomach. I gulped and quickly evaluated the situation. Was I about to throw up all over poor Heh's regalia? I'd nearly done that to the demomili, no need to repeat here. But no, it wasn't that, just a lurch. Then it happened again.

Then I was somewhere else. I heard a roar that sounded very much what I imagined a bear would make. It was very dark. I knew I was not in the round-house anymore, though I can't tell you how I knew that. But I could clearly hear the chanting and drum. I couldn't see the fire; I couldn't see anything at all. The heat was gone. I felt as though I were in a deep, cold cave, resonant with Miwuk chants and smelling of sage, pine, and smoke. A very old part of me wondered if that bear was there too, and what to do about that if it were.

I tried to get up and found I couldn't move at all, not even my head, but I could move my useless eyes. I just stared into the darkness. I felt very cold. I felt as though something was just outside my peripheral vision, and if I concentrated, it felt like the goddess Ma'at, I could glimpse her erect posture and white dress and the feather atop her head. Ma'at was remote, distant in an emotional way. She ignored me. I stretched my eyeballs back and forth to try to catch a real glimpse, and I thought bizarrely that Ma'at had a body and hair of gold. Then a Miwuk man strode into my sight out of the darkness, right in front of me.

For a moment, I thought it was Heh, because the man wore a feather head-band and apron, but I could see the coppery face was different, though familiar. Then I saw the man dressed in a Remetjy shendyt, the linen kilt all Remetjy men wore on formal occasions, but bare chested with his skin and his face green, the green of the dead, no longer coppery brown. He held a w'as-scepter, the staff of power of a god, in his right hand, as in all the old pictures, and I saw it was Heh's walking stick. Then I saw the man had the head of a coyote. It was very strange: I still saw the Miwuk regalia, but I saw the Remetjy at the same time, and I saw the human head and the animal head at the same time. They weren't switching back and forth or anything, I just saw them at the same time on the same man.

"Shesmu." The man spoke my name, though his mouth never moved. It was a normal voice, just conversational in tone. "Son." My heart exploded with the emotions of the five-year-old child I had been. I have no memory of my father's face, how he stood, how he acted. My heart told me that this was indeed my father. Miwuk, Remetjy, Coyote—where was the reality of it? What was I really seeing?

Behind the Coyote appeared an incredible valley, like Heh's valley of Hetchetci but much grander, cliffs rising to the sky, waterfalls dashing down from great heights to the valley floor. I didn't actually see this place, I felt it. I felt Coyote's presence in it. Coyote said, "Come." My heart said go to him, my feet would not move. I had to choose which was right, my heart or my immobile body. Coyote said, "Learn. Atone. Come."

I said, "Akhen, father" without moving my mouth. The Miwuk man looked up at me, growing smaller.

"Danger. Watch where you tread, and who treads with you," he said.

He spoke in Miwuk, which I don't know but somehow understood. He raised his arms toward me, palms outward, elbows at right angles, the ka-sign, holding the staff in both hands over his coyote head. He shrank down as I grew. He spoke in Renkemet, "'Ankhu-djet, alive forever." I barely heard this last, really just felt it, and I felt the Coyote raise the walking stick in my direction, emanating power of some kind. The blackness became absolute as my father shrank into a small point of light and disappeared. My emotions boiled over, my need to find Khenmes dissolving into a greater need: to find my father, to find Coyote, somewhere in this darkness.

The darkness dissolved into the fire and the roundhouse and the circle of Miwuks. Heh was frozen, one foot still raised, looking at me with terror on his face, teeth bared and eyes wide under the feather headband. I fell off my log, sprawling helplessly to the dirt floor of the roundhouse. The last thing I saw before I blacked out was Heh rushing toward me, his mouth opening, but I never heard what he said.

ary domain. It was a large room full of desks and computers, with

CHAPTER TEN
MacIntyre Starts Work

MacIntyre reported for work the next day dressed in clothes matching her idea of a minor administrator in the Security Department: black and coral pantsuit with coral sandals.

She ascended to the second floor of the Temple to the Security Department's offices. Her new workplace turned out to be in the opposite wing from Pashed's administrative domain. It was a large room full of desks and computers, with monitoring screens on one wall showing surveillance videos of different areas of the building and of Menmenet.

"Can I help you?" A beefy security guard stopped her at the door. MacIntyre put on her best new-employee persona.

"Yes, officer. Thank you. I'm Cheryl MacIntyre, and I'm looking for Sheritr'a, the Atchet-Netjer of the department. I'm a new employee, starting today."

The man grinned wolfishly. "A very nice one, too. But we have to search any American who comes in here." The man's tone convinced MacIntyre that he had made this up on the spot.

"Touch me and die." MacIntyre smiled to soften it into a joke and raised her arms to be searched, but the man just laughed and signaled her to follow him.

They wound their way around lots of desks to the far end of the room. As they went, MacIntyre's eyes focused on a woman sitting at a desk raised up a little on a platform, clearly The Boss, the atchet-netjer of the Security Department. As they got closer, MacIntyre saw a Remetjet in her mid-forties, a little on the corpulent side, with sharp brown eyes, mid-length brown hair, and a grim set to her mouth. She wore a Remetjy business dress, white with black trim along the wrap line across her large breasts. The sharp brown eyes followed MacIntyre's progress with disfavor. MacIntyre stepped up on the platform behind the guard, who introduced her.

Sheritr'a smiled without warmth. "MacIntyre, hmm. The memo from the Hem-Netjer-Tepy's office said that you would start this morning." She stared at MacIntyre with a pinched expression. MacIntyre wondered if she had a food spot on her pantsuit but decided that Sheritr'a just hated her on sight. Not a good start to her first day of work.

Sheritr'a broke off her disdainful stare and shuffled some papers on her desk. "I suppose we'll have to find something for you to do, despite the fact that we are overstaffed as it is." She picked up a folder and opened it. "You've been working for the medjau for five years, got all the way to hutyt-er-semetyu, I see." Her voice sounded as though she had a hard time believing that. This was clearly a woman dedicated to stepping on the fingers of other women climbing the cliff of success. MacIntyre's route would need some adroit rock climbing.

Sheritr'a studied the folder some more, then closed it and dropped it on her desk. "I'll team you up with Meryr'a for now, he'll show you the ropes. He's working on a disciplinary matter, he can fill you in on his progress on that. So Neb-Waset Setehnekhet sent you down here personally?"

MacIntyre nodded. "He thought I'd be a good addition because I'm familiar with Americans and how they think, ma'am."

"Hmm." Sheritr'a looked her up and down. "Well, it isn't the first time the Hem-Netjer-Tepy has had a brain wave. American. Hmm." She did not sound convinced. "Oh, very well. Come along."

She got up, and MacIntyre followed her across the room to a desk in the far corner of the room. The farthest corner of the room.

As they approached, she saw a young man look at them with apprehension. He looked almost like a teenager, with a receding chin, sparse brown hair, sleepy black eyes, and a weak mouth with a sparse pencil-thin mustache nestled unattractively above it. His shirt and pants were disheveled.

"Meryr'a, this is Hutyt-Netjer MacIntyre. Show her the ropes." And with that, Sheritr'a turned and left without giving her a desk or even a chair. MacIntyre looked around.

"Got a chair?" she asked. Meryr'a looked at her helplessly, so she took an extra chair from a nearby desk over the objections of the desk's resident, whom she stared down. She dragged the chair over next to Meryr'a's desk and sat down and looked at him and smiled.

"OK, show me the ropes, Meryr'a," she said.

"Ropes? I don't have any ropes. What was she talking about?" The boy seemed very confused. MacIntyre knew just by looking at him that he spent a lot of time being very confused.

"Ropes. Show me the daily routines around here. What do you do every day?"

"You're American."

"Ah, you're a detective! Great."

"I mean, we got rid of you all."

"Except for me."

"But…"

"The ropes, kid, the ropes." Got to have ropes to climb cliffs, after all.

"Well, I spend most days sitting here doing paperwork." He waved a hand over the papers scattered on his desk and fingered one nervously. She reached and snatched it from his hand. He made a futile grab at it as it left his control.

"Hmm. This is a receipt for lunch dated two years ago."

Meryr'a looked down at his desk without saying anything. MacIntyre shuffled through a few other papers and realized they were all garbage. Putting two and two together, she said, "They don't give you anything to do, right? And so you got these out of a waste basket somewhere and put them on your desk to look busy." She, too, was a detective. "And now you have to admit that to an American woman who outranks you, making you feel like one of the smallest worms on the planet, is that right?"

Meryr'a blushed and looked at his desk.

"Not to worry, Meryr'a. We're a team now, two worms working together on nothing at all. Think of the synergy!"

"But you're *American*." Meryr'a stressed the last word in a way that loaded his simple statement of fact with more dismay, distrust, and dislike than MacIntyre could tolerate. But she was undercover, and she quickly recited to herself all the ridiculous aphorisms about how to catch flies with honey and so on.

"We'll overlook that for now, won't we? Besides, worms don't have countries. Look, kid: Neb-Waset Setehnekhet sent me down here to gen up on all the security doings, despite my being American, or maybe because of it. The Bitch-Netjer over there doesn't much care for me, and I can tell that you don't much care for me either. We'll overlook all that for now, won't we? Because we have a job to do, protecting the Republic, right? Am I right?"

Meryr'a stared at her, mouth open.

"And since they haven't given you much of a chance to get on with that mission, I'm here to help. The Atchet-Netjer teamed me up with you to make sure I couldn't do any harm. So, think positive. Think of me as a resource. Think of me as somebody who has your back. Think of me as somebody who can get you promoted if things go well."

Meryr'a groaned. "I suppose so. I have to follow the Atchet-Netjer's orders, anyway, to show you the strings."

"The ropes, kid." She saw that she wasn't going to get very far by prompting the boy, so she started working him over. MacIntyre pumped Meryr'a with question after question about the department, turning the poor lad inside out, shaking all the dust out of him, washing him thoroughly, and hanging him up to dry. By the end of this, she had a pretty good idea of who was important in the department. She also gathered that Sheritr'a ran things with an iron hand.

Finally, she probed the conundrum of Meryr'a and his non-job. He admitted after stumbling around a bit that he owed his job to his father, who had a high-up position in the Temple of Imen-R'a.

"Why didn't he just get you a position in that temple?" she asked.

He looked down at his desk. "He was…he told me that he couldn't afford to have me on staff there because it would damage his reputation, so he pulled ropes and got me this job."

"Strings, kid, pulled strings. And Sheritr'a made sure you wouldn't damage her reputation by sitting you here with nothing to do rather than just kicking you out, because of the strings your father pulled."

He nodded with shame reddening his face.

"And then dumped me on you without a desk or a chair or any job to do at all." She looked at the clock on the wall. "OK, kid, I think that's enough for the morning. How about lunch? Where's the employee dining room? Have lunch with me and we can get acquainted, and I can see how the local fauna drink at the watering hole."

Meryr'a tried an excuse. "I usually eat at my desk," he said. "I can't really afford—"

"It's on me. Let's go."

Looking around the employee dining room, MacIntyre saw lots of the people she'd observed in the Security department eating and talking. She replied, "So you don't interact much with the folks you work with."

"No, not really. They don't like me much."

"I can't imagine why. But never mind—we'll adjust." She considered ways and means of moving herself out of Sheritr'a's isolation strategy. From her talk with Meryr'a, she understood that their Security Department coworkers were not likely to take to her. She decided that the direct approach would work best to get their attention, and thereby get Sheritr'a's attention. Sheritr'a would then realize that dumping her on Meryr'a wasn't going to work. MacIntyre didn't know what Sheritr'a would do, but stirring things up was better than shuffling garbage papers on Meryr'a's desk for the next few weeks.

She picked up Meryr'a's plate and her plate and moved over to a table already occupied by a couple of the Security people. "Mind if we join you?" She sat down and put the plates down before they had a chance to answer. Meryr'a reluctantly followed his plate and sat down next to her.

"Who the fuck are you?" asked the larger of the two Security men, addressing MacIntyre.

She replied, forking her salad, "New girl on the block. Hutyt-Netjer Cheryl MacIntyre. I'm working with this dazzler here, Meryr'a. I'm sure you know his work."

"Yeah. We do." The smaller guy smiled unpleasantly. "And we don't like Americans."

"That's OK, I don't like 'em either. So, what do you guys do around here?"

"Eat," said the bigger one.

MacIntyre chortled, then to the smaller one said, "Your friend is pretty funny. Has he learned to read yet?"

Somehow the pair didn't warm to their new guests. The two men picked up their plates and moved to another, smaller table.

MacIntyre acknowledged the failure to Meryr'a. "OK, maybe they weren't the right choice. Let's try another one."

Meryr'a put his foot down. "No, please, hutyt. Let's just stay here, eat, and leave."

"But I need to meet people."

"Do it on your own time, not mine. I don't like these people, and they don't like me, and they certainly won't like you."

"Meryr'a, that's the longest speech I've heard you make. You must feel pretty strongly about it."

"You have no idea. Look, I know I'm not the brightest bulb in the room. I've accepted that. My father got me this job. I hate it. And then Atchet-Netjer

Sheritr'a put me on an internal affairs case, and now they all hate me so much I can't do anything at all. Please. Just leave me alone."

MacIntyre just shook her head. "Look, yourself. If you're going to do internal affairs work, you've got to get a tougher hide or buy some body armor or something. Tell me about it."

"About what?"

"The case. We're a team, so it's my case now too."

MacIntyre saw the rusty gears grind away in the confused eyes across from her, then Meryr'a got a look of horror on his face. "You mean you're going to investigate?"

"Why not?"

"They'll shoot me."

"Over my dead body."

"That too."

"So these guys are pretty tight, as a group?"

"They're like a Russian vori gang."

"That's not too bad, I wiped one of those out last year. With a little help." She paused for effect, then continued, "You can help me, Meryr'a."

Meryr'a closed his eyes. "I'm not up to this, I'm really not. I wanted to be a librarian, but I wasn't smart enough."

"At least you can read."

"About that…"

"Never mind, it's not important." MacIntyre felt as though a bog of absurdity sucked at her feet. "Let's just focus on the case. Tell me about the case."

"Well, there's this Huty-Netjer in another department, a man named Pashed…."

"No! Not Pashed! Could that fine, upstanding man be corrupt?"

Meryr'a looked confused again. "You know him?"

"He hired me." Subtlety was not a strong point with Meryr'a, and she felt protective of the poor lad and didn't want to ruin the rest of his life by exposing him to the realities of a woman in the workplace at the Temple of Mentju by telling him about Pashed and the contents of his lower desk drawer. "I can see how he might have stepped over the line a little now and then."

"A couple of the other Security men came by my desk and told me that if I found anything I should keep my mouth shut or they'd sew it shut just before they dumped me in the Bay."

"And you can't swim, right?"

"Right." He didn't see the humor in it. MacIntyre was pretty sure Meryr'a saw very little humor in anything in his life.

"Which two guys? Are they here now?"

"The two sitting over by the wall mural by the door." He glanced over, and she saw the two gorillas in question. "I really can't...."

"No, I guess you can't. But I can." Sensing an excellent opportunity to distinguish herself on her first day of work, she got up and walked over to the pair of gorillas. They looked up at her from their chairs.

"Hi, guys!" she smiled.

"Who the fuck are you?"

"My goodness, the fellows in this Department are friendly as sailors on shore leave, aren't they?"

"I asked you a question."

"You did, you suave devil, you. Hutyt-Netjer MacIntyre, I'm new. I'm on the Pashed case, and I understand from my sources that you are heavily involved in his corrupt activities, is that true?"

The pair looked at each other. Simultaneously, they arose from their chairs and stood on each side of MacIntyre, towering over her with dark, threatening looks.

MacIntyre smiled, pointed, and said, "Look, Meryr'a has a gun."

They turned their heads and looked toward Meryr'a, who had resumed eating his lunch, head down. MacIntyre kneed one man in the testicles, then, pivoting and picking up momentum, sucker-punched the other in the jaw with a jireugi she'd learned from a particularly nasty Tae Kwon Do sabum, then kept the momentum going and knocked down the first man, who was just straightening up. That ought to get their attention.

She bowed slightly, and said, "Enjoy the rest of your lunch, I'll be around later this afternoon with some questions."

She walked back to the table. Meryr'a was sitting with mouth open. The room had fallen silent.

"I guess lunch is over," said MacIntyre.

MacIntyre, sitting at Meryr'a's desk, saw Sheritr'a leave her desk and walk out with one of the Security men she'd sucker punched. She grinned in anticipation of the atchet-netjer's reaction to the news that her latest employee had already broken the Pashed case, or at least the jaw of one of the corrupt perps. Hearty thanks and a promotion were not on the table, but at the very least Sheritr'a was bound to move her out of the do-nothing chair she occupied. Somewhere down deep, Ma'at approved of MacIntyre's tactics. So MacIntyre sat and did nothing except watch Meryr'a doing nothing. This non-activity was by far the most difficult task MacIntyre had ever undertaken in her career, exceeding even the boredom of a stakeout. Fortunately, it didn't last long.

An hour later, in the conference room with the door closed, MacIntyre explained several times the logic of her actions in the employee dining room to her boss. She calmly explained that she had tried to make friends but hadn't had much success, so she had decided to take on Meryr'a's open case, and the fight had been purely self defense against the threatening behavior of the two Security operatives.

Sheritr'a looked at her. "Hutyt, I'm taking you off that case, right now."

"I'm fine with that, really, Atchet-Netjer."

"Pashed is off limits to you from this point on."

"Yes, ma'am. I understand. I don't like Pashed that much, to be honest, and I'd prefer not to deal with him."

"Stay away from Meryr'a; he's off limits to you too."

"Yes, ma'am. I understand."

"And stay away from my Security people, I will deal with discipline myself."

"Yes, ma'am. I understand. I don't want to damage the men in the department any more than necessary."

"You are very lucky the individuals involved do not want to pursue the matter any further. They understand you are new here and that you don't understand the rules. I'll overlook it this time, but personal violence at work is a firing offense."

"Yes, ma'am, I understand."

Sheritr'a pursed her thin lips and reconsidered her warning. "Do not talk with anybody in any way at all, period. Just go home now and reflect on how to behave as a member of the department. Tomorrow, we'll see. If this happens again, you're gone, understand? Whatever Neb-Waset Setehnekhet thinks."

"Yes, ma'am. I understand."

"I swear, if he hadn't sent you down here himself, I'd have you thrown out the temple door or drowned or something. And I *will* inform Neb-Waset Setehnekhet of your exploits."

"Yes, ma'am. I understand." She was getting the hang of these unfamiliar phrases now after so much repetition, though her emotions were quite mixed at having to say them to preserve her job, pretending a humility she did not feel.

"Get out of here." Sheritr'a waved a hand in disgust at the door.

"Yes, ma'am." MacIntyre walked back to Meryr'a's desk, dozens of eyes on her the whole way shooting metaphorical daggers into her back.

"Hi, there," she said to Meryr'a.

Meryr'a just groaned in despair, holding his head in his hands, elbows resting on the garbage papers strewn over his desk.

She told him, "I'm off the case, so you're free of me. Just a piece of advice. Find a new job. Better hurry." She took her chair back to the desk where she'd borrowed it, thanked its dagger-eyed owner profusely and insincerely, and went off to her stick-fighting gym to work out the kinks she'd acquired from the stress of her first day of work at the Temple of Mentju.

CHAPTER ELEVEN

MacIntyre Uncovers a Nest of Vipers

MacIntyre showed up for work the next day ready for the challenge. Though she knew she could not bring in a gun or a knife through the metal detectors, she figured that nobody would find a nice, hard-plastic collapsible baton if well-positioned. An American stick fighter she knew had given it to her as a present at the ceremony awarding her werkhet status, the equivalent of a black belt in stick fighting. She tucked the holster in the small of her back, under her business suit jacket.

Between her stick-fighting expertise and the Tae Kwon Do skills she had learned back in Boston, she hardly ever needed to use a gun in her work. As she was fitting the baton into place, she thought of Shesmu, who also wore the little swallow hieroglyph of the werkhet on his stick-fighting sleeve. She'd left two more voicemails on his phone, but still no callback. She phrased the last voice-mail with care, as she was not used to boyfriends that didn't return her calls, and her natural response wouldn't help their relationship.

At the Temple of Mentju, the walk of shame in the Security Department took her back through all the desks and up to Sherit-R'a's podium, the metaphorical daggers still flying at her from her co-workers. Sheritr'a had an extra-grim set to her double chins and just pointed at a chair. MacIntyre sat.

"Have you had a chance to think through what I told you yesterday, Hutyt-Netjer?" Sheritr'a's voice, properly applied, could have chilled the walk-in freezer at Shesmu's restaurant.

"Yes, ma'am," she replied. She presented the little speech she had prepared while getting dressed at home. "As a w'abet of Mentju, my loyalties are to the

Hem-Netjer-Tepy and Mentju, and I wouldn't want you to consider me disloyal to you or to the Republic."

"Fine words. Just remember that you are American, and however much you profess loyalty, there are going to be people on the staff here who distrust you. Let it ride, hutyt. They're good people, smart people, and you need to earn their trust. Not hitting them might help with that."

MacIntyre attempted to reframe the conversation. "Ma'am, if you give me something to do rather than putting me in a closet with Meryr'a, you'll see that you can trust me. I'm at my best when I'm working on something real."

"Hmm. Perhaps." Sheritr'a considered. "But you need close supervision. My assistant, Imenka, could use some help on a security matter with the Temple of Imen-R'a. He is an excellent monitor for problem employees. Which you are." She turned to the desk right below her podium. "Imenka, may we speak with you for a moment?"

MacIntyre looked over the man who arose from his desk and approached. He was about 40 years old, 2 meters tall with a tough and wiry body, dark wavy hair, full mustache, sensuous lips with no smile to them, slightly hooded black eyes, and a sharp nose. Altogether, Imenka reminded MacIntyre of a falcon—a hungry falcon. Not a man to underestimate.

"Yes, Atchet-Netjer?" Imenka sat down in an empty chair next to MacIntyre.

"I want you to work with our new Hutyt-Netjer here, Cheryl MacIntyre, on the Imen-R'a matter, if that suits you. She says she needs real work."

"Can we trust her?" This seemed like a bold remark to make in front of a new employee, but it was clear that Imenka was very close to Sheritr'a and her way of thinking about management.

Sheritr'a replied, "No, so you need to keep her on a very short leash."

MacIntyre lips quirked in irritation. "I have my own dog collar if you need it."

Sheritr'a frowned. "What did I just say a minute ago?"

"Sorry, ma'am. I'll try to be as compliant as I can. You can trust me. I'm fine with whatever Imenka needs me to do on whatever kind of leash he wants to use."

Sheritr'a and Imenka looked at each other and nodded simultaneously. He said, "Hutyt-Netjer, let's adjourn to the conference room so I can bring you up to speed."

Imenka led her across the room to the glassed-in conference room. He pointed at a seat and closed the door, then sat across the conference table from her.

He began, "First, let me say that I don't mind working with Americans, I've done it many times in the past and have no animosity because of the latest events."

"But you don't trust me."

The lines of his face moved and sharpened his falcon's nose. "Of course I don't trust you. I don't trust anybody until I know them. Let's see how long a leash you need, Hutyt-Netjer. Are you familiar with the Temple of Imen-R'a in Menmenet?"

"Only by reputation. Never had any medja business there, and I worship Ma'at and Mentju pretty much exclusively."

He fixed his raptor's eyes on her. "Here's the situation: we think there's a spy in that temple, possibly an agent from a terrorist group based in South America, but we haven't found anything concrete. Perhaps you can use your local medjau contacts to find out if they have heard anything or harbor suspicions of anyone in particular."

"You can't just ask the medjau?"

"Not at the moment. Relations are quite strained between the local medjau and the sepat right now. You should not reveal that you have sworn a w'abet's oath to Mentju. Have you told anyone about that yet?"

"No, I haven't. Just as well, I guess."

"Yes. All right. Give your contacts a try, and we'll see where we go from there. And you must report in detail on your contacts, with names, ranks, and the information you get from them. A short leash, all right?" The dark-haired man sat back in his chair and stroked his mustache, looking at her. He continued, "Do you have any American security or diplomatic contacts? Do you have an American security clearance?"

"No, I left America behind when I came here. I wasn't in policing or security when I lived there. I've met the American Consul General recently, though I doubt that will help. Why?"

"There are…complications, with the Temple of Imen-R'a and their relations to the United States Embassy." Imenka smiled again, his black eyes sizing her up as prey. MacIntyre adjusted to the baton pressing into her back. He continued, "But don't worry about that now, we can work on that when it becomes important."

"I see." Should she comply meekly on her short leash, or try something else to shake things up? MacIntyre didn't take to leashes, but the leash appeared the right way to go for now. Shaking things loose only worked if you had things to shake, after all. "So, for now, work on plumbing the depths of the Temple of Imen-R'a with my contacts, and later we'll see."

Imenka bowed his head a little in acknowledgement of this summary. They both arose and walked out of the conference room. MacIntyre asked, "May I grab a corner of your desk? You can attach my leash to a desk leg or something. And you can call me Cheryl, if you like. Sir."

MacIntyre's medjau counterintelligence contact, Idnu Merysekhmet, delivered his comeback to her initial probe about a spy at the Temple of Imen-R'a in his gravelly voice. "MacIntyre, what are you into now?"

"Can't tell you, Sekh, need to know basis only."

"If you need to know, I need to know why."

"Look, I really appreciate how much we've worked together over the years, Sekh. I do. Trust me on this one."

"Fuck that. I trust no one, especially Americans." This last was said with enough sarcastic inflection to let MacIntyre know that he was joking.

"Temple of Imen-R'a, Sekh. South American spy. Everybody else I've talked to doesn't know anything. What do you know?"

"MacIntyre, you've been in Menmenet long enough to know that talking about the internal workings of the Temple of Imen-R'a is not likely to be beneficial to one's career."

"It will be beneficial to mine, Sekh. And if there's a spy, we need to deal with that."

"Do you understand how much power that temple has?"

"Yes, which makes it even more important—"

Sekh laid it out for her. "The hekasepat himself is the head of the temple, as the Hem-Netjer-Tepy of Imen-R'a. That may be ceremonial, but that temple is in charge of so many things, including my budget and my retirement fund, not to mention kickbacks from corruption schemes, that I absolutely cannot risk making them aware of me, personally. MacIntyre, this is the highest level of the Republic's government you're asking about."

"I'll keep it between us, Sekh. Really."

More silence. "There is no spy."

"How do you know."

"We'd know."

"How?"

"You don't need to know. There's no spy."

"Just supposing, Sekh, that there was a spy. Where might I start looking for him? Or her?"

Merysekhmet hung up on her. MacIntyre excused herself to the ladies room and found an empty stairwell, then called Karkin.

"Karkin?"

"Yep."

"Cheryl MacIntyre here."

"Yep."

"I'm working—"

"For Imenka."

She was silent. "How did you know that?"

Silence.

"OK," she said, "Yes. I need to know things about him. And about—"

"The Temple of Imen-R'a. Here's two. Imenka is a killer, and he's complicated."

"Thanks," she said, "but I need something more concrete. Something I can investigate."

"Dangerous."

Exasperated, she replied, "How come *you're* so worried about *my* safety when I can take care of myself?"

Karkin replied to this question with what sounded like a combination of a snort and a grunt, which MacIntyre interpreted loosely as meaning "You have no idea what you're doing."

Even more exasperated, she said, "That's why I need to investigate, Karkin. So I'll know things."

"Don't. Back off. Especially from the Temple of Imen-R'a." He hung up.

Well, wasn't that just fine. Irked, MacIntyre returned to Imenka's desk determined to probe this complicated and dangerous assassin to his depths. Who had he killed? Was he a serial killer, or did he just do it for fun on occasional weekends? Karkin's warning had an energizing effect on her; the fact that Imenka might kill her if she slipped up just speeded up the pace of her secret investigations.

On the one hand, she was pretty sure there was no spy at the Temple of Imen-R'a. Sekh wouldn't actually lie to her, despite his reticence. On the other hand, the interest of the Temple of Mentju in the internal workings of the Temple of Imen-R'a suggested that Imenka and Sheritr'a were interested in the internal security of the Republic in ways that she did not yet understand. If she had a third hand, she would say that they knew perfectly well there was no spy and that they were using it as an excuse to pump her about her contacts in the medjau. Karkin was right: complicated.

At lunchtime, Imenka told her he was heading out to lunch and would be back in an hour. He took a lunch bag from his desk. MacIntyre waited a little then walked out after him, careful not to let him see her following. He did not go to the dining room, he walked down the stairs and across the street to Mentju Park. When he was far enough into the park, MacIntyre followed. She kept her distance but was careful not to lose sight of him among all the people and statuary in the park.

Imenka sat on a bench by a large sphinx statue that was the centerpiece of the park. The head was that of a general who had won a strategic battle against the Japanese in the Great War. MacIntyre leaned against a large statue of the god Mentju a little distance away and pretended to talk into her phone, watching him from behind the statue. He ate something from his bag. After fifteen minutes, he got up, put the bag in a trash receptacle next to the bench, and walked back to the Temple of Mentju. MacIntyre watched him up the stairs of the Temple before moving.

As she was preparing to follow, she saw the American Consul General John Smith approaching from the other side of the park. She hid behind the statue again. She knew the embassy was a couple of blocks away in that direction. He sat down on the bench where Imenka had sat. After carefully looking around, he reached into the trash receptacle next to the bench and pulled out the bag Imenka had deposited there. Unless Mr. Smith supplemented his income by dumpster diving, he had just retrieved some kind of message from Imenka. Smith arose and left the way he had come. MacIntyre realized she had just seen a dead drop, and that Imenka was definitely more complicated than she had thought. And much more dangerous, too. She would bet money that the Americans now knew what she was doing at the Temple of Mentju.

"Where were you?" Imenka asked when she returned to his desk.

"Lunch," she answered. His eyes pinned her as she sat down in the uncomfortable chair. She raised her phone to make another call about the Temple of Imen-R'a. The short leash was getting old fast.

After a time, Imenka arose and went up to talk with Sheritr'a. They both glanced at her. Imenka smiled at his boss and returned to his desk. MacIntyre now had her suspicions about both Imenka and Sheritr'a—perhaps they were both complicated. And dangerous. Should she warn Setehnekhet that his Security

Department was a nest of corrupt, traitorous assassins? Perhaps, just perhaps, he already knew. She caught the eye of the gentleman she had sucker punched the day before and waved at him. He made a snarling motion with his mouth.

"Stop that!" said Imenka.

"You're right, not productive. What should I do next?"

Imenka leaned on his desk, looking across at her. "Atchet-Netjer Sheritr'a thinks it might be useful to visit the Temple of Imen-R'a, just you and me. Undercover. I can give you a ride. Tomorrow, first thing."

MacIntyre grinned and said, "Terrific, a field trip. Looking forward to it!" But she wasn't. Being alone in a car with a traitorous serial killer who had every right to be suspicious of you was not high on her agenda. She would be lucky to enter the Temple of Imen-R'a; more likely she would see the Temple of Inpu from inside mummy wrappings. She would have to figure out a way to evade her new mentor's killing ways.

CHAPTER TWELVE

Shesmu Awakens

"He's awake, Dad!"

My eyes had opened to look straight up at the blue sky. I lay flat on my back on what felt like a bed of dry, sharp pins. I looked up at the tall, green trees that framed the sky, smelled the pine in the air. Pine needles. I turned my head and saw Tahefnu squatting and looking down at me, her long black hair hanging down around her beautiful, upside-down face.

"Unh," I said, meaning "Please somebody tell me what's going on and what I can do about it."

I turned my head in the other direction to see Heh approaching, still in full Miwuk ritual regalia. With R'a shining brightly above, he really did look like my image of a Miwuk god, the sunlight bouncing off the shiny feathers surrounding his head.

"Hey, boy, glad to see you back with us," he said as he knelt down beside me.

"What..." I said, then my throat locked up. "Water..." A completely dry throat refused to let me say much of anything else. All my muscles had stopped working, and I couldn't move, just twitch. So I twitched, frustrated.

Tahefnu turned her head and said, "Get some water for him, please!" I looked around and saw the whole valley's worth of Miwuks looking at me, nudging each other and mumbling things I did not understand. Tahefnu smiled at me, but nobody else did.

A waterskin appeared, and Tahefnu carefully dribbled some into my open mouth. Blessed relief! "More," I croaked. She squirted enough for a mouthful, and I swallowed carefully.

I said, when I could get the words out, "What happened? What's wrong with me?"

Tahefnu said, "Shhh, now. Rest."

Heh said, "You got something big in you, boy. Something really big. It took over when I started up the healing spell. I could feel the pull, like a big wind in reverse sucking me toward you. But it didn't want me, it wanted you, and Bear took hold of me and pulled me back. I saw your eyes go blank, and you sat there for a couple of minutes frozen, then you came out of it and fell over." The shaman shook his head. "We brought you outside here to get some air. I never seen that much power surge in one human being. Not in all the years of knowing the Bear."

"I…didn't see a bear, heard him though, roaring. Out of the dark."

"Yeah, he does that when he's pissed at something. Big roar. Where did you go?"

Heh was looking at me with a concentrated expression on his face under the feather headband.

"I…don't know. It felt like a huge cave, dark, cold. I saw…a man."

"Man or spirit?"

I tried to shake my head but could only make a wiggle. "More water, please?" Tahefnu obliged with the waterskin.

"Man or spirit?" Heh insisted.

"How the fuck would I know?" I said. I took a breath to calm down. "What does a spirit look like? It was a man, but…it was strange, I saw multiple versions of him all at the same time." Memory flooded back. I explained what I had seen with as much detail as I could muster. Even as I said it, it all seemed crazy to me.

"That man with the animal head—what kind of animal?" Heh's face behind the feathers was urgent.

I visualized the god and replied, "Coyote." But there were no Remetjy coyote gods. Just jackals. But I'd seen a coyote head, I was sure of it.

Heh closed his eyes. "Spirit."

"He said I was his son."

Heh's eyes flew open. "Akhen. Akhen?" The feathers on his headdress shook.

"I don't know, I can't remember what my father looked like. I can tell you he didn't have a coyote head. It just *felt* like him."

"Akhen. As a spirit. Using Coyote to help him find you, find your heart. Coyote, huh. That's gonna be a problem, Coyote's a tricky one. But all the

Remetjy stuff, that's new to me." Heh looked worried. "Something big…" he muttered.

"Dad." Tahefnu's voice was sharp.

Heh looked at her, and so did I. She was looking at him with a stern expression.

"OK, OK, daughter." Heh looked back at me. "But he's gotta get ahold of all this as quick as he can. A spirit vision with this power…things are gonna happen. Big things."

"I…can't get ahold of a pine needle, too weak," I said.

"*Dad.*"

"OK." Heh turned to the crowd and said something in Miwuk. Two of the bigger men came up. Somebody brought two long poles and a tarp which they made into a stretcher, and the two men rolled me onto it, none too gently. Somebody dropped the walking stick onto the tarp next to me, and I curled a hand around it. At least I could think about walking, even if I couldn't generate the energy to do it.

I felt too weak to assert myself to Heh, but I couldn't see his shaman's view of all this as a so-called powerful vision—it was just a dream, with the strange images brought on by my concussion and my desperation to find Khenmes, my surrogate father. Akhen, Coyote—maybe my subconscious was struggling with the issues of a 5-year-old abandoned by his father. Maybe Heh was right, something big was going to happen, and it had to do with my search.

I assessed my situation, which felt dire. These dreams could kill me, slowly but surely, if I didn't figure out what was going on inside me. I needed to search for my father, or at least figure out what he meant to my life. I had to start with Khenmes, because I had no idea what else to do. Khenmes knew my father and could tell me what I needed to know.

Tahefnu said, "Shesmu, they're gonna take you to our house so you can rest up."

"I don't want to rest up, I want to *stand* up," I said, uselessly, as I could only twitch a toe or a finger.

"Think about Coyote, Shesmu," said Heh. "I got the feeling you're gonna have to move pretty quick. Get strong, boy. You're gonna need a lot of strength."

Tahefnu got up and spoke to the two men, who carried me off to the house. I could feel the warm breeze and hear the rushing water of the river as I watched the few clouds in the blue sky above. I watched Tahefnu walking beside the stretcher. So beautiful, her walking, her profile, her eyes looking at me with concern. I could hear others walking with us. I thought about the dream. Akhen, my father? What now? Why see him after all these years? Why such a powerful dream? Why Coyote, why Miwuks?

I gripped the walking stick harder, working my hand to get back my strength. I remembered my impression that Ma'at stood right outside my sight, looking on. At least the goddess had not completely abandoned me. But I had no idea why she didn't help me, just ignored the spirit god of my father. And she had golden hair and a golden body, beautiful but very cold. What was my subconscious telling me about the right path? I shivered at the memory.

CHAPTER THIRTEEN
MacIntyre Climbs the Cliff

"Good morning, Hutyt MacIntyre." As she looked down at MacIntyre from her podium, Sheritr'a simultaneously smiled and frowned, and the double chins quivered.

"Would you please have a seat here?" Sheritr'a indicated a chair across from her desk.

MacIntyre stepped up onto the podium and sat down across from Sheritr'a.

Sheritr'a spoke with a very formal tone. "Hutyt-Netjer MacIntyre. You know very well that I disapprove strongly of your presence in our temple."

"I serve at your pleasure, ma'am," said MacIntyre, the grin belying the words.

"After discussion of your *exceptional* contributions to our department," said Sheritr'a, "Neb-Waset Setehnekhet decided he would prefer to take over supervision of your exploits himself. I am sure that Imenka will be very disappointed at not being able to assist you further in your career." Sheritr'a was clearly not on board with this decision. As for Imenka, the only assistance he might offer would be to wrap her in mummy linen after assisting her off into the Duat.

"So, the field trip is off?"

"Indeed. Neb-Waset Setehnekhet desires your presence in his office at your earliest convenience."

"Better get up there, then." MacIntyre arose, eager to get on with it and very eager to avoid the field trip with Imenka.

Sheritr'a hesitated, then said, without any smile or trace of humor, "Hutyt MacIntyre. I feel compelled to let you know that the Hem-Netjer-Tepy often, ah, *adopts* young w'abut such as yourself. As a mentor, of course, as a mentor. Now, while this may sound enticing and exciting and exhilarating for you, please be aware that it might have many negative consequences for your career, as the Hem-Netjer-Tepy often discards his protégés. He discards them rather quickly, and brutally, if they prove unreliable, tiresome, or unwilling to, ah, *commit* to his guidance and principles and needs. Especially his *needs,* Hutyt. And should that happen, Hutyt, I would no longer be in a position to help you gain the trust and support of the temple. I would not in fact have any desire to help you whatsoever. I have a sense that you would not be compliant to Neb-Waset Setehnekhet and his needs; no, not in the least. I hope you understand my advice?"

"Yes, ma'am, I understand." There was that phrase again, running smoothly enough off her lips. And she did understand: Sheritr'a was warning her off any relationship with Setehnekhet.

Sheritr'a waved a hand to dismiss her and turned her attention to the papers on her desk.

Setehnekhet seated himself on the couch in his office. Over his shoulder loomed the large statue of the falcon-head god Mentju. Opposite the couch were two large, antique chairs with lion-paw feet. In her previous visit, MacIntyre had classed these as "uncomfortable;" now, she took a longer look before she sat down and classed them as uncomfortable but extremely valuable. They might even go back to the original Empire of Kemet, but she was no antiquities expert.

"Is there something about the chair that distresses you, Hutyt?" asked the hem-netjer-tepy.

"I was just checking whether it might collapse underneath me, Neb-Waset Setehnekhet," said MacIntyre, smiling.

"Hasn't so far. But if you're worried, sit here." He patted the couch next to him. "We need to have a little discussion about your career."

MacIntyre walked across to the couch and sat, gingerly, about a meter away from the hem-netjer-tepy, who regarded her with what he probably considered a smile: closed, downturned mouth and hooded eyes that looked at MacIntyre with no humor at all.

"First, let us clear the air, Hutyt. When you last spoke with me, you asserted your loyalty to the Republic. You said you could use your knowledge of what it is to be American to help understand the United States during the current crisis. You said to give you a try; we have done that. The report from Sheritr'a—well, let's just say it isn't warm. There was the incident in the dining room, of course, but Sheritr'a says there was nothing in that other than a lapse of discipline." He eyed MacIntyre, looking for a response.

"I assured Atchet-Netjer Sheritr'a that it wouldn't happen again, Neb-Waset Setehnekhet."

"So she said. Very well. I have inquired a little into your background and history in Menmenet."

MacIntyre braced herself for the onslaught, as she was sure that her background was not likely to impress this master of discipline. Djehutymes's comments on her performance had never been warm, and filtered through the discipline of Mentju, she felt sure the creative ways she had employed to get results would not mesh well with the culture of the Temple of Mentju.

Setehnekhet smiled his almost-smile, eyes still hooded. "I am well aware of what you are doing, Hutyt. Your record of success as a hutyt-er-semetyu, and your reputation among your colleagues and masters is very clear. You hope to infiltrate the Temple of Mentju and to learn exactly what we are doing and how and why we are doing it, particularly as regards getting you fired. I can only assume that your oath of loyalty to Mentju does not override your oath to Ma'at. I can only conclude that you come here solely with the desire to get your job back, laying waste to everything that obstructs your path to that goal."

MacIntyre listened to this excellent summary of her innermost thoughts and feelings with dismay, but there was something about the body language of the man that indicated all was not lost. There was also the fact that they were alone rather than having a cohort of armed guards removing her to the unspeakable dungeons in the basement of the temple. She didn't actually know anything about those dungeons, but given the nature of Mentju, she felt sure they were there.

"You mentioned clearing the air. It smells pretty clean to me after that speech, Neb-Waset Setehnekhet. Why am I here and not rotting in the dungeons in the basement?"

"I don't use those for people like you, they're too…crude. I prefer to persuade, when I can. Can I persuade you, Hutyt?"

"To what, sir?"

"To work with me."

"Doing what, sir?"

"Whatever I ask."

"That's a little broad, sir. There's Ma'at to consider."

"Fuck Ma'at."

"Yes, sir. But still." MacIntyre fronted a reluctance she did not feel.

"Hutyt, in these situations, I usually describe a career at the temple with great rank and privileges. That career comes with the opportunity to make a great deal of money and hold a great deal of status and consequential power in the Republic. Given your desire to remain a medjat—and I do not doubt that desire is real and urgent—and your boldness in pursuing that desire, I will not offer you such a career. Instead, I want to make use of you, just as you suggest. Our goals, Hutyt, are not incompatible. Not at all. I could warn you about your overzealous tactics, but I would rather just tell you what you need to know and set you loose to do your job. That job entails a promotion to djaret-netjer, reporting directly to me. It is a title with a good deal of power and status within the temple, and I do not bestow it lightly."

MacIntyre, shifting her undercover persona closer to her real one, said, "This sounds too good to be true, Neb-Waset Setehnekhet. Who do I have to kill?"

The hem-netjer-tepy smiled briefly with his downturned mouth to show he appreciated the humor; his eyes said that he didn't want to see any more of it. He said, "I need to approach the American Embassy in Menmenet. The man we work with—you know him, John Smith, the Consul General at the United States Embassy—he is at the center of the nest of snakes undermining our government. For various political and practical reasons, I cannot approach him myself. You would be an ideal liaison with the man. You can even speak his language."

"I can do that." Should she tell him that he already has people working with Smith? Not just yet; she didn't know enough. "But what do you want from this operation?"

"A back channel."

"Lord?"

"I want to establish a line of communication with the American military through which we can trade diplomatic suggestions and information that will never see the light of day. Any crisis as fraught as the one we are in, with a nuclear power no less, could go sideways in a minute. I need a back channel to ensure that everyone understands exactly what the other is really thinking. I need it to allow the Americans to float alternatives to sending in NATO troops or raining down missiles upon us. I need it to lull Smith into complacency over our capabilities for defending ourselves. I need it to gather information from Smith that he does not understand he is giving to us."

MacIntyre peered through a veil of creative disinformation. "I don't need capabilities for that, sir, just my blue eyes." She focused the attributes in question on his face. "Why me?"

"I want someone who can read between the lines and take action if necessary." He smiled. "I don't think everything that Smith will tell us will be the absolute truth, and I need someone who can investigate and determine the facts. I need someone he thinks is a compatriot. And I need someone who is fearless, deceptive, and ruthless."

"My best attributes, sir. What about the Numunuu Empire and the rest of NATO? And the American government itself?"

"In this case, the channel is between the militaries, not the politicos. And it is the Americans we need to deal with, we can ignore the indigenes, they are just NATO allies being controlled by the Americans. But we'll consult with the hekasepat. Do you want to meet him?"

MacIntyre smiled. "That would be wonderful, sir. It would legitimize all this for me."

"Very well, I'll set up a meeting."

"Do I get a cover? A story to tell to Smith?"

"No need. You've met Smith, correct? At your dismissal."

"You're very well informed, Neb-Waset Setehnekhet."

"He knows you and he knows your situation. He probably knows more about you than I do, and I know quite a lot. Explain the facts of life to him and refer him to me if he needs to verify anything, and reassure him as to your loyalty to the 28 states, whatever, I don't give a fuck. Just have him be discreet about contacting me. Do you agree to do this for us, Hutyt?"

"What about pay?"

"Triple what we're paying you now and a bonus for excellent performance."

"Agreed." At least she'd be able to eat now, independent of Shesmu's charity, maybe save up some money for that house she'd been dreaming of for so many years. Possibly Setehnekhet was setting her up for something nasty. Between that and Imenka, MacIntyre thought she'd better check out that mummification insurance scheme she'd read about. The motto in the White House was "don't trust, verify;" MacIntyre speculated that the hidden motto in the Temple of Mentju was simpler: "don't trust." But for now, she was where she needed to be.

Setehnekhet got up and went to his desk. She stood up. He retrieved a piece of paper and gave it to her. "This is an appointment as djaret-netjer, signed and registered with the temple scribes. You now can go anywhere and read anything except materials and rooms that require A-Plus level access. I'll let Sheritr'a know you won't be going back to the Security Department. I am sure this will be a relief for her, poor woman." He smiled his raptor's smile. He had the appointment paper ready, assuming she would take the job. Very sure of himself, was Setehnekhet, she thought.

He continued, "One thing, Djaret-Netjer. You must keep this promotion a secret within the temple. No one outside must know about it. We don't want the United States Embassy to get word that a djaret-netjer is taking an interest in Embassy affairs, even if she is American. Yes? You are just an American citizen taking care of personal business."

"Yes, Neb-Waset Setehnekhet."

Setehnekhet walked her next door to his administrative office and had the supervisor allocate a new desk for her. He then introduced her around to the staff and told them she was a special appointment working directly for him and to stay out of her way and to not discuss her with anyone outside the office. He might as well have been a despot announcing his latest concubine to his harem. She sat at her new desk and contemplated the joy of being a go-between for two of the most detestable players in Menmenet.

The next morning, Setehnekhet's limousine and entourage headed north up the hill toward the Palace of the Republic, set among the palaces of the very rich that stretched out along a ridge on the tallest hill in Menmenet.

"Welcome to the real world of power, Djaret-Netjer," smiled the hem-netjer-tepy.

"Smooth ride, Neb-Waset Setehnekhet."

Setehnekhet relaxed his excessively military posture and took a drink from a waiting water bottle. "I think it is time, Djaret-Netjer, to leave formality behind. Please call me Set, at least in these informal surroundings. May I call you Cheryl?" He offered her a second water bottle, which she took and drank from.

"Sure, why not? OK, Set, why are we really going to see the hekasepat?"

"Cheryl, do you have any idea how much trouble we are in?"

"Um. By 'we' do you mean the two of us or the Republic?"

"The Republic, of course; I am in no trouble at all, and you are only in as much trouble as you manage to create for yourself." He smiled his downturned smile again.

"Then I think the Republic is in a lot of trouble." A Republic that fires you for being American, for example. That's a lot of trouble.

"Cheryl, after you have met the hekasepat, you will begin to understand the true parameters of that trouble."

MacIntyre absorbed this for a minute, then said, "So the hekasepat might not be the strong, positive leader the voters elected in a landslide at the last election?"

"The hekasepat is a farmer from the Central Valley who does not know which end of a missile is which unless I tell him. As for the voters, they get what they deserve." The hem-netjer-tepy stared out the window at the passing houses and shops as the limo purred up the hill.

"So you're the power behind the throne?"

"Yes, though I prefer to think of it as the key advisor to His Excellency in these times of trial."

"Sorry, Set, I like to say what I think."

The man was truly full of himself, but until she actually saw the hekasepat in action, she would withhold judgment on the size of the glass. After all, a man could be the biggest narcissist in the world and yet still be the most powerful man in it. For a time, anyway. But MacIntyre knew that you could never really trust such a man. Especially the man that had had her fired.

Setehnekhet replied, "Refreshing; but it might be best to guard your tongue a bit more than you do. Not with me; I don't care for flattery or euphemism in my djaru, and your tongue suits you quite well, I think. But a reasoned restraint in public communication is good with men like the hekasepat."

"Noted." Shut the fuck up, in other words, she thought, or you won't get your job back.

"In that regard, are you aware of the protocol for addressing the hekasepat?"

"Nope, it's never come up in my lowly work as a medjat."

"His Excellency Hekata'an Menma'atr'a Sebekemheb is addressed as Your Excellency or by his full title. My guess is he will dispense with this and allow you to call him by his nesubit, Sebekemheb, and possibly just Seb if you get to know him really well. Don't. He is *excessively* informal, at times. And you should expect some initial disapproval just for being American."

"So the democratically elected leader of the Republic uses the same naming protocol as the Emperor, with both a za-r'a name and a nesubit name?" She'd never really gotten up to speed on the higher levels of government in her adopted country.

"There was a need, in the early days, to establish the legitimacy of the Republican leader in the eyes of the Empire and its leaders. Taking the various throne names was one way to do that; it asserts a presence worthy of the same respect as a global leader. Now it is a well-understood custom, in the same way such customs surround the Queen of England, for example."

"We, meaning Americans, went the other way. George Washington decided to dispense with all the formality and just went with 'Mr. President'. He was making a point about the British."

Setehnekhet smiled and replied, "And the British king and most of the other European rulers looked down on him for that, despite his having handed them their heads in his Revolutionary War."

"Americans didn't much care back then."

"But that perceived weakness was the key to why the Americans fought so many useless wars before their technological prowess clearly established their legitimate role as a world power. We have chosen to project our power directly instead."

MacIntyre silently translated "technological prowess" into "nuclear weapons," which the Republic still did not possess, as it was an early signatory to the Nonproliferation Treaty.

"But you say the hekasepat is weak," she brought the conversation down to the earth they were about to tread.

"Not externally; he and I present a good front through my advice and his ability to act the part. You will see, Cheryl."

The limousine pulled up to the security gate of the palace with its identity checks and car inspection. Once through security, the car rolled up the sweep and stopped before the palace doors. The driver got out and opened the door for Setehnekhet. MacIntyre scrambled out behind him. They walked up the travertine stairs to the huge bronze doors. An army guard in dress uniform opened one door for them, and they went into the palace.

After walking through a seemingly endless series of corridors, the pair arrived at the private office of the hekasepat. They entered the anteroom, where a lone scribe sat at a large, ornate desk with multiple phones and a rather elderly computer.

The scribe looked up and smiled. "Right on time, Neb-Waset Setehnekhet. His Excellency will be right with you." He indicated the sofa, and they seated themselves to wait. It wasn't but about two minutes before the inner door opened, and a handsome man of about 60 peered out, smiled, and said, "Set, great to see you. Come in, come in." He swung the door wide.

The hekasepat looked just like his pictures, thought MacIntyre. Tall, strongly built, dark hair with grey along the sides, and all his features crinkling in a welcoming, politician's smile. He backed into his office, and Setehnekhet and MacIntyre went in after him. The hekasepat sat in a large armchair and indicated the couch across from it. They seated themselves after bowing. MacIntyre gazed out the huge windows, which gave onto a long balcony overlooking the northern part of Menmenet, the Bay, and the bare, brown hills beyond.

The hekasepat looked at her in astonishment. "An American? What the fuck, Set, you brought an American to my office?"

"This is Djaret-Netjer Cheryl MacIntyre, my newest staff adjutant, whom I wanted to introduce to you, Your Excellency."

"Now, Set, you know damn well that I don't like fucking Americans. That's why I've removed all of them from government positions." He smiled at MacIntyre, but his eyes were cold.

"Djaret-Netjer MacIntyre should prove very valuable to us, Seb. She is a loyal citizen of the Republic and has proved that loyalty to us over many years of service. I am personally very fond of her, and I hope you can overcome your dislike; she is worth it."

"Oh, very well." He nodded briefly. "Ms. MacIntyre. I will do my best."

"It's an honor, Your Excellency." She bowed with her deepest bow.

The hekasepat unbent. "I suppose I can relax the formality with you as well, then; call me by my nesubit, please."

"Thank you, sir." She bowed again. He returned the bow by nodding his head and smiling the smile that got him elected.

"What's the latest, Set?" He turned toward Setehnekhet.

"I brought Djaret MacIntyre here, Seb, to introduce her and to let you know what she's planning to do. We're going to open a back channel to the American military through the American Embassy in Menmenet."

"Are we? I thought we were going to throw everything we had at them. Why do we need a back channel?" The hekasepat looked bewildered.

"It is a nuanced situation, Seb. At the same time we need a strong military response to the NATO provocations, we need to make sure we are communicating our real needs to the people that matter, and that's the CIA and the US Special Operations Command, USSOCOM. We have good information that Consul General John Smith has a direct line to the leadership in both those organizations."

"Well, goodness. Why would we need to communicate with them? Real needs? Aren't our real needs to make them go away and stop bothering us? And why are we harboring an American spy as a diplomat? We ought to expel the son-of-a-bitch!" He slapped his forehead. "Forgive me, Ms. MacIntyre, no disrespect!" He delivered the winning smile again.

"Not a problem, Sebekemheb, I'm on your side."

Impatience showing in his voice, Setehnekhet explained in detail. "There will always be spies, Seb, as I've explained before. The trick is to know who they are, not to get rid of them. And, in this case, we need—or may need—a way to talk to USSOCOM without delay to make sure our acts and intentions are properly understood in the context of our public stance. Remember that we have ties to the NATO countries that we don't want to break. But the NATO people and the US Northwest Command aren't important right now, only the CIA and USSO-COM."

"Shouldn't I just talk to the president? He's a jerk, but we can still talk, I guess." A flash in the hekasepat's eye suggested he was still mad enough at the president to shout rather than talk.

"I don't think talking to the president is going to get us very far with military things, Seb. He doesn't understand those things well and has his own agenda. And he tends to react badly to any kind of talk he thinks is disrespectful of his power, as you are well aware given what happened to you last week at the White House. It's the special ops people, the CIA, and NATO who are running this show."

"That kind of takes me out of the loop, doesn't it, Set? I don't know...."

"I'll make sure you stay in the loop, Seb, trust me on that." There was that word again, thought MacIntyre, *trust*. She was pretty sure she shouldn't trust either of these guys out of her sight, or in it either.

The hekasepat looked at his feet in dismay. "It's just that when I have to decide things quickly, they spiral out of control, you know? I don't want to be blindsided by things. I don't like it. It wouldn't be good for me or the party, you know, if it looks like I've screwed up again. In the next election, that is; it wouldn't be good." He added as an afterthought, straightening up, "Or for the Republic, either!"

"Yes, I know, and I'll make sure you're not blindsided, Seb." Setehnekhet's tone was faintly patronizing; MacIntyre wondered whether Sebekemheb picked this up.

He apparently did not. He thought the problem over. MacIntyre could practically hear the rusty gears clanking, reminding her of Meryr'a. After a minute or two, he gave up, smiled, and said, "Very well, go to it!"

He stood. Setehnekhet and MacIntyre stood up too. "Great to meet you, Djaret-Netjer MacIntyre. Good luck with your mission, and don't let your

countrymen pull the wool over your eyes. Vicious, evil thugs, the lot of them."
He paused. "No offense."

"None taken, Sebekemheb! Thank you for your blessing."

"Was it a blessing? I suppose it was. Set here is better at that sort of thing. I'm just a simple farmer, you know. I do preside over the daily blessing in the public chapel of the sepat, but that's as far as it goes. Say, it's time for that: I have to go!" The humble hekasepat smiled and bowed his head in dismissal. Setehnekhet and MacIntyre bowed more deeply and left the office. MacIntyre resolved to read the voting booklet for the next election more carefully than she had read the last one —if she were still a voting citizen by that time!

CHAPTER FOURTEEN

Shesmu Finds Forbidden Love

I OPENED MY EYES, AGAIN staring at the cracks in Heh's ceiling. Same blanket, same feeling of utter weakness. I opened my mouth to speak and came up with only a croak—my throat seemed consumed by a raging thirst.

"He's alive again, Dad," said a voice from the other room. Tahefnu appeared in the doorway and looked at me inquisitively. I croaked again. "I think he's channeling the Frog, Dad."

"Frog is powerful, daughter, never underestimate him."

I croaked louder and made futile moves to get out of the bed. Tahefnu hurried over and pushed me back in the bed. She helped me sit up, arranging some pillows behind my back and turning the blanket up over my lower body. They'd taken all my clothes off and piled them on a little table in the corner of the room.

"Sorry, Shesmu, just having some fun. I'll get some water, sounds like you need it." She hurried out of the room and came back with a cup. I took the cup and sipped until my throat was more reasonable.

I sat back and savored the taste of the wonderful water and the soothing feeling it made as it rehydrated my throat. I stared at the cracks in the ceiling and imagined all kinds of things, like lying in MacIntyre's arms in her bed and ordering my line cooks around and walking down the hill from my house in Menmenet through the fog.

A hand gripped mine, softly. I brought my eyes down and saw Tahefnu sitting by the bedside, a half-smile on her lips and her black eyes fixed on mine. I don't know what the Miwuks believe, but we Remetjy believe all thought and emotion center in the heart, the brain doesn't count for anything. Not really true, but it makes for a good metaphor. The heart is where the gods speak to us, according to tradition, though I can't say I've ever had the pleasure of speaking to a god, at least until the last few days. The trouble with my heart was that it was far too weak at that moment, along with the rest of my body parts.

"How are you feeling?" asked Tahefnu, letting go of my hand and smoothing back the hair that had fallen over my forehead. "You were out for quite a while."

"What day is it?" I asked.

"The ceremony was yesterday, you've slept all evening and night, and now it's afternoon again."

"What happened to me?" I was still as weak as a kitten and could barely move. I'm a pretty athletic guy, in my way, and I'd never felt like this.

"The best Dad and I can figure, you took on a god. Dad says he's your father, but that don't really make any sense to us. Or at least, to me. Dad is…he's real quiet about it. He's got something in mind, but he won't talk about it." She shook her head in disgust. "Old man stuff. I'm supposed to be a shaman, but these old guys won't talk to me. They just say stuff like 'Hummingbird flies fast, you'll get there, little one.' Crap."

"What I'd like to know is, what kind of herbs were you throwing on the fire?"

"Just sage, none of the heavy stuff. It was a healing ceremony!"

I consulted my body. No pain at all in my ankle; but I couldn't move it, and there were other issues I worried more about. "It might have worked, I'll let you know when I can find a way to get out of bed."

Tahefnu stripped off the blanket and checked my ankle. Her fingers rubbing around the joint and bottom of my foot made my foot feel better but made my other problem worse.

"Stop that."

"Does it hurt?"

"No, it does not hurt. It…stop that!"

She jerked away like she'd touched a hot coal.

"Sorry! I didn't mean to hurt you."

"You haven't, yet. Look, I'm in bad shape right now. Having you here is good, but I seem to be pretty sensitive right now to touch, so…"

She smiled. "I get it. You're ticklish, right?" Her eyes fastened on a part of me that wasn't under control. "Oh, now I get it! Wow! OK, it looks like you're getting better!" She turned and called, "Hey Dad, come and look! Your medicine is powerful, Bear's taking care of business."

Now, in the ordinary course of things, I am a one-woman man. When I'm in love, it just feels right. Over the last couple of years, I'd developed very strong feelings for MacIntyre, and she for me. But whatever had happened in the Miwuk ceremony clearly shook something loose. When Tahefnu touched me, it was an electric shock. Where MacIntyre and Menmenet once filled my heart, a Miwuk woman poured herself into it.

Heh came into the room, and Tahefnu pointed at my rebellious body part. Heh smiled. "Dang, how about that, daughter? And the ankle don't hurt any-more?"

"He says not much, Dad." She turned back to me. "I don't think you're in any shape to do anything about it yet, right?"

I just made a weak Remetjy no-gesture with my hands, as I was speechless with embarrassment.

Heh came over to the bed. He inspected the ankle and looked into my eyes. "No swelling, at least in the ankle, and your eyes are clear."

I finally found my voice. "No pain, but these feelings—it's really strange, I have no idea where they're coming from."

Tahefnu smiled, and said, "Sure you do. Or am I that ugly?"

"No," I said, "not ugly at all. But I'm in love with someone in Menmenet." I checked my heart, and MacIntyre still occupied most of it, but there was this large lump that represented Tahefnu now. "Can you cover me up, please?"

"That's OK, Menmenet is far away and you're here and now. Just go with whatever feels right. Right, Dad?" She didn't cover me up.

Heh looked at me with a grin. "I don't know, I'm not ready to have a son-in-law yet, I'm too young. How about the bride-price? He's already in debt to me for the healing ceremony. I got no idea how much money he's got. And are you a good hunter?"

"Very funny. I'm not ready to have a father-in-law yet. I am good with a bow, though." I closed my eyes and tried to think about the most boring math textbook I'd ever studied. That usually worked.

Heh said, in a serious voice, "Boy, I don't mind anything daughter doesn't mind, but I think you got something when you say strange things are going on. I been thinking a little about what I heard in the ceremony. I got suspicions about your new god, and I'm betting you'll need to get ready for some pretty different feelings about life from now on. Things are gonna pull you in ways you ain't been pulled before, you know? But I got no idea why daughter is pulling you so much. It's OK, but strange."

I opened my eyes and let the math go. "Why all the mystery, Heh? What do you know? Why is my father in all this? Why don't you just tell me what you're thinking?"

Heh just smiled. "Lots of questions, huh? Coyote's involved now. Gotta be careful with that animal. With spirit-things like this, especially with Coyote involved, it is best to let the spirit guide the man to where he needs to be and not to get in the way."

Tahefnu snorted. "That's the kind of old-man crap I was talking about, Shesmu. Well, hell, Hummingbird's fast, maybe Coyote's fast too, and you'll figure it all out before I'm an old lady hummingbird." She reached over and rubbed my cheek with her fingers. Electric shocks. Let's see, the eigenvalues of the coefficient matrix of an elliptic partial differential equation…. Even math wasn't working today to get things quieted down.

Tahefnu finally had some mercy and drew up the blanket over my embarrassment, leaning over me, which helped the situation not at all.

CHAPTER FIFTEEN
MacIntyre Listens Hard

MacIntyre called the United States Embassy the next day and made an appointment to see the Consul General, John Smith. She then called Shesmu and left another voicemail. She hinted vaguely about her new position but couldn't help but snark a little more. Where the fuck *was* the man?

She rooted around in her old Boston boxes and finally turned up her somewhat dog-eared American passport, European and Hawaiian visas from long-ago family vacations reminding her of the worst experiences in her life: family vacations. The only thing that had positive connotations for her was the entry visa stamp for the Ta'an Imenty Republic. She rejected her earlier self in the rotten picture with the crappy American hairstyle that her mother had insisted she wear, then noticed the expiration date: three months from now. An opportunity, a cover.

She took care over dressing, putting on a black business suit over a white blouse with a silly little scarf she had bought on a whim many years ago as a teenager. She unearthed her high-heel shoes, which were apparently still worn by businesswomen in Boston, according to the movies she'd seen. She put the collapsible baton in its holster in the small of her back and checked to make sure that the suit jacket didn't bulge. She didn't expect an attack on her at the Embassy, but you never knew. This spy game had her a little spooked.

The United States Embassy was on Liberty Street in the American sector of Menmenet, in the southern part of the city along the north shore of Iahmes Creek. MacIntyre had patronized an American stick-fighting gym near there for several years before moving to Shes's stick gym up north. The embassy was just a few blocks east toward the Bay from her apartment.

MacIntyre walked the few short blocks down Iunu to Liberty Street and looked the embassy over. She had never had occasion to go inside. It was a two-story mansion in the old Remetjy style—no street windows, a flat roof, and presumably an inner courtyard. A stone wall about 3 meters high and topped with razor wire surrounded the building. Blast barriers made the sidewalk very narrow. MacIntyre could see a flagpole flying the American flag with its 28 stars, one of which represented her home state of Massachusetts, a place she hoped never to see again. The flag brought back far too many painful memories.

She showed her passport at the metal gate and told the marine guard that she wanted to see the Consul General. The guard phoned in, then opened the gate just enough to admit her. The ambience suggested that the Americans had some security concerns. MacIntyre smiled to herself, thinking that the concerns were fully warranted.

She crossed a parking area through more blast barriers and a small courtyard occupied by a lawn and several oak trees. She walked down a flagstone path meandering through and up to the door of the Embassy. She spotted seven different security cameras covering her as she walked. She rang the bell on the embassy door, which clicked open to admit her. She walked into the reception area, where a short, fat Remetjet with dark hair and eyes inspected her, then indicated a well-upholstered chair. "Mr. Smith will be with you in a moment, Ms. MacIntyre. May I see your passport?"

MacIntyre gave the woman her passport, then went to sit down. The woman typed into a computer, scanned the passport, and looked a little worried, but said nothing.

After a few minutes, John Smith walked down the stairs behind the reception area. Smith was a thin-lipped man, and his wire-rimmed glasses glinted in the fluorescent light, concealing his eyes. He stopped by the reception desk, picked up MacIntyre's passport, and examined it. He then walked over to MacIntyre, who rose out of the chair and shook his offered hand.

"Come this way, Ms. MacIntyre," said Smith, "We'll use the conference room." He led the way down a short hall into a conference room with floor-to-ceiling windows onto the central courtyard, which looked like a typical Menmenet courtyard but had chairs and tables, presumably for the employees to sit at while eating lunch.

Smith sat in a chair at the conference table and put her passport on the table in front of him. "Have a seat, Ms. MacIntyre. What can I do for you? You did not seem anxious to avail yourself of our services the last time we met."

"Sorry about that, Mr. Smith." MacIntyre smiled. "I was pretty stressed that day, as you can imagine. I truly appreciate and value your work here as the representative of the United States. I really hope you can help me with a couple of problems."

Smith replied, "I'm very sure we can help."

"All right. First, my passport will expire soon. Can you expedite renewal for me so I won't have any problem traveling back to the States in the near future? It seems likely that I will have to do that."

"Certainly. You have dual citizenship?"

"Yes, that's right."

"Shouldn't be a problem. I'll keep this," he said, tapping the passport.

"All right, thanks. Now, for the big ask."

Smith folded his hands and waited.

"After the medjau fired me, I decided to try for a position at the Temple of Mentju, and due to some luck and hard work, I'm an adjutant to Hem-Netjer-Tepy Setehnekhet. Do you know Neb-Waset Setehnekhet?"

"I have met Neb-Waset Setehnekhet at social occasions, yes, but I don't know him well. Congratulations on the new job, Ms. MacIntyre. What can I do for you?"

MacIntyre looked around the room. "Are you recording this meeting?"

Smith looked taken aback. "Why, no; should I?"

"No, definitely not. Please keep what I'm about to ask you confidential for now, if you would."

"Certainly; you're being very mysterious, though, Ms. MacIntyre."

"Neb-Waset Setehnekhet wants to establish a back channel to the US military, specifically the USSOCOM, and also to the CIA. He wants me to be the conduit from his office to yours. He wants you to keep the channel entirely confidential."

Smith sat back in his chair, a look of surprise on his face. "That's a pretty unusual request, Ms. MacIntyre." He considered it for a minute, then continued, "I'd have to clear it with the State Department Bureau of Diplomatic Security."

"Neb-Waset Setehnekhet wants you to keep this very confidential, sir. Perhaps you can just clear it directly through the Secretary of State? Or even just with the appropriate people in the military—I'm sure you have your contacts, sir. We'd like to involve as few intermediaries as possible, to ensure rapid and accurate communication. The escalating situation has the Hem-Netjer-Tepy very worried about miscommunications causing problems between the countries."

Smith rubbed his mouth, thinking about it. "Out of curiosity, where do your loyalties lie, Ms. MacIntyre?"

"I'm loyal to the U. S. A., Mr. Smith, but I live and work in the Republic and I want things to work out between the countries." A little dissimulation as to loyalty never hurt anything except in Shakespeare.

"And this comes directly from Neb-Waset Setehnekhet?" His cold blue eyes probed hers.

"Yes, as far as I know, only he is aware of it."

Smith mulled this over again, then said, "Very well, I'll talk with some folks and see what we can do. Very confidential folks. All right? Where can I reach you? Do we need secure communications?"

MacIntyre gave Smith her cell number and said, "No need for secure phones, but any serious information will be transmitted in person and not recorded, OK? I'll come to the embassy, my citizenship gives me cover for that. And my passport renewal."

"Very well, I'll let you know. And, you know, we might expect something in return."

"I'm sure Neb-Waset Setehnekhet will be most grateful, and most helpful."

"I'm counting on it," said Smith. He showed her out all the way to the gate and shook her hand warmly before the marine let her out and closed the gate behind her with a loud clang.

The next day, MacIntyre sat at her desk pretending to read papers, having adopted Meryr'a's strategy for appearing busy while doing nothing. Finally her phone rang. Mr. Smith said, "It's a go. My contacts are very interested, Ms. MacIntyre, and everyone hopes things will work out to everyone's satisfaction."

"Thanks, sir. I'll let Neb-Waset Setehnekhet know."

Setehnekhet. Time to take control. MacIntyre hesitated. Was this really the right thing to do? What did right mean? She'd made her purchase surreptitiously from a small shop near her apartment that she knew about from her medjat work. MacIntyre extracted the small black box from a desk drawer and put it in her pocket, then walked across to Setehnekhet's office and asked to see him. After a few minutes, the assistant told her to go in.

Setehnekhet stood near his desk, looking out the window. He turned as MacIntyre walked in and said, "Well?"

"Mission accomplished, Set. John Smith is on board with his contacts."

"Thank you, Cheryl, I knew you were the right person for this job. Drink?" He gestured to the bar over on one wall.

"Sure. Glass of white wine?"

Setehnekhet walked over and poured two drinks. While his back was turned, MacIntyre attached the small box under his desk. She stood behind the desk and looked out the window. He came back and gave her a glass of wine, and she toasted. "To America!" He smiled and raised his glass of brandy. They chatted, sitting on his couch. When she finished her drink, she left him to savor alone the success of his measures to avoid war. She had some listening to do.

MacIntyre went down a floor to the Records Department. She introduced herself to the clerk, then asked for some records on the Imen-R'a investigation that she'd been working on with Imenka. She took the folders, then found a small desk nestled in between some tall shelves, completely invisible to anyone. She took what looked like a smartphone from the bag she carried and plugged some earbuds into it. She spread the folders over the desk to look as though she were studying them, then turned on the phone, which was not really a phone. It was a powerful receiver linked to the bug under Setehnekhet's desk.

"—successful operation." Setehnekhet's voice was firm and loud; the bug was working. "Yes, this line is secure. You handled the situation well, John. She didn't suspect a thing."

A hand fell on MacIntyre's shoulder, and she jumped in surprise. She turned her head; it was Sheritr'a. She removed an earbud.

The fat woman smiled a thin smile. "Hello, Djaret-Netjer. The records clerk said you were over here. I just wanted to congratulate you on your promotion." She looked down at the desk. "Doing some work for the Hem-Netjer-Tepy?" She picked up one of the records.

"Following up on my work with Imenka." She removed the other earbud and turned off the phone.

Sheritr'a grunted. "Humph. I think you can let that go. Imenka has everything under control. That's an order."

"Yes, ma'am." MacIntyre probably outranked Sheritr'a now, but she wanted to get rid of the woman, and she thought that being meek would speed that process up. It did; Sheritr'a put the file down on the desk. "Take care, Djaret-Netjer. My advice still stands."

"Thanks; I'll be fine."

Sheritr'a's glare should have turned MacIntyre to stone, but in the absence of magic, this failed. Sheritr'a turned and left, and MacIntyre turned the phone back on, put the earbuds in, and listened.

A few minutes later, she heard Sheritr'a's voice through the bug.

"Set, I want that bitch as far away from you as possible. She's trouble. She's down in Records looking at Imenka's work. It's too dangerous. What if she finds out about Smith and Imenka? Imenka just gave him our troop arrangements yesterday. Maybe she suspects him."

"Sher, Sher, calm down. I've got her under control. Assuming you mean my new djaret-netjer?"

Sheritr'a voiced her very direct opinion. "How many other women are you fucking, Set? You think any woman is under your control. You're fucking her, aren't you?" Sheritr'a's voice was contemptuous.

"*You* are the only woman under my control. And, no, I'm not fucking her. Yet."

"I'm under your control only because I like doing what you like. But that bitch worries me. She's not stupid, Set. She's dangerous. She's a bomb waiting to go off."

"I just talked to Smith, he says she's convinced she's working with him in confidence. I don't see anything to worry about. I like danger. I like explosions. Come here, you. You need some of my control."

There was a silence for a time and some rustling.

"How about right here, right now?" Setehnekhet's voice was hoarse.

"On the couch? Here, I'll…oh, that's…. Tighter."

After a few more confirmatory sounds, MacIntyre took out the earbuds, shut off the phone, gathered the records and returned them to the clerk, and went back to her desk to think. She was on the right track, but that track twisted around in all kinds of complicated ways. John Smith had asked where her loyalties lay, but the situation was such a mess that she didn't even know what the sides were, much less whose side she was on. The scary thing, the porn scene in the hem-netjer-tepy's office excited her in ways she didn't care to acknowledge. She put that thought away and focused on what to do about Sheritr'a and the grace granted her by Setehnekhet. She sat, very quiet, and had no idea what to do.

CHAPTER SIXTEEN

The Gods Tempt Shesmu

I WAS DREAMING. I HOPE I was dreaming.

Ma'at had come loaded for Bear. Not finding Bear, she turned her sights on my spirit-god—my father, a Miwuk shaman, and some kind of Coyote-god all wrapped up in one. Dreams have a logic all their own, and impossible things happen. They mean nothing, really, they're just the heart's way of reconciling the incompatible things you've learned, hoped, and felt. That's all they are.

I wandered on a mountainside on a path full of boulders, clambering over and around them to get to where I was supposed to be, but I had no real idea where that was. All I knew was the path.

I sensed a presence behind me and looked around. There was the goddess Ma'at in all her glory, drifting along behind me without strain—she just floated over the boulders. Ma'at is young and beautiful with glossy, dark hair spread over her shoulders and held back from her face by a thin headband with a feather sticking through it. I understand that feather is very heavy when you weigh your soul against it. She wore bracelets around her upper arms, her wrists, and her ankles, and her red sheath dress showed off her body's perfection.

Her right hand held a stick, a w'as scepter of power and dominion, and her left hand held an ankh, the symbol of life. I recognized the w'as scepter as Heh's walking stick. Now, while all this presents a picture of loveliness and desire, that is not what you think about when you see her face. It is a terrifying face, for all its loveliness: no smile, and the eyes pierce you to the core, rooting out any conflict or disorder in your soul. Truth is beautiful, but very hard. I turned back to the path and scrambled a little faster over the boulders. This was Ma'at's path.

I came to a flat place on the mountainside, snow-covered and cold. I saw a cave, and I knew for a certainty that this was the cave of my earlier vision. A man stepped out of the cave—well, a god, really, the Remetjy man with the head of a Coyote. I felt no fear, only loneliness and exhaustion.

Suddenly, Ma'at stood in front of me and confronted the Coyote spirit-god. Her arms now had great wings, which she folded in front of her body. She held the walking stick in front of her body as the scepter of dominion over the gods; Ma'at asserted the right to judge a god's behavior.

The Coyote cocked his animal head slightly to one side and raised a lip in a sneer.

"You have no dominion here, goddess. I am not part of your collection of misfits and nature-lovers."

Ma'at's face never changed. "I may not have dominion, but I have a voice, a strong voice to which you must listen, or die." Her voice was strong, but not loud; you could feel the force of it.

"I cannot die, I am already dead." The Coyote grinned with all his teeth.

"Shit, that's true." Ma'at considered this for awhile, then shook her head impatiently. "Well, just listen, then. Now, this man, this Shesmu, is a good man who pursues ma'at with all the power he can muster."

"That is true, goddess. He is my son and was raised in the right way, though not in my way."

"He is not the son of a coyote."

"Coyote is my spirit now that I am in the spirit world; I was not Coyote then."

Ma'at brought the conversation back to me. "This Shesmu has seen you in all your forms. He wants very much to understand you and why you are part of him."

"Yes, now that he is here on our land. Before, I could not reach him."

"OK, let's get real. All this abstraction is nice, but you're making him nuts."

"How so?" The Coyote was not sneering, just inquisitive.

"By tempting him with the Miwuk woman. You're trying to connect him to that people."

"Tempting…in what way?"

"By making him feel strong feelings for her, by arousing him whenever she touches him, by guiding his heart toward her and away from my w'abet." Her voice was strong and accusing.

"Ah, so that's what this is really all about. Your w'abet. That MacIntyre. She's a real piece of work. My son loves her, though, and I would never interfere with that."

"Really. That's exactly what you're doing. I've spent a long time creating this relationship and I'm damned if I'm going to let a fucking Coyote break them up. Together they are a powerful force for creating ma'at in the world."

"First, I'm not actually a Coyote, just hanging around one. This—" he slapped his furry jaw, "this is just cosmetic, it keeps things sane between us, and gives Shesmu something to think about. Second, I'm not tempting him, maybe you should find out who is. Third, I don't care about ma'at in their world, only mine."

"I don't give a shit about your face, your lies, or your world. You've got to stop tempting him with the woman."

"I'm not."

"You are."

"Nope." The Coyote grinned and shook his head.

Ma'at spread her wings wide, suddenly, with a loud rushing noise of feathers beating air, blocking my sight of the Coyote. Then she was gone, and so was the cave. There was only a path, a path I knew I must take. I felt a push in the middle of my back, looked over my shoulder, and there she was, no wings now, pushing with the head of Heh's walking stick. She gave me the stick, and I walked on.

I awoke in the morning to find Tahefnu sitting by my bedside, holding my hand. I faced the fact that her touch had a very stimulating effect on my body, or at least on certain parts of it. I gently disengaged my hand from Tahefnu's and rubbed my aching head with it. She sat calmly in a chair by the bed.

"You were dreaming," said Tahefnu. "I came in to check on you a couple of times in the night, and you mumbled and tossed and turned. It was bad, I think, but I didn't want to wake you, that can turn things very bad."

"It…was complicated."

"Then, this morning, you tried to push something away, but I grabbed your hand and held it, that seemed to help. Then you woke up, just now."

"About that…."

She took my hand again, which didn't help. "I like your hands. They feel good to me, they feel right when I hold you."

"Tahefnu." I withdrew my hand again, feebly. "I can't do this."

"I'll help you recover, Dad will too. We'll get you back on your feet real quick."

"No, I mean…. My feelings, for you. I can't do this."

"Feelings? You have feelings?"

I smiled. "I know, I act like a block of ice."

"Well, you may think you do, but your hands and your penis betray you. Kind of obvious, in fact." She smiled and took my hand again.

"I really can't do this. My dream tells me I can't."

Tahefnu lost her smile and let go of my hand. "What happened? Did you see Bear? Did he say something?"

"No, not Bear. Ma'at, and some crazy god with the head of a Coyote."

"Coyote? What did he look like?"

"Like a Remetjy man with a coyote head. We don't have any god like that."

Tahefnu's brow went up. "Remetjy? But Coyote? That's…difficult to understand." She took my hand again. "Maybe it doesn't really matter. For us."

I gave up and left my hand in hers, but said, "I have no idea what is going on in my libido. My heart is my lover's."

"What's her name?"

"Cheryl, Cheryl MacIntyre. She's a medjat."

"That's not a Remetjy name."

"She's American. But she's a Menmenet medjat and a w'abet of Ma'at, she wears the feather of Ma'at. I love her."

"But you have feelings. For me."

"Yes. Ma'at called it a temptation and accused the Coyote spirit-god of creating that temptation with you."

"So, I'm a temptress?" Her eyes locked on mine, and she wasn't smiling.

"In my dream, yes."

She took back her hand and put both hands in her lap. "Let me think about this." She closed her eyes and started humming. I looked over at the walking stick and wished I could walk, or at least get out of bed.

After a few minutes, the humming subsided, and Tahefnu's eyes opened, slowly. She looked at me with a smile. "Hummingbird guides me well. She tells me my feelings for you are pure and joyful, and that we would make good children, many good children. She tells me that your feelings for me are strong and potent, full of spirit and desire, but muddy."

I just looked at her.

"She's very clear: what you must do is your choice, not mine. Your own spirit, whatever or whoever it is, must guide you. I must accept your choice. If you want to sleep with me, I am yours, but you must marry me, and I will bear you many children. I will leave the valley and live in Menmenet, if that's what you want. I will abandon the old ways, if that's what you want. But if you don't want me, I must find someone else or accept that I will remain childless and full of longing for someone I cannot have." She smiled, sadly this time. "All that stuff is a direct quote. But I can't do that; I gotta choose a path that carries our family forward, I am my father's only daughter. Fuck, I'm my only me." She squeezed my hand.

I squeezed back, but said, "However much I want to be with you, Tahefnu, I can't marry you. This thing that's happening to me—it's screaming for me to finish it, to discover what it all means. I can't jump off the path now."

She let go of my hand and sat back in her chair. With a cocked head, she looked at me and said, "Hummingbird also tells me that your desire, your feelings for me, are not natural. I didn't want to say, but if you're gonna go away, I have to tell you."

"Not natural—in what way?"

"No fucking idea," she grimaced. "Hummingbird isn't very good at describing things, too much of a hurry all the time. She forces me to ask the right question. And I don't always know the right question. I just got an impression of wrongness about the feelings, just zip and gone, but it was there. I kind of realized that if you were a good man you would not sleep with me, but I had to make you choose. That wasn't Hummingbird, and it wasn't whatever is tempting you. It was me. I am willing to be with a bad man if my feelings are pure for him."

"Are my feelings for Cheryl wrong too?"

"I am not going to talk about another woman, even as a shaman, you prick." She smiled to take the sting away, but she reached up with her hand and gently slapped my face. "Take that and go on your path. Or talk to Dad, he's always got some great fatherly advice to ignore."

She got up and walked toward the door.

"Tahefnu." She stopped and turned. I asked, "Could you give me the stick?"

"What?"

"Heh's walking stick. Leaning on the wall, there. Could you hand it to me?"

She shook her head. "Shit. Ruined a perfect dramatic exit for a stick. Here. Knock yourself out!" Her tone implied she meant it literally. She tossed me the stick, tossed her head, and walked out of the room. I held the stick and felt it ease my complicated feelings. Ma'at was not a goddess that gave much comfort, but following her path was always a good idea. A walking stick was always a good thing to have, on a path. Maybe tomorrow I would get out of bed and use it.

CHAPTER SEVENTEEN

MacIntyre Discovers Imen-R'a

THE NEXT DAY, MACINTYRE CAME in to find several minor defense authorization reports on her desk, suggesting that Setehnekhet was trying hard to find things for her to do that would not strain his trust in her. Given what she'd heard through her surreptitious surveillance efforts, she wasn't particularly surprised.

She took her time reading the reports, which were excellent substitutes for hard-core, coma-inducing drugs. Read a little, sip some tea, read a little, go for a walk. And so on.

About half-way through the morning, her dopamine levels required stimulation, so she pocketed her listening device and headed for the records department. She again requested records on the Temple of Imen-R'a and went to her little table in the back.

She sat at the table and spread out her records, then set up her device with its earbuds and listened to Setehnekhet dealing with personnel issues for a half hour.

A janitor smiled at her as he emptied the wastebasket next to the table. She smiled back and continued listening. She noticed that the janitor had missed a crumpled piece of paper on the floor and leaned over to pick it up to put it back in the trash.

She saw her own name written in large, bold-face hieroglyphs. Curious, she smoothed it out on the desk. She read the hieratic scrawl: "**Cheryl MacIntyre**, if you are truly interested in the relationship between the Temple of Imen-R'a, Setehnekhet, and the Temple of Mentju, come to the boiler room in the second basement at 2 p.m. Please destroy this note and tell no one where you are going."

Well, wasn't that just fine. Having evaded an assassination plot from the Security Department, now she faced one from the janitorial services. She wondered whether the entire personnel structure of the Temple of Mentju was out to kill her but rejected that as too paranoid. Still, even the paranoid have enemies. And if the janitorial staff knew what she was doing, could Setehnekhet and Sheritr'a and Imenka be far behind? MacIntyre suspected that getting her job back might prove more difficult than she thought.

As Setehnekhet was apparently not in conspiracy mode today, she abandoned her listening post and went to an early lunch. She stopped at the ladies room on the way and flushed the note.

MacIntyre searched for the boiler room in the second-level basement by following the pipes. A lot of pipes. She couldn't exactly ask passers-by where the boiler room was so she could meet a mysterious admirer.

Standing at the door, she loosened the collapsible baton in its holster and arranged her jacket for fast access. She did not put it past Imenka and Sheritr'a to get her into this out-of-the-way location to complete their original plans for her.

She opened the door and went in. The noise in the room prevented her from using her hearing to detect anyone lying in wait, so she moved slowly, looking carefully around. She stepped around one of the large boilers and saw the janitor that had dropped the note. He rose from his chair and bowed to greet her, showing empty hands.

He was a small man with a grizzled almost-beard reaching down a scrawny neck, a beard favored by the lower middle class of Remetjy workers. His prominent nose and large ears gave him a faintly comical look, which his sad smile accentuated. His eyebrows sloped downward toward his ears, giving his eyes an enormously sad look, and his cheeks pushed the edges of his mouth down.

"Ms. MacIntyre. I am so glad you have come." He bowed again.

"What is this all about?"

"First, let me introduce myself, my name is Hori." He bowed again.

"Stop that."

"Sorry, habit." He grinned, sadly.

"OK, who the fuck are you and why are you trying to kill me?"

He cocked a sad eyebrow and said, "Why do you think I am trying to kill you?"

"Everybody else is, why not you?"

He shook his head and said, "Such a lack of trust does not become you, noble lady," using the traditional title of respect.

"How come everybody knows who I am, and I don't know who they are?"

"That is the way of things in Menmenet lately, noble lady," said the little man.

"Oh, please. Now all I need is for you to tell me you hate me because I'm American."

"Should I?"

"No. You should hate me because I can kill you with my little finger."

Hori ignored this threat. "Forgive me, noble lady, I choose not to hate you at all."

"Thanks. So, what can I do for you? Does the temple need another janitor?"

"No, it needs somebody with some kind of moral compass."

"Ooh, raising it to a philosophical level. Nice parry. Let's get real, Hori. Who the fuck are you?"

"You have shown a continuing interest in the Temple of Imen-R'a."

"Ah. Imen. The Hidden One."

Hori nodded with a smile. "Exactly."

"And you are aware of what I've been doing here?"

"Investigating the illusory presence of a South American spy in the Temple of Imen-R'a for the estimable Imenka. And generally pretending to be interested in furthering your career at the Temple of Mentju while in actuality trying to obtain information that will let you reclaim your valued job. And listening surreptitiously to a very holy and entirely corrupt man with advanced technology that is available only to medjau such as yourself. And to certain others, such as myself."

MacIntyre decided that being a spy was not likely to be a career path for her. It wasn't so much that she was an open book as a series of massive billboards that announced her intentions and actions to the world. She was, apparently, a brand, not a spy.

"OK, I'll bite. What do you want?"

"The temple—that is, the Temple of Imen-R'a—has an interest in what is transpiring here at Mentju."

"My. I seem to be caught between 'the devil and the deep blue sea.'" She rendered this metaphor in English.

Hori smiled politely. "Perhaps."

"You speak English?"

"Less than fluently, but I have read enough to understand the analogy; perhaps Skylla and Kharybdis might be a better one, if one were to go to classical European mythology."

"Thank you for correcting me." MacIntyre gave the little man a little bow of acknowledgement. "Now, what the fuck do you want?"

"Pardon me for not inviting you to sit, there is only the one chair here. Would you care to take it?"

Interpreting this deflection correctly, MacIntyre said, "I'm not going to be polite. I'm American, for God's sake." Again in English.

"You may be able to use that identity to further your career, noble lady."

She waited him out.

He smiled, sadly, but showing teeth. "Very well, I'll get to the point."

"Finally."

"Here." The little man extracted a thumb drive from his pocket and handed it to MacIntyre.

"What's this?"

"Read what's on there in private, not connected to the Internet."

"And what will I learn?"

"Something to your advantage."

"Oooh, I hope it involves large amounts of money secretly transmitted to my secret Cayman Islands bank account."

"You do not have a secret Cayman Islands bank account. Your Menmenet bank account contains DBN 1265.23. I had no idea the medjau paid so little."

"My efforts at encouraging corruption have not been successful. And right now they are not paying me anything at all."

"We could arrange...." Hori waved a hand, conjuring up fantasies of golden coins flowing into her pockets.

"No, thanks. I've got all the food I can eat, and I have a very good salary now working for Setehnekhet."

"But you do not yet have the position you would like to occupy. Or the power."

At this, MacIntyre broke the narrative.

"Hori, I can't work this way. I need real. I need to trust."

Hori smiled, sadly. "I am constrained, noble lady, by my temple."

MacIntyre paused and considered this. "Your temple does not trust anyone."

"My temple, my most dear noble lady, *controls* everyone. If it cannot do that, it takes measures."

"Not always successfully." The history of Imen-R'a and its priests was ancient and bloody.

"No, not always. That is the danger. The danger to you." The sad smile seemed to MacIntyre to be tinged with a certain reproof, as though she were forcing him to make threats he did not wish to make. She tried again.

"What is Imen-R'a's interest?"

"The temple cares for the well-being of the Republic." He paused. "You must know that Imen-R'a has cared for the Remetjy people through the millennia, even when wrong-thinking factions tried to sideline him. The hekasepat—our Hem-Netjer-Tepy—must be secure in his ability to take the correct decisions for the Republic." He paused again, his eyebrows contracted, making his face even sadder. "The current plans of the Temple of Mentju and its leader, I fear, may well impair our hekasepat's ability to take such decisions. Decisions acceptable to the rest of the temple." He paused again and cocked a sad eyebrow. "We cannot tolerate such a situation."

She held up the thumb drive. "Can you give me a hint."

"NATO. Setehnekhet. Sebekemheb. Thousands dead."

"An American reality TV show? Did they at least get Remetjy actors for the main roles?"

He smiled. "As to that, you must judge for yourself. We are hoping, noble lady, that you may take action, however difficult for you, that will allow Imen-R'a to continue to provide his light to the Republic. The alternative is entirely too harrowing to pursue, for me and for you. Tomorrow, you must choose your fate. Now, I must go, I have toilets to clean. Let us leave separately." He bowed again, sad eyes never leaving hers, and walked away. Two minutes later, MacIntyre went back out into the corridor and saw no one. The toilets of the Temple of Mentju, she felt, must be much cleaner than she had suspected.

MacIntyre locked her apartment door deadbolt and drew her blinds. No sense in not taking precautions. She considered unplugging her landline, removing her SIM card, donning an aluminum foil hat, and looking at the thumb drive under a blanket. No, too hot. But she did turn off the wireless on her laptop.

No, her career was not likely to include the kind of infinite tradecraft needed by an agent in place or anywhere else.

She plugged the thumb drive into her laptop and brought up the list of documents. They were, helpfully, numbered and labeled. "1. Coup participants."

"12. Internment camps." "19. Execution list." "23. Troop plans." "30. Timetable."

MacIntyre soon found herself lost in details. Two hours in, the dread overtook her. That was about the time she discovered her own name on the list of Americans to be interned immediately in the new camps in the Central Valley, designed to provide forced labor in the agricultural sector or the gold mines in the foothills. That was followed by a strategy document showing the longer-term planning behind the Remetjy takeover of the NATO military forward bases and the internment of the NATO troops after their successful defeat of the "loyal" Republican troops.

Trust, trust, trust. Not a career-enhancing emotion at the Temple of Mentju.

The last file, the timetable, told her that the coup would start in three weeks. MacIntyre ejected the thumb drive, shut her laptop, and poured herself a triple bourbon, no ice.

CHAPTER EIGHTEEN

Shesmu Gets a Visit from Mentju

A LIGHT APPEARED IN THE darkness. In the gloom I was in, I could now make out that I was standing in a temple of some kind, with a large hetep altar. The room was huge; I could see large statues of gods but they were too far away to make out details in the dim light. That light moved toward me; it was a huge bull, the light emanating from his body in some way. When the bull drew close, I saw it was a human with a bull's head holding a w'as scepter of god's power. I saw the figure at the same time as a human with a falcon's head topped with a solar disk and two tall feathers: Mentju. The man/bull/falcon strode toward me, closer and closer until it came up to the altar.

"Shesmu." The incredibly loud voice of the falcon-god shattered the silence of the room. It was meant to awe. I was awed. I was also trying to run like hell, but my legs would not move. I did not have my stick, and the falcon-god controlled me.

"You intend to find the man Imen-Khenmes."

"Yes, lord," I replied.

"You must not do so."

"I must, Lord, Ma'at commands it." I was polite but firm.

"I command otherwise."

"I must follow Ma'at, Lord." I looked around but no winged goddesses appeared to back me up. I looked back at the falcon-god and stayed firm.

"Then you will suffer forever."

"Ma'at will protect me, Lord." And she'd better show up soon, because Mentju was looking like he wasn't going to take no for an answer. And in fact, he did not.

"*Nothing* will protect you, you weak fool." The falcon-god lifted the w'as scepter and I rose with it, turned over in the air, and crashed down onto the hetep altar. "This is what will happen to you; I am giving you notice and informing you fully so you may make the correct decision. Please bear in mind that I can be a merciful god when I so desire, but that I do not so desire at this moment. Please me, and that may change—at some future time."

The falcon-god's angry eyes bored into mine as he swept a curved khepesh sword from his belt and down to cut off my little finger. Blood spurted, and I screamed, more out of the sight of it than the pain. The pain came a little later, and I screamed again. Then the falcon-god got to work. The sword descended again, again, and again, taking fingers, hands, arms, severing tendons, arteries, bones.

My blood flowed and collected into a deep crimson pool around the altar, and the rusty-iron smell of it overwhelmed me, but I never lost consciousness, never stopped feeling the cuts and the pain. The falcon-god laughed, standing in the deep pool of blood, the hacked-off pieces of me splashing down one by one.

In between screams I reconsidered my search for Khenmes, but I used what little logic remained in my heart: the falcon-god meant this as a warning, so I'd be all right in the end, I'd be able to follow Ma'at's path. Then the falcon-god cut out my heart, and I knew only the pain, white-hot, blinding, stunning pain that went on forever.

All this would have been just another dream, but for the pain. I could *feel* each cut, I could *feel* the blood flow, I could *feel* the life coursing from my body, I could *hear* my own screams and the gurgle of my life's blood filling the room, a sea of blood. Then he started flaying the skin from my torso until it was just a solid mass of blood with my head on top. I could see all this, somehow, as though I were outside my body at the same time I felt everything. At some point I stopped hearing my screams and just looked at my open mouth as the god Mentju pulled out all my teeth, then cut out my tongue.

If I'd had a heart then, I'm sure it would have wanted death, but I lived on. The pain just went on and on. After finishing up the dismemberment, the god Mentju cleaned his sword with a cloth, put it away, then called in his friend the god Inpu, the jackal god of the necropolis.

"I can't work with all this blood, you idiot," said the jackal to Mentju.

"Sorry," said the god, and the blood disappeared.

"That's better," muttered Inpu. He raised a tool and opened my mouth with it, the first part of the mummification ritual. Over the next several hours, Inpu took each small piece of me, sewed it back to its approximate place, filled me with natron and other preservatives, extracted my brain and other organs, and then began to wrap my body in mummy wrappings. There was dead silence during all this; my screams had stopped, but I could still feel all the cuts. I could feel my life draining away, but it would not leave completely, so I was aware as the god Inpu gradually wrapped my head up tight. I could not breathe, and I did not breathe pretty much continuously for the many hours the god spent mummifying me. If you have ever been underwater just a bit too long, you may know the feeling. I had not, but I understood what was happening. I just kept not breathing. I felt Inpu lift my body, stiff with wrappings, and I saw (from outside my body) my mummy placed in a series of coffins, nested within each other, unending.

"Given Life," said Mentju in his loud voice. I was back on my feet, in one piece, only the remnants of pain tweaking my nerve endings.

"So, you see, Shesmu," said Mentju, "you must not attempt the discovery of the man Imen-Khenmes. Or you *will* suffer."

He seemed not to expect any response. I suppose the treatment had worked enough times in the past that he didn't need any response.

My eyes opened. Heh and Tahefnu were standing next to my bed, looking terrified.

"What…." I croaked.

Tahefnu ran and got a cup of water and I sipped, easing my sore throat.

I asked, "What happened?" The memory of the pain was superseded only by the memory of not breathing.

Tahefnu sat on the bed and took my hand. "You…you've been screaming, for hours. We couldn't wake you up. The last hour, your voice gave out and you were just jerking around in the bed!"

Heh was shaking his head in wonder. "This is far beyond anything I've seen, son. Something seriously wrong in your world. What did you see?"

I struggled to sit up, and Tahefnu helped by arranging a pillow. I checked various body parts to make sure they were really still attached. After my nerves quieted down a bit, I gave the Miwuks the short version, though I remembered, with clarity, every single cut and the long, agonizing time not breathing in my coffins. MacIntyre had told me she never remembered dreams. I envied her.

"Whatever this is, it don't have anything to do with Miwuk spirits, son." Heh sounded somewhat indignant, as though foreign gods had no business doing this kind of work in his valley.

I rubbed my sore throat and drank some more water. Warned off by Mentju, in a way I found impossible to ignore. Just a dream, I told myself. Just a dream. What about Ma'at? Where the hell was she in my dream? It was *my* dream, after all—why not help me out when gods I never even thought much about came in and chopped me up like a side of meat? What was my heart telling me through this dream?

I thought back to all my imaginings of Ma'at and her influence over me. I realized Ma'at was a leader, not a rescuer. Ma'at told you where to go and what you must do, but the rest was up to you, and too bad if you encountered disasters along the way. Figure it out and get it done, that was Ma'at. And she held you accountable for it all: when Inpu put Ma'at's feather on the scale against your heart, Ma'at never put a finger on the scale to help you out. And I really didn't like the sound of her crocodile/lion/hippo sidekick, 'Ammet, the Eater of Hearts, who only got fed when the feather came up short.

So I had a choice: faith and the choice of endless suffering versus endless wandering without a soul and heart; or no faith, ignore my dreams, and work it out on my own. I am not a particularly religious man. I chose self reliance.

I was going to have to press on and ignore the gods. My resolution to find Khenmes hadn't changed, but it was clearly going to be a more difficult path than I imagined, at least according to my dreams. I'd need help, the help of the people around me.

I squeezed Tahefnu's hand and told her that I appreciated her support and care. I wanted MacIntyre beside me badly. But MacIntyre wasn't here, so I'd have to make do with whatever strength the Miwuks and their shaman-channeled bears and birds could give me. It would have to be strong enough; I had to find Khenmes.

CHAPTER NINETEEN

MacIntyre Proves Her Loyalty

MacIntyre sat at her desk the next morning pretending to work, looking at the defense authorization reports without seeing a word. She struggled with herself over what to do about what she'd learned. The coup was so massive a thing that she could not immediately see a clear path to stopping it, at least not by herself. She reflected that this thing had gone far beyond just getting her job back, the stakes were a lot higher now. She needed to save the Republic if that job was to exist at all. She thought about Shesmu and fantasized that with him at her side, they would stamp the coup into the mud from which it had emerged. Damn the man! Where was he? The pencil she was holding snapped in her fingers, and she took a deep breath.

The desk phone rang, and she heard Sheritr'a's voice.

"Djaret-Netjer MacIntyre, would you please join us in the Security Department conference room? We have some questions on the work you did a few days ago for Imenka."

"Certainly, Atchet-Netjer. Now?"

"Yes, please."

In the conference room, Sheritr'a sat, waiting, with Imenka at her side. She indicated a chair across the table, and MacIntyre sat.

"What's up?" she asked brightly.

Sheritr'a's dour expression froze the air between them. "Djaret-Netjer. We have reviewed your reports on the Temple of Imen-R'a, and we noticed that, while you gave it a clean bill of health through your medjau contacts, you did not actually talk with anyone at the Temple itself, is that true?"

"Yes, that's right. I didn't have any contacts, and the time involved in developing one would have been a waste given the information I'd already gotten from my friends in the medjau."

Imenka stirred. "You did not ask me whether I already had such contacts."

"I assumed you would have already used them. Why all the concern? Has something happened? Is Imen-R'a planning to murder us all?"

Sheritr'a replied tartly, her chins quivering, "I do not appreciate your humor, this is a serious matter. We need to determine your intentions and loyalties. You told Imenka that you had no previous contact with anyone at the Temple of Imen-R'a. Do you still say that?"

It was time to push back, as Sheritr'a's language was borderline accusatory, and she no longer reported to Sheritr'a and owed her no deference. They wanted to pin something on her.

"I state it as a fact. Do I really need to justify myself to you?" She looked Sheritr'a in the eye.

Sheritr'a sat back in her chair with a look of disfavor. "No, you do not. Very well." She picked up the phone, punched in an extension, and said, "Ready for you, Lord." She then put down the phone, folded her hands on the table, and waited. Imenka shut his eyes and apparently went to sleep in his chair.

"What is this about, Sheritr'a?" asked MacIntyre in a pleasant voice.

"Just wait a moment."

The conference room door opened, and Setehnekhet stepped in. Sheritr'a's face brightened at his appearance, Imenka was wide awake suddenly and smiling, and MacIntyre added to the atmosphere by a welcoming grin that she made as convincing as she could. Setehnekhet strode over and sat next to MacIntyre, adjusting his chair down so that he was at eye level with her.

He said, "I am sorry for the necessity of this questioning, Cheryl. I needed Sheritr'a and Imenka to see your loyalty for themselves in order to deal with this problem."

"What problem, Set?" Sheritr'a's face flashed a look of intense hatred at MacIntyre's use of the nickname.

"We have discovered a traitor in the temple."

"The Temple of Imen-R'a? So my contacts were wrong?"

"No, indeed. Our own temple, the Temple of Mentju. A traitor to the Republic!"

MacIntyre braced herself for the big revelation: was she about to be moved from the internment-camp list to the execute-immediately list?

Imenka stirred. "May I explain, Neb-Waset Setehnekhet?"

Setehnekhet smiled on him. "Certainly, Imenka. You discovered the traitor, after all."

Imenka, himself a traitor, turned his gaze on MacIntyre. "Djaret-Netjer MacIntyre, after you confirmed your findings about the Temple of Imen-R'a, I did indeed use my contacts there. A very secret asset near the head of the temple himself told me he had discovered that Imen-R'a had placed a spy in our temple."

"A spy? What does that mean?"

Imenka replied, "It means that the Temple of Imen-R'a does not trust the Temple of Mentju and is intent on undermining us, or worse. We have identified the spy as a janitor named Hori."

"That is why we called you in, Cheryl," said Setehnekhet. "I fear I must test your loyalty to Mentju one more time." He smiled. "I am sure you will perform the task well."

He's going to have me kill Hori. Let's nip that in the bud. "If you are asking me to kill this agent? I won't do it, even to prove my loyalty. I don't kill people, I find and punish those who do." She had to find a way to warn Hori before these homicidal maniacs were able to act.

Sheritr'a said, impatiently, "Imenka has already taken care of that. But in doing so, we have created another problem, one that Set—Neb-Waset Setehnekhet, that is—feels you are the best person to handle."

MacIntyre turned her gaze on the burly man sitting next to her. He smiled his toothy smile and said, "We want you to dispose of the body. It's a mess, and we need you to clean it up without alarming anyone in the Temple of Mentju or alerting anyone in the Temple of Imen-R'a to the killing."

MacIntyre had known Hori for only a brief time, but his death was a personal loss. She felt nothing but revulsion at the thought of desecrating his body for these maniacs. Her heart leapt from feeling to feeling, the consequences of this murder cascading through her and winding up in a steely resolution. This had to end in justice, and that was her job. She controlled her immediate urge to knock them all unconscious and said calmly, "Certainly. Where is the body?"

Imenka said, "Second basement, in a little room off the main corridor. I'll take you there."

"Please report to me when you have accomplished the task, Cheryl," said Setehnekhet, with a nod. "I will be prepared at that time to reward the proof of your loyalty to me." Sheritr'a gave him another dour look but said nothing.

Imenka got up. "This way, Djaret-Netjer."

* * *

In a room deep in the second basement, Imenka and MacIntyre entered a room awash in blood, the blood of the sad little man in a chair, his head hanging back and his throat a gaping wound.

"A messy way to kill, Imenka," said MacIntyre. "This will ruin my shoes."

"Professional. It's how they train us to make sure the target is finished." He smiled. "I never use the garrote. Garotting works up to a point but you're never quite sure it's enough. The knife makes sure."

MacIntyre walked over to assess the body, carefully avoiding the pools of blood on the floor. After sizing it up, she turned back to Imenka. "I'll need a waterproof body bag, a large crate big enough to contain the body, a cart, and a truck I can use to transport the thing. My car is a sports car, won't fit in that. Oh, and one of the w'ab cleaning kits from the hetep-altar room, I'll need that to clean everything. Gee, it's good to have had the training in that, I thought I'd never need it again!"

"I'll arrange all that, Cheryl," replied Imenka with a familiarity that MacIntyre wanted to shove down his throat. He smiled again, objectionably. "You know, if you're going to be around here much longer, you'll need training in the killing techniques I've used here. I think you'll find that refusing to kill traitors is not going to advance your career."

"Thank you so much for the advice, Imenka. I'm sure Set will put me in the way of learning everything I need to know," said MacIntyre, crossing her arms. "Now, can we get to it?"

Imenka's smile became a little forced, then he took out his phone and summoned up all the things she'd asked for. He said, "I'll explain to everyone that this is a secret operation transferring some arms to a special unit at the request of Neb-Waset Setehnekhet. They'll deliver the items at the service elevator in the back, down that side corridor we passed."

"All right. Arms. Right. Legs too." She could barely stand to look at the body, in spite of the many she had seen in her homicide work. This one was personal.

Imenka left. MacIntyre waited a couple of minutes, checked the corridor, then closed the door. She took carefully positioned photos of everything of interest in the room and uploaded them to her private cloud account, then removed the photos from her phone. Imenka texted her that the supplies were in the freight elevator. She took the supplies back to the room, donned the w'ab cleaning suit and gloves, and packed Hori's body into the body bag, then crated it.

She said a little prayer to Ma'at and hoped Hori would find peace and justification in his journey to the Duat; but he wasn't going to be mummified, at least not yet. MacIntyre reflected that she hadn't quite yet made the journey to faith in the Remetjy religious beliefs about mummification preserving the person's body to pal around with the gods in the Sekhet-'Aru. But she knew that Hori was Remetjy and belonged to the Temple of Imen-R'a, and she would make sure his body was available for the full ritual at the right time and place. But not just yet. It wasn't at all clear to her whether justice would come from her getting back her job as a medjat or from her power as a player in Setehnekhet's new universe. Once this all played out, justice would come.

She cleaned up the blood using the hetep cleaning kit. Nowhere near as much blood as a bull, but he was a tiny man, really. You don't even notice the smell after awhile. She broke up the wooden chair into pieces. She took off the cleaning suit, then bundled everything in the room up and threw it into the crate with the body. She looked silently at the body for a moment, then carefully placed the thumb drive Hori had given her onto his chest, a kind of protective amulet for his journey into the Duat and a great way to hide the thing.

MacIntyre drove the government pickup truck down toward the southern part of the city and double-parked in front of a little electronics store of dubious reputation that she knew about from her work as a medjat. She went in and emerged with a new cell phone, a burner. A little later, she pulled up at a poorly maintained park in the south of the city and sat quietly for a moment, reciting to herself a prayer for the good journey of the dead that she'd learned from Mes a long time ago; it was his way of dealing with his feelings about the dead bodies that he encountered so often. She felt that Hori deserved a little prayer or two. She put away her feelings of revulsion at what she was about to do. She then brutalized the blister-pack, extracted the burner phone, and punched in a number.

"Karkin? Hi, it's Cheryl MacIntyre. Listen, you were so anxious to help me out a few days ago, remember? Well, I've finally got something you can help me with."

"Like what?"

"Just a little thing."

"Like what?"

"A disposal."

"Of what?"

"A body."

A pause. "In over your head again, aren't you?"

"Definitely. Hence this call to you. Are you coming?"

"Sure. Where are you?"

MacIntyre told him where she was and sat back to wait.

Karkin rolled up in a car that looked like it had been through several wars. He parked, got out of the car, punctiliously locked it, then walked over to the pickup truck.

"Hi there," said MacIntyre, getting out of the truck. "How're you doing?"

The small Ramaytush man said nothing but walked over and peered into the back of the truck.

"Is that it? The body?" he asked.

"Yep."

"Would you," he said carefully, "care to expand on what you said earlier?"

"Nah."

Karkin looked at her with a deadpan expression. "You learn fast, little rabbit." The many creases on his face moved in amusement, but you couldn't call it a smile.

"I'm in a good school now."

MacIntyre knew this was not going to be easy, but she had to find out if she could trust Karkin.

"You knew him."

Karkin's face said nothing whatsoever about what he was thinking.

"He said to tell you, 'Waset.' That's it, just 'Waset.'"

Karkin closed his eyes briefly, then said, "Hori."

"Hori."

"'Disposal'?"

"My job is to make this body disappear so that no one knows what happened. I need you to help me do that—but I want the body somewhere I can produce it when things get to the Court of Ma'at. If ever." She shook her head. "And I don't want the body turning up until I'm ready. The crime scene forensics are completely fucked, but at least we'll have the body. And it will need to be in great shape so we can mummify him and all that."

Karkin nodded.

"I knew I could count on you."

MacIntyre looked at the wiry Ramaytush man and wondered why she trusted him when he told her so little, but she did. Something to do with his rescuing her from the Russians that time. Shesmu trusted him too.

Karkin went back to his car, opened the trunk, and took out a green, rectangular device that had a control pad and an LED display. He carefully ran it all over the pickup truck. When he finished, he put the device down, rolled under the truck, then emerged with a small box in his hand. He put the box in his trunk. He then went back to the pickup and ran the device over the truck again, then returned the device to his trunk and closed it. He got into the passenger seat of the pickup.

"Always check twice. Only found one," he said.

MacIntyre mentally added an item to her list for the future; she was learning the tradecraft fast. At Karkin's direction, MacIntyre drove through the southern streets of Menmenet and down past the small mountains to the south to an industrial area near the bay. As they drove, she told him a little about what she had done at the Temple of Méntju and everything about the plans Hori had shown her.

Karkin asked, "Do they know?"

"Not unless these guys are playing a very deep game, and I don't think they're all that deep. They're 'testing my loyalty', which I think would not be on the table if they thought I was aware of the details of their conspiracy. What do you think?"

Karkin nodded. "Poor Hori. Told me he would not die in his bed. Excellent hem-netjer, just as he claimed to be."

"Hem-Netjer? Hori?"

"A hem-netjer, a prophet, priest of Imen-R'a who foretells the future. Great spies, always one step ahead."

"I think that's bunk. Given what's in the crate, I mean."

Karkin nodded, sadly.

Karkin directed her through the back streets and warehouses and finally into a loading dock behind a large concrete building that no one had painted since it was built, many years ago. Karkin went inside through a door, then came back with an older Ramaytush man wearing a white apron. Karkin did not introduce the Ramaytush to MacIntyre. The Ramaytush man looked down at the crate in the back of the pickup truck, nodded, then disappeared back into the building. Shortly, the door of the loading dock rolled up, and the man was there with a forklift.

Karkin, the Ramaytush man, and MacIntyre pushed and lifted the crate up onto the loading dock. The Ramaytush man then used the forklift to carry the crate into the building. Karkin and MacIntyre followed him as he drove slowly across the warehouse. There were a few men at work at various tasks; they all ignored the little group as it crossed to a large sliding door at one side of the building. The Ramaytush man opened the sliding door.

The room was a walk-in freezer. There were an enormous number of unidentifiable things hanging from hooks and many more things in boxes stacked around the freezer. The Ramaytush man drove the forklift into the freezer and took the crate all the way to a back corner, where he deposited it. He drove the forklift out, then slid the door shut. He bowed to Karkin and went away. Not one word had passed between any of them during this entire operation.

Karkin and MacIntyre left. MacIntyre drove Karkin back to his car with only a few prompts as to turns. Karkin got out of the truck. MacIntyre leaned through its open window.

"Karkin! What will your organization do?"

He stopped and turned. "Plan for contingencies."

"I mean, what will they do about the coup?"

Karkin shook his head. "Nothing."

"That seems…counterproductive. Just what is this organization?"

"International security. Europeans and Chinese who think action is usually counterproductive."

"Given my experiences with you, you don't agree with that strategy."

Karkin cocked his head but said nothing.

"Sometimes," she said, "action is incredibly hard." MacIntyre saw in her inner mind the sad little man she had just consigned indefinitely to a very cold place. Her resolve to put a stop to all this grew and hardened. "Karkin—if I need more help on this, can I count on you? Not your organization, you."

"Maybe." His eyes were as cold as the freezer they had just left, little black stones looking at her.

"Fair enough. Then *maybe* I'll let you know when things heat up. Oh—you'd better put that tracking device back on the truck. And dispose of this." She gave him the burner phone.

He nodded and went back to his car. He got the small box out of the trunk, rolled under her truck, rolled back out, went back to his car, and drove away.

MacIntyre drove her government truck back to the loading dock at the Temple of Mentju. She then took the rest of the day off.

CHAPTER TWENTY

Shesmu Finds His Path

IT WAS ANOTHER DAY BEFORE I stopped remembering the pain of dismemberment and mummification, and another day after that before I wanted to get out of bed and walk around with the help of the walking stick. I did eventually get some sleep, thankfully without dreaming. Heh supplied me with a little leather bag to hang around my neck that he said contained some "strong medicine" that would ward off spirits as I slept. I guess it beat a sleeping pill. Then he mounted guard over me while I slept.

On the third day, I sat at their dining table with them, eating a dinner that I'd helped to prepare on the little stove. It was the first square meal I'd had in days. Tahefnu's shopping expedition had yielded some excellent preserved duck Mennefer style and some Remetjy noodles. I experimented a little with the various familiar and unfamiliar herbs they had in their cupboard; the result was a very satisfactory meal.

Pushing my plate away after a second helping, I assessed the state of my heart and decided it was time to understand what was going on. Remetjet have interpreted god-given dreams for millennia. I wasn't a strong believer in god-given dreams, but that didn't stop me from wanting to understand them.

"Heh, what do you think these dreams mean?"

Heh was silent, picking his teeth and considering the question. After a little while, he said, "The stuff you said your gods were telling you, it don't make no sense to me. Now, you're sure Coyote wasn't there? Or Bear?"

"No sign of them. Just Mentju and Inpu."

"Yeah. Like I said before, not a Miwuk thing then. Just who is this Mentju?"

"God of war. God of just war. He's the warrior god, the companion of R'a in fights against those who would deny the pera'a's power. He has the head of a bull or a falcon with a sun disk and two big feathers, the headdress of a warrior."

"Why would he want to torture you?" Tahefnu was indignant.

"I'm trying to make sense of this in a rational way, Tahefnu, interpreting the dream. I don't know what my heart is trying to tell me, but in my dream Mentju was obsessed with stopping me from looking for Khenmes."

"Was Khenmes a warrior?"

"Not that I know of."

"A head-scratcher," said Heh. "I think you should take these dreams more seriously, son. Gods are real, they use dreams to talk to us. It's why you're here, at least that's what those Waashiw guys claimed. That first dream had Coyote?"

"Yes, claiming to be my father."

"Akhen." Heh rubbed his mouth. "Hmm. Have to think about that. What about this Inpu?"

"Inpu is the god who protects the dead. Head of a jackal, in charge of cemeteries and mummification. There's a big Temple of Inpu in Menmenet at the top of the cemetery district in the west part of the city."

"What gets Inpu involved in your problems?"

"Don't know. Maybe Mentju just needed some mummification work done and got him in as a consultant. He didn't seem really enthusiastic about things, just doing his job." I tried to imagine what my heart meant by Inpu and came up dry.

"And Mentju just wanted you to stop looking for your Waashiw friend?"

"Khenmes...." I cleared my throat. "Khenmes means a lot to me. When my parents died, he stepped in, he and Tuy. I owe them a lot. I love them. Ma'at wants me to find him."

Tahefnu said, "Explain a little about Ma'at."

"Ma'at is the goddess of justice, truth, and the right way of doing things. I don't honestly believe much in all this stuff in a religious sense. It's really a philosophy of life as much as a religion. I've really just gotten into the habit of saying Ma'at is guiding me when I make choices about what's right and wrong. High-level cooking requires a strong commitment to quality, to doing the right thing, and Ma'at is a great metaphor for that. She promotes balance in the universe. There's also the law enforcement aspect; my girlfriend is a w'abet of Ma'at and a medjat."

Tahefnu snorted. "Sounds like the right god to follow. Cozy. Why would Mentju want you to go against Ma'at?"

"He wouldn't, ordinarily. That's what I don't understand. And Ma'at didn't much care for the Coyote, my father."

Heh said, "You got a lot of conflict in your dreams. Our gods are always pissing each other off. How about Ma'at? What gods get her dander up?"

"The main one would be Seteh, god of the desert. He's the god we associate with isfet, chaos, the opposite of ma'at, balance."

Tahefnu commented, "Sounds a lot like Coyote, doesn't it, Dad? Complicated. Wasn't Seteh the bad uncle who killed Wesir, dismembered him, and tried to take power? I know that much from school." Tahefnu was showing off.

I nodded. "Yep, one of the main myths that came out of Kemet. Wesir's sister Aset put him back together, mummified him, and he became king of the Duat. But Seteh is also a strong god who has a lot of power, so a lot of people worship him."

"So why not Seteh, then? In your dream. He likes chopping people up. Why Mentju?"

"I just don't know. I haven't thought about Mentju since my middle school religion classes. Why would he show up in my dreams?"

Heh put his hand on the table and looked at me with his mouth set. "Son, said it before: you got to take these dreams serious, it's the gods talking to you. You don't take this serious, you're gonna get your butt handed to you. Gods are real, son. Your gods are telling you they don't want you looking for your friend. You go against that, you gotta make sure you either got ways to pay them off or you got other gods that have your back."

I just nodded; I didn't want to offend him, but I wasn't there yet. Gods, religion, the justified dead: all made sense from a certain point of view, but it just wasn't *my* point of view. If the gods were real, the pain was real, and I wasn't ready for that. I wasn't even really sure Khenmes was alive. That was why I insisted on climbing that cliff: I wanted to see Khenmes, to see whether he was really alive in the prison compound. A wrinkled old Waashiw shaman's fever dream wasn't enough for me. But I had to find Khenmes if he was alive. Religion was fine. Psychology was fine, but Khenmes was real. He was part of me. He was all I had left of a family.

"What are you thinking you're gonna do?" asked Heh.

"I need to go back to Washeshu, to the black site we found, and see about Khenmes. Heh, can you drive me up there? Back to the Serqu Pass?"

Heh looked at Tahefnu. "What do you think, daughter?"

"I think we should do it. Got no idea what's going on, but with Coyote involved, I think we have to move on it."

Heh said, "OK, son, we'll do it. Daughter will do the driving, though, I hate dirt roads. I'll watch for coyotes. A road trip!" He leaned back in his chair and smiled his shaman's smile at me, his face crinkling in pleasure. He patted his stomach.

Tahefnu gathered up the dinner plates and took them away, then came back and said, "Dad, I think Shesmu needs some rest, all this talk is worrying him. I'll watch over him for awhile if you want to get some rest yourself."

"OK, daughter. No monkey business, though."

Tahefnu rolled her eyes. I hobbled back to my bed with the walking stick. She chastely arranged the covers and the medicine bag and sat in a chair by the side of the bed. I slept well, without dreaming.

Well, here we go again, I thought to myself. The old pickup truck rattled and rolled along the dirt road up to the Serqu pass. This truck definitely had no new transmission or motor, unlike the Waashiw ones. It wheezed and rattled as we toiled up the slope, crested, then came down into the little valley where I hoped we would find my friend Khenmes.

"Fucked up road." Tahefnu was not happy, but she was doggedly steering the old truck along. "Are all the Washeshu roads like this?"

"No," I replied, jolting in the middle of the truck's bench seat. No seat belts. I wondered just how old the truck was. "We're a bit out of the way, here."

Heh, sitting next to me on the left, looked out the side window and said, "Lot of good hunting up here, lot of deer, rabbits, that kind of thing. Never been up here, heard about it."

We'd gone through the Washeshu border post back on the main highway. There was no one there, just a little sign saying "Welcome" in three languages. I supposed that Washeshu was not terribly concerned about Miwuk immigrants from the south. I was again wearing the hunter's outfit. My ankle was much better, but I borrowed Heh's walking stick for the duration.

I said, "We don't want to alert the soldiers to our presence, so we need to stop up here and work our way in by following the creek, cross country."

"Great. Just great." Tahefnu didn't sound like her heart was in it.

I showed Tahefnu the spot where the Waashiw sergeant had parked. It was the middle of the afternoon. I was still a little slow on my legs, so it was near sunset by the time we got to the little valley where the black site was. Except it wasn't.

I stood under the cliff from which I had fallen, looking out at the clearing. It was just a clearing, now, no compound. There were signs—truck marks and various disturbed areas—but nothing like a building or fence.

"It was here," I said.

"Sure it was," said Tahefnu. She was definitely disgruntled now. "Fucking mosquitoes are the only thing here now."

"I told you to bring the bug herbs, daughter, did you not listen?" Heh reproved her mildly.

"Forgot."

I couldn't stand it. I walked away from them out to the center of the Meadow where I could feel Khenmes had been and sat down on the trampled grass. I closed my eyes and the images flew through my mind: the Coyote, the picture of my mother, dead, on her hospital bed, Khenmes smiling and throwing me a ball. All gone, leaving me here, abandoned again, sitting in an empty meadow with nowhere to go. I wanted to know why no one would tell me about my father's secrets. If I didn't find Khenmes, all I had left was Karkin, who made a stone wall seem garrulous.

Somebody sat down next to me and I felt an arm around my shoulders.

"Shesmu?" Tahefnu's voice was gentle.

"He's gone." I shook my head in frustration and pain. Tahefnu pulled me toward her and my head dropped onto her shoulder. She was quiet, resting her head on mine. At least she and Heh were here for me.

"What do I do now? I need to find him."

"He surely ain't here," observed Heh, who had come up behind us.

Tahefnu let go of me and said, "Maybe there's something along the road?"

The creek ran into a gushing river just past the meadow. We walked back up the path along the river to the road, looking carefully for anything that might tell us where the soldiers had gone. Just before the road, we found a campsite with a Waashiw man building a fire. He too was dressed as a hunter. He was about fifty years old, with thin, greying hair and a whipcord body. When he saw us coming, he stood, arms folded, waiting until we came up, then said something in Waashiw.

Heh greeted him in Waashiw, pointed to me, and said "Shesmu. And my daughter, Tahefnu." He added, "Shesmu's a Remetj, don't speak our languages."

The hunter turned to me and said, "Hey, good to meet you. We'll talk Renkemet, then." He turned to Tahefnu and said, "Pleased to meet you, miss." He looked us over in a friendly way. "Hunting? Where're you camped?"

"Up by there," said Heh, pointing up the road. "Out for a walk."

"Huh. Well, say—I was just about to start dinner, always good to have folks to talk to, care to join me? Got some rabbits need cooking."

Heh looked at me, and I nodded. "Sure, happy to. Where you from?"

"Little village up north of here, come down here for the hunting."

We sat with him while he built his fire and put the rabbits on a spit. He turned it over to Tahefnu at her request. We talked about hunting, acorns, pine nuts, and the general state of affairs between Washeshu and the Miwuks in the Republic. Very congenial.

I asked, casually, "Seen anything of the soldiers that were here last week? We passed by, didn't talk to them."

The man looked contemptuous. "Bastards wouldn't let me hunt down here, had to go up to the pass. Gone now, though."

"Any idea what was up?"

"Nope, never got close enough to see. Stripped out a lot of vegetation in the river valley, though. You can see where they bivouacked." He pointed up the path we'd come down. "You must of seen it up there."

"Yeah," said Heh. "Wondered what it was all about."

The hunter shrugged. "Long as they're gone, I don't give a shit. Things are a little loose around here, sometimes. We're kind of out in the back country here, you know?"

We ate the rabbits. I complimented Tahefnu on the cooking, they were just right. She smiled and slapped a mosquito.

"Say," said Heh, "You got any bug herbs? Daughter here forgot hers."

"Sure, let me get some for you," said the hunter, who went over to his truck and brought back a bag. Tahefnu thanked him and rubbed the herbs over her exposed skin, then gave the bag to us and we did the same.

"So, where's your village?" asked the hunter.

Heh replied, "Kikyapapli, little place in a big valley, south. I'm the Bear shaman, daughter here is training to be Hummingbird shaman. Shesmu here is a friend from Menmenet. He's a cook."

"Hey, no shit—I'm a shaman too!" The hunter smiled. "My village only has me, they don't like it when I come down here to hunt, always complaining, you know? Just got to get away from it all sometimes, you know?"

Heh nodded sympathetically. "Yeah, me too. Everybody's so needy these days, I guess. Say, you notice anything like a lot of visions happening lately? I'm kind of like thinking something's going on."

The hunter/shaman chewed his rabbit. "Huh. Yeah, now that you mention it. Don't quite know what to make of it." He waved a hand. "You know, lots of symbols, portents, but not a lot of facts. It's a lack of training in school, is what it is. People come in with dreams and don't know how to frame 'em for you."

"We got back to the old ways, in our village," said Heh. "Helps."

"Huh. Good luck with that. If my people don't have television for an hour they complain. Just have to make do. Sons of bitches come in, they say the dream was like some episode of a TV show they just saw. Hey—at that, maybe you can help. I had this vision, last night, right here, don't know what to make of it. I was standing in the forest and a herd of bulls ran by, so I followed them and they ran until they came to a big valley, beautiful, cliffs, trees, water everywhere. Then the bulls turned and ran right over me and I woke up."

"Huh. Bulls in the forest? Bullshit." Heh smiled at his own joke.

The hunter nodded. "I guess. We got no bulls up here in Washeshu, just pine nuts and rabbits. And tourists. Pretty strong vision, though. Maybe the bulls symbolize tourists. Funniest thing, I knew the valley, seen pictures of it." He turned to Shesmu. "It was that big valley you Remetjet took over down south, to bury your important people in." He rubbed his mouth. "Maybe I been thinking about that place a little. Sure looked pretty."

I said, "Ta Sekhet." I'd seen pictures in occasional newspaper and magazine articles, and I too had always felt a pull toward its beauty. "We don't actually bury them, we put them in tombs." Suddenly I remembered the first vision I'd had in Da'owaga'a, the valley with cliffs: Ta Sekhet. Where my dead father was? I froze up completely, my heart nearly stopping.

"Yeah, that's the one. Kinda recognizable, you know? All those cliffs." He paused and considered. "I guess it was on my mind, I heard a couple of those soldiers talking about it when I was arguing with the guy who wanted me to turn around. The rest of 'em were just standing around their big armored thing jawing about interesting things they'd seen in the mountains. Funny thing, I think they were First Peoples, just from their accents, you know? Couldn't tell a thing by looking at them 'cause they were all covered up. Not Waashiw or Miwuk either, foreigners. Maybe those soldiers were the bulls in my vision!"

My heart unfroze. I sat up a little straighter at this idea. "Where exactly is Ta Sekhet? Do you know?"

"It's over a couple of hills from our village, south," said Tahefnu. "I grew up walking around the mountains near there, pretty rugged. Not bull territory. Marmots. Lots of marmots. And bears."

We talked a little more about visions and the three shamans traded some shop talk. I sat chewing over the new information and forming resolutions. I didn't tell them I'd seen Ta Sekhet in my own vision. I didn't believe in visions, shaman dreams; they weren't real. But soldiers talking, that was real. Something I could grab onto.

After an hour or so, it was getting pretty dark. Tahefnu stretched and said, "I think we better get back."

We stood up and thanked our new hunter friend, then walked up the road. It only took us a half hour to reach the truck because we weren't clambering over rocks and through scrub along the creek. I leaned on the walking stick more and more, and it was good to see the truck when we walked around a bend in the road. Tahefnu turned the truck around and we drove back up through the pass and down to the highway.

"Ta Sekhet," I said. "I didn't realize it was so close to you. How do you get there?"

Tahefnu gave another snort. "You don't. It's pretty much right over the mountain, kind of a hike though. 90 kilometers. No roads, just the one from the Central Valley that the army uses. And the Republic don't let anybody in. Republican Guard, crack troops. They kicked out the locals when they took it over." I heard something in Tahefnu's voice as she told me this. She kept her eyes on the dark road, and I could tell she wasn't smiling. "Like they kicked us out of the foothills when they found the gold there." She sounded like she didn't like the Republican Guard much.

I probed a little. "Were the locals Miwuks?"

Heh said, "Nope, called themselves Awanichi, something to do with the Paiutes over the mountains in the Federation. We didn't get along with 'em, them being kinda obstreperous, but having the military moving them out seemed a little extreme to us. Nothing came of it, though, nobody from Paiute country started a war or anything, I guess they got compensated somehow; so we all settled back down. A long time ago now, way back in the 18th century, right after you folks came over from Africa. Kinda sticks in the craw a little, though, still." Tahefnu grunted in agreement.

Bulls in the forest. I could think of a god that might have something to do with bulls in the forest. And the demomili had given the Sergeant specific instructions to dump me on the Miwuks in Hetchetci, right next to Ta Sekhet. I didn't believe in visions, but I also didn't believe in coincidences.

"I think I'd like to see Ta Sekhet," I said into the gathering darkness.

CHAPTER TWENTY-ONE
MacIntyre Gets to Know the Boss

MACINTYRE AWOKE AFTER A NIGHT of tossing and turning, acutely missing her bedmate. If she'd dreamed, she didn't remember any of it, but she was sure any dream would have been full of revoltingly bloody bodies and wild but successful escapades. She reached for her phone and called Shesmu, but again the call went to voicemail. She left a short, incoherent message about missing him and hung up, her feelings in a tangle of revulsion, elation, loneliness, and hunger. She then realized she'd never actually had dinner the night before, she'd just dived into binge-watching her favorite feel-good comedy show about a pair of lackwit w'abu of Inpu and their wives who found a new way in each episode to screw up a mummy, then make it all right. She needed to see the humor in her own situation. Then she crashed into bed, exhausted.

Hunger was the only feeling she could do anything about, so she made a solid American breakfast of eggs, bacon, and toast. She burned none of it, which boosted her self confidence no end. There's a first time for everything.

From that point on, the morning became a period of self-reflection, self-doubt, and self-pity as she chose her clothing for the day's business: meeting with Setehnekhet to get her reward. Solving the knotty problem of dress did, however, let her untangle her knot of emotions.

What was most appropriate to wear at a meeting about the successful disposal of a brutally murdered spy's body? Red might be a little aggressive, too reminiscent of all the blood she'd cleaned up. Just thinking about that made her queasy. She also didn't want to remind Setehnekhet that he'd made her into a cleaning lady again. No, not red.

How about black? No, too funereal, at least to her, being American. She needed uplifting, not the depression of apparent grief for the dead. No, not black.

How about white? White with a gold edge? No, too sexy. That dress showed off a little too much figure for this day's work. Shesmu loved that dress, and she didn't want to think too much about Shes right now. And white was the Remetjy funeral color. Worse than black. No, not white.

Well, that left the green thing Henutsenu had bought for her that day they went shopping together last year. Other than jeans and t-shirts, the green suit was the only thing in her closet that she had not already rejected for philosophical, tactical, or emotional reasons.

The green suit was not something MacIntyre would have bought for herself, both because of price and because it was a little more elegant than she was used to. Actually, a lot more elegant. Henutsenu had admired her greatly in it, and MacIntyre felt warm in remembering her touch. Too elegant, perhaps? But perhaps elegance struck the right note here. And it didn't show off too much, but it didn't hide anything either—except for the baton, just, under the jacket. The way the fabric pleated and folded created just enough texture to hide body flaws, and the baton was just another such flaw. Just right. OK, green it is, she thought. And of course the matching shoes, green with low heels, and the little gold girdle belt. She carefully arranged the collapsible baton in its holster, making sure it was invisible behind her back.

She added the gold bull pin over her breast. It was really kind of cute, a snorting bull tossing its horned head with red carnelian eyes, asserting its masculine power and confidence. The feather of Ma'at had its own charms, of course, but direct power was certainly an attractive alternative now.

MacIntyre climbed the steps up to the second-floor entrance of the Temple of Mentju, attracting the stares of her co-workers because of the elegance of her dress. Most people dressed down for work these days or wore uniforms at work. But it was the right thing to wear for what she needed to do.

Setehnekhet was not yet in. After telling his assistant she needed to see him, MacIntyre settled down at her desk to wait. She surreptitiously set up the burner phone as a voice-activated recorder and attached it to the box she used to listen to the bug in Setehnekhet's office.

Setehnekhet was clearly not an early bird. Two hours later, word came down that he was ready to see her. She checked the voice recorder, which had duly recorded his arrival in his office, so that was good to go.

Setehnekhet stood at the window looking out at the city. He turned and smiled when she came into the office.

"I trust, Cheryl, that you have good news to report? I expected you yesterday."

"Very good news, Set. I decided I'd worked enough, took the afternoon off."

"Close the door, please." He looked her up and down, apparently liking what he saw.

MacIntyre closed the office door, and they were alone. She said, "I hope you've checked this office for listening devices?"

He grinned. "Security is very tight."

"But Set, You let an Imen-R'a spy in." She tried to make this disarming rather than confrontational.

"But he had no access to anything important," he said, dismissing her fears. "He fooled us for a short time only."

It was clear that Setehnekhet, while he was a powerful and decisive man, had very little actual sense of what was possible, his pride getting in the way of his common sense. In her experience, male pride led to male unreliability. She also assessed this particular male as just a little on the crazy side, which added to his unpredictability.

She said, "Why kill him?"

"He had outlived his usefulness to us. Where did you dispose of the body?"

"No one will ever know."

He smiled. "I knew we could count on you for this service."

Good—he was assuming that he knew where the body was, as the truck had stopped for a long time at the little park in the south of the city—or so the tracking device told them. MacIntyre was sure that Imenka would have reported back on the tracking device's location by now, which was one of the reasons she had waited to report success. She wanted Setehnekhet to believe he was all-knowing and able to manipulate her. She wanted to make him think she was a useful tool in his plotting. His recorded verbal confession added the last element to the case file.

He waved a hand at the couch. "Please have a seat, Cheryl." He sat next to her on the couch, just a fraction too close.

She perched on the couch with her legs crossed at her ankles and her back not touching the back of the couch, as her mother had taught her at a young age. It was a posture designed to catch the attention of young, shy, and repellent Bostonian gentlemen, but MacIntyre saw no reason to doubt that it would also attract the attention of middle-aged, confident, and sensuous Remetjy priests.

He said, "I'm sorry I had to have you do all that cleaning work, but I needed somebody very reliable to do it. We can't afford to let just anyone in on this kind of thing."

She smiled and replied, "No problem, Set. I understand you needed to test my loyalty. I hope I've proved myself now?"

"You have, Cheryl." He shifted a little closer. "I would very much like to celebrate this moment with you. How about dinner tonight? My house?"

"Thank you, Set, I'd love that." She paused, thinking furiously. She sat back and felt the baton dig into her back and adjusted. She said, "But I think I have more obligation to you than you do to me. I'd like to treat you. A private dinner at the Neferti. Have you eaten there?"

"Yes, certainly—one of the best restaurants in Menmenet."

"I have an in. I know the house manager, she can set us up with a very nice and very private dinner. *Very* private."

Setehnekhet looked thoughtful. "And your boyfriend won't mind my entertaining you in his restaurant?" Her dossier must be very complete, she thought.

"Sure he'd mind, but who cares? I can handle that. And he's not there right now, he's out of town." She smiled a sardonic smile. "Anyway, he's always been very supportive of my career choices, Set."

"As am I, Cheryl." Setehnekhet showed his teeth in a predatory grin, then said, "I think it is time to move you a little deeper into our plans. We can talk about that tonight, among…other things. At dinner, and later."

MacIntyre felt she had wound him up about as far as was advisable. She stood, adjusted her dress and jacket, and said, "Let me just call them to set it up." She took her phone out of her jacket pocket and called the Neferti. She spoke with the hostess, then with Henutsenu, arranging everything. She hung up. He got up from the couch. She smiled and said, "Well, I should let you get back to work, Set. I look forward to tonight."

"Shall we meet at the front doors at 1900?"

"Yes, can't wait!" She bowed respectfully, and he returned the bow, and she left. She found herself shaking a bit from the release of tension as she walked back to her desk, the sexual and emotional energy from the meeting slowly dissipating. Elegant rather than sexy had been the right choice for her dress. Sexy would have made things…difficult, if not dangerous.

She sat at her desk for a few minutes to gather herself, then went out and found an empty stairwell and called Henutsenu. Her friend was all questions, but she interrupted.

"This is all part of the undercover stuff, Henutsenu. I'll be showing up with the hem-netjer-tepy of Mentju. Private dining room?"

"Am I right in thinking this is remarkable progress?" asked Henutsenu, her voice taking on a certain warm quality of approval.

"Too right. So, this guy is a killer." And she hoped Henutsenu took this to be a sexual reference rather than literal, but both were true. "I need help. If you could have the wait staff interrupt us at strategic moments, it would help a lot. He's...a bit much to handle."

"You're playing him?"

"Seriously. He proposed dinner at *his* house. I counter-offered."

"Ah. Fine, we'll make sure opportunities for intimacy are limited, but we'll do it discreetly."

MacIntyre smiled. "Thanks."

"I'll tell Sebek, too." She paused, then said, "Shes will find out, when he gets back."

"I know. I'll fill him in. Have you heard from him?"

"No, not a word."

"He's not answering my voicemails or returning my calls, the prick. I'll tell him I'm seeing other people out of loneliness. That should get his attention."

Henutsenu's voice was warm. "Cheryl, you'd do well in the Temple of Bastet. Take my word. See you!"

They disconnected. MacIntyre smiled. This game was fun, and she was playing it well—at least up to the point of the death of the players. She stopped smiling as Hori's sad little face formed in her mind.

MacIntyre made sure that she was at the big bronze doors to the temple at five minutes before 1900 hours. She read Setehnekhet as an on-time kind of guy. Yep; he appeared from the elevators at precisely 1900.

"Cheryl, good to see you! Are you ready?" He had changed from his uniform to more formal civilian apparel, wearing a shendyt kilt instead of pants and showing a lot of muscular leg.

"Yes," she responded with a smile. "How shall we go? A cab?"

"No, I have my car waiting in front," he said, returning her smile. He steered her out the doors to the front stairs of the temple. At the bottom, in the "Absolutely No Parking Here on Pain of Death" space sat his car: a stretch limo emblazoned with banners showing the martial figure of Mentju.

"No entourage?" she asked.

"Definitely not. I gave them all the night off. Just you and me."

Perfect; she was sure he would abandon any remaining reserve in private, just the two of them. MacIntyre surreptitiously patted the hidden pocket in her elegant green dress to make sure her phone was there recording everything.

The drive to the Neferti only took about 15 minutes. The restaurant looked out onto the bay from the base of Kha-Hota, the rounded hill in the northeast corner of Menmenet. The driver of the big car parked in front of the Neferti and waved off the tip-hungry valets, and MacIntyre and Setehnekhet emerged from the voluminous back seat of the car and entered the restaurant. The valets averted their eyes from their boss's girlfriend accompanied by another man, making Setehnekhet smile in anticipation of an excellent evening ahead.

The Neferti had been very popular with the more discerning VIPs of Menmenet ever since it opened, which is why Shesmu knew people like 'Aapehty. Shesmu had turned the restaurant over to Sebek and had promoted Henutsenu from hostess to business manager as a reward for their help in earlier adventures, but he still owned the restaurant and made sure it was a destination for the people who wanted to see and be seen, but also for people who wanted privacy.

The Neferti's private dining room was a small room off to the side of the restaurant that was closed off with a door and decorated with tromp-l'oeil murals that created the atmosphere of a palace of Kemet overlooking the great river. VIPs used the room when they wanted to dine with special guests, private guests, guests with whom they had serious business or covert pleasure to conduct.

Henutsenu stood next to the hostess at the welcoming stand in the restaurant entry, two beautiful Remetjet waiting for the VIP. MacIntyre, whose last visit to the Neferti had resulted in a semi-comatose taxi ride, felt her reputation at the restaurant wouldn't suffer from the fawning pomp lavished on her companion. Henutsenu acknowledged her with just the right level of recognition and status, then spent her real energy on welcoming the hem-netjer-tepy of Mentju. After this effusion, she asked the hostess to see the honored guests to their private dining room, where everything pleasurable for the evening awaited them.

The Neferti's menu offered what Shesmu called the New Two Lands cuisine, his interpretation of Remetjy cuisine enhanced by the use of modern technology, local ingredients, and his own inventiveness. Sebek layered his own blend of pragmatism and art over Shes's original concept. MacIntyre loved the place, though she missed some of the food she grew up with, but not enough to patronize any of the terrible American restaurants in Menmenet. Shesmu had ruined her for that kind of food. Her thoughts again strayed to the man who still refused to return her voicemails.

Setehnekhet told Henutsenu to send in whatever the chef desired. The wine steward brought a complimentary bottle of French Champagne. "Here's to a long and fruitful partnership between us, Cheryl," said Setehnekhet. "I feel certain we are off on the right foot."

MacIntyre clinked the elegant tulip glasses and smiled warmly. "I feel sure that's true, Set. Um, do you mind a little work while we play?" She savored the wine that she would never be able to afford on a medjat's salary.

"As long as we keep it short, my dear, I have so much to talk about with you!"

"I'm underutilized."

"Disposing of inconveniences doesn't give you enough work?" he smiled.

"Well, that, but I mean in the normal course of things. I've rearranged my desk drawers so many times they're starting to come apart. And that's only for two days." Waiters came and went, and the wine steward suggested and uncorked a bottle of excellent Sauvignon Blanc from a vineyard just over the border in Russkaya Amerika.

"I think that now you have demonstrated your capabilities to my associates and myself, we can integrate you more into everyday affairs. Yes, I think that is what we will do, Cheryl." He nodded sagely and took a bite of the crab cup they were sharing as an appetizer, a lotus-shaped cup of fried noodle filled with bits of the local crab and wild mushrooms from the north of the Republic.

"Your associates?"

"Sheritr'a and some of the other department heads work closely with me on a daily basis. Very closely. I had to satisfy them about you before we could really make use of your talents."

"And what about special projects? I love special projects, you know? Taking on new challenges." MacIntyre thought with some irony that she had taken on just about every challenge that existed in Menmenet. How many flaming swords could you juggle?

"Oh, I think we can accommodate you there, Cheryl, my dear." He grinned. "You remember the American diplomat you spoke with?"

"The ever-serious Mr. Smith, yes. Do you need to activate your communications idea with him?"

"Not exactly. Things are underway that he will communicate to us, and I think you are the perfect person to carry those messages. Your visits to the Embassy will not be suspicious."

"Suspicious! That sounds exciting." She ate some crab and washed it down with a sip of wine.

Setehnekhet smiled and sipped wine. "You'll need to keep very quiet about the work you're doing for us."

"I'm very good at quiet, Set. If you say it's classified, it never leaves my lips."

"And beautiful lips they are, Cheryl, closed or open."

OK, things are moving along now. Push for more.

"Can you fill me in a little on what Smith might tell us?"

"Only a little, I'm afraid. Need to know."

"Oh, I need to know, believe me. I do much better when I know what's going on."

He set his wine glass down on the table and leaned on one elbow, looking into her eyes. "What did you think of Mr. Smith?"

MacIntyre said, carefully, "I think he is a typical American diplomat." She didn't tell him her suspicion that he was also some kind of intelligence agent for the United States.

"Then he is working hard at his public face for you. He isn't."

"Isn't what?"

"A typical American diplomat. He's on our side."

"I see," replied MacIntyre. "And you're getting serious information from him about American intentions and troop movements?"

"Yes, but he's having trouble getting the information to us, and you can help with that. As I said, you can do it without raising suspicions."

The image of Imenka sitting on the park bench dead-dropping information to Smith filled MacIntyre's mind with questions, and her eavesdropping on Setehnekhet raised more, but she immediately answered all of them: Setehnekhet was stringing her along. She could believe nothing that he was telling her.

"How?"

"You're American. Who has better reason to go to the American Embassy and talk with the Consul General than an American fired from her government job?"

MacIntyre smiled and nodded approvingly. "Sure, you're right about that. But I've got a new job now, won't that queer the pitch for the rest of the Embassy staff?"

"Not if they don't know about it. That's why I've had you conceal your promotion. We'll arrange to spread the rumor that you're being fired from the Temple of Mentju for security reasons."

"I see," she responded, smiling.

"And you should tell him anything he wants to know about the medjau, Cheryl, to give him cover for talking with us. He'll need to satisfy his chiefs as to his bona fides." MacIntyre inferred from this instruction that Setehnekhet knew she had promised Smith information for information in their meeting. Smith was definitely in his pocket.

The waiter entered with the main dishes, all small plates with various local delectables arranged in startling configurations that tasted and smelled of Kemet. The wine was gone, and Setehnekhet ordered a second bottle, this time of expensive French Bordeaux. The wine steward entered, decanted, smiled at Setehnekhet's approval, and left, closing the door.

"No reason to stint ourselves, Cheryl. And this is on me, of course."

"No, no, it's on me, Set. Really. I have special privileges here," she smiled. "I never pay a dime." She sipped the gorgeous Pomerol her boyfriend was paying for, unbeknownst to himself. She set off the dinner against the arrears he was incurring by not returning her voicemails.

"Well, then, a toast to—what's his name?" He knew the name perfectly well.

"Shesmu."

"The god of olive oil! How appropriate. To Shesmu!" His shark's smile and willingness to toast the boyfriend of the woman he was seducing firmed her resolve even beyond the forged steel it had been: this man must be flayed alive after all was said and done.

"To Shesmu!" She sipped more Pomerol.

Setehnekhet drank some wine, put down his glass, and got serious. "Very well, Cheryl. Let me explain a little about what we are doing so you can see your role clearly. With the information Smith supplies us through you, we will be able to thwart the NATO incursions into our territory before they start. People in the Republic have no idea how serious the situation is with the Americans and the Numunuu Empire right now; they are building up forces in a quite threatening way. We need Smith's information to counter them." Or to work *with* them, concluded MacIntyre.

"I am thrilled to be part of this, Set!"

"Cheryl, you're a true patriot, I am sure. I am trusting you implicitly." And she wasn't trusting him at all, recording everything he said.

"I'm so glad I can help, Set," she responded warmly. The rest of the dinner was a little on the heavy side—not the food, just the company. Now that she had her orders and her place in the plan and her recordings, she could proceed. Setehnekhet's clumsy attempts at seduction were just fluff to be brushed away. But she had to be careful not to offend him or put him off to the extent that he would exclude her, or worse. Henutsenu helped out by constantly sending in waiters with more small plates and the wine steward to pour more wine, so things never got too heavy.

As they sat in the car after leaving the restaurant, Setehnekhet embraced and kissed her, and she felt his hand on her leg. She returned the kiss but stopped his hand from progressing any further up her leg.

She said, softly, "Not on the first date, Set, I don't like to think of myself that way." She had to admit to herself that his touch was not that of a fat slug. Her attraction to him disconcerted her; was she really that easy? The power in the man....

The burly man smoothed away some hair from her face and kissed her again, pushing his hand further up her leg. She shifted a little, moving away from him, and said, "Please, Set, not now. We need to get to know each other better. I don't want to move this fast. Please?"

Setehnekhet smiled and raised his hands in acceptance, taking her refusal well. "Of course. How very American you are! And how elegant. We will have many more opportunities together, Cheryl, my dear. *Many* more opportunities. You are so beautiful, and I love your American eyes!" MacIntyre, anxious to avoid any further demonstrations of affection, just smiled and sat back. She noticed the eyes of the driver on her in the rear-view mirror and considered sticking out her tongue but restrained herself, carefully avoiding letting the driver know that she knew he knew what he knew.

"Have the driver drop you at your apartment, Cheryl." He leaned back next to her, replete and as satisfied as a man could be without having actually consummated the relationship.

"I appreciate that, Set, and the really nice evening, one to remember forever." And she would; she had it all on record on her phone. She leaned forward and told the taciturn driver where to go.

CHAPTER TWENTY-TWO
Shesmu Finds Paradise

The cab of the old pickup truck was dark, but I could feel the incredulity leaking out of my companions. We were an hour into the trip back to Kikyapapli when I said, "I need to get to Ta Sekhet if there's any chance Khenmes is there. But how do I get there?"

Heh just shook his head and said I was crazy. Tahefnu snapped on the sound system and hummed along with some Miwuk-infused country music. Her mood had improved a lot since we left Washeshu, but she radiated doubt. A few miles along, she turned down the music, and said, "If that's what you really want to do, we walk."

I contemplated this for a kilometer or so, then asked, "Walk? To the valley? What do you mean 'we'?"

Tahefnu smiled in the darkness—I could feel her smile, somehow—and said, "Yep. Walk into the valley, with a guide—me."

"But you said it was 90 kilometers, it'll take days."

"Yep. About three days."

"Three days! Tahefnu. I do not have three days." I flashed on an image of Khay and Webkhet standing at the door to my kitchen, waiting for me impatiently. This dissolved into an image of MacIntyre, the last image I'd had of her stomping out of that same kitchen angry that I was not going to be there for her.

Tahefnu snorted. "Oh, like you're doing something else here? If you're gonna find your friend, you're stuck here. What are you gonna do, grow wings and flap over the mountain? Even Hummingbird won't do that for me. Walk. That's it."

I cast around for another solution. "Why not roads?"

Heh stirred and said, "Army, son. Only road in is from the west, and the Republican Guard has that locked down. See, there's a river through the valley, and it's a big one, just as big and dangerous as the Hetchetci river. You need to cross three bridges, and the Guard has every one manned and shut down. Guard troops only allowed through there. Not a chance."

"How about horses? Or donkeys?"

"Haven't got any, Shesmu," said Tahefnu. "Besides, they only go a little bit faster than a walker. Easier on your feet, harder on your butt. Good eating, though, in a pinch."

I left that one alone. "I'm still walking with a stick."

"You're doing OK. That wonderful little cross-country jaunt up in Washeshu toned you up, I could see you doing better toward the end."

"*You* say." Now I was the disgruntled one. "Three days? 90 kilometers? Can I borrow your stick permanently, Heh? My ankle could use some more Bear treatments. Or maybe you have a spell that will turn my legs into magical bionic limbs. Or maybe I can travel there by spirit and rescue Khenmes that way."

Heh just laughed. "Everybody walks up here, son. If you want to hunt, you got to walk. Sure, I got spells, and a few herbs that might help. Deal with the mosquitoes, too. Lots of them on that walk. Don't forget your bug herbs, daughter."

Tahefnu voice came, the mischief in it clear. "Oh, and did I mention the thousand-meter cliffs?"

I shut my eyes and wished I could shut my ears.

Tahefnu laughed. "I know the paths down, you won't need ropes and stuff."

Heh said, "I been in Ta Sekhet once, son, when I was a kid. The big trick is to avoid the patrols near the tombs. At the bridges, they turn you back. At the tombs, they shoot to kill."

Tahefnu added, "And there's a bridge over the river, there in the valley, with guards, but I know a way there too. Can you swim?"

"You're serious, aren't you."

Heh said, "Water's awful cold, but you won't be in it too long. We can practice a little in our river when we get back."

"Great. This is a real vacation adventure. Khenmes will pay for this if I ever find him." I thought that Ma'at would approve of this plan, as she didn't particularly care about horrible details like cliffs and shoot-to-kill guards and swimming icy, raging torrents; I just hoped Mentju wouldn't get wind of it. I remembered my vision of the Coyote and the valley behind him and the tomb. Khenmes was there, I was sure. My father's tomb was there, I was sure. I had to be concussed to even consider doing *any* of this. But I'd do it. I had to do it. I needed answers, answers to questions I'd never asked myself or anyone else about who I was. And I was a little afraid of what I'd find out.

I must have muttered to myself, because Tahefnu laughed again. "Boy, you sure are grumpy for a guy who's getting exactly what he wants." She turned the Miwuk music back up and started humming again.

The next morning, Tahefnu and Heh dragged me out of bed at sunrise and took me down to the river. They pointed at a little beach on the other side.

"Now, what you got to do," advised Heh, "is breathe. Got to remember to breathe. Don't think about anything else: get to the beach, breathe, get to the beach, breathe. OK, son? And aim above the beach, the current will push you downstream."

"Right."

"And Tahefnu will rescue you if you go down."

"Right."

Tahefnu took off all her clothes, which had the effect you might expect on me. I hesitated.

She said with a grin, "Come on, Shesmu, strip down. We got work to do."

I obliged, my erection notwithstanding, and endured the grins of both my Miwuk companions.

"Just dive in, it's deep enough here," said the naked woman. She pushed me toward the riverbank. "I'll be right behind you."

I dove in, happy to let the water cover everything. Frankly, I do not remember much about the next few minutes. I apparently did remember "get to the beach" but I can't say I remember breathing at all. Cold does not say it, for that river. So much adrenaline pumped into my system that every limb on my body moved far beyond my normal capacity. I remember pulling myself up on the beach and breathing in huge gasps. I sensed rather than saw Tahefnu swim up to the beach and get out.

"Boy, you're fast! A little on the panicked side, though, got to control that. A bigger river, you'll have trouble once you run out of steam. You know?"

I just flapped and gasped.

"OK, now we swim back."

"No."

"Come on, Shesmu. We got to get going if we're going to get to the place I want to camp at tonight."

"No."

"Do you want me to warm up your body?" She held up her arms, her breasts gleaming wet, her long, dark hair plastered around her face and shoulders, a grin on her face. I lay on my back and got my breath back.

"No!" Not that it mattered. My erection had disappeared somewhere in the river, unsurprisingly.

"Then get going." She kicked me in the side with her bare foot.

I remember a little more, going back, and I breathed at least once, and I was a bit less panicked, but I did not linger. Heh had towels and blankets waiting for us. We returned to the house, and Tahefnu rummaged around finding camping equipment suitable for our adventure. The equipment included two lightweight hunting bows, surprisingly modern, with arrows Heh said he made himself.

Two hours later, Tahefnu was hugging her father goodbye and listening impatiently to his many admonitions about staying safe. He gave me a friendly hug and said, "Keep that medicine bag on you, even when you're swimming. It will help with the spirits." I fingered the little pouch hanging from my neck; I had no idea what was in it, but he just told me to leave it alone. Finally, he presented me with his walking stick.

"Take this stick, Shesmu. With those visions you had, I think it has special meaning for you. It is yours now, treat it well and use it wisely. A little part of me goes with you."

Heh slapped me on the back, and Tahefnu and I set off for Ta Sekhet. We hiked up along the river for half the day, meeting and greeting the various families that lived in the valley as we passed. Tahefnu suggested that we tell anyone we met on the trail that we were on a hunting trip up the river. Once we left the river, we'd say we were heading for the 'Anr Pass, the big pass through the mountains leading to the Paiute country in the east.

In early afternoon we reached a creek that flowed from the south down to the river, and we toiled up the trail for hours until we reached a small, beautiful lake and decided to camp there. This was hard country, and Heh's walking stick was more than welcome. We didn't even make a fire, just ate some dried food and went to sleep, exhausted.

The following day, Tahefnu bounced up at dawn and spent the next hour making breakfast, being chirpy, and badgering me to keep moving or we wouldn't get to where we needed to be. My legs had gone on strike, but once Tahefnu got us moving, the pain and stiffness eased. The walking stick felt good in my hands. The hiking that day was more reasonable, moving over ridges and through little passes through the mountains.

As we walked, we talked in snatches about our lives. I told her about my life in Menmenet, growing up there, becoming a chef and opening my restaurants, and falling in love with MacIntyre. She told me about her growing up "in the old ways" with her father and going to school "in the modern ways." She wasn't sure yet which life she wanted to live, but she was putting off college until she could claim to be a fully qualified Hummingbird shaman, just in case the old ways won out.

"How far along are you?" I asked.

"I can talk the talk, but I'm still a toddler, not walking. Dad's taught me what he knows, and a couple of women shamans have filled in some, but Hummingbird is a little different, really. Faster, always out in front. Dad guided me in choosing Hummingbird, he said the spirit was in me, and I feel her every day."

"Could you still feel Hummingbird living in a Remetjy world?"

"Don't know. Things get…indistinct, when you go outside your land."

I thought about my visions. "I think things get sharper, myself." Tahefnu grinned.

We trekked along awhile as she pondered this. Then she said, "It's not usual for people to have the kinds of visions you've had. Dad was absolutely terrified when it hit you. And the last one…. That was extreme. I've had a couple of Remetjy boyfriends who came up to the Valley to meet Dad and see the scenery, and they never had visions. Granted they were kind of dopey, which you're not; still, if it were a thing, you'd think they'd have popped up with worms or flies or whatever was moving their spirits."

I laughed. "It sounds like you've been unlucky in love." I bit my tongue the minute I said it. She looked at me over her shoulder with a frown.

"No shit."

"Sorry, didn't think."

"Try it sometime, you'll like it."

We proceeded in silence for awhile, which I broke.

"I haven't had any remarkable dreams since that nightmare with Mentju."

"Dad gave you some protection."

"I respect your dad, a lot; but I don't believe in magic, Tahefnu."

"And yet here you are." She spread her arms wide as she walked. "Look around you. Pretty magic, if you ask me."

"You've got me there," I smiled. "But I can't believe in all these gods and visions and what-not. I just want to find Khenmes."

"Sure. Let's see: shamanistic visions guiding you to a secret prison, vision after vision, that hunter's dream, your hunch about Ta Sekhet—none of that makes you believe in magic?"

I shook my head. "Just dreams, Tahefnu. And a hunch about Khenmes."

"What about the walking stick appearing in your dreams? What did you call it? A w'as scepter?"

"Just a stick. A good stick, but just a stick."

More humming. After a few minutes, she said, "I still don't understand how a Remetj like you has visions like that. It's almost like you're a part of our land somehow. But you've never been here." She shook her head. "Very puzzling. Dad says he's got some ideas but he's not ready to act on them. So he threw all the magic he knew into your medicine bag to try to keep you safe from your spirits. And it's keeping them quiet, isn't it?"

"Thank the gods," I said, halfway meaning it but unconvinced.

She left off trying to persuade me into magical thinking. We camped that night by a large creek, to which we descended down a hill late in the day. Tahefnu said this creek led right into the big valley to the south, with a huge waterfall at the end, near where we would camp the next night.

The third day, we talked more about ourselves, and I found myself increasingly liking this odd, magical Hummingbird woman, so different yet similar to MacIntyre. I thought more about things and said less, restraining my baser instincts. Tahefnu kept humming, off and on, and it grew on me. I learned a lot about the flora and fauna around us. At one point, we unshipped our bows and went hunting at a spot that Tahefnu knew was good for rabbits. We camped that night along the creek. Tahefnu said it was an hour more until we came to the valley, but we needed to stay back to have a fire that would not be seen.

"I want a decent last meal, if that's what it's going to be," she said, building the fire and roasting the rabbits on a spit. I handled the side dishes to her satisfaction, taking a few liberties with her recipe for acorn mush by adding some herbs I'd found along the trail to some of our stash of ground acorns. I'd also found some excellent mushrooms that went really well with the roast rabbits. An excellent last meal indeed. Comfort food.

Over the campfire, we talked about ourselves, opening up a little on our feelings.

"Your American girlfriend sounds like a good person," Tahefnu said.

"She is. She's the essence of Ma'at, which is both good and hard to be around sometimes."

"Well, if you love her, you love her. And your place is there, not here, though I wonder sometimes."

"And *your* place is here, Tahefnu, not Menmenet. You belong in these forests and mountains."

"Maybe." She didn't sound completely convinced.

We sat next to each other, staring into the fire, watching the flames dance. Tahefnu put her arm around my back. I felt echoes of the electricity I'd felt at her first touch, and I put my arm around her shoulders and we nestled, keeping warm.

"Tahefnu…" I said. "I can't."

"You will, sooner or later." She nestled. "It's part of the magic."

"I don't believe in magic," I said, my chin resting on top of her head. She smelled of wood smoke and herbs and mysterious things and earth.

"You will, sooner or later." She seemed content with that.

The next morning, we ate breakfast, then packed up, and Tahefnu led me south to the big waterfall. I could hear the roar long before we got there, and as we walked up the flat rocky area, the view opened out to the east and west, then opened out again until I saw a sight I will remember all my life: the Ta Sekhet-Imenet-Ma'at, the valley that was the final resting place of our great Remetjy men and women and one of the most beautiful places on Earth.

CHAPTER TWENTY-THREE
The Consul Reads In MacIntyre

MacIntyre again stood at the open door of her clothes closet choosing what kind of clothes to wear for a special day. No need for elegance anymore; she was now a powerful insider, a full partner in the conspiracy to overthrow the Republic. She had a power meeting with the American Consul General, a step up from the murder suspects she usually met with, though probably not that different overall, she suspected.

She reconsidered the red dress: aggressive, yes, and an association with blood to convey her willingness to take no prisoners. Black, always a good choice for dominatrix behavior. White, signaling a humble and pure yet powerful presence in the new government? Green, symbolizing, what—an elegant yet down-and-dirty support for the environment? No, a stretch. Not green.

Being on the inside rather than on the outside might simplify your choices: it didn't matter what you chose to wear or who you chose it for anymore, because you were *in*. Not *out*. She longed to be *in* again at her real job in homicide, but that was still only a distant possibility. Yet, simplicity went out the door when you considered the raw fact of being a woman facing powerful men, even when you're *in*.

Today she would see John Smith, who would now treat her as *in* but would first and foremost treat her as an American woman. The red dress, its lines were more recognizably American without being absolutely un-Remetjy in character. Heels or sandals? Sandals would throw her power in his face, never a good idea. Heels it was. She added a jacket to cover the collapsible baton in its holster.

She walked down the street to the American Embassy, and the marine guard admitted her without a second glance. The same short, fat Remetjet who had welcomed her the last time greeted her at the door.

"Consul General Smith will join you in the patio for coffee in a moment, Ms. MacIntyre. Would you care to wait there?"

"Thank you." A step up from the standard reception she had received the last time. The receptionist used the English word "patio" and smiled as she used it; the reality was a classic Remetjy interior courtyard with garden and very elegant fountains in the modern Remetjy style, angular abstractions spouting water that suggested the gods rather than representing them explicitly. MacIntyre imagined that the Americans had just bought an old Remetjy palace for their embassy, refurbished it, then wrapped it in razor wire and marines. Tables scattered around the courtyard were empty until MacIntyre sat at one.

The receptionist poured her a cup of real American coffee, which she sipped, enjoying it immensely. Wonderful coffee; she had still not switched her allegiance over to the ubiquitous herb tea so popular in Menmenet. Perhaps the real justification for the coup was to import better coffee! MacIntyre doubted that would happen, but it was worth considering as another reason to support the coup. She was sure that as a highly placed conspirator, she could finagle a supply of great coffee out of the American partners.

"Ah, Ms. MacIntyre, it's good to see you again!" She looked up with a smile at the English greeting.

Smith approached the table and offered a hand. MacIntyre stood and shook hands, another American custom but one she didn't miss. Filthy habit. Smith reached into his suit's inside pocket and produced a passport.

"Here is your new passport, all signed and sealed."

"Why, thanks! That was fast." She opened the new document and checked it over: nice and clean, a fresh start. She put it in her own pocket and sat back down.

"We help out our citizens as quickly as we can, Ms. MacIntyre," he said as he took a seat across from her. The receptionist poured him a cup of coffee which he desecrated with some cream and far too much sugar. As far as she could tell, he hadn't noticed her dress at all, or her sandals. His eyes were cold and blank behind his little wire-rim glasses.

MacIntyre sipped coffee, savoring it, then said, looking at him over the cup held in her hands, "Damn, I'd come here just for the coffee!"

"Any time." He smiled; his eyes didn't.

She shifted gears to business. "John, Setehnekhet sent me as primary communication conduit between your folks and his folks."

"I thought it might be a good idea to meet outside, Cheryl. Fewer flapping ears."

It appeared that Smith had decided on informality now that she was on the inside of the conspiracy. He knew that she knew that he knew…. But he didn't really know, did he?

She smiled. "Suits me!" She put down the coffee cup on its elegant saucer. "Now, John, what have you got for us?"

Smith leaned forward a little and lowered his voice. "Progress on all fronts, Cheryl. The Numunuu are all in on this one, and we're one step away from getting the Anasazi in as well. The Plains Federation is all in as the major player in NATO, and the local Plains Federation Paiute leadership over the mountains is fully apprised of our plans and on board. How much do you know about the proposed troop movements?"

"No details, no briefing yet, not enough time. Setehnekhet wants the latest information so we can integrate it in the planning."

"Good. Well, let's see. We have the 6th Armored Division of NATO secretly stationed in Paiute desert territory to the east of the Tihachipia pass along with support infantry, ready to roll the tanks and APCs through the desert south of the mountains into Southern Ta'an-Imenty. I just got word yesterday that the NATO takeover of the Ta Sekhet is complete. I understand the Temple of Mentju issued orders to redeploy the Republican Guard to the Central Valley, with NATO troops dressed in Republic uniforms replacing them."

"The Ta Sekhet?" MacIntyre was only vaguely aware of the great burial place in the mountains; why would NATO…? "That's the valley with all the tombs?"

"Ta Sekhet-Imenet-Ma'at, yes, the tombs—and the treasure. Especially the treasure! The ops are self-funding, with all that gold. The NATO troops set up the bivouac in the Ta Sekhet as a staging area for the NATO Special Forces coordinated by USSOCOM. Once they're fully staged and ready, in a week or so, they'll be able to deploy out of the mountains and across the Central Valley in a day using the new McDonnell Osage transport choppers we'll fly in from Salt Lake. They'll deploy in the north while the armored troops will deploy in the south."

Things were a lot further along than she had anticipated. Armored divisions and special forces deployed and ready. Tanks and choppers. Ma'at was not thrilled with these developments, she was sure. MacIntyre ran through some scenarios:

should she do everything she could to end the coup before it started, a hard task, or run with it, use her inside knowledge and position to get more power, and make a difference there? A complicated decision that would need more investigation and thought. She put it aside as Smith continued his information dump.

"And the Paiutes are readying their own Special Forces NATO units to overrun Washeshu and Modoc when the time comes. We're coordinating with the Russians to make sure they don't interfere there."

MacIntyre froze, then made herself smile.

"Well, great, John! This whole thing is a fabulous piece of work!" She grinned, and he grinned back. "With this great new order of things, we can finally be real Americans here!" Her mind wasn't on the New Order, though, it was on Shes, and on where he was: Washeshu. If wild Paiutes intended to lay waste to the country, being a Remetj there wasn't the best thing to be, since the ultimate goal of the Paiutes was to help the Americans take over the Republic. As a development, this was dire. The fall of the Republic was bad enough, but she could in no way accept Shesmu tortured and buried in a mass grave by Paiutes.

Smith smiled in return and said, "Yes, it will. It will be a great day for the U. S. and of course for the NATO allies."

"Anything else to report?"

He considered. "Setehnekhet's request for recognition of the new government is a priority, all the paperwork is done and the State Department has it, and the president has been read in, so we should have a good start on worldwide recognition of the coup as the legitimate government. Especially since the hekasepat will still be in power—theoretically."

MacIntyre's image of Sebekemheb's head being chopped off as the first thing that happened in the coup changed to one of him waving to the crowd with Setehnekhet behind him pushing his arm. Apparently his limitations were his advantages. Does Sebekemheb know about any of this yet?

"Great. That's great, John!" MacIntyre finished her coffee.

"Another cup? I'd like to ask you some questions about the Menmenet medjau."

"John—can we circle back to that? No bandwidth. I gotta get back to the Temple with all this stuff, it's totally urgent. I'll ping you when I get time, OK? Thanks so much for the wonderful coffee! You have no idea how much we—how much *I*—appreciate all this."

"Certainly, no urgency on our side. We'll have plenty of time to get things in order. Cheryl—don't be a stranger! And," switching to Renkemet, "alive, sound, and healthy, my lady," the standard blessing. He grinned again, and the sunlight glinted off his glasses, obscuring his cold, green eyes. He was clearly proud of his mastery of Remetjy forms. Ma'at groaned within MacIntyre.

She shook hands with Smith and left the Embassy stuffed with knowledge, her mind working feverishly. First things first: she called Shes. Voicemail again! Where was the man? Why wasn't he picking up? She left a cryptic message about her progress and advised him strongly to get the fuck out of Washeshu as soon as he could. She disconnected and walked, distracted. She needed him home. She really could use the support, but she'd also just like him back alive, warm, and in bed with her.

Then she shook her head and put him out of her mind, as there was nothing more she could do for him. From where she stood, Setehnekhet was the key; ideas for pumping him tumbled around in her brain as she walked down the quiet Menmenet streets to the Temple of Mentju. She couldn't assume anything, Setehnekhet could turn on her in a heartbeat if he found out what she was really doing. Taking precautions wasn't really in her nature, but knowing she was heading for the storm, she'd need to keep her wits about her. Her decision about which way to go with the coup had to be imminent. The city burned with subterranean action, and the cool Menmenet fog wasn't going to help this time.

CHAPTER TWENTY-FOUR

Shesmu Finds the Miwuk Tomb

THE WALKING STICK WAS FIRM in my hand as we trudged down the heavily switch-backed path to the valley floor. We zig-zagged down the side of the mountainous valley wall separating a series of granite cliffs from the great waterfall that crashed and sprayed into the valley below.

I dredged deeply for something to say beyond what was cycling through my heart: why didn't we sleep together last night, Tahefnu? Or why don't we just make love right here, Tahefnu, in the midst of all this beauty we have to ourselves. Why?

"Why aren't there guards?" I asked.

"Who would be crazy enough to come in this way?" She appeared oblivious to my obsessive and close-held regrets. "They just guard the road down there. And the tombs. Always the tombs, with their gold."

"Short-sighted."

"There are rumors," said the Miwuk guide, "that some Miwuks have more money to spend after hunting trips around the tombs here. Small scale, though. What the Republican Guard doesn't know won't hurt them, much."

About ten minutes down the trail, my phone beeped wildly. "There's service here! Stop a minute."

"We need to keep moving. We have a river to ford, got to do it soon."

"OK, just let me see…." I saw the voicemails indicator, went there, and saw 30 voicemails from MacIntyre. "Sweet Aset! I hope I still have a girlfriend when I get back to Menmenet. 30 voicemails. I'd better call her."

Tahefnu rolled her eyes and turned to the trail and started off. She said, over her shoulder, "Come on. And if you call your sweet little girlfriend, I swear I'll push you off this cliff."

"Hold on, hold on. This is important." I brought up the phone and…the phone died. Out of power. I'd forgotten to plug it in back in Kikyapapli.

Tahefnu had stopped and regarded me, arms folded. "Well?"

I held up the phone, shook it, and said, "I'm totally fucked. Dead."

"You're not fucked, and you're not dead. Yet."

"The *phone* is dead, Tahefnu. I can't.…"

"Let's go, day's getting older by the minute." She turned and started off again, faster.

I couldn't even make lemonade. I put the phone away and followed. My ankle was doing all right with the stick, but the faster pace challenged me, as did dark thoughts about my relationship.

The last part of the trail was straight down over a series of granite boulders arranged in a kind of stair pattern that would have been fine for somebody about 5 meters tall but required us to rock climb down through the spray of the waterfall. The valley floor was forest punctuating a series of rolling meadows, with a meandering river running down the middle of it forming pools and rapids.

"Which way do we go?" I asked loudly as we rested briefly at the base of the falls, the roaring loud in my ears. The noise was so intense I decided not to even bother to listen to more MacIntyre snark.

"Not a clue. Shall we?" She arose and turned toward the river.

I got up and picked up the stick. It pulled my arm out toward the south, along the creek that cascaded from the waterfall toward the river in the middle of the valley.

"What," said Tahefnu.

"The stick. It's pulling."

Tahefnu turned back to me and reached out for the stick, which promptly swung my arm away.

"It doesn't appear to want you to hold it," I said.

"Prick. Give it to me." Tahefnu, arms akimbo, looked furious, her banked anger flaming up.

"No, really. Here, let's try this." I dropped the stick on the ground. Tahefnu leaned down and picked it up. She shook it and swung it up and down.

"Nothing. Not. A. Thing." Her voice dripped with sarcasm.

"Let me see it."

She handed it to me, and again my arm immediately swung around toward the river.

Tahefnu, re-banking the flames of her anger, considered the stick with her head cocked to one side. "Got to be Coyote. Only Coyote would screw around with a stick. Evil bastard. Probably a phallic symbol. Hummingbird and Bear would have more sense. They'd just tell you where to go, nice and simple. OK, we follow the stick."

I thought back; had I eaten any suspicious mushrooms or maybe some bars from Tahefnu's pack thick with unknowable ingredients? No. Well, it was a decent stick, a solid stick. It was a stick with character. It was a Miwuk stick. Maybe we'd better follow it. Never look back. There are times when you need to submit to the unreality that's happening to you. This was my time.

We hiked along the creek to the river that ran noisily through the center of the valley. Looking upriver from our hidden vantage point among the trees, I saw a bridge with troops stationed at both ends.

"We need to find a good spot to cross," said Tahefnu, looking at the bridge. "Out of sight of those troops. We need to do it now before the runoff from the melting snow later in the day brings down more water."

"Why not here?"

"Too narrow, too deep. See that big pool? And the water's running really fast."

"What about swimming?"

She grinned. "We were kind of just getting you up for it, Shesmu. If you have to swim across a river, you're in the market for a nice boat. We need a spot where the water doesn't come up to our waist. *My* waist. You need to be able to see where you're putting your feet. And I need a stick."

We walked down the river, away from the bridge. Tahefnu found a nice stick-branch and trimmed it off. We kept going until we came to a widening of the river. I could see the water running over the rocks in frothy little rapids. I looked back; the bridge was invisible now.

Tahefnu said, looking out across the river, "So, you see that little slope there? With the sandy beach? That's what we're aiming for, it'll be easier to climb out there than anywhere else. So we go up a little ways and then cross down the river diagonally, working our way across the current to that slope. You face upriver and ford sideways and downriver, with the current. You use the stick to brace yourself and make three points of contact; hold it with both hands. This river is pretty rocky, so we'll have to wear our boots and dry them out later. Go slow and try rocks before you put your weight on them. You'll go first, and I'll help you if you stumble or fall, try to grab my stick. If you can't do that, try hard to float on your way down to the ocean."

I looked longingly at the now invisible bridge and wondered about water babies. "Wouldn't it be simpler to just shoot the soldiers and cross the bridge?"

"Ha ha. Ready?"

"As I'll ever be."

At the deepest point, the water flowed a little above her knees, but Tahefnu never wavered. She encouraged me to move on and suggested new routes as I hesitated. The sticks made all the difference in balancing over the rocks. The water was icy and the current was moderately strong, and we moved as quickly as we could. No water babies, but I stumbled once on a shifting rock, and Tahefnu was right there, bracing me with her arm, which was surprisingly strong.

It took us about five minutes to cross the river, very cold minutes indeed, and we came up on the little slope and headed into a grove of trees to rest and assess what came next. I took off my boots to drain them, then sat quietly, my arms wrapped around my knees, thinking warm thoughts about my toes.

"Shesmu! Down, flat, quiet." Tahefnu was suddenly hissing at me. As I impaled myself on a sharp rock under my chest, my head down, I heard what she had heard first: a couple of men talking in low voices. A patrol of 5 men appeared, walking down the river on the other side. As they got to the point where we'd gone in, I was able to see them clearly. When the patrol passed out of sight among some trees, Tahefnu rolled over and looked at the sky.

"That was close," she said. "We just made it across in time."

"Tahefnu. Something's wrong." I shifted off of the offending rock and rubbed my chest.

Her eyes shifted to look at me. "No shit. We're here. Wrong is not strong enough."

"No, those aren't Remetjy troops."

"What?" She lifted herself up on her elbows and looked at me, puzzled.

"Those weren't Republican Guards. Did you see the arm patches? Those are NATO troops."

"Shit. Why would NATO troops be here? This is one of the Republic's most guarded spots."

"Exactly. Something's wrong."

We were silent for awhile, then she said, "Those troops you saw at the Washeshu site. Were they NATO?"

"I don't know. They looked like First People, but with all the gear you couldn't really tell. They spoke Remetjy. I didn't recognize the accent. I don't know enough about the military to recognize the vehicles or anything, and they weren't wearing insignia."

"If they were NATO, they might have closed up shop and brought your friend here, and that's why the bulls in that Waashiw shaman's dream ran here. And why we're following a magic stick."

I stood up and held out the stick. It swung east—upriver. "NATO troops, with guns and no inhibitions about Remetjy citizens. Should we just go back?"

Tahefnu considered this. "Up to you, but I'm game."

"OK, let's follow the stick and see where it leads."

"Following a fucking stick. Do you realize what this does to my self esteem as a native guide?" She grinned.

We put on our still-damp boots and squished east through the forest.

"This must be it."

The stick rested in my hand without pulling.

"Not much, is it?" asked Tahefnu. We stood in a little clearing in the woods, right next to the giant south cliff of the valley. A small chapel projected out from the huge cliff face. The tomb would be behind the chapel, tunneled into the cliff. No inscriptions on the chapel's exterior face told us whose tomb it was. An orange protective tape stretched across the door with NATO insignia all over it.

I said, "Unguarded, already checked. I guess that means no gold there anymore. Let's go in." My usual Remetjy revulsion at tomb robbing roiled my heart. And this could be my father's tomb.

We tore down the tape and stepped into the unlit chapel. I set my pack down on the stone floor and dug out my torch. Flashing it around, I saw there were inscriptions and pictures covering the stone walls. I started at the beginning and quickly saw that the inscriptions were a mixture of spells from the Book of Going Forth By Day and a recitation of the heroic exploits of the resident of the tomb. I kept reading until I found a word that wasn't Renkemet.

"Tahefnu, what does the name 'Uipyaka' mean in Miwuk?"

"Say it again?"

"Uipyaka."

"I think that's 'Bald Eagle.'" She pronounced it differently, Wipayakuh. "Why, is that the guy who's buried here?"

"Yep. Apparently some kind of hero." I read further, and it got interesting. The dates were a little unclear, but the style and nature of the content made it pretty modern. But the history was bizarre, certainly nothing I'd ever heard about.

"It says that this warrior, a Miwuk named Uipyaka, fought in a great battle in the mountains to protect his land from evil."

"What kind of evil?"

"Not specified. They're using a metaphor, 'Aapep the snake who envelops and destroys the world. It's an old legend—R'a and Seteh destroy the snake and start the normal world going."

"Wait—a Miwuk, as R'a?"

"Seems to be." I continued reading. "A great battle in which the Miwuk warrior and his Remetjy troops defeat all the massed enemies."

"Shesmu, come look at this."

"Wait a minute, I'm just getting to the good part...."

"No, come here. Now."

I walked over to where Tahefnu was standing by the door to the tomb itself.

"Look at the cartouche, there. Above the door."

The priests of Inpu usually reserved cartouche names for only the most important VIP dead. In the old days, it meant a pera'a; nowadays, major government figures and priests rated them. Basically it meant you became a god when you died. I put the torch on it so we could see it clearly.

I froze when I read the hieroglyphs. The first cartouche had the birth name Uipyaka, with an epigram that read something like "Chief of the Noble Band." The second—I couldn't believe my eyes. "Akhen."

"Wasn't...." Tahefnu paused.

"My father."

"But...."

I leaned against the wall, my heart on fire. Akhen was a Miwuk, and Akhen was a hero, and Akhen was a Remetjy god in the Sekhet-'Aru. Akhen was my father. Who was I?

"Shesmu, this explains a lot." Tahefnu looked at me, her face smiling in the torch light. "Like why I'm attracted to you so much—you're part Miwuk." She reached out and touched my face, and I fell back against the wall as though she'd punched me, and then I was somewhere else.

"You did not listen properly the first time." I was back in the black void facing Mentju, and again I could not move. "Perhaps you did not feel my wrath sufficiently. I must address that." And he pulled out his khepesh sword and started in again. I won't bore you with the details, though I still remember to this day each and every cut. When he was done, I expected Inpu to show up again, but Mentju said, "I want you, Shesmu, pretender to being God of Wine and Olive Oil, Butcher of Souls, to understand fully the futility and waste of what you are doing." He picked up each piece of me and piled it up into a really disgusting little mound of body parts, with my head on top, upside down, eyes open and terrified. He then went away and came back with a bundle of wood, which he distributed around the pile. He then set the whole thing on fire. The instant when the flames exploded, I felt the fire's heat but I saw a face upside down through the flames and it was not Mentju's falcon head but another animal that I could not clearly make out, and it quickly burned away and I saw Tahefnu's face, which burned away to nothing. The fire went on and on.

I woke to see Tahefnu's face again, this time leaning over me as she rubbed my hand. The torch lay on the floor, broken. There was only the light from the door.

"Are you awake? You've been screaming."

"How long," I croaked.

"Only a few minutes. But you were screaming. I couldn't wake you up," she stammered.

I gazed groggily at that beautiful face.

"It's you."

"What?"

I pulled myself up and sat against the wall, against my father's heroism, and looked at the face of evil. It turned out the face of evil was pretty easy to look at, overall.

"I don't know how, but it's you, your presence, Tahefnu. It's letting Mentju into me. Somehow he's using you to punish me. In my dreams." I thought back to what I'd seen. "And there's somebody else, some other god, behind Mentju, he's the one really using you."

"Nobody's 'using' me." Her face turned angry.

"Ask Hummingbird." I'd already accepted a magic stick and a bunch of nasty Remetjy gods, why not an imaginary bird friend?

"What?"

"You heard me. Ask Hummingbird." I figured that whatever the actual reality of her gods, a little meditation would show her the truth.

Tahefnu glared at me, then sat, cross-legged, against the other wall, a little ways away from me, her face in darkness, and meditated. She relaxed, slowly, then suddenly her eyes popped open, white in the dark, and she gasped and jumped up.

"It's true, Shesmu. Hummingbird says it's true, something bad, something foreign, got into me. Hummingbird says it's why I can't decide between worlds. She says I never asked before. She says I need to decide or I'll die childless and alone in agony." She closed her eyes and stood, trembling, leaning against the wall.

Miwuk. I wasn't the Remetj I thought I was, and Tahefnu wasn't entirely the Miwuk she thought she was. I wandered, lost, in the complexity thrust upon me. One thing was clear: we couldn't stay here and wait for NATO to find and kill us. I couldn't stay here and lose body parts at every touch of my beautiful Miwuk companion and her gods. My gods?

"You're going to have to help me, Tahefnu. We need to get out of here and figure things out. I think…." I kneeled, then slowly got to my feet with the help of the walking stick. "I can walk but I'm wobbly, you'll have to help me. I need some time to recover, and we can't stay here. If NATO finds us, we're dead. We need to hide outside somewhere."

She nodded as she helped me out of the chapel. "We'll head up to the south rim, lots of places to hide up there." She reattached the tape across the door so that NATO wouldn't know we'd broken in.

Over the next few hours, we slowly climbed up a steep trail to a heavily forested area that overlooked the valley from the south, with Tahefnu supporting me on one side and the stick on the other. We said nothing to each other. Once out of the chapel, her touch did not trigger anything in me, not even the desire for her that I'd felt earlier. The sun went down, and we collapsed into our sleeping bags, exhausted. And, thankfully, I did not dream.

CHAPTER TWENTY-FIVE

MacIntyre Learns the Hard Way

MacIntyre walked into Setehnekhet's outer office just as the door to his inner office opened and Sheritr'a and Imenka walked out. Seeing her, they bowed the small bow and smiled smiles that did not reach their eyes. MacIntyre returned the bow and smile as she walked past them into the inner sanctum. She closed the door.

Setehnekhet sat on his couch, hunched a little forward, reading a report on the small table in front of him. He looked up at the closing of the door, arose, and bowed.

"Cheryl, good to see you. I assume you come from Smith. Good news?"

"Excellent news, Set."

"Sit, sit." He sat back down and patted the couch next to him. She sat. "Tell me all." He put his arm up along the top of the couch as he turned to listen to her.

MacIntyre related the details that John Smith had given her about the NATO troops and their intentions. As he absorbed the full import of the preparations, a light grew in his eyes and his raptor's smile emerged, teeth gleaming sharply.

"Excellent indeed, Cheryl. I have just been meeting with Sheritr'a and Imenka, and our plans are proceeding apace! Just think: we will be ready within days to…"

MacIntyre smiled. "You can say it, Set. I'm not blind. You're taking over the government with a coup. Smith told me as much. He was not particularly reticent about anything." She paused, then continued, "You know, he could be a weak link. He's not very bright."

The predatory smile emerged. "Hmm. My assessment as well. Let us just say that he is in an excellent position to be of use to us, at least temporarily."

"Fuck yes! Troop movements, diplomatic initiatives, the president's plans—it's like a hundred free lunches delivered on a plate!" Showing a little enthusiasm for the boss's plans never hurt anything, and certainly not when the boss was an arrant narcissist. Sexy, but definitely full of himself. She needed to get him in the right frame of mind to put her into the right position of power after the coup so she could do something about it all.

Setehnekhet got up and went to his bar, where he extracted a bottle of French champagne from the cooler, opened it with a ceremonious but restrained pop, and poured two glasses. MacIntyre joined him, taking a glass.

MacIntyre said, "Now that I'm up to speed on everything, I want to help. I want to be closer to everything." She toasted him with her glass and sipped the excellent champagne.

He smiled and reached and put a finger to her lips. His eyes looked into hers. Startled, she drew back a little. He put his glass of champagne on the table.

"I want to talk about the future, your future, your…"

She waited.

He lifted his chin and looked down at her eyes. "Your beauty, your power, everything about you. You've shown I can trust you. I can give you the world, make you the most powerful woman in Menmenet, in the Ta'an-Imenty." His hand caressed her cheek, then moved down behind her neck and pulled her to him. He kissed her. Caught by surprise, she returned the kiss, but then pushed back, gently. He was actually a pretty good kisser. But this wasn't the time or place.

"Not here, Set. It's work, it's…somebody could come in." She tried to sound a little scandalized.

"Nobody's coming in, Cheryl," he said smoothly, caressing her back with one hand and her hair with his other. "The door is soundproof." He kissed her again. She again pulled back.

"No, Set, let's wait for later."

"Now, Cheryl," he said, his voice was a little hoarse, his hands holding her more strongly, pulling her against him. "Now."

"No."

"Yes." He forcefully pushed her down onto the couch, holding her arms, leaning over her with his predatory grin. Her glass of champagne fell out of her hand to the floor and shattered. "Yes. Now, Cheryl. I can't help myself." But he *was* helping himself. He was loosening his robe with one hand, getting to the point. Her darker self, the self she had only sensed briefly while listening to Sheritr'a and Setehnekhet's tryst, pushed for attention. She throttled it as she had done so many times before. Giving in to that part of herself, the part that knew that letting the man do what they wanted was the way out, long buried in dark closets, would not help matters. It would ruin everything she cared about.

"Set, Set. It's…Let me get out of these clothes, if we're going to do it, let's do it right." She smiled and went limp.

"That's what I want to hear," he whispered, his eyes locked on her. He sat up and let her go. She rolled off the couch and stood up, crunching broken glass under her sandal. She could still feel the force of his hands on her arms. He was deadly serious.

"You're so forceful. I want you so much, Set. Let me…." She adjusted her dress at the side, then reached behind her as though to take off her jacket. She whipped out the collapsible baton. The baton shot out into its full meter-long length.

Training kicked in, and she said in a hard voice, "It's over, Set. Let's just settle down and deal with things in a reason—"

Setehnekhet's shoulders bunched and he grabbed for the baton. MacIntyre stepped back, bringing the baton around, picking up momentum as she swung at his head. Setehnekhet. His arm shot up to ward off the blow. The stick connected with a thud, and his arm broke with an audible snap. He gasped but did not shout. His eyes, usually hooded and sharp, now burned fiercely. With his good arm, he swung a fist at her head, which she blocked with her left arm. She grabbed his blocked wrist and pulled him downwards past her, then swung the stick again and connected solidly with his back, knocking him to his knees. She stepped back—was it enough?

With a grunt, he pushed off the floor and rammed his head into her stomach, knocking her back against his desk. Up against her, he rammed his body repeatedly against her, smashing her back against the desk. Gasping for breath, she thrust her knee into his exposed groin, and he again collapsed toward the floor, groaning in pain. She pushed off the desk and jumped over him, heading for the door. He caught her shoulder before she got halfway across the room.

But in the open space, he was at a disadvantage; blunt force couldn't compete with her better knowledge of her own body and its capabilities, and she still had the baton in her hand. His hand went from her shoulder to her neck, she blocked, twisted, and swung the baton with as much force as she could given the short distance in a cross-strike to the side of his head. It was so fast and forceful that he had no opportunity to block. He collapsed to the floor without even a grunt.

MacIntyre, breathing hard, collapsed the baton and sheathed it. She knelt by the felled falcon and felt his head. A rising bump, but she could feel no moving bones. Out cold. She thanked Ma'at for her fortune in not adding to the relatively small list of people she had killed.

Setehnekhet's robe had opened as he fell, and he was still erect. She watched his manhood wilt as she got her breath back. She successfully resisted the urge to inflict more damage on vulnerable parts as she leaned over the unconscious Setehnekhet and took his bull pin as a kind of souvenir of their romantic encounter. She knew she would treasure the pin in the years to come, if there were years to come. Ah, the memories of lost love. She shivered. All this would hit her at some point, but now was not the time to go under.

She immediately discarded the routine next step, calling the medjau. Too humiliating; and it would end any possibility of dealing with the coup. She might even wind up in jail or worse. Kidnap him? She'd never get him out of the building. Kill him? That might shut down the coup and make her feel better, but her glimpse of the organization behind the coup suggested other possibilities that she refused to contemplate, such as Sheritr'a running the country. And killing people wasn't something that she was prepared to accept at this point, not this way, not in cold blood. Was her blood cold? She thought of R'aia and knew her blood was definitely warm to hot when it came to murder: she was on the homicide squad for a reason.

What she needed was some quiet time to think things through.

She straightened her clothes and patted her hair into place as much as she could. She opened the office door, went through, and shut it behind her. She walked over to the assistant and said, "The Hem-Netjer-Tepy doesn't want to be disturbed for an hour or so, he wanted me to tell you."

"Thank you, Djaret-Netjer," the man said. She despised the knowing look the man bestowed on her. He must be well versed in Setehnekhet's one-on-one team-building style. She bowed slightly and left. She didn't stop to retrieve anything from her office but left the building as quickly as she could without attracting attention.

CHAPTER TWENTY-SIX
MacIntyre Gets Help

MacIntyre boarded a bus that took her down to the Bay. She had to go to ground, fast. She surreptitiously removed her own bull pin and put it in her pocket with the souvenir she had taken from Setehnekhet.

She got off the bus a block before the waterfront stop, then worked her way up some back streets along the little bay that stretched up the east side of the city until she came up to the back parking lot of the Neferti restaurant. The lot had a few cars in it, but no one was around. She stood in a shadow against a wall and checked for anyone watching, then walked across the small parking lot to the kitchen door behind the loading dock and went in.

She peered into the busy kitchen through the prep room door. Everyone was hard at work getting ready for the lunch rush. She saw Sebek, the executive chef and Shes's best friend, standing over by the plating station going over the menu with a waiter. She waved, and he saw her and came back to greet her. They stepped into the prep room to talk.

"What's up, Cheryl? Why the back way?" Sebek asked. Looking at his smiling face, humiliation again washed over her as the realization of what she'd done finally hit her. MacIntyre finally understood something, somewhere down deep in her soul. She couldn't do this on her own, with her own superpowers, with her own independent action. That was done. Setehnekhet had taken that from her. His assistant's leer of knowledge made it worse. Now she needed the help of friends. She needed to ask for it, too, and she found that the hardest thing of all.

She forced it out past her enraged pride. "Sebek. I'm kind of, that is, I…"

"Just say it, Cheryl."

"I need help."

"What kind of help?"

"The kind only a really good friend can give. I…see, I sort of, well, I kind of, sort of…knocked the hem-netjer-tepy of Mentju unconscious with a stick when he tried to rape me." This last came out in a rush. MacIntyre blushed with the humiliation of it.

Sebek's face showed his shock in raised eyebrows, narrowed eyes, and as pale an expression as a dusky-hued man can get, and he said nothing for a minute. Finally, he rubbed his mouth and asked, "Henutsenu said you two came up with something, but I'm guessing that didn't work out."

"I…don't know if I can tell you."

"You can tell me, you know you can. You can tell us anything."

"This might be too much. It might…well, it might put you in danger."

"Like with the Russians last year?"

"Way worse."

"What the fuck could be worse than dealing with four guys with AK-47s intent on killing anything that moved?"

"An army with tanks intent on killing anything that moved."

"What the fuck are you into, woman?" Sebek sounded exasperated, but he reached out and took her into a hug. Won't cry, won't cry, won't cry.

She muttered into his neck, "I need to get somewhere safe…."

"Shes's house? My apartment? Henutsenu's apartment?"

"Once I get out of sight I can probably get a friend to get me into a safe house somewhere. But I have to get off the street, right now. Now, Sebek!"

"I'd suggest our walk-in, but it's set down to freezing, and you're underdressed."

"Oh, ha-ha. No jokes right now, Sebek, I can't handle it. Besides, I'm off walk-ins, and I don't want to talk about it." The image of Hori, covered with blood, staring sightlessly at her—she'd been obsessed with faking her loyalty and with the gory details of body disposal. Now the horror of that savage death came to her, and the understanding that without Karkin's help she might not have pulled off that deception. The horror joined with the emotions she still tried to suppress. Near breaking, she gripped Sebek as though he were the only thing holding her up.

"Hmm." he said, holding her, "let me get Henutsenu and we'll go from there." He sat her down on a stool by the prep counter. "Are you going to be OK here?" She nodded. He walked out, closing the door behind him. MacIntyre leaned her head on her hand, elbow on the prep counter, and closed her eyes to think things over.

"Cheryl, you beat the hem-netjer-tepy of Mentju with a stick? He was raping you?" asked Henutsenu, a little breathless with shock. MacIntyre's eyes flashed open as she awoke from her narcoleptic attack. She jumped up and hugged Henutsenu, and Henutsenu hugged her back.

MacIntyre said, "Our plan worked, but…things got complicated. Really, really complicated. I can't tell you everything, it would put you in danger."

"I can't imagine what you must be feeling right now. What a pig!"

"You have no idea how much of a pig."

"But he didn't…actually…"

"No." Won't cry. "But, hitting him with a stick: I've gotta stay invisible until I can get to a safe house."

"My apartment isn't safe?" Henutsenu released MacIntyre and held her arms, looking into her eyes.

"Not for this." MacIntyre shook her head. "Once they start looking, it won't take long for them to start on Shes's friends. They'll find you, question you. We probably have a day, max. I need somewhere I can get it together, get help, find a safe place."

"Who is 'they'?" Henutsenu asked. "Mentju?"

"Yes, and half the other authorities in Menmenet! Maybe all of them. I… Henutsenu, I really have nowhere else to turn. I'm sorry, I feel so…helpless. And humiliated."

Henutsenu hugged her again. "How about this? I've got the key to a neighbor's apartment, I'm taking care of their cat. If you stayed there for a night or two, nobody would find you, and if they came to my apartment, you wouldn't be there. We just have to get you there without anyone seeing you."

"The restaurant delivery van," said Sebek. "No windows in the back and plenty of room for you."

Henutsenu and Sebek turned things over to their assistants, then got their coats. Sebek pulled the van around to the loading dock, and Henutsenu helped load MacIntyre into the back, then sat in the front passenger seat. MacIntyre sat on the floor, feeling the warmth of having good friends, the desperation receding for the moment. Her thoughts went to Shesmu again, but she couldn't risk calling him on her phone. The van drove the short distance down to Mentju street and right into the basement parking garage. They sat in the van and talked tactics.

"There are cameras in the garage and the elevator, does that matter?" asked Henutsenu.

"Probably, yes," MacIntyre replied. "The medjau have access to all the cameras all over Menmenet, and they've got software that can track people."

Sebek asked Henutsenu, "Any cameras in the stairwells?"

"Not that I've ever seen. The stairwell doors are locked on each floor, only unlocked in the basement."

"You go up on the elevator," said Sebek. "We'll go up the stairs, then you let us in on your floor."

"I'm on the 23rd floor!"

"I know you are, my dear," replied Sebek. "I've been there. Better get going! See you in a little while." He kissed her, then pushed her toward the elevator.

After the elevator doors had closed on Henutsenu, Sebek drove the van around to the stairwell door and let MacIntyre out of the back.

"The camera can't see you, go inside and wait for me," he said. Once she was inside, he drove to Henutsenu's parking space, parked, and joined her. They started up the stairs. At about the 13th floor, MacIntyre thought it wasn't worth it. At the 20th floor, she knew it wasn't worth it, she was perfectly willing to accept her execution by the minions of Mentju.

"Come on, only a couple more," cajoled Sebek, who gasped for air himself.

"Fucking mountain goats," grumbled MacIntyre, pushing herself up another flight.

Sebek knocked lightly on the stairwell door, and Henutsenu opened it. They crossed the hallway and went into her neighbor's apartment. MacIntyre collapsed on the couch. Henutsenu went into the kitchen and brought back glasses of water, which MacIntyre and Sebek thirstily drank down.

"Thanks," gasped MacIntyre. "For everything." The resident cat, curious, jumped up on the couch and looked over the gasping fugitive, then left, apparently unimpressed.

Henutsenu asked, "What are you going to do?"

"Fuck knows," admitted MacIntyre. "I need a real safe house, I need serious help, and I need to get you two out of the line of fire. I need to get a new plan. And I know who I have to talk to about it all. "

Henutsenu considered, then asked, "That Karkin person?"

"Yep. That Karkin. And Shes."

* * *

MacIntyre sat on the couch the next morning, waiting. She had tried to read a book from Henutsenu's neighbors' small library and got lost on page 2, she couldn't concentrate on the glyphs. She turned on the TV and watched a news program. The Remetjy anchor reported on a mass shooting in Charleston, North Carolina, which the anchor apparently thought was somewhere near the Everglades. She switched to a cartoon, a Japanese anime production that reflected a world view so foreign to her that she gave up. The image of Setehnekhet looming over her, pressing her forcefully against the couch, the fear of it, and the humiliation of his assistant's leer, kept intruding. The cat, nestled next to her on the couch, took note of none of it.

She waited.

Finally, midmorning, the door opened. Henutsenu unloaded the packages in her arms onto the small table next to the couch. "Hi, Cheryl. Sorry it took so long, I've never been down that way before." The cat's eyes opened and looked sleepily at this invasion of her domain. Ah, the black-haired food-giver. The cat curled around Henutsenu's ankles.

"Did you get it?"

"Yes, of course." Henutsenu took up a small package and handed it to the American.

MacIntyre struggled with the plastic clamshell packaging. "Fucking..." She finally got the package open and extracted the small burner phone she had asked Henutsenu to buy for her. Maybe she should get a dozen of these things with a big discount, it looked like she needed to be off the grid awhile. First thing on the bus, she had turned off her own phone and removed its SIM card to take it off the mobile network.

She thanked Henutsenu with a brief kiss, then looked over the other packages —some clothes, a small backpack, a hoodie, pajamas, chips and some Aztec molli (gotta eat something besides all that rich restaurant food), fruit (maybe, maybe not), ibuprofen tablets, a small bag containing tea according to the label, and a couple of bestseller political thrillers, in English. The cat jumped onto the table and sniffed the bag of tea.

"What the hell are these?" she asked, holding up one of the books.

"I thought you'd get a kick out of some hometown thrills." A mischievous smile lighted up her face. "The pharmacist said they're the best thing he'd got on American politics."

MacIntyre burst out with a hysterical little laugh. "Sorry," she said, covering her mouth, eyes wide. American politics! "Really, I appreciate it all, Henutsenu. But mostly this," she said, holding up the burner phone. "Now I can get to work."

"It's prepaid with 50 debenu, I hope that's enough."

"If it isn't, I'll be making calls from the internment camp public phone anyway, using American quarters," MacIntyre replied. "I'll pay you back when I get money, after all this."

Henutsenu smiled. "Don't worry about it. And that bag of tea, that's a special tea from the Temple of Bastet, I asked a hem-netjer who specializes in pharmaceuticals what would be good for someone who was really stressed. Try it! Boiling water, six minutes. So, if you've got everything you need now, I've got to get to the restaurant. Today's fish delivery day."

"Um—any sign of the authorities?" MacIntyre's stomach felt a little queasy at visualizing the minions of Mentju led by Sheritr'a descending on her friend. She picked up the bag of tea and smelled it, just to be doing something other than looking at Henutsenu. The cat, interrupted in her investigation, jumped back to the couch and glared at MacIntyre.

"No, nothing so far. Cheryl, you know you can stay here as long as you need to, my neighbors will be gone for the next three weeks. Or even at my apartment, once you think it's safe." The cat butted MacIntyre on the leg. MacIntyre put the tea back on the table and mechanically stroked the cat, then looked at her friend.

"That's the best offer I've had in awhile, or at least since the last time you offered. Tempting. But I can't stay, Henutsenu. I have to call Karkin, and I won't be here when you get back. It's dangerous for you as well as for me. I haven't told you everything that's going on, and I'm not going to, I can't. Those books…may just be useful. But I absolutely can't keep putting you and Sebek at risk." She got off the couch and hugged her friend. "Thanks for helping, you have no idea how much it means to me: it's literally life and death. Thanks for the love. I needed that more than anything. Tell Sebek I love him too." A gentle reminder to Henutsenu about the significant others in her friend's life.

Henutsenu smiled, her curving lips showing her resignation to the realities of tradecraft. "Take care, and let us know if we can help, and what's happening, if you can. Make sure the door's locked when you leave." She looked a little wistfully at MacIntyre, holding her, then traced a gentle finger along her cheek and tried the direct approach. "Cheryl. When some shithead tries to rape you, and you beat the shit out of his head, that's a good thing, no?"

Taken aback at this direct insight into the depth of her fear, MacIntyre could only look silently into Henutsenu's eyes.

Henutsenu continued, "It's not humiliating. You're a powerful woman. In my temple, Bastet teaches us to wield the knife of the Great Cat of R'a to defeat isfet, and hitting the bastard with a stick qualifies."

Henutsenu had, as Hemet-Netjer-en-Bastet, felt it was her responsibility to tutor MacIntyre in the complexities of Bastet worship. The story of the Great Cat referred to the militant aspect of Bastet, who chopped the 'Aapep snake into pieces as it tried to destroy the world. The cat, curled up on the couch, purred with satisfaction. Cheryl MacIntyre, for the first time in her life, was completely lost for words. She hugged Henutsenu fiercely and let go and backed away. Henutsenu, who could tame lions, was the essence of peace and love. And power, the power of Bastet. Not her goddess, though, who had her own views on the nature of power.

Henutsenu shook her head in resignation and left to deal with her fish and her lover.

MacIntyre put the phone on the table, sat on the couch, gently deposited the cat on the floor when it tried for her lap, and considered how to approach Karkin. The cat disdained her and vanished to wherever affronted cats vanish.

"Karkin?"

"MacIntyre. Thought you'd call. Burner?"

"Sure. I'm—"

"In deep fucking trouble. I know."

"What do you know?"

"Geneva telex. Very nasty French. What happened?"

"I hit a hem-netjer-tepy with a stick. While he was trying to rape me. I'm in hiding at a friend's apartment. I need—"

"A safe house."

"Right."

"Where are you?"

"375 Mentju Street, the big apartment house. 23rd floor."

"OK, service door, back of the building, 10 minutes. Don't be seen."

"I'll be wearing a black hoodie."

Karkin disconnected without saying anything. After packing up the clothes, the chips and molli, and the books (you never knew) in the backpack, MacIntyre put on the hoodie and made sure nothing showed. She looked at the fruit and shook her head. The cat could eat it. And the pajamas: she slept nude, no need. She thought about Henutsenu's interest in pajamas and put that away for another time. She left the apartment and walked down the hall to the stairwell.

"No fucking way I'm walking down all those stairs," she muttered to herself. She went on to the elevators and kept her head down to avoid the camera in the control panel. The doors opened on the garage, and she walked back and through a small door labeled "Employees Only." It was OK, she was an employee of something, or maybe not anymore. She walked down a little hallway past boilers and a storage area and came to a door marked "Exit." She exited. First time in her life, she reflected, that she obeyed orders.

Karkin's small car was there. She got in, and Karkin set off at a sedate pace.

"Hi," said MacIntyre from inside the hoodie. Karkin gave her one eye and his lips twitched. He said nothing but drove in circles for awhile, looking around carefully. Then he worked his way over the hills in the middle of the city, over the Tjesut ridge with its spectacular views of the Bay and down into the Asian quarter that nestled in the northwestern part of Menmenet.

She made one attempt to look out the side window, at which Karkin said, "No face." So she just sat and pulled the hoodie forward.

They turned down a little side street, and in the middle, a garage door opened automatically when Karkin pushed a button in the car. He drove in and the door closed behind them.

"Safe house?" asked MacIntyre.

Karkin nodded. They got out of the car and walked through a door into a nice little house, sparsely furnished.

"No windows." Karkin went around closing the blinds, shutting them in from the already foggy afternoon.

MacIntyre deposited her backpack on the minimalist couch and looked around.

"First things first, Karkin. I need to know I can afford this place. What are the terms, and I'm not talking about rent. Am I getting sucked into your shadowy international police organization and incurring all kinds of liabilities that will trap me forever in a web of international deceit and corruption?"

Karkin finished drawing the last blind and turned to her, finally growing loquacious. "Nope. Place is off the books. Cayman Islands corporation owned by a Jersey company, which owns quite a few companies and properties in the Ta'an-Imenty Republic."

"Karkin: I need to know what I'm getting into here."

Karkin asked, "Know many First Peoples here?"

"As much as any medjat, I guess, I know important names and a few individuals, I've met the local leaders. And a few local crime lords."

"Part of the scenery. Vote in Republic elections and keep the Remetjy brothers and sisters honest, right? And cultural centers, lots of cultural centers. And crime lords."

"I haven't seen any activists marching or throwing bombs looking for independence, anyway."

"Govern ourselves. Secret organization. Need to know. No debt to us for this."

After mulling this cryptic information over, MacIntyre asked, "Given the situation, I have to ask: where do your true loyalties lie?"

He just shook his head. "It's an awful thing to have so little trust in people," he said, with regret.

"I just disposed of a body, Karkin, with your help. Is that on the local level too?"

"Pretty much. Meat warehouse is ours, for storing stuff. Like your corpse."

"Loyalties, Karkin. Answer the question."

"Situational. I have debts, paying them off standing here. You're with Shesmu, that's all you need to know. Don't worry about me, worry about you."

"OK, what now? Things are getting hot, Karkin. The Americans—"

He held up a hand.

She laughed without any humor. "You already know."

"Satellite data. Geneva. Troop movements."

"But you said your organization wasn't likely to do anything about it."

"Nope." He shook his head in disgust. "Wrong. Kind of existential for us here, and for Washeshu, those Paiutes. Waashiw shamans are worriers."

Shamans. OK. Waashiw, OK. Paiutes, OK. MacIntyre's father used to say, "Trust in the Lord and hope will never die." She didn't believe in the Christian God any more than in the Remetjy gods, but what the hell.

MacIntyre sat down on the couch and opened her pack. She rummaged a bit and took out the chips and molli that Henutsenu had rounded up for her. "Snack?" she said, opening the sauce. "What am I going to eat?"

"Freezer. Knock yourself out." He took a chip and dipped. "Hot."

"I like it hot."

"Clearly. Just…try to keep the heat down a little, OK?"

"We'll see. I can't just let this happen, Karkin. I'm on the interned list, and I think I probably just got upgraded to the 'immediate execution' list once I beat the shit out of the hem-netjer-tepy of Mentju. My current plan, I want to talk to Shes, and I want to talk to Djehutymes, my boss on the homicide squad. He's a curmudgeon but he has good instincts, he'll help."

"Shesmu…may be hard to reach. Last I'd heard, he was headed for Ta Sekhet-Imenet-Ma'at."

Alarmed, she said, "But that's—"

He nodded, raising his hand again. "I know. Bad comms up there."

MacIntyre got louder. "But he's—"

"He's good. Friends up there. *My* kind of friends." Karkin wasn't looking her in the eye when he said that, and MacIntyre got suspicious.

"What are you not telling me?"

"Need to know." He took another chip and some molli. "Hot."

Exasperated, she picked up her burner phone and dialed a number. After a minute, she disconnected.

"His voicemail is full. I can't even leave a message, and he still doesn't answer."

Karkin said, "Djehutymes, best bet. Keep all this to yourself. Upsets the locals." Now he was looking her hard in the eye, his little mustache asserting a strength of feeling not obvious from his words.

When he'd gone, she thought about the danger Karkin himself was in for about two seconds, then dismissed it. A secret web of indigenous secret agents fighting a secret coup attempt with massive, secret international implications. MacIntyre marveled at the depth of knowledge about the local world she'd acquired in three weeks, compared to the superficial understanding she'd accumulated over ten years of medjat and detective work in the beautiful city of Men-menet. Summed up in one word: *fuck*.

Need to know. She sat on the couch, safe for the moment. More molli on another chip. Hot. Need to fucking know.

CHAPTER TWENTY-SEVEN

Shesmu Is Given Life

I AWOKE IN MY SLEEPING bag nearly unable to move; my muscles had locked up. The immediate consequence of this was that I could not manage to unzip the bag. And I desperately needed to empty my bladder.

"Tahefnu."

"Mm."

"Tahefnu!" A little louder.

"Ur."

"Tahefnu!" Louder still.

"What!" Tahefnu turned over and looked at me with barely open eyes framed with black hair.

"Got to pee. Can't unzip my bag." I looked at her with what I hoped was what little pride I had left. It wasn't a lot.

"Shit."

"No, just pee. Please. Don't make me beg."

Grumbling, she emerged from her bag, naked, and quickly put on her clothes, shivering in the cold. She stumbled around the remains of the small fire she had made the night before and knelt down beside me. She unzipped the bag. I had crawled into my bag fully dressed the night before, exhausted, so I didn't need to dress, but I found I couldn't stand up.

"Fuck." Tahefnu found the walking stick and gave it to me then helped me up. "Do you need help with—"

"No!" I grunted. I hobbled off behind a tree and struggled with my icy fingers, finally undoing myself and letting loose a stream. I was not able to redo myself, so I hobbled back and presented myself for more humiliation, which Tahefnu duly imposed by zipping me up. I flinched, fearing that her touch would push me into another dismemberment dream, but it didn't.

"It will get better once the sun clears that mountain," she said.

"Thanks." I was hoarse and could not hide the humiliation in my voice. It wasn't going to get better, not for a long time to come.

"You're pretty damn surly for a Miwuk warrior."

"I'm not a Miwuk warrior," I said. I tottered over to a fallen tree and sat down.

"OK on the warrior part, but it looks like you got the genes."

I closed my eyes. My father the Miwuk. And now some kind of honorary Remetjy god. It made sense of the dreams, the Miwuk man that was also a Remetjy Coyote god.

"What does it mean, Miss Shaman, that I see my father in my dreams as a Remetjy god with a Coyote head?"

"Fuck knows, Shesmu. I'm just a trainee. Dad was pretty suspicious about that Coyote, though." She came over and sat next to me.

"Don't…sit so close."

"Fuck."

"And stop saying that. Please. It doesn't help."

"Sorry," she said with a grin. "Habit."

"It's a dirty habit and you should be ashamed of torturing me." I was trying to joke, but it came out wrong. It came out whiny. I'm not whiny.

"Whoa, you're surly." She got up and rummaged in her pack. "Better stick with energy bars this morning, a fire might attract too much attention in daylight."

I sat, munched, and glumly considered my heritage. Miwuk. It explained so much. My mom's unwillingness to talk about my dad, Khenmes's and Tuy's reticence. They all didn't want me to know. And all the dreams.

Little by little, the sun crept through the trees, finally reaching the little clearing we had found off to the side of the trail. The night before, Tahefnu had insisted we move a few hundred meters away from the trail to avoid anyone stumbling over us.

"What do you want to do now?" she asked.

"It isn't really what I want to do, it's what I *can* do, which is pretty much fuck all. I can barely move."

"OK, so we won't go mountain climbing today." She smiled and looked around, listening. There were birds and wind and not a lot else. "We'll need water by tonight if we're staying here. I don't hear a creek, so I'm going to have to walk back to the river and fill up our water sacks. Why don't you sit here and rest, and we'll talk when I get back."

I nodded without speaking, and she rolled her eyes and took herself off.

I sat thinking about my heritage. It wasn't a bad thing, to be part Miwuk, it was just so new. It called into question a lot of things I'd internalized about myself over the years, but it also opened up a range of possible futures that boggled my heart.

Tahefnu finally returned about mid-day with full waterbags. She set them down by our packs, then came over and stood over me, arms akimbo with a smile on her face.

"Have you moved since I left?"

"A little. Peed again, on my own." A little pride left.

"F—sorry, promised not to say that. Shesmu, you have to get a grip."

"I can't seem to get past this Miwuk thing."

"You don't like being part Miwuk?" Tahefnu's voice raised in incredulity.

"I do, it's just…I'm not used to the idea yet. I've been full-blooded Remetjy all my life, now I'm not."

"Big change, huh?"

"Very big."

"Changes like this, we usually take the time to go through everything, have some ceremonies, talk about it. Endlessly." She smiled. "So, talk."

"Do I belong to a band or tribe or something?"

"Probably. If we knew what band your father was part of, that would be a start. Who might know that?"

"It might be in the tomb. Khenmes knows."

"Neither of which is of much help right now."

I asked, "Do you know any mixed-blood people?"

"Nope. Pretty uncommon with us mountain folks. We keep ourselves to ourselves." She grinned. "Like I said, I had some dopey Remetjy boyfriends that didn't work out, gave up on that." The grin disappeared. "Maybe it was those Remetjy boys that put this whatever it is in me. Maybe being with you is where I'm meant to be."

"Let's not make any quick judgments."

"Prick."

"You said mountain folks." That opened up another strand of thought. "Mountain—could I be valley or coastal?"

"Sure. In the old days, we used to care a lot more, these days not so much. Different bands do talk a little different."

"Language. I'll need to learn the language."

"If you want, though most everybody speaks Renkemet. Be nice, though, makes you feel at home with people, you know?"

"And what about a name?"

"Now that's complicated. We'll need to talk to Dad about that one. Names are kind of special, and we'll need to work on that with you, once things settle down a little."

"There's so much…."

She patted my leg. I flinched at her touch, but nothing happened, no dream or gods or pain. She said, "What you've been talking about is Miwuk stuff. How do you feel about your father, now you know all this?"

I hadn't thought much about my father for years, and now all the repressed things rose up and swamped me. I picked out one thing I remembered.

"He gave me a bow, a reproduction of a Remetjy acacia military bow, when I was really young. It's my earliest memory. I can't remember his face, but I can remember his voice telling me that when I could pull it, I'd be all grown up."

"A bow, really? And you're good with one?"

"More than good."

"Puts you way ahead in the Miwuk stakes, then," she said with approval. "We'll have to compare sometime."

More memories. "I shoot with the bow all the time at the Menmenet archery range. Last year, I was shooting and another archer came over, a guy named Karkin that I'd seen around but hadn't talked to before. A local Ramaytush man." And what a story that turned into. "It's complicated, he turned out to be a secret international policeman, helped me save my girlfriend. But…he told me, later, that he helped me in order to pay off part of his debt to my father. He never told me what the debt was, though."

"Wow. OK, the bow connects you to your dad, but somehow the details never made it to you."

"Right. Khenmes…was a substitute for my father, I think. He knew things but never told me." I reached into my heart and uncovered a fact. "When I heard he'd gone missing, it was like my father dying all over again. It's why I dashed off to Washeshu and Tuy."

"It sounds like you miss him."

"More than that, if there's any chance of finding Khenmes, I have to do that. And my father; his mummy must be in the tomb, I need to know. You have no idea what it means to a Remetj when a close relative is just missing, no mummy, no idea whether they've made it through the Duat. Even non-religious guys like me feel it. My dreams are surfacing that feeling too. Maybe that's the source of all these dreams: what's in the tomb."

Tahefnu's face was a little skeptical. "Maybe, but some of that stuff…Dad was pretty sure they were real, spirits welling up inside you. Maybe it's all related, but you need to treat that as real, not 'just dreams'."

"Spoken like a true shaman," I joked. She didn't laugh. She just looked at me, brooding silently.

"So," she said, changing the subject, "the other thing that happens when boys lose their fathers is trouble starts. We've had a few families like that, boys were always trouble. Did you have all kinds of trouble as a kid? Bad behavior, anger, that kind of thing?"

"No, because Khenmes filled the void, and my mother was wonderful."

"One thing I've seen in men with dead fathers, they get a little weird when they grow up, they have trouble with commitment, trouble figuring out what to do with their lives."

Well, that was a hit to the heart. "Yeah, that's me. Hopping from restaurant to restaurant, relationship to relationship." I didn't want to hop away from MacIntyre. I needed to listen to those voicemails somehow, I didn't want to lose her. I feared I'd already lost her.

"But no marriage?"

"No, and that's the thing: I didn't know why, but I think it must be part of the father thing. I just can't see myself married and raising a family. In love, caring, helping her, committed to the relationship, but no marriage."

"Yeah, I got that," she said sardonically.

"Sorry," I said.

"Now you want to learn how to be a Miwuk."

"Well, at least…do something else."

"What? Start a Miwuk restaurant?" Tahefnu's lips formed the sardonic grin that I was beginning to know well.

I grinned in return. "Specializing in acorn mush? I don't know. I really don't know." And it bothered me that I didn't know. "I need…to talk with someone."

Tahefnu raised her eyebrows. "You are talking with someone."

"Sorry, I mean someone who knows about my family, about my past. Khen-mes. He's there, I know it," I said, pointing toward the valley. "He's still alive and I need to bring him back. I need to know what he knows."

"There may be a more direct way," said Tahefnu. She shifted her seat a little. "Those Coyote dreams, and…I have my own problems. Remetjy gods jerking me around." She stared off into the trees that surrounded us. "I need to figure out what to do about them."

I sat, thinking about how rough the log was on my butt. I'd pretty much imprinted the bark patterns on it. Another pee? Was this too male a response to a woman's internal concerns?

"I've got to do it," said Tahefnu, who'd been silent and morose for an hour.

"True. What, precisely?" I eased my butt up off the log and tried to decide where to pee.

"Peyotl."

I considered this for a minute. I was out of my depth.

My silence prompted more information. "I want to journey with the spirits using peyotl."

I asked, "What is peyotl?"

She fished in her pack and took out a good-sized leather pouch. "Medicine supplies. This is peyotl." She showed me a roundish, organic object.

"What is it?"

"A kind of cactus thing, from the Aztecs."

"And this will help how?"

She looked at me with opaque eyes. "It…it's a very powerful kind of medicine." She closed her eyes.

"It's a drug of some kind."

"It's an experience. A revelation. A gateway."

"You're being a little mysterious."

She opened her eyes. "Exactly. And I don't…I can't…I don't know whether I can control it."

"OK," I said. "So, what do I have to do? Keep watch? Wake you up if things get really bad?"

"Peyotl." She held out a peyotl to me. I took it and looked it over carefully. Dried, a little round piece of the Earth. I could feel Ma'at stirring within me, but I couldn't tell what she was telling me. Religious bullshit.

"Shesmu." Tahefnu reached out and closed my fist around the peyotl. "I want…I need you…to come with me."

"Where?"

"I don't exactly know."

"This does not sound like a well planned vacation."

"It will be good. In the end. As long as you're with me."

"Am I going to be dismembered again, then burned and each grain of ash crushed into nothingness, or something even worse? How is that going to help you?"

"I don't know. I know you can help me."

"How?"

"I just know. Maybe by distracting your gods for awhile."

"And what then?"

"When I'm free, I can decide what to do. Hummingbird will help me. And you."

"Free…of Mentju?"

"Yes…sort of."

"What do you mean?"

"There's…something else. More powerful. Behind Mentju. Hummingbird was afraid."

I'd felt it myself, in my dream. Seteh, Lord of Chaos. Isfet.

"And you think the peyotl will help free you?"

"I know it will. But…"

"It's going to be powerful."

"I've only done this once, it was overwhelming. I found Hummingbird through it. I trust it, but it's…very powerful. But I can't get to Mentju, and what's behind him, without it. I need your help. And we'll need a strong journey." She dug into the pouch and extracted more buttons, giving me nine more.

I said, "I think I may be closer to my gods than I have ever been. This may kill me, but if it doesn't, it will make me—"

She smiled. "A lot more fucked up than you are, even now." She popped a button into her mouth and started chewing.

I looked around at our campsite. "What about the NATO troops? What if they come by while we're journeying?"

"If they were gonna come by, they'd have done it by now. I didn't see anything when I went back to the river."

"Right." I smiled back. "Let's do it." I popped the peyotl into my mouth and chewed. Bitter, nasty. Another. And another.

The sun was setting behind the trees of the forest. R'a fell through the horizon.

I was holding a sauté pan over a fire, shaking it back and forth. The pan had a heart in it, and I knew it was Tahefnu's heart. I was cooking her heart.

I was sitting at a table, eating a meal, a feast. The noise clamored and blasted my ears. I looked around, saw all the gods, in their thousands, their hundreds of thousands, sharing my meal. I looked at my plate and saw the heart I had cooked. All the gods ate pieces of it. There was enough for everyone.

I swam in the River, the Great River, at full flood, I saw the rapids ahead. I hit the rapids and died.

I washed up on the shore at a temple.

I climbed up ten thousand steps to the temple sanctuary.

I saw Tahefnu's heart on the hetep altar.

I saw myself take a ritual knife and slice through the heart; no blood, it was cooked, after all.

I ate a slice of heart.

I flew across the desert, isfet. I felt the chaos inside me.

I felt my hand touch another hand. It was MacIntyre's hand.

I ate her heart too.

I flew above all the gods, and they laughed to see a man making such a spectacle of himself.

I flew above the desert, isfet. Chaos filled me.

I sat, cross-legged, in front of Ma'at. She was huge, beautiful, looking down at me, stern, feather not moving, w'as scepter solid in her hand. She raised her arm, pointed behind me. I looked, Tahefnu stood behind me. She did not see me, she looked off into the distance, into the desert. I saw MacIntyre behind her, her smile warm and inviting, and utterly unreachable. I reached anyway.

I reached but found Mentju instead. The last time I had seen Mentju, he had taken various bits of me slowly with lengthy, burning cuts. He seemed frozen. I found the w'as scepter in my hand and lifted it and Mentju vanished.

I flew above the desert, isfet, Heh's walking stick in my hand pulling me. The chaos inside me clattered and shrieked.

I fell.

I fell.

I fell.

I looked up, flat on the ground, into the eyes of the Coyote.

The Coyote's body, arrayed in mummy wrappings, became that of the god of the afterworld, Wesir.

Utter silence, everywhere. Coyote-Wesir ran away, and R'a came to me, birthed anew, carrying me through the horizon into the dawn.

Ma'at came, with Tahefnu, as Hummingbird, birthed anew.

Ma'at came, with MacIntyre, who extended a hand holding the 'ankh, the symbol of everlasting life.

'Ankhu djet, alive forever, I took it, birthed anew through R'a and Ma'at and Tahefnu and MacIntyre.

Next to the expiring campfire, Tahefnu and I lay wrapped in each others' arms. It was just before dawn, you could see the stars disappearing one by one. R'a arose from his trip to the underworld, coloring the sky with fire behind the trees, clouds shining with an orange promise. I was cold, drenched in sweat, and shivering. The peyotl, wearing off, still affected my senses and perceptions.

I felt Tahefnu's embrace, but I felt it as MacIntyre's embrace, and I knew I was good. I wasn't too sure about Tahefnu, though. She was out cold. I shook her, but she was dead out. I stuffed her slack body into her sleeping bag, hoping that would warm her up to life again. Her journey was to a different place than mine, clearly.

I was enormously hungry. I put on my coat and rummaged in my pack and got two energy bars and ate them, shivering in the early morning cold. R'a went on his journey, unconcerned, and warmed the world. About the time R'a reached the tops of the trees and shone his light on us, Tahefnu stirred.

"Uhh," she groaned. "Oooh," she moaned. Her eyes remained closed, her face half visible in the sleeping bag, her black hair splayed out around the top of it.

"Tahefnu," I said.

"Um?" she asked.

"Wake up."

Her eyes swept open and looked up at me.

"Did we fuck?" she asked.

"Not to my knowledge."

"OK, well, whatever happened, it was at least as good as that. Oooh."

"It was…complicated."

"F—sorry. Everything's complicated with you, Shesmu." She humped down in the bag.

"It is what it is."

"Fucking old man talk again." She closed her eyes. "Oh. I'm an Old Man now."

"What?"

"Training's over. I'm one with Hummingbird. I'm a shaman, now. Fucking peyotl. You never can tell."

"What about Mentju?"

"Gone. Son of a bitch. And the chaos behind him, all gone. I'm ready."

"Ready?"

"Ready. For whatever your fucking gods have in mind. I'm seconded."

"What?"

"My gods have lent me to your gods. Hummingbird says, whatever Ma'at wants, Ma'at gets. Things are that fucked up." Tahefnu's black eyes looked up at me. "Speaking of which, why don't you come in here and help me recover? It's the least you could do since you didn't come with me like I wanted."

"I don't think so." In actuality, even if I weren't obsessed with MacIntyre and her wonderful ways of love, I was in no shape to perform. It appeared I was cured of my spirit-driven obsession with Tahefnu, or at least my body was. Or maybe this was the residual peyotl too. That was Tahefnu's disgusted conclusion.

"Fucking peyotl. You never can tell." Her head disappeared into her sleeping bag, then reemerged. "Thing is, I've got Coyote in me now."

"What?"

"The bastard came in at the last minute and told Hummingbird she'd have to put up with him for awhile, while I was seconded to the Remetjy gods. It was quite a scene. Feathers and fur all over the place. So. I'm your father, for now."

"Great," I said. "Hi, Dad." I leaned over the sleeping bag and planted a good one on her. Incest? I don't think so. Fucking gods. It explains a lot about all that stuff about pera'a marrying their sisters. I don't believe in gods or incest, or at least I didn't before the peyotl. Not so sure anymore. Coyote in her?

I think all this was a burst of residual peyotl logic. Bright colors flashed through the sky and trees. Sounds of the forest cascaded around my ears. I carefully refrained from doing anything that might be taken wrong, later. I think. MacIntyre was in there too, beckoning, shining in the sun. I think. Got to listen to those voicemails.

Tahefnu smiled dreamily, then her eyes sharpened at my reluctance to do more and she said, "OK, don't worry, Shesmu, you're safe from me, at least for now. But look, speaking as your native guide, we need to get warm, and the best way to get warm on the trail is human bodies together in a bag full of feathers. Same idea as burying yourself in your horse's entrails, but it smells better. I'm fucking freezing. Come in here."

Tahefnu unzipped her sleeping bag, and I crawled in with her to get warm under the light of R'a. We held each other for awhile, brother and sister, until the crazy peyotl shit subsided and we warmed up with the sun. Coyote in her? Did I believe that? At that moment in time, I did believe it. Maybe the trickster Coyote would help me find Khenmes. Maybe Coyote would help me to understand who I was.

Birthed anew, alive forever, 'ankhu djet.

CHAPTER TWENTY-EIGHT

MacIntyre Appeals to Ma'at

MacIntyre worked on the chips and molli while plotting her next step. The biggest problem with her plan was Djehutymes. Mes was a good man, though a bit of a curmudgeon, but first and foremost, he was a medja. At the moment, she was the most wanted person in Menmenet, and it was his duty to collar her and turn her over to the executioners at the Temple of Mentju. She had to craft an approach to him that would short-circuit his sense of duty.

That sense of duty came from an absolute devotion to Ma'at, and Ma'at was all about truth. She was a w'abet of Ma'at, though not a religious one, and she ought to be able to parlay that into something, but only if the truth was clear to Mes. If Mentju pulled the wool over his eyes, she was dead meat.

And, after all, he was the man who started her down this whole thing, by betraying her, firing her from the job she loved, because she was American. He hadn't liked it, but he did it, and now was his time to pay.

MacIntyre picked up the burner phone and dialed a number she knew by heart.

"Djehutymes." His voice came loud and clear.

"Hi, Mes."

Silence.

She said, "Find somewhere you can talk to me."

"Hold on." A little time passed, then his voice came. "MacIntyre? What the fuck do you think you're doing?"

Same old Mes.

"I'll explain, but first, I have to know—are we good friends?"

He stuttered a bit. "You are the most wanted person in Menmenet right now, MacIntyre. *The*—Most—Wanted!"

"Going to turn me in?"

"Give me a good reason not to. You attacked the fucking hem-netjer-tepy of Mentju, MacIntyre! Hit him with a stick. Capital offense. Do you know what a capital offense is in cases like this? They'll cut pieces off you and make you eat them. That's if you're lucky, if the gods don't get you before the priests! The only thing I can't figure out is how you're still walking around!"

MacIntyre felt a surge of anger. "May I remind you that you fired me, for nothing? Betrayed me after all our years working together?"

"I did what I had to do."

"So. Did. I. This is about Ma'at, Mes."

"I didn't hit anybody with a stick. Talk to me, MacIntyre. Now."

So she talked. She got the big stuff out of the way first, then argued him down from his complete state of incredulity by giving him details, chapter and verse, including troop movements and the involvement of the American Consul General. She capped it off by explaining that she knew he was safe to talk to as his name was on the internment list as a possible foe of the conspiracy. That got his attention.

"How do you *know* all this?"

"A spy from the Temple of Imen-R'a named Hori. Small man, sad face, agent with a cover as a janitor in the Temple of Mentju. He filled me in on the secret plans he'd uncovered. The next day, they discovered him and killed him, then made me dispose of the body. Mes, time is running out, you know? We don't need to go into all the details right now."

"How did you get in this deep, MacIntyre?"

"That's kind of complicated, Mes, but it comes down to I'm a detective. When it all comes out, I'll need you to help me explain Hori's body, which I've got on ice. I had to destroy the crime scene, but I have images of everything, and I have the corpse, so maybe we can make it work in court."

"Fuck me. Now bodies from the Temple of Imen-R'a. Just one more question: why did you attack the hem-netjer-tepy of Mentju? With a stick? I can't believe I'm even asking this question."

"More complications. I wormed my way into their confidence, and Setehnekhet...." MacIntyre hesitated. This was hard, harder even than telling Sebek and Henutsenu.

"Talk!"

She closed her eyes and got it out, speaking very quickly. "He tried to rape me, in his office. So I hit him with a collapsible baton, then ran. Look, cut me some slack on this, Mes. I had to do what I had to do. And this goes no farther than you, OK?"

"He tried…. This isn't going to be one of those he-said she-said things, is it, MacIntyre?"

"I don't think so. If he gets a say, he'll just have me shot or something."

"And I'm supposed to just take your word for all this?"

"Ma'at. You know me, I know you, we both know how we feel about Ma'at. Right? And why the hell else would I hit a high priest with a stick?"

"OK, say I buy all this bullshit, MacIntyre." He laughed without humor. "Bullshit is the word, too, with Mentju involved. Say I buy it. What the fuck am I supposed to do about it? I'm just a homicide medja. A lowly idnu trying to get to retirement without pissing off any gods. Or any top medjau brass who are probably in on the coup."

"Investigate. Light of day. Arrest somebody for murder, Ma'at knows they all have blood on their hands already. Pray to Ma'at. I don't know, just figure it out. I'd be doing it but I'm kind of constrained right now, you know? Surely you know people in the medjau and the government that could act to stop it all. I've got time, I can do the praying part, how's that? Oh—here's the number of a guy named Karkin that might be able to help, he does international work." She gave him Karkin's number.

"I've heard of Karkin. A local, supposed to be a good man." Mes's voice was calmer as he absorbed her seriousness and started thinking about what to do. "What are you going to do?"

"Stay put."

"MacIntyre, in all the years I've worked with you, you have never once 'stayed put.' It's why you're still a hutyt, not an idnu. If there were a first time for it, this is it. Get it? Stay! Put!"

"Will you rescue me if they catch up with me?" She said this as a joke, but he took her very seriously.

"If they catch up with you, MacIntyre, you'll be dead before you see the street. Stay put." He hung up.

CHAPTER TWENTY-NINE

Shesmu to the Rescue

WE MADE PRETTY FAST TIME down the trail into the valley, then took a different trail heading along the river in the eastern part of the valley.

Tahefnu said, "The main force is across the river on the north side of the valley, near the middle."

"You've been here before." I wondered if she, too, had become a little richer from time to time around these tombs.

"A few times, just looking around on hunting trips. Dad has some friends in the Guard, I think. And I mean, look at it!" She waved a hand, and I had to admit that the valley was spectacular. But we weren't sightseeing on this trip.

We walked along the river for a time then worked our way around to the south side of the valley, near a huge pile of rocks that had collapsed from the cliff above a long while ago. The forest gave us cover right up to the rock-fall.

Tahefnu paused and looked around. "I think I need to consult," she said, and sat down, cross-legged, on a rock. She closed her eyes. After a couple of minutes, she opened her eyes again and got up.

"This way," she said. She was facing a heavily forested area where there did not appear to be any path.

"Um," I said. "Are you sure…"

"This way. Coyote knows exactly where your friend Khenmes is, and he says it won't be hard to rescue him."

I held up the magic stick to get confirmation, but there was nothing. Just a stick, now. Back to normal. Sure.

It was all or nothing, apparently: either I bought into this nonsense completely and believed whole-heartedly in Miwuk spirits and gods, or…what? I realized I had very few choices left. I stood in a narrow valley with a tough but young Miwuk shaman facing a division of NATO special forces that held my almost-father prisoner. My only hope was to follow the instructions of an invisible spirit-god who might or might not be my father into a bushwhacking adventure. Right.

"Let's go," I said. She led us along the valley wall looming high above us. About every 500 meters there was yet another rock-fall that had cleared out some of the forest in its attempt to reach the river. I looked up at the towering granite above me and felt its weight.

I voiced my concern. "I wonder how stable this cliff face is, Tahefnu. Maybe we should go a little more into the valley?"

"Don't you have some kind of rock god you can pray to? No patron god for stonecutters or something?"

"That's for making them fall apart, not stopping them from falling apart. Anyway, no, no such god."

"Well then, keep your eye out and if you see rocks move up there let me know and I'll dig you out after it's all over."

She kept walking along the cliff wall, skirting the rockfalls without any apparent concern. Feeling lucky, I guess. I've always liked being with lucky people, so I kept close behind her. We stopped when a gap in the forest let us see a bridge across the river, well guarded. We carefully sneaked through the gap meadow, keeping low, and there was no warning shout from the patrols.

We kept at it for another kilometer or so of heavy going. By the time Tahefnu stopped and looked around, it was late afternoon.

"We'll stop here and wait for dark, wait and watch. There's no moon tonight, pitch black. The prison compound is right down there, by the river." She pointed through the trees, and I could see a chain-link fence topped with razor wire. Beyond that was the same kind of temporarily roofed cage layout I'd seen at the Serqu Pass black site. Ugly and forbidding.

I voiced yet another concern. "I want to make sure Khenmes is there." That's what had got me into trouble before, but I didn't want to risk everything unless it was Khenmes. And this time the cliff would fall on *me*. Having already dismissed that concern, Tahefnu dismissed my new one as well.

"He's there."

"Tahefnu…."

"He's there. I'm not going to die proving it. Coyote knows it. I know it. Sit down and shut up."

We concealed ourselves in some bushes and got comfortable, as comfortable as you can get sitting in a bush. I lashed the walking stick to my pack, as I'd need both hands free for action. We waited, and we watched. The patrols passed by on both sides of the river every half hour or so. The soldiers looked bored but kept their eyes moving. We stayed still.

Tahefnu said, as darkness descended, "Coyote tells me that there are two guards in the compound. He says the ones at night are not attentive, we can easily kill them. I think we will have to do that quietly, to give ourselves a chance to take your friend and escape. If he's in bad shape, we'll have to decide what to do." She looked at the darkening sky. "We'll go in about 4 hours from now, once the darkness is complete." She paused and looked at me. "We'll have to kill them, Shesmu, it's the only way."

I nodded and looked away.

Tahefnu clarified what she was saying. "Can you do it?"

"Yes, but I don't like it." My mood darkened a lot faster than the sky. This trip unceasingly exposed more things about me than I could handle. Was there bedrock somewhere, or was my entire life just a mess of quicksand?

Tahefnu was satisfied. "Good."

I was not sure whether she meant it was good I could kill them or good that I didn't like it, but I chose not to ask.

The night was very dark, with no moon and no electric lights. A flickering light sprang up when the guards built a small campfire. They sat on logs arranged around the fire, presenting a nicely lit target. We waited until the roving patrol passed out of earshot, then crept down to the compound.

Tahefnu touched her bow, and I nodded. I nocked an arrow. It would be a little tricky shooting through the chain-link fence, so I took another arrow and kept it in my hand in case I needed a second shot. Tahefnu looked in approval in the dim light and did the same.

"So, what did Alvin say?" One of the soldiers said, suddenly, in American English. The other one looked up. It was a black woman, her eyes the only thing visible in the dark, the bulk of her body armor shifting uncomfortably. The voice of the first one suggested she was a woman as well. The question was quite loud in the quiet of Ta Sekhet-Imenet-Ma'at. You could hear only the gurgling water of the river.

"He's taking the kids off to the water park in Tampa Bay for the weekend."

"You know what I mean. What did he *say*."

"Shit. You know what he said. He said he didn't hook up with the broad at all, it's all lies."

"And you believe him? If Jerry did that to me…."

"Fuck no I didn't believe him. But what the fuck can I do about it out here? My kids….I don't know what I'm going to do, Beth. Stuck here watching a fucking Indian sleep."

My quicksand heaved. It was too much. I touched Tahefnu's arm and leaned toward her. I whispered, "Back off. I need to talk to you."

We crept back into the forest until we could no longer hear the two women. We kept our voices low.

"What." Tahefnu was less than pleased. "We need to get on with it."

"Did you hear them?"

"I don't speak whatever language they were talking."

"English, they're Americans. Women."

"OK, so what."

"They're talking about the kids and what they're doing tomorrow." I hesitated, then said, "I can't kill two working moms. Tahefnu, don't make me do this."

"Shit." Tahefnu's hiss expressed her anger. "Shesmu, these people are invaders. I don't know what they're doing here, but they're on our land and they have your friend and they mean business. Those two are soldiers in an enemy army. They're special forces, they're perfectly able to rip your arm off with their bare hands and beat you to death with it. And you're worried about their kids. They'd be happy to tell their kids the story of how they beat the Remetjy chef to death with his own arm on their way to conquering the West. As a bedtime story. To be continued with the story of how they roasted and ate the little Indian shaman bitch! And you're worried about killing them?"

I replied, "Well, I am. Look, there's got to be another way." Arguments, I had to convince her. "Two things. First, killing a couple of guards, especially women, will piss off the rest of the NATO troops a lot. Second, they're wearing heavy body armor, they're behind two chain link fences, and we don't have the kind of arrows that would be able to deal with that."

Tahefnu was silent, then said, "Kind of arrows?"

"We need special points, they're called bodkin points. Long, needle-sharp, and hard, can pierce anything."

"Shit." She was quiet for a long time.

"Tahefnu?" I hissed.

"Shut the fuck up. I'm consulting."

Great. I waited.

"OK, here's the deal, according to Coyote. He's pretty pissed at you, by the way. They're going to move Khenmes in the morning, they're taking him up the valley for questioning. It'll be these two. They won't be paying enough attention or expecting an attack on the way. Do you think," she said in a withering tone, "that you'll be up to immobilizing them if we get the jump on them? Them being women and all? With kids? I mean, I don't want to do it all myself."

"I believe I can do that," I replied with dignity.

"Prick." After five minutes of silence, she took my hand. She whispered. "Sorry."

"That's OK, I understand. Adrenaline."

"Yeah. I get a little aggressive sometimes."

A movement from the compound got our attention. The black woman had approached the fence, looking out into the darkness. She was looking right at me, eyes white in the darkness. I squeezed Tahefnu's hand, and she squeezed back. We were quiet after that. And she didn't let go of my hand until the light came up in the east, over the big granite domes that shadowed the top of the valley.

The two guards gathered their equipment a few minutes after sunrise. One of them, the white one, went into the cages at the center of the compound and came out leading a bleary-looking Waashiw man. Khenmes. I breathed a little faster. He looked tired but OK.

His arms were fastened behind him. When the soldier pulled him up to her friend, the black woman extracted a black cloth from her pack, shook it, and pulled it over Khenmes's head—a black bag, a hood.

We cut through the forest at an angle to get ahead of the guards. Tahefnu pulled ahead of me; she was able to move quietly and quickly, while I had to take a lot of care not to make any noise, and I was limping and couldn't use the walking stick. My career in the kitchen had failed to acquaint me with all the skills I needed to deal with life. At least I knew how to use a knife.

Tahefnu stopped, and I caught up with her.

"I'll cross to the other side of the trail, and when they come up to us, we jump them and immobilize them. I noticed the white one has a bunch of plastic ties hanging from her pack, we'll use those to tie them up. OK with all that?"

I nodded, and Tahefnu went across the trail. We concealed ourselves and waited.

The advantage of surprise was with us. It helped that the pair had loaded themselves up with equipment and that they weren't worried. There was a little noise until we got them gagged. We dragged the pair off into the bushes and tied them together back to back. The two soldiers struggled against their bonds, and their eyes betrayed their inner desire to chop us into small pieces as they grunted their anger. Working moms, no doubt; but this was work.

During all this commotion, Khenmes in his hood and tied arms was turning around and around, trying to figure out what was going on. I walked over to him and took his arm. He tensed. I reached and took off the hood.

"Shesmu! What the fuck are you doing here?" His eyes were very large.

"Rescuing you, old man." I slapped his back. Tahefnu came back from the bushes and unsheathed a knife that would be perfectly capable of gutting a grizzly bear. His eyes got big again. I smiled to reassure him. She cut through the plastic ties on his wrists, and he rubbed them in relief.

"Khenmes, this is Tahefnu. She's a Miwuk shaman. Hummingbird."

They nodded to each other. Tahefnu looked him up and down as she sheathed the knife. "Hmm. Pleased to meet you. I'll be right back." She took the hood and walked back into the bushes, then came back after a few minutes without the hood.

"Now let's get the fuck out of here before the next patrol comes through, OK?" She smiled in a "let's dispense with all this bullshit and get going" kind of way.

"One thing," I said. "Khenmes. Tahefnu somehow can channel Akhen, he helped us get you out."

He shook his head. "That man is dead, buried over there." He pointed in the direction of my father's tomb. "You shouldn't say his name, you know?"

I replied, "You have some explaining to do, old man. He's a god now. And I don't think you need to worry about attracting his spirit, it's already here."

He shook his Waashiw head again. "Fucking Miwuks. Everything is a spirit dance. OK, let's go."

CHAPTER THIRTY

MacIntyre Drinks the Tea

AFTER A SINGLE DAY IN her safe house, MacIntyre had explored the depths of stir craziness. The chips were long gone. She checked her phone; nothing from Karkin. And nothing from Djehutymes, either. At this point, she'd be grateful for the minions of Mentju bashing the door down, just for a change of pace. The sun shone in through the edges of the shuttered windows, sending two little white stripes across the dimness of the room.

She had slept well; but she always did. She searched through the kitchen cabinets and found a very old box of barley flakes and some instant coffee. The instant coffee was not up to her standards, which were pretty low. She drank three cups anyway; it was something to do. She'd checked out the small library, which was a combination of Remetjy classics and random junk. Travel books. She flipped through a book about China and thought about how much she'd like to be at the Great Wall right now. There was even a book about the sights and sounds of Boston, which she avoided. You can't go home again.

Another cup of coffee? No, too jittery already, and the nasty taste lingered in the back of her throat. She rummaged in the refrigerator and found a bottle of bloody mary mix, which she juiced up with vodka from a cabinet. She sipped it, making it last, thinking about possible things to do and rejecting them all. She finished the cocktail, which cleared out the nasty coffee remnants from her throat. Another one? No, too early to get sloshed. How about some of the Remetjy tea that Henutsenu had bought for her? Stress relief, yes indeed. Why not?

She dug out the little bag and opened it. She smelled it; kind of flowery, and in fact she could see little pieces of flowers nestled among the tea leaves. Nice, gentle, and lovely, like Henutsenu. Maybe there was something in this Bastet business. She boiled some water and dumped in about half the tea. That should be enough for two or three cups. She let it steep.

She settled down on the sofa with one of the American spy novels and a cup of the tea and started reading. She had another cup of tea and thought about lunch. The novel was no more than OK, a thrill a minute but totally unbelievable American spies. She lost the jittery feeling from the coffee; the Bastet tea was definitely having an effect. In fact, she was getting sleepy. She kept reading and started a third cup of the tea but dozed off after a couple of sips.

MacIntyre never remembered her dreams, and she claimed never to dream at all. But now, she fell into a dream that seemed all too real.

Not in the safe house anymore, she stood on a featureless, burnt-red plain. There were mountains in the distance. The blowing wind whistled in her ears. She could feel the coldness of the wind on her face. She turned around and saw that the plain was the same in all directions. Her hair blew past her face with the wind behind her. She felt a little odd, then realized her clothes were different. She looked down and saw what looked like ancient Remetjy armor. She wore a leather jerkin that extended below her waist. Bronze plates covered it. A nice change from Kevlar. Heavier, too. A mace filled her hand without her having any idea where it had come from. She lifted it. Heavy enough to crush skulls with a blow. Better than a collapsible baton, but hard to hide.

A voice behind her said, "We must hurry." She turned to find the goddess Ma'at, a large feather above her head. The goddess, armored and holding a mace, stood in a chariot. MacIntyre stepped up into the chariot, and Ma'at gave her the reins and pointed. At MacIntyre's urging, the two spirited white horses pulled the chariot faster and faster across the smooth plain. Ma'at picked up a shield from the floor of the chariot and gripped her mace tightly.

MacIntyre asked, "Where are we going?"

Ma'at looked at her with a stern expression. "You know."

"Mentju?" She did know.

"We must stop this before it is too late."

"How do we stop Mentju?"

Ma'at looked at her with a sardonic smile. "What do you think these are for?" she asked, holding up the mace. "Pounding grain? We will fight him to the death."

"Ours or his?"

Ma'at ignored this sally. The chariot was now rushing so fast the wind was nearly impossible to withstand. It didn't seem to affect Ma'at at all, her hair stayed long and perfect. MacIntyre found her own hair blowing in all directions. She had to strain to stay upright as she urged on the horses. She couldn't see much, as the wind blinded her. The chariot hurtled ahead, faster and faster.

"There he is!" shouted the goddess, pointing forward. "Here's your shield!"

Ma'at handed her a shield. MacIntyre held it with the same hand with which she was controlling the horses. A chariot rushed at them, a blow fell on her shield. Ma'at took a blow to her shield and swung her mace at something in the other chariot as it rushed past.

"Turn!" Ma'at commanded, and MacIntyre whipped the chariot around to follow the other chariot. The pace and the turn itself felt physically impossible but very real. The chariot ahead slowed, and MacIntyre slowed hers as well as they caught up.

"Be ready," said Ma'at, holding up her mace. MacIntyre raised hers as well, preparing to strike at whatever presented itself.

As they drew close, MacIntyre saw the god Mentju handling the reins of two fiery black horses. His falcon head twisted to look back at them. His companion, the one with the mace, stood foursquare in the chariot, waiting for the pair of women to catch up. With a strong sense of foreboding, MacIntyre recognized the second figure as the god Seteh himself, the arch-enemy of Ma'at. The goddess beside her growled and called out, "You will not succeed this time!"

MacIntyre wasn't so sure. Seteh had a long, curved animal head ending in a round muzzle and large, squared-off ears poking up like horns. The mouth opened, revealing sharp wolf-like teeth in a dog's grin, tongue lolling out.

"I will always win, goddess, isfet is the way of the desert. My chaos is stronger than your truth!" The god's voice was deep and resonant, as though he spoke through a loudspeaker hidden in the chariot.

As the two women drew near the side of the enemy chariot, Seteh's blow descended on MacIntyre's shield and tore it away. She heard a bone snap and felt the searing pain of it. MacIntyre dodged, then swung her mace at Mentju's falcon head. He had no shield, but he raised his own mace and hit hers with it, very hard, and her mace flew out of her hand. She saw from the corner of her eye that Ma'at had swung her mace at the god of chaos. He caught it in his hand and held it above his animal head. MacIntyre felt the next blow from Mentju strike her body, knocking her out of the chariot. She rolled and rolled across the hard, red plain. She sat up and watched the two chariots disappear in the distance.

MacIntyre stood up and took stock. A broken arm, her armor shattered where the blow had fallen on her side. The pain from the blows felt real, yet she somehow knew she was dreaming and that none of it was real. She walked toward where the chariots had disappeared. The wind died down and disappeared.

She walked and walked, for hours. The day faded into blackness and back into day again as R'a completed his journey through the underworld in his sun chariot. Could have used a ride, but no luck there.

She walked and walked, hungry and tired, overwhelmed by the pain from the mace blow. She had to find Ma'at and help her, no one could fight the combination of Mentju and Seteh alone.

She walked and walked, stumbling and exhausted. Her thirst grew. Finally, she collapsed onto the hard, red plain.

Two shepherds found her and gave her water. They carried her on one of their camels to their village in the distant mountains, cunningly carved into a cliff and invisible to the gods.

She was back on the couch in the safe house, blinking, her mouth dry, her body slumped. Her hand went to her arm, pushing the book she'd been reading onto the floor, but there was no break, no pain. She remembered every moment of the dream, even the pain, but mostly the longing to help Ma'at that had kept her going across the arid red plain.

The shuttered windows showed no edges of sunlight; she'd been asleep for hours. "What the *fuck* was in that tea?" she asked aloud.

CHAPTER THIRTY-ONE
The Spetsnaz Capture Shesmu

THE RIVER PROVED EASIER TO cross with three people. We formed a chain, holding onto each others' packs. Tahefnu led us across with no problems.

"Where are we going next?" wondered Khenmes. "Just curious, no pressure or anything."

"Fuck you." Tahefnu had been in a foul mood since I'd refused to let her kill the guards. But she answered his question by pointing at the top of the big waterfall ahead of us. Khenmes lifted his head and held the pose, looking at the cliff we were about to climb.

"Um. Ain't gonna do my bum leg any good." As Khenmes had never had a bum leg since I'd known him, I smiled and offered him the use of Heh's walking stick. He took it and looked it over, rubbed it, and said, "Beautiful piece of work. Reminds me of something, can't think of what. But I can't take it from you, Shes. You'll need it more than I will." I was still limping a bit on my injured ankle. He gave me back the stick.

"Can we move it along? You're all rescued now, I'd hate for a patrol to come along and ruin our day," said Tahefnu.

"Surly little thing, ain't she?" commented Khenmes. Tahefnu started up the trail, walking fast.

"Tahefnu!" I stopped and waited. She turned and walked back to us.

"What, Shesmu?" She stopped in front of me, arms akimbo, eyes narrowed and looking straight at me.

"We have a three-day trip ahead of us," I said. "I can't see how we can do it if we don't work together. What's going on with you, Tahefnu? Can I help?" I'd had management problems in my kitchen like this. A few kind words, a little career counseling, done. Hummingbirds, magic sticks, NATO troops, and shamans were definitely above my pay grade, but I thought I'd give it a try. I had a handicap, though; I couldn't use my usual fallback position of firing the problem.

She looked at me, then at Khenmes, then out at the glorious view. "I don't know why I'm so mad, Shesmu, but I am. You and your pappy here feel like chains keeping me from where I need to go."

"Where is that?" I asked.

"I don't fucking *know*. With Hummingbird on board and Mentju gone, I need to get home, I need to talk to Dad." She crossed her arms.

"And home is three days?" asked Khenmes. "That would be Kikyapapli, right? Bunch of hermit Miwuks?"

"We're not hermits, old man," rejoined Tahefnu. "We're followers of the old ways."

"Matter of opinion," replied Khenmes. "Anyway. You got any plans for how I'm gonna survive three days and nights without any sleeping bag and wearing these things?" He pointed to his feet. I looked down, I hadn't realized it, but he was only wearing felt slippers designed for prisoners. They were now pretty much the worse for wear, squishing with water from the river. They were flimsy enough to suspect they'd last less than five minutes on the trail up the cliffs.

"What, Waashiw have tender feet?" snarked Tahefnu. But she took off her pack, reached in and brought out a pair of combat boots. She said, "That big, black American guard looked to have feet about as big as yours. Try 'em." She tossed them down in front of Khenmes, then took a pair of socks out of her pack and tossed those down as well. Khenmes smiled, sat on the trail, and put on the socks and boots. I hadn't seen her take the boots off the black American guard; she must have done it when she checked that the guards were secure. The charitable soldier had even donated her socks to us. I grinned as I imagined her explaining to her squaddie mates why she was walking around barefoot.

"A little tight but they'll do for now. Thanks!" Khenmes got up and stamped around a little in the boots.

Tahefnu put her pack back on and said, "Got a survival blanket that you can use."

"I can see why you brought her along, Shes," said Khenmes. "Worth her weight in pine nuts."

"Fuck you," replied Tahefnu. But she grinned when she said it. We hiked on and started up the cliff path.

* * *

We reached the top of the cliff next to the waterfall in the middle of the afternoon. We collapsed for a time at the top to recover from the arduous hike.

"Damn fine view," noted Khenmes, who had removed the combat boots and was sitting nursing his feet.

"Privyet, druz'ya." The melodious Russian female voice spoke up from behind us. We looked around to see five large individuals in camouflage uniforms, with full body armor. They had blacked-up faces and an impressive array of armaments, all pointed at us.

I don't speak Russian, but I knew enough of it to ask her if she spoke Renkemet.

"Surely," said the woman in perfect Renkemet, "but why should I when you're about to die?"

"Now, is that any way to start a friendship?" asked Khenmes.

"Is that what we are about to start, a friendship?" The woman, very blonde short hair visible beneath her camouflage peaked cap. "Up, please. You have one minute to live, you can use it to explain why we should care."

We looked at each other. "Hey, Shesmu," said Khenmes. "You're in charge of this escapade, why don't you explain it to the major."

She looked at him sharply. She had no insignia of rank, just an arm patch with a slavering wolf and a rifle.

I said, "I'm pretty sure we're on the same side, Major. Major?"

"Talk to me." She did not sound convinced.

"We've freed our friend here from a prison compound. You can see it down there," I said. I pointed to the valley, where you could make out the little compound by the side of the river. "We're on our way back to her village to figure out what to do next." I pointed to Tahefnu.

"I have learned not to treat any troops as friends in the last few days. What brigade are you with?"

"Um." I looked at Khenmes, who shrugged.

"Tridsat' sekund," noted the man next to the major. He smiled. His excellent teeth gleamed from his black-face.

"Thirty seconds until we shoot," translated the major.

"We're on our own," I said, rushing the words out. "No affiliation. My friend here, he has his own reasons for being here, I don't know what they are, but I had to rescue him." I thought about explaining about the visions and the spirit-god and decided that would not help us much. If at all. "And Tahefnu's our trusty native guide." Tahefnu gave me an evil look but said nothing.

"You." The major pointed her rifle at Khenmes. "Why are you here? And how is it that you are able to recognize a Spetsnaz major without insignia?"

"Used to be Waashiw special forces, in better days, worked with some of your units in the Secret War. And you got the look."

"What Secret War?" Her tone was dismissive.

"Wouldn't be secret if everybody knew about it, now would it? And I'm here because the NATO folks down there know who I am, want to know what I know, and want to keep what I know to themselves. Until they finish what they've started."

"Now that's something. What you know." Her tone was icy, her face showing no humor whatsoever.

The man next to the major said something in Russian. I'd exhausted my limited knowledge with "privyet."

"Nyet. Zatknut'cya." OK, I lied, I knew what "nyet" means too. I liked the sound of "nyet." The sour expression on her subordinate's face showed he did not, but he complied. She continued, in Renkemet, "We have no time. Very well, we will let you live for the moment."

The major took a liking to Heh's walking stick and decided to walk with it. She detailed two men to walk behind us, and we moved out. Rather than moving toward Kikyapapli, we went east, along the top of the cliffs. We covered a good deal of ground along the cliffs in the next few hours. As darkness descended over the forest, we stopped and made camp.

The Spetsnaz sat us down against trees and posted a guard.

I asked Khenmes, "What's 'Spetsnaz'?"

He answered, "Spetsialnovo naznacheniya, 'special purpose' forces."

"No talk," said the Spetsnaz soldier guarding us.

The Spetsnaz pulled plastic bags of food and a camp stove from their packs. When the major finished her meal, she came over to us. She opened Tahefnu's pack and rustled around in it, pulling out some energy bars. She gave these to the guard, who carefully examined them for hidden weapons, then gave them to us. When we finished, the major came back and sat on a nearby rock.

"Now, then. Let us talk a little," she said. She addressed Khenmes. "What Secret War?"

"Sorry," replied Khenmes. "Can't tell you. Wouldn't help you much anyway."

"I can have my men beat it out of you," said the major.

"You can try."

One of the men got up with a smile. The major waved him away. She asked me, "Who are you?"

"My name is Shesmu za-Akhen, I'm a chef in Menmenet."

She smiled. "A chef."

"A good one."

"And you are here hunting for game or mushrooms for your restaurant, Shesmu-the-chef?" She looked at Tahefnu. "With your special forces friend and your trusty native guide?" She got up and walked over to me and bent down to my face. "And your powerful bows? What lovely features you have, Shesmu-the-chef. It will be a shame to destroy them." She tapped my cheek lightly. "Who are you?"

"Honest. Shesmu. A chef."

She tapped my cheek harder. "Liar," she said in a smooth, dreamy kind of voice.

She walked over to Tahefnu, who had a blank look on her face. "And this one? Who is this little one?"

I said, "Tahefnu. She lives in a little village called Kikyapapli, three days north of here. She agreed to get me into the valley and out again with Khenmes."

"A small amount, a tiny amount of persuasion applied to your 'guide' might open you up, Shesmu-the-chef?" She lifted Tahefnu's head up with a hand on her chin. "So beautiful, so easily damaged. And as far as I can tell, she doesn't need her tongue. Odd, for a trusty guide." She pulled an evil-looking knife out of a sheath on her belt and held it up to Tahefnu's neck.

"I'm already open," I insisted.

The major moved her hand and a line of blood appeared on Tahefnu's neck. "Indeed? I think not. Might it be possible to be a touch more open, then?"

I shook my head while Tahefnu looked stonily at nothing. The major smiled and pushed Tahefnu away. "And this," she said, stepping across to Khenmes, "is Khenmes? Who will not tell us what he knows and who knows quite a lot. And will suffer anything to keep his secrets. We might see his insides in the dirt." She tapped the tip of her knife on Khenmes's belly.

"We're on the same side," I said. "Against NATO and the Americans."

"I am not sure," she said, coming back to me, "what a 'side' is in this conflict that is not even a conflict yet." She slapped me hard. Tahefnu stood up, and a soldier gripped her and sat her down again and held her. The dribble of blood stained her shirt collar.

I shook my head a little, then said, "Look, you can beat the crap out of us all you want, but it's not going to get you anywhere. I'm a chef, she's a guide, and Khenmes is an old man with a war story. What the fuck. It's not like you don't have something better to do, right?"

She turned and sat back down on her rock and got comfortable again. "Do you know, Shesmu-the-chef, you may be correct. I am letting my curiosity get ahead of my mission. I sit here talking when I ought to be killing people. You, for example."

"Back to that again." I looked over at Khenmes. "Khenmes, you should consider helping these kind folks out with their mission."

Khenmes was apologetic. "Shes, I would love to, but I haven't got the faintest fucking idea what their mission is." He looked at the major. "Is it a big secret?"

The major smiled, on/off, and said, "Our mission is to find the leadership of the forces down in that valley and kill them. And as many of their troops as may be." The major seemed to have an excellent grasp of her mission and a clear way of expressing herself. Her superiors must love her in meetings. "Why is of no importance to you."

"Well, hell, Major, I can help with that." Khenmes smiled. "The trick is to get them outside their base. I could come up with a way to do that. I've been all over that camp in the last few days, one way or another. Can we sleep on it and figure it out in the morning? Kinda punchy, ya know? We been hiking all day and I didn't get much sleep last night anyway. Need to kind of rest the brain and get it working again."

The major got up. "Very well. But if this plan does not materialize tomorrow morning, you will all three be sitting there with bullets in your brains by lunchtime. Better, we shall just cut your throats, no need to waste bullets or the food for breakfast." She carefully wiped Tahefnu's blood off the edge of her knife on Khenmes's pants and put it back in its sheath.

Khenmes smiled and said, "Got it. I don't suppose you have an extra sleeping bag?" One of the Russians snickered; the major smiled and left us to ourselves. Faced with sharing with either Khenmes or Tahefnu, I gave Khenmes my bag. Khenmes was a little too large to share with. Sharing with Tahefnu would not help me sleep, and the Russians might misconstrue things. I used the survival blanket from Tahefnu's pack.

I felt very noble and very, very cold.

CHAPTER THIRTY-TWO
MacIntyre Introspects

MacIntyre had slept well again, no dreams, or none she could remember. But she could remember every detail of her dream of Ma'at. She microwaved some instant oatmeal and ate it without tasting it, not that there was much to taste.

She walked over to the shuttered window and stared at it. She walked back to the table and stared at her empty cereal bowl. She walked over to the couch and sat down. She picked up one of the spy novels and put it back down. She stared into space.

MacIntyre was not a particularly introspective person. She did not spend a lot of time with herself. Spending time alone with herself led to downward spirals of self loathing and doubt that she refused to tolerate. This was because of the last time she'd spent a lot of time with herself. At age 10, her father locked her in her closet for a day as a punishment for some imagined infraction of his rules.

Not that she didn't like herself, that wasn't it. Aside from the humiliations imposed on her lately, she had been pretty successful at running her life. She was a success as a homicide detective. Though her spying efforts were not playing to her strengths, she'd survived quite a few reverses so far in that career. But that career was gone now too. She'd even managed to find and more-or-less keep a great boyfriend. Where the fuck was he, anyway?

She picked up the burner phone and dialed Shesmu's mobile number again. It rang through to voicemail, which again notified her "Voice mailbox is full." For good measure, she texted him, "call me you fucking idiot". Nothing. She called Karkin. The call went to voicemail, and she left a short message asking him to call her. She called Djehutymes, and that call went to voicemail. Frustrated beyond measure, she left no message at all. She put the phone down on the little table and stared at the far wall for another ten minutes.

Unable to restrain herself, she picked up the phone and tried Shesmu again, same result.

MacIntyre considered the vodka, with or without bloody mary mix. She rejected it as too easy a solution and not one that would do her any good in either the short or long run. She considered making some coffee and decided against, she was jittery enough as it was. Tea? Not a fucking chance. But the tea reminded her of Henutsenu, who always had a firm grip on reality and a wonderful ability to console the afflicted. She needed to hear a human voice. One that meant something to her.

MacIntyre picked up the phone and called Henutsenu.

"Henutsenu?"

"Yes."

"Cheryl."

"Oh—the caller id wasn't your phone!" Henutsenu was not up on spycraft.

"Right, it's the burner you bought me. I needed to talk to someone, I'm going crazy here."

"It's all right, Cheryl, it's all right. What are you doing?"

"Well, that's just it, I'm sitting here in the safe house, staring at the wall. For three days. I can't get ahold of any of the people who should be helping me."

"Well, I can tell you that there's a lot of people who'd love to talk to you. Both Sebek and I have spent hours with medjau. Both Menmenet and Sepat. Lots of questions."

"I'm so sorry for getting you involved, Henutsenu."

"We just told them the truth, leaving out the apartment and that Karkin."

"Good. I'm worried that the Temple might have found out about him."

"Have you heard from Shes? Neither of us has heard anything from him since he left."

"I get a voicemail-full message from his phone. I'm worried about that, too. Henutsenu, I'm going crazy here."

"You said that before. Look, Cheryl, you're a w'abet of Ma'at, right? Don't you have some meditation exercises or something you can do to find ma'at?"

"That reminds me. What the fuck was that tea you gave me?"

"I'm sorry?"

"The tea from the Temple of Bastet, what was in it?"

"All the Hem-Netjer said was that it was good for stress."

"I drank a couple of cups of the stuff. It blew me away into a massive hallucinatory dream about Ma'at fighting an epic chariot battle with Mentju and Seteh."

"Goodness!"

"The vodka might have played a role there too, to be honest. I've quit drinking now."

"My. Goodness." The Remetjet struggled for a moment with her response. "Well, Bastet is a very helpful goddess, you know, so the dream is telling you where you need to be."

"Fuck, I hope not." Men, maces, and Ma'at: not a place she wanted to be. Did she need to be there? Why did she need to be there?

Henutsenu, struck by MacIntyre's unwillingness to accept Bastet's truth, probed more deeply. "Can you tell me about the dream?"

MacIntyre told her the story in detail. She remembered the pain of the broken arm and the overwhelming need to help Ma'at as she related the last part of it.

Henutsenu was quiet as she considered the details. Then she said, "Interpreting dreams is hard. This one seems to have a lot of anger and pain in it. Wanting to help Ma'at seems natural for you. But why Seteh?"

"The only thing I can think of is that Seteh is the natural enemy of Ma'at. Mentju I can understand, what with Hem-Netjer-Tepy Setehnekhet trying to rape me and all."

"It sounds as though Seteh is helping Mentju, just like you were helping Ma'at. Who are the shepherds? They sound helpful. It's not you against Mentju, Cheryl, there's all this other stuff going on. The dream is telling you that you've got friends, and that you need to go with them into battle."

"Yet here I sit, talking to you on a phone about dreams."

Henutsenu's voice was warm. "Dreams are important, Cheryl, they connect us to the world of the gods in ways we can't access in daily life. And I'd like to be there talking to you in person."

"You have no idea how much I'd like that," replied MacIntyre.

Noise in the background. Henutsenu said, "Look, I need to go, they're starting setup for lunch. Call me if you need to talk more, I'll make the time."

"You're a good friend, Henutsenu. And thanks for your help. But I'm not drinking any more of that damn tea."

After Henutsenu was gone, MacIntyre sat and thought about Ma'at and the battle against isfet. It didn't help her restless, edgy feelings much. She needed something to do, something that helped Ma'at. Anything, really. Anything.

CHAPTER THIRTY-THREE

Shesmu Stays Alive

"This survival blanket is crap," I said to Tahefnu in the morning. She shrugged and huddled in her sleeping bag, staying warm in the chilly morning air.

The major said from her own sleeping bag, "Shut up, Shesmu-the-chef. I should have killed you all last night and left you to rot in the forest. I must be losing my grip."

"Grumpy this morning, aren't we," muttered Tahefnu.

"What?" asked the major, removing herself from her bag with an angry glint in her eye. Tahefnu ignored her.

"Fuck me," remarked Khenmes, out of his bag and pumping his legs to get the blood flowing. "It's hard on old people. Have you no heart?"

The major smiled a charming smile, crinkled her eyes in pleasure, and said, "No." And left us to find our own breakfast.

As far as I could tell, the Russians had slept in their body armor. I think they slept with their rifles, too, inside their sleeping bags. The major looked as though she had spent the night on the town in the Novoarchangelsk bars. Her men looked like two or three nights on the town.

Khenmes spoke up. "I have an idea."

"Do tell me what it is, Khenmes," replied the major, turning to look at him. Her voice was melodious and persuasive. She unsnapped the holster for her sidearm, just in case she needed to use it suddenly, I supposed.

"What is your name and unit, Major?" asked Khenmes.

"Does it matter?"

"Does to me."

She smiled her charming smile. "Yekaterina Antonevna Suvorova, Major, 42nd Independent Spetsnaz Naval Reconnaissance Point. Happy?"

"So, you're the daughter of Anton Viktorivich? Colonel-General Suvorov? Antosha?"

"Yes, old man, I am. What's it to you?"

"A good man. Well, not good, but you know what I mean."

"Yes, old man, I do."

"Now, Antosha would just order up tanks or gunships or tactical nuclear missiles and blast away. Am I right? That won't work, here. Agreed, Katya?"

"That is why we are here, not my father. And you will address me as Major if you wish to avoid having your tongue removed."

"OK, then. No offense, Major, just so we're clear. Now, first, you need to understand the gods."

A funny look came over the major's face, a sad smile. She fingered her sidearm. "Get to the secret war, old man."

"Nope. Got to understand the gods. You don't have to believe in 'em, but you have to appreciate 'em. The Americans don't give a shit, and that's why they're so damn clueless."

"Very well, tell me about the Remetjy gods." The major stood in front of Khenmes, looking down at him with a smile. "But first, explain to me how a Waashiw gives a shit."

"We honor all the gods. Ours, theirs, yours."

"I have no god, old man."

"Fine. I'll honor the god you don't have, Major. Pay attention."

"I am all ears. Keep it short."

Khenmes said, "The valley, here—Ta Sekhet-Imenet-Ma'at—is the burial ground for key people, people who become gods, deified by rebirth in the Duat. Hey Shesmu, just break in here if I get this stuff wrong, it's your religion, not mine."

"Sure," I said. My religious knowledge stopped at middle-school religion classes and a comprehensive knowledge of where the temples were in Menmenet. Oh, and visions. Don't forget spirit visions.

The major fingered her sidearm again. She was making me nervous.

"Now, it's not just anybody that gets to become a god. Most people, they're just mummies. They get to enjoy the Sekhet-'Aru, your 'paradise.' But they're not gods. And their tombs and chapels are a little poky. They're in the necropolis in

Menmenet, not in Ta Sekhet. The ones here get an army brigade to guard them. And their gold."

"You are strangely interesting, old man."

"Now, there's this tomb, see, down in the valley. It's small, out of the way, no treasure, but it's one of the important ones. A man named Akhen."

"And what was this Akhen's importance that he became a god?"

"He won the war."

Won a war? My dad? A god because he won a war? The major was as bewildered as I was.

Khenmes continued, "You remember the Secret War? He won it."

"And when was this?"

"25 years ago. You were just a kid, and the Russians stayed out of it. Kinda busy becoming Russia again after the Soviets packed it in. See, Akhen was not your ordinary guy. He was a Miwuk, a valley band member. Akhen was his Remetjy common name. His Miwuk name was Wipayakuh, Bald Eagle. Now, we Waashiw don't speak the names of the dead, especially their secret names. Since Tahefnu here has a spirit thing going with him, worrying about attracting the spirit ain't a problem. The spirit is already here."

Tahefnu said, "Why is his name Wipayakuh and not 'Asheli? The Coyote? That's how I see him, as a coyote, not as a bald eagle."

"If he's a coyote for you, it must be a Miwuk thing."

Tahefnu mused, "Maybe being a Remetjy god and a Miwuk man shakes things up, makes changes necessary. Maybe the back-and-forth with Seteh taking over his identity made him choose a different name and spirit animal, so the foreign god's actions wouldn't pollute his secret name. Huh. Gonna have to talk about this with Dad, for sure. Coyote, too—dangerous spirit, tricky. Especially as a spirit guide."

The major pulled her gun out of its holster.

"Enough of this superstitious nonsense. Vasha, Andrei, Pyotr—get these idiots up and take them into the woods. I will do the work." The soldiers arose. I scrambled to my feet, and Vasha grabbed me and pushed me against a tree.

Khenmes continued, "Now, you just hold on, major. Here's the part you're interested in. I won't go into details on the Secret War and why it happened. It had to do with the Americans and Numunuu wanting more land to accommodate their growing populations. The Americans wanted the gold. And oil, always oil. Akhen figured out a way to stop them. The Republic covered everything up as part of the deal, but they made Akhen a god after he died."

The major holstered her sidearm and waved off Vasha and Andrei and Pyotr. I sat back down.

"A fantasy," she said. "You imagine the current situation—NATO infiltrating troops into this tiny little republic—that will interest us, so you make up this ghost story."

"Nope, hard reality. Except for the god parts, you don't believe in them. But you're right. A generation later, the Americans and Numunuu are at it again, but they believe Akhen's tomb has a secret that will compromise their operation. They can't find anything and think I know something about that. It's why they took me. You need to see the tomb."

I knew right then that I too had to get back to my dad's tomb—with Khenmes. This was a story I had to know. I might need some help in staying alive long enough to get there, though. The major was not compassionate, but if she knew Akhen was my father.... Who knows, she might care enough to get us all there. Alive. My jaw hurt from clenching my teeth.

The major's face betrayed nothing about her plan. Execute us or use us to learn more? Maybe the why of her mission had something to do with it. NATO moving in on the country next door to Russkaya Amerika might provoke them to action.

"Very well, Khenmes," she said. "To the tomb, then. Where you will tell us everything. And we will see what is to be done about NATO." The major's gaze turned to Tahefnu. "And you, my little Miwuk hummingbird with the so-delicate throat that makes me itch to cut it. What is your interest in this?"

Tahefnu looked up at the major with a set face and said, "I am a Hummingbird shaman in my band of Miwuks. This Coyote, this Wipayakuh, made himself part of me through a vision. I can speak with him."

"Indeed." The major cocked her head. "A shaman who speaks with the gods. And what is Coyote's opinion about all this?"

"He says you're a fucking bitch goddess, but he says you'll do what needs doing at the tomb."

"Hmm. Well, if he's right about one thing, he's probably right about the other. We will leave your throat intact to enable Coyote's further communications." She turned back to me. "And now you, Shesmu-the-chef. How do you figure in all this Akhen bullshit? Why should you live to see this tomb?"

I loosened my clenched jaw and committed myself. "He's my father."

CHAPTER THIRTY-FOUR

MacIntyre Follows the Path of Ma'at

THE NEXT MORNING, MACINTYRE AROSE from a deep sleep, certain she had the answer to her questions about the battle against isfet. But, as usual, she didn't remember the dream.

She walked into the compact kitchen to make herself the morning cup of instant coffee, disgusting as it was. She couldn't face another day of staring at walls. She caught sight of the little bag of tea that she had thrown onto the counter after her battle dream. No, no, no. It wasn't worth it. No? No.

She stared at the tea, reconsidering. Shit. It was worth a try. What did she have to lose? She didn't even have a hangover after the last adventure, just awful memories. She'd pack those away with the rest of her terrible memories in the baggage she carried.

She boiled water and put a tiny pinch of the tea in one of the paper cups. She poured in a few tablespoons of boiling water and let it steep for ten minutes. She sat on the couch, let the tea cool, and drank it off.

Nothing happened. MacIntyre meditated with closed eyes, waiting for the collapse or whatever. Nothing happened. She decided to make more tea on the theory that more was better.

She opened her eyes to get up from the couch. Now she was in a dim hall filled with papyrus-shaped columns, all marked with Renkemet glyphs. She walked over to one column. It told the story of how she had knocked her father unconscious. OK, this must be the right place.

MacIntyre walked down the hall toward a door, or what appeared to be a door. When she got there, she saw it was a false door over an offering hetep. The good news was that the iconography on the door showed Ma'at in her winged form spreading ma'at through the world. Definitely the right place. But she had nothing to offer. Did she? She found her collapsible baton in its holster in the small of her back. She pulled it out and, with what little religious pomp she could muster, placed it on the hetep.

The door opened, and she climbed up onto the hetep and stepped through. She walked forward in the dim, dusty light toward a distant figure. Soon the full figure of the goddess Ma'at was before her, wings spread wide and welcoming.

MacIntyre said into the deep silence, "Sorry about the other day. I hope everything worked out with Seteh and all."

Ma'at ignored this apology and said, "You must go."

"Uh, huh. Where?"

"To the hekasepat."

"And how would you suggest I do that, Oh Goddess?"

Ma'at, being a very diligent goddess with resources beyond those of mortal men and women, handed MacIntyre a papyrus scroll. MacIntyre unrolled the scroll to find a digital map. It highlighted a path from the safe house to the public chapel of the Palace of the Republic. There was a small avatar of herself at the safe house.

"You will find the hekasepat—alive, sound, healthy—performing his duty in his public chapel." A small avatar of Sebekemheb, the hekasepat, appeared on the map. "Go to him and tell him what he must do."

"Right." She rolled up the papyrus and stuffed it into her belt. "Anything else?"

"You must tell him of the battle. You must both fight against the forces of Seteh, who has corrupted Mentju, the god of just war. You must tell him that Imen-R'a is missing in action. My brother has left the fight. You must fight isfet alone. You must also fight your own impulses. Not necessarily in that order."

"Right. I can do that."

"You must go *now*. You're late." The goddess reached up and took the feather from her head. "Your heart is in the balance with this feather of ma'at, w'abet: do not fuck this one up."

"How—" started MacIntyre, and she was sitting on the couch, blinking. She felt a lump under her butt and got up to look—the baton. She holstered it. Finally, something to do.

* * *

MacIntyre needed a disguise. The closet in the tiny house's bedroom contained a limited array of strange clothing, all for men. MacIntyre figured this was a sign, so she dressed in loose pants and a dirty white linen shirt. She put on a camouflage jacket at least two sizes too big for her; it hid the collapsible baton well. There was a baseball cap with no logo on a shelf, and she stuffed her hair up into it. The mirror told her she was downscale enough to avoid notice on the streets unless the government conducted one of its periodic homeless removal sweeps.

She called Karkin's number and left another message. She told him that, on orders of Ma'at, she must go to the Palace of the Republic to see the hekasepat. That ought to get a response from the bastard. She considered calling Mes but abandoned the idea at the memory of his last words to her: Stay. Put.

She walked two blocks to a principal street to see what she could find in the way of transportation. She stood on a street corner looking at the unintelligible Chinese signs for inspiration. Two medjau cars passed by, the occupants scanning the crowd. She turned away and looked at trinkets in a window, glass animals in action poses. She studied a reddish glass hummingbird extracting nectar from a yellow glass flower. She didn't much care for it; there was something about its charm and industry that she found repellant. She sneaked a peek. The medjau had moved on.

She decided the burner phone was now a liability. It had been around too long and used too much. She ditched it down a sewer grate after removing the SIM card, which she broke in half and deposited deep in a nearby dumpster. Then she hailed a pedicab; she had just enough money to get her to the Palace of the Republic.

The Asian pedicab driver checked out his new passenger's clothes, rolled his eyes, asked for money up front, and sighed at the destination because of the hills. MacIntyre sat back and enjoyed the ride.

MacIntyre walked up the Wesekhwat, the main street of the Tjesut. A line of supplicants trailed from the door of the chapel, which was next to the public entrance to the palace. She looked over the people: tourists and a few Remetjy supplicants who had problems that only Imen-R'a could solve. Her best bet was to imitate a tourist.

She noticed at the end of the line an obese man in a polyester shirt, baseball cap (Alabama Gators), and shorts, obviously American.

She said, in English, "Excuse me, is this the line for the public blessing by the hekasepat?"

"Sure is, honeychile. Just got here myself, but this sure is it. Keep me company! Joe's the name."

"Cheryl. Good to know you, Joe."

Joe inspected her. "You sure look down, darlin'. Got a place to stay?"

MacIntyre replied in a sweet voice, "Yes, my wife and I just got into town, but we lost our luggage at the airport." That ought to shut him up. Nice enough guy, if a bit easy with the come on.

The line inched forward when the doors opened. Everyone filed into the well-appointed room after paying the hefty 5 debenu entrance fee. Joe offered to pay hers, and MacIntyre smiled as he paid the fee out of a wallet almost as fat as he was. Joe sat too close to her on a bench toward the back.

"Sorry, it's kinda crowded, darlin'."

After about ten excruciating minutes, there was a stir from the back. Sebekemheb appeared in full priestly regalia accompanied by a quartet of guards with spears.

"There's the SOB," said Joe in English, assuming no one around them understood it. "Stupid bastard. Had to come, you know? After the President took his number and showed him the door. I was gonna be here anyway, you know? On business. No meetings today, so I came on down here to check out the fuss. Nice dresser for a dumbshit, though."

MacIntyre smiled a slight smile and nodded. Oh boy, she thought. I'm a dead woman if any of these people around us understand English. She looked around apprehensively but saw no sign of comprehension on anyone's face. People avoided looking at her. Sebekemheb, the hekasepat and hem-netjer-tepy of Imen-R'a, stood in front of the grandiose hetep adorned with an image of the sun god. He'd raised his arms in a ritual gesture to the sun, which hadn't yet made an appearance through the fog. He was majestic as he spoke the ancient prayers to Imen-R'a in the deep, resonant voice that had gotten him elected. She wondered whether he'd refuse his blessing to the American tourists. He said a short general blessing, along the lines of "Here we all are and may Imen-R'a bless us for paying money to do that." He squared his shoulders, and the reception line began.

The tourists and the few Remetjet filed past, bowing and receiving his blessing. A few of them spoke to him and got a short word in return. Joe stuck out his hand to shake. A guard lowered his spear and shook his head, and Joe moved on. MacIntyre stepped up and looked into the hekasepat's eyes, which widened.

She whispered, "I need to talk with you, Seb, about what's going on."

Sebekemheb jumped back and turned to the guard. "This woman is an enemy of the state, she attacked a hem-netjer-tepy and she's trying to kill me!"

The guards started for her, ceremonial spears lowered. Joe said in English, "Hey, what the shit, leave her alone, you bastards!" A guard stepped in front of him and pushed him back with the middle of his spear. The distraction let MacIntyre dodge back behind the hetep and into the palace. The guards came after her.

As she ran, MacIntyre formed a vague plan of barricading herself in the hekasepat's office. Then she could figure out how to save her mission. She dashed around a turn into the big hallway that led to the office. Unexpectedly, the door had two guards, one on each side, dressed in combat gear and carrying assault rifles. They eyed her running toward them and moved to intercept. She spotted a side corridor and dashed down it, evading the advancing guards. Mentju won this round; Ma'at had stepped out for tea, and Imen-R'a was not going to take her up on her offer to help through his hem-netjer-tepy, who *really* didn't like Americans. She was on her own. The shouts came, but no shots; they probably didn't want to shoot up the marble walls, they'd have to pay for it out of their own pockets.

She pounded away around another corner, and there was a door marked "Exit." She concluded that an exit was exactly what she needed. She burst through it, and an alarm went off, whooping after her like a demented, trumpeting elephant and telling the guards precisely where she was. So much for Ma'at's plan, thought MacIntyre. Next time she'd make her own plan instead of dreaming one.

CHAPTER THIRTY-FIVE
Shesmu Revisits the Valley

Another cold night under the survival blanket, another cold energy bar for breakfast, and another cold conversation with Major Suvorova. We hit the trail shortly after sunrise and our meagre breakfast. I got my walking stick back, as the major had other things on her mind: getting to the tomb as fast as possible. As the alternative was dying where we stood, we all adapted our pace to the major's desire.

The trail was even more precipitous than the waterfall trail Tahefnu and I had taken. The trail took us between two granite cliffs into the upper part of the valley, near a reflecting lake that doubled the surrounding beauty. As we hiked, the major pumped Khenmes for any information he had about the layout of the NATO forces and their base. She also tried for more information about the events of the Secret War, but on that she was unsuccessful. Khenmes clammed up again.

"If we make it to the tomb alive, Major, the tomb inscriptions will tell you the story. I know most of the background, so let's wait until we get there and we'll have it all."

"It would be better to tell me now, Khenmes. I could motivate you with the help of your friends Tahefnu and Shesmu-the-chef. I am sure they can stand a great deal of pain."

"Better wait for the tomb. You'll see why when we get there."

"I could castrate you. Slowly. After eviscerating your friends while you watch."

Khenmes smiled and kept walking. Major Suvorova, irresolute, decided on a change of subject rather than pursuing her plans for pleasure.

The major cared only about killing. She pledged to kill as many NATO troops as she could. As we force-marched to the valley, the story came out in pieces.

The major was from a naval group stationed in Novoarchangelsk in Russkaya Amerika. Although it was a separate country, Russkaya Amerika had Russian troops all over it, a pattern in many countries that had been part of the old Soviet empire.

The major had personal issues with NATO. Specifically, they had "neutralized" 30 of the troops under her command. She was a little vague on why those troops had approached the NATO roadblocks on the road into Ta Sekhet, given that both groups had no business at all being there in our Republic. She was much more clear on the unfortunate results of a surprise ambush on the road right before the first bridge. She excoriated the bad intelligence that had told her there was nothing but "friendly" Republican Guard troops at the bridges. It had told her that NATO had not yet arrived. She wanted NATO skin, as much as she could flay off of any NATO troops that she found in front of her. Her orders were clear, she said, without further detail on what those orders were.

One soldier behind us snorted on hearing her relate this to Khenmes, and we got to talking. He was the only one of the five soldiers who spoke Renkemet, and he wanted to practice, he said. His name was Vassily Alexeyevich, and he said to call him Vasha. His sister worked in a bank in Menmenet. He had a job lined up with her bank when he finished his current deployment. I wondered where the bank's money was winding up but said nothing about that. A nice enough guy for a war criminal. He said that if we survived, I could be a reference for him. He did not sound confident about that resolution of our situation.

We took a brief rest while the major went off for a crap or something, and Vasha sat next to me.

"The Major seems like an outstanding commander, caring so much about the men and women under her command."

Vasha grinned. "Not at all," he protested. "The Major wears wolf patch of Spetsnaz. She has reputation, important to keep it. NATO troops outflanked her. That she cared about. If she take wolf patch back to Novoarchangelsk without at least as many NATO scalps as lost soldati, she not hold her head high, get patch taken away."

"When you say scalps—" I stopped there. I didn't ask whether "scalps" was a metaphor or a depressing reality. I filed away this psychological evaluation of Major Suvorova in case the war crimes people ever showed up. Vasha hinted that stopping NATO from moving any further into the Ta'an-Imenty would gratify the Kremlin.

When I related all this to Khenmes and Tahefnu, she said with a certain intensity, "We've got to do something."

"Such as?" I asked.

"Fuck, I don't know, Shesmu!"

"No talk!" This from the Russian guarding us—not Vasha. When we took a brief rest stop, our guard went off to piss, and we whispered amongst ourselves.

"We've gotta do something. Escape, run, anything. We can't just walk along and die." Tahefnu seemed adamant about not dying. I didn't much care for the idea either. Khenmes shook his head.

Tahefnu said, "Look, how about we create a diversion, then—"

"No," said Khenmes. "Can't do it."

"Why the fuck not, old man?" Tahefnu asked this with a low, vehement hiss.

"Got to get to the tomb. Only way to do that is to go there with the Russians."

Tahefnu drew back and squinted at him. "Are you fucking insane? The only thing that tomb has for us is an untimely death."

Khenmes smiled and shut his eyes. "Got to go there. That's why I'm helping them."

"Is this some kind of Waashiw bullshit magic stuff, or do you have reasons?"

"Reasons."

Tahefnu waited for the reasons, but none came. Khenmes clammed up again.

"What does Coyote say, Tahefnu?" I asked.

She gave me an impatient look. "To go, of course. It's his tomb! I can't believe I'm channeling a fucking Miwuk dog with a death wish."

I said, "Tahefnu, I'm sorry. I have to go along with Khenmes. We need to go to the tomb. *I* need to find out about my father. But you can escape if you want to, it's not your family, not your fight."

She grimaced. "Fuck. I am fucked. We are fucked. I cannot believe I got myself into this mess. One-and-a-half Miwuks and a deadbeat Waashiw elder with dementia against NATO and the Russians." She shook her head. "OK. I'll stick with you, somebody's got to be the brains of this operation, with everybody else leading with their balls."

"Surly little thing, ain't she?" commented Khenmes, eyes still closed.

I and my testicles thought the same, but I said nothing, as the Russian appeared from the trees and motioned for us to get up. We proceeded down the trail in a resolute line behind the major.

* * *

Once down into the valley, Tahefnu guided us across the valley to Akhen's tomb. We passed three NATO patrols down by the river but avoided them.

The major stopped in the woods out of sight of the tomb. She sent Vasha to scout out the situation. He came back and whispered that there were now four guards around the tomb, alert and ready for action. Something must have spooked the NATO troops since our earlier visit—probably Khenmes's escape and our disabling of the two guards.

The major whispered to her men in a huddle. They broke out of it and grabbed us and tied our arms and legs with plastic ties, gagged us, then used a length of climbing rope to tie us all to a tree. The major leaned over and whispered to me, "We must deal with these NATO pigs. We will return shortly."

The major synched up watches. She crept off through the woods toward the tomb with her men. A short, fraught time passed. I heard an interrupted yelp, barely audible through the trees. The major and Vasha returned, walking normally. They cut us loose and removed our gags.

The major said, "Come along, dushki. We've neutralized the guards. Nothing to worry about now."

We walked out of the forest into the little clearing before the tomb. The tape across the chapel door looked just as we had left it after our first visit. The squad had the four NATO guards flat on the ground with their hands tied behind their backs and with gags keeping them silent. One was the black American woman soldier we had tied up earlier; she seemed to have no ill effects from it all, but she sure was unlucky. New boots on her, though.

"Let us see. First things first. Go into that building," the major said, pointing us to the door of the tomb chapel. We walked over and opened the door and walked in. Khenmes looked around.

"The same as the last time I was here, 25 years ago," he said. "Nice job they did with your dad's life here, Shes." He paused, then whispered, "The real stuff is inside there, in the tomb, with the coffin. I'll make sure you get the full story when this military crap is finished."

The tomb itself pulled me like a magnet. I walked over to the sealed door, leaned the walking stick against it, and put both of my hands flat on the door. Tahefnu joined me and put her hand on my arm. "Coyote...." she began.

A series of coughs from outside drew us over to the open chapel door. I looked in dawning horror at the realization of the major's plan: four dead NATO soldiers, executed with the Russians' noise-suppressed rifles. The powerful bullets had made quite a mess. The major pulled out what looked like an entrenching tool hanging from her belt. Vasha told us later that Spetsnaz use this MPL-50 tool with its very sharp edges like a throwing axe and only rarely as a spade. I thought she intended to bury the bodies, but no such luck. The major leaned over each body, raised the tool, and brought it down like an axe to chop off the heads of the dead NATO soldiers, one by one.

The major turned and noticed us in the doorway. She smiled, wiping blood off the entrenching tool with some grass and putting it away. "We need to send a message to get the NATO troops to come here. A bag of heads should do the job nicely."

I thought she was right. I felt hollow; this did not bode well for our own survival. I'd seen dead bodies before, but the level of brutality was new to me. Tahefnu, usually tough as a brick, had stumbled over to the side of the chapel to throw up. Khenmes was unmoved. I handed a water bag to Tahefnu, who rinsed out her mouth and spat. She looked grim. Her earlier assessment about an untimely death now seemed prophetic.

The major sent a two-man team with the bag off to the NATO base. She said that once NATO identified the heads, they would realize where they had come from and would take measures, sending troops. She would then deal with those troops with a well-considered tactical response. The two Russians were back within an hour and reported successful infiltration of the base. The bag rested on the doorstep of the NATO commandant.

The major had her men scout out the best locations for their intended ambush. Once they hid themselves, she told us to get back into the chapel, then closed the door on us. Absolute darkness and silence shut out what was about to happen.

CHAPTER THIRTY-SIX

The Medjau Claim MacIntyre As Their Own

MACINTYRE CHARGED THROUGH A SHORT alley that ran between two wings of the palace, the door alarm squealing in her ears. At the end of the alley was a tall, chain-link fence with razor wire atop it. She got a running jump and hit the fence and started climbing.

She'd scrambled about three-quarters of the way up when hands grabbed her ankles, a soldier pulling at her. She kicked at his hands but couldn't get enough leverage to break his grip. Rethinking, she let herself fall on top of the soldier, who collapsed under her weight. MacIntyre scrambled up and whipped out her baton and extended it. She faced off against the soldier that had grabbed her, feinting hits to get some distance. As the second soldier approached, she kept them at bay with sharp blows.

A lucky grab by one soldier immobilized her baton, and the other soldier rushed in. She let go of the baton and fist-punched him, knocking him backwards. The first soldier two-handed the baton into her back, pushing her face against the fence and holding her there. The other soldier grabbed her arms and twisted them behind her. They wrestled her around and frog-marched her back to the building. She struggled to no effect as the soldiers gave her no opportunity to use her martial arts skills.

As they neared the door, four uniformed medjau appeared. The alarm continued to squeal its outrage.

"What's going on?" shouted one of the medjau over the noise. "What's with the door alarm?"

"Wanted fugitive, tried to get to the hekasepat, then busted out through this door," replied one soldier, breathing hard. "We're taking her to the Temple of Mentju."

"Mentju? A security thing?" The medja paused and examined the culprit. "Hey, don't I know you? Not too many Americans around that look like you. Huh." He reached and took off her peaked cap, and her hair fell onto her shoulders.

"We'll take it from here, no need for you guys to get involved," said the soldier. "Mentju will handle it."

"I got it—you're the homicide hutyt, let's see, MacIntyre, right? The one everybody's been looking for." The medja grinned. "Yeah, that's who you are. MacIntyre."

"Like I said," reiterated the guard in a firm tone. "Republic security matter."

The medja shook his head. "Yeah, but we gotta take her in. She's ours."

"Not anymore," the soldier replied with a grim smile, twisting MacIntyre's arm tighter.

Fuck! Once in the Temple of Mentju, she wouldn't come out in one piece. She twisted and said to the medja, her voice loud over the alarm, "I wanted to turn myself in. These guys scared me with their guns. Call Idnu Djehutymes, he knows me, he'll know what to do."

The medjau looked at each other. The lead one said, "We'll have to call in for instructions. Nakhy, can you go do something about that damn alarm? I can't think with that noise." One of the medjau ran back inside to turn off the alarm. The lead medja continued, "Now, let's take her to the security room until we can figure out what to do. And *we* have jurisdiction here, we're not under martial law, you know."

The soldiers looked at each other. "OK, but one of us has to stay with her. The Hem-Netjer-Tepy needs her in jail, you know? He's raising hell about it." He twisted MacIntyre's arm for emphasis, then pushed her toward the door.

Two hours later, MacIntyre sat in a chair in a small room in the palace's basement with one arm handcuffed to the chair. One soldier and a uniformed medja sat on chairs across from her. Her phone and other belongings lay on a table along with the collapsible baton. Nothing had moved in at least an hour, and MacIntyre's patience was nonexistent. She jerked at the cuff, and the two men, startled, got up out of their chairs.

The door opened, and Djehutymes walked into the room. Behind him came the other soldier, looking grim.

"Yes, it's Hutyt-er-Semetyu MacIntyre," said Djehutymes. "MacIntyre, you're under arrest for assault of a state official. I'm taking you in."

The soldier complained, "The Hem-Netjer-Tepy won't be happy about this, Idnu. He's mad as hell and wants her back in the Temple of Mentju."

Djehutymes smiled an icy smile and said, "I don't doubt it, but I don't care, either. She's ours and we're taking her. I have a warrant. Mentju will have to wait his turn. She's ours first." He signaled, and the medja unlocked the cuff from the chair, then cuffed MacIntyre's hands behind her back. Djehutymes picked up the baton and looked it over, then shook it to expand it and swung it back and forth to get its feel. MacIntyre noted in one cool part of her mind that he used more wrist than he should; he wouldn't get full force behind the swing. The rest of her mind fixated on not screaming at him to get her out of there.

"Nice thing to use on a poor, defenseless priest, MacIntyre. OK, let's go." He collapsed the baton and gathered up the rest of her things and put everything into his pockets. He turned to the soldier. "We'll be in touch with the Temple of Mentju once the brass figures out what to do with her." The soldier's face said he wanted to do something about Djehutymes's decision. Djehutymes calmly waited while the soldier thought it through and gave in.

Djehutymes walked MacIntyre out of a side door of the palace to a waiting medja car and put her into the back seat, then belted her in. He got in the other side and sat next to her. He grimaced, pulled the collapsible baton out of his back pocket, and set it on the seat between them.

"Where to, Idnu?" the driver asked.

"Temple of Ma'at, we'll put her in a detention cell," replied Djehutymes. "Use the siren and get a move on." He sat back, arms folded, as the car moved off at speed.

"Mes…." said MacIntyre, shifting in discomfort at having her hands cuffed behind her with the seat belt fastened. She'd laughed off complaints from suspects she'd restrained this way in the past, but now her frustration gave her a new outlook. Maybe a new career in prisoner's rights advocacy?

"Not now, MacIntyre. Not now." The idnu ignored her as the car sped through the crowded streets of Menmenet. MacIntyre wasn't sure which was worse, the threat of a gruesome, slow death at the hands of Mentju or the chilly silence of her former boss.

* * *

"Can you take these stupid things off, Mes?" MacIntyre shifted her aching arms in the hard chair in the detention room at the Temple of Ma'at. Mes sat across from her in another hard chair.

"I'd better not. Procedure." Mes's voice was even and judicious. MacIntyre couldn't tell whether he was being sardonic.

"Fuck."

"MacIntyre, did I tell you to stay put?"

"Yes, but—"

"And you didn't stay put."

"Yes, but—"

"You walked away from your safe house. And now you're here, lucky to be alive."

"Yes, but—"

"Shut up, MacIntyre. You're staying cuffed." He considered her with a frown. "Or, better, talk to me. What's going on? Tell me the whole sordid story, have it make sense to me. Why were you trying to kill the hekasepat?"

"I wasn't—" she began, the indignation sounding in her voice.

"Never mind. Tell me the story. Start at the beginning. Start when you ignored my reasonable request that you stay where you were."

She did. Mes settled himself in his chair and stared at her, frowning, until she got to the part about her Bastet-tea dream. He closed his eyes and continued listening without looking at her. She finished up with Ma'at's failed plan to get the hekasepat involved and the resulting chase.

"I don't believe it."

"It's true, Mes. Honor of Ma'at."

"Why aren't you dead?"

"Luck. As you said. Ma'at is on my side."

"In your dreams, MacIntyre. Only in your dreams. And your luck may have run out."

She smiled, unconvinced. "I don't dream. What are we going to do?"

"What *you're* going to do is sit here, cuffed, while I figure this situation out. What you're not going to do is more damage."

"Yes, but—"

"Shut up, MacIntyre. Don't say another word." He got up and walked over to the door and pushed the button. A medja opened the door. MacIntyre saw the soldier who had caught her sitting in a chair in the hall, like an angry, evil ba hovering over a cursed enemy. Djehutymes pointed at MacIntyre and issued instructions to the medja guard seated next to him. "Check on her every fifteen minutes and make sure she doesn't escape. Don't take the cuffs off, and don't let her talk to anyone—*anyone at all*—until I get back. And don't let her get the jump on you, or you'll be pounding a beat forever, if you're not dead. And if you're not dead, you'll *wish* you were dead. Understood?"

"Yes, Idnu."

Djehutymes glanced back at MacIntyre, shook his head, then went out, closing the door. She got up and walked over to the door and looked out the little window, meeting the stony gaze of the soldier. She slumped and sat on the floor against the wall. Her eyes closed, and she wondered whether she had hit bottom this time.

CHAPTER THIRTY-SEVEN
Shesmu Negotiates with NATO

THE SILENCE IN AKHEN'S CHAPEL weighed on my ka. The walls were thick, the doors were thick, and the atmosphere was even thicker. I heard a rustling noise, and a light flared. Tahefnu had taken an electric lantern out of her pack. The woman was impressive.

Khenmes sat against one wall, his legs extended in front of him. The American combat boots looked ridiculous on him, and they reminded me of the American heads.

"What do we do now?" asked Tahefnu, her voice sounding small as the thick walls absorbed it.

Khenmes smiled up at her. "Get comfortable and wait. It won't be long."

"Wait for what?"

"Whatever happens."

"I feel sick."

"I noticed. Stinks the place up." Khenmes smiled to take away the sting, but he was right—Tahefnu's vomit contributed a great deal to the thick atmosphere.

I looked at the door. I reached out for the handle.

"I wouldn't do that if I were you, Shes," said Khenmes. "Bound to be lots of stray rounds whizzing around out there soon. We're best off in here."

"I can't stand much more of this," said Tahefnu.

"Sure you can," replied Khenmes. "You've done OK so far. Aside from being a little surly."

"They cut off their heads! Just like that!"

"They do not train the Russian Spetsnaz to be deeply caring people, you know?" Khenmes smiled with what he thought was a reassuring smile. This observation did not reassure Tahefnu.

"I know now. Like Coyote said: bitch goddess. We can't stay here, Shesmu, not with these people. They're not even human!" I could hear the panic in her voice.

"Calm down, Tahefnu," I said. "We need to be ready for whatever happens. Take a deep breath and be ready." Excellent advice, I took it myself.

Tahefnu gave me another evil look and sat against the opposite wall from Khenmes and closed her eyes, her mouth a tight line.

I said, "Hey, Khenmes—since we aren't doing anything and we've got lots of time, why not tell me about my Dad? And his heroic actions in the Secret War? That kind of thing?"

Khenmes opened his mouth, but Tahefnu interrupted. "Coyote says no, it's too soon. He says you're not ready, you don't know enough yet." I swung back to her and saw nothing but surprise on her face. "That's it, Shesmu. Just that. You're not ready, he says." She closed her eyes again.

"Won't hurt to see what happens, Shes." Khenmes leaned back against his wall. The strange thing was, I felt nothing but relief. Maybe I didn't want to know. Maybe there was too much to know. Maybe, maybe. Maybe I wasn't ready, like the spirit said. Maybe I was afraid of what I'd learn. I'd learned I wasn't who I thought I was. This knowledge could make it worse. Is knowing the truth always better? I sat against the wall next to Khenmes to wait.

After an hour, I heard a noise at the door. It swung open, and Major Suvorova stumbled in with Vasha, the Russian who spoke Renkemet, and slammed the door shut. She breathed in hard, quick gasps. She was carrying two of the Spetsnaz rifles, and Vasha carried another two. I scrambled to my feet.

The major leaned back against the door and got her breath back. Her expression was ferocious.

"What's happened, Major?" asked Khenmes, who was on his feet. Tahefnu remained sitting, eyes closed.

"What do you think?" she snarled.

"On past form, your guys killed a bunch of NATO troops before they took out the three comrades who aren't here with you."

The major glared at him.

"What next?" I asked.

Vasha, also breathing hard, put his rifles on the floor and slumped against one wall.

The major transferred her glare to her subordinate. She hissed through gritted teeth, "Vasha! Prigotovitsya!"

He waved her off with one hand. She raised one rifle, hesitated, then lowered it again, shaking her head with sharp jerks and clamped lips. She put down the rifle and changed the magazine on the other one, saying nothing further.

"What next?" I repeated.

She grimaced as she checked the settings on the rifle. "Kill as many people as I can before they kill me, Shesmu-the-chef." Her face got thoughtful. "We can prolong this mission with your help."

"Help how, Major?"

"Hostages. I will use you three as hostages to negotiate my way out of here and kill as many people as possible."

"How is this new strategy going to play out?" I asked.

The major smiled her nastiest smile. "I will send Vasha out to negotiate. I will send out a body or two. The shaman first."

I said, "Let me negotiate, Vasha doesn't convey confidence right now." Vasha sat against the back wall, eyes closed. He smiled without opening his eyes. I didn't tell him he was sitting in the pile of Tahefnu's puke. This would become obvious to him in time and wouldn't improve his negotiating skills. "And I'm good with words when I want to be."

The major contemplated me with fierce eyes and pursed lips. She asked, "How can I trust you not to go over to them?" She answered her own question before I could. "The shaman. You fuck up, she's dead, and I still have Khenmes. Very well. Here's the arrangement you offer them. We walk out without weapons. You and the shaman go free and Khenmes comes with us out of the valley. After that, I'll kill as many of them as I can. I need more to take back to Novoarchangelsk, or I'm a dead woman."

"I'll see what I can do." I thought the major's plan had flaws regarding the fate of the hostages, but I didn't think she wanted constructive criticism. We'd have to cope with whatever NATO threw at us.

I fashioned a white flag out of a pair of used underwear from Vasha's pack, which I tied to the walking stick. I opened the door a crack and waved the flag. Nobody shot at it, so I stuck my head out. I called out, in English, "I want to talk, negotiate."

"Come ahead. Unarmed." I couldn't see the speaker through the dense under-growth.

I eased out of the chapel and walked toward the voice with both arms raised and the flag held high. In my hunter's suit, I suppose I looked military.

"Stop there." I stopped. "Name and rank?" asked the voice.

"Shesmu, no rank, I'm a civilian." I spoke in English.

"Remetjy?"

"Yes," I replied in Renkemet.

"What the fuck is going on?"

I still could not see the person speaking. I looked around and saw at least five American NATO soldiers dead on the ground and two of the Russians, also dead.

"A crazy Russian and her squad kidnapped us, and she's holding my friends and me hostage."

"Who are you? And who are the other hostages?"

"I'm a cook from Menmenet, and the other two are a Miwuk guide and a Waashiw gentleman who joined up with us and the Russians. Major Suvorova wants to negotiate a trade. She'll release my guide and me for freeing herself, her soldier, and Khenmes."

"Khenmes! Not a chance. We want him."

"The Russians will fight to the death and destroy the tomb." As a best alternative to an agreement, this was weak. But you play the cards you're dealt.

A brief silence, and the voice spoke again. "Counterproposal. We'll free you and your guide and intern the Russians and the Waashiw until this operation is over. Or we can even intern you and guarantee your safety during the operation."

"What operation?"

"Never mind what operation. That's what she'll get. No way we can let her go. Or the Waashiw."

"Why?"

"Go back in there and tell her that. She has 30 minutes, then we're coming in."

I backed away, turned around, and reentered the chapel. I relayed the terms to the major, who expressed dissatisfaction with my negotiating skills.

"Why haven't they sent a rocket through the door?" she mused.

Khenmes stirred. "They want what's in here, and they want me to explain it to them."

The major said, "I'll send out the woman's body to let them know we're serious. Then Vasha's."

Vasha, without opening his eyes, picked up his rifle and smiled.

Khenmes said, "Major, you're out of options. If you kill us, you won't have any hostages left. Make the best of it, enjoy NATO hospitality for a while, then pick up the pieces."

I added, "It's for the best, Major."

"Yob tvayu mat', Shesmu-the-chef." The major gave me the two-finger salute. She took several magazines of ammunition from her pockets and dumped them on the floor, then methodically checked them. Behind her back, I saw Vasha rise in silence, raising a finger to signal us to stay quiet. Moving fast, he came up behind the major and put her into a choke-hold.

"Shesmu!" Vasha's voice was urgent and loud in the chapel's silence. "Get ties from pack, there!" He pointed to the pack with his chin.

I scrambled over to his pack and brought the ties back. Khenmes and Vasha held the struggling major's arms twisted behind her back. Tahefnu was there, ready to help. The major screamed what I took to be Russian verbal abuse at her subordinate. I got behind her, and the two men held her arms together while I tightened the ties.

"And legs!" said Vasha. "B'stra, tavarishch!"

Khenmes and Tahefnu came to help and got two vicious kicks in return before they secured the major's legs. I tightened another tie around her ankles. Vasha got a shirt out of the major's pack, ripped off a section, and gagged her. Silence descended on the chapel.

"What now?" I asked.

Vasha used the torn shirt to wipe the sweat from his face. "Now negotiate. Using her."

CHAPTER THIRTY-EIGHT
MacIntyre Gets a Career Direction

MACINTYRE PUSHED WITH HER LEGS and slid up the wall, then walked back to her chair and sat. With her arms cuffed behind her, she found just about any position she took uncomfortable. The ache pulsed across her shoulders, but there was nothing she could do about it.

Shifting in the chair, she remembered sitting in her closet after her father had locked her in. She sat for hours thinking she was going to die of thirst or starvation or humiliation. She didn't die that time, and she remembered every awful moment. This new ordeal was shaping up to be worse. Mes's job was to put her in jail for life, or longer. She didn't want to wind up with as much hatred for Mes as she had for her father. But there was nothing she could do about that pain either. Not while she was cuffed and locked in a detention room. She jerked on the cuffs in frustration, but that only made her wrists hurt.

She shifted her shoulders again, her head drooped, and her brain shut down on her, sending her to sleep.

No special tea, no hallucinogenic drugs, nothing like that: just the dream. MacIntyre found herself in a great, sunny temple, standing among huge lotus columns looking out at what she assumed was the Great River of Kemet. She'd seen the Mississippi River once, but there was something primal about the river she was watching now, something timeless and forever. The Mississippi was the edge of an America pushing at its limits; the Great River of Kemet was the boundary between two worlds, the world of the living and the world of the dead. If you believed in that sort of thing. The Mississippi represented new worlds, slow eddies of time moving everything along in a kind of dreamy, muddy American dynamic that she had grown away from during the last few years.

"W'abet MacIntyre. It is good to see you here, where you belong."

The goddess's voice was warm and welcoming, and it filled her with a joy she had felt only on occasion. She turned, and there was Ma'at, smiling and holding out her winged arms. MacIntyre walked forward into the embrace that warmed her deep inside.

The goddess released her and said, "Walk with me, w'abet. We must discuss your situation, and the future."

The two women walked through endless rows of lotus columns, going deeper and deeper inside the temple, away from the bright light of Ma'at's brother R'a. MacIntyre found herself explaining every part of her life to the goddess. Ma'at listened well and rendered her judgments kindly. Eventually, they came to the temple sanctuary, the inner room kept in darkness and clean of any human trace so that the goddess could reside there in peace.

The goddess said, waving one hand, "This room is your future, w'abet. This room is the perfect center of ma'at."

"Am I then about to join you in the Duat, goddess?" MacIntyre, startled, realized she was speaking the formal Renkemet of the temple. The odd thing was that she had never learned that language. She had become a w'abet only because the medjau grapevine had told her it was the easiest way to help the approval of her transfer to homicide and her movement up the ranks. Being a w'abet let her put as many murderers behind bars as she could while angling for the deserved promotions that would give her control over her life.

"That future is uncertain, w'abet, even for an all-knowing goddess such as myself," replied Ma'at with a smile. "One way or another, your ka will go forth by day and promote ma'at through the Duat and the invisible universe, to the end of time. But we must speak seriously of the here and now."

"My here and now seems very limited at the moment. I am certainly ready to hear any advice that might help me escape my fate."

"One does not escape fate, w'abet, that is the very nature of it. All one can do is to go forth with ma'at every day and lead others to the same place."

"I have tried to be true to ma'at, Lady, every day."

"I require more of you now. You have plumbed the depths of the current situation. You have fought with Mentju and Seteh on the Great Desert of Isfet. You obeyed my instructions to see the hekasepat to help him to understand the situation."

"And I failed each test miserably. I am abject before you, Lady."

"No, you merely left the battle for a time. My strength was not and is not sufficient to prevent the blows you will take for me. That is the nature of goddesses. Except Aset, of course, who does whatever she wants." This last was said with a touch of cattiness; Aset was the goddess who found the chopped-up pieces of the god Wesir where Seteh had dumped them, then sewed him back together. She apparently had some special privileges in the invisible world.

With a touch of asperity, MacIntyre asked, "What would you have me fail at next, then, Lady?"

Ma'at, suddenly furious, blew MacIntyre backwards by lifting her winged arms and flapping, creating a violent burst of wind. MacIntyre hit the wall and fell to her knees.

The goddess's voice deafened MacIntyre. "Failure is not what I need, w'abet. You must succeed. I cannot succeed for you, I can only guide you toward the light of ma'at. You must take the reins of the war chariot and lead the armies to their final victory. You must regain your position in your world, then follow me into leadership that will guarantee the triumph of ma'at over isfet. Only by leading can you turn Seteh toward ma'at and send him and his poor, misled minion Mentju back to the desert where they belong. Should you fail, you have only the Great Devourer 'Ammet ahead of you. As I judge your failure, she will devour your heart, and you will never pass the gates of the Duat. You will never enter the blessed Sekhet-'Aru. You will exist alone in darkness with your failure for all eternity!"

Ma'at flapped her arms more and more strongly, the wind rising to gale force. MacIntyre knew that she must accept the direction by the goddess, she must not fail in the fight against isfet, she must escape the gods arrayed against her and her goddess. Funny how eternal damnation focuses you. The Winds of Ma'at blew MacIntyre through the endless columned halls until she rolled right out the door and out into the strong, pitiless glare of R'a. She hit the ground with a scream.

MacIntyre jerked awake as the chair fell over. She screamed and just managed to avoid slamming her face into the concrete.

The medja and the soldier rushed into the room and stopped, laughing at her predicament.

"Stupid bitch," said the soldier.

"Here, Hutyt, let me help you up. Come on, you, let's get her up." The medja got the soldier to set the chair upright while he helped MacIntyre to get back into the seat. The fall had not helped the ache in her shoulders.

"OK, Hutyt, try not to hurt yourself. The Idnu won't like it, you know?"

"Stupid bitch," repeated the soldier. MacIntyre gave him the Eye but it didn't seem to take. He just grinned with disdain and shook his head. "Stupid."

The two men left her sitting in the chair in the center of the room, facing the door, back where she'd started.

Two hours later, the door swung open, only to confront her with the unwelcome face of Sheritr'a, her old boss from the Security Department at the Temple of Mentju. Sheritr'a's double chin quivered as her humorless smile showed her satisfaction at seeing her former employee in dire straits. The two women stared at each other without words.

"Sorry, Hutyt," said the medja guard from behind Sheritr'a. "She's got a warrant, says she can take you. We're trying to get hold of the Idnu, but he's not answering." He held up his phone.

Sheritr'a motioned the soldier into the room and handed him the bag she was carrying. "Here, you, put these shackles on her, then take off the cuffs." The soldier reached into the bag and extracted a mass of thinnish chains. He sorted it out, taking a key from Sheritr'a, and shackled MacIntyre's legs and waist. He unlocked her arms, and she took the opportunity to exercise them.

"Stop that," said Sheritr'a.

"Get fucked," replied MacIntyre, continuing to swing her arms. But Sheritr'a and the soldier grabbed her hands, and the soldier then shackled them into the system of chains. MacIntyre was fully shackled, hands to waist to legs. Sheritr'a contemplated this work while MacIntyre simply enjoyed not having her arms stretched behind her back anymore. Any development beat another hour of watching the clock change.

Sheritr'a, smiling again, smoothed a hand over MacIntyre's cheek, then grabbed her by the hair and shook her head from side to side by it. "You're dead. Your heart's still beating, but you're dead. You know that, don't you, you little blue-eyed, blonde-haired pain in the butt."

"Hey," objected the medja.

"Shut up. National security." Sheritr'a sent him a black-eyed look of dismissal.

"We need to talk to the Idnu," he protested, standing his ground.

Sheritr'a glared at him but didn't waste any more time. She took back the shackles bag and extracted a black cloth hood from it, then pulled it over MacIntyre's head. MacIntyre shook her head impotently and bunched her shackled hands in protest.

"Bring her," said Sheritr'a. "There's an unmarked van by the side entrance."

The medja got on the phone to his superiors, but the sound of him disappeared as hands pushed the blind, stumbling MacIntyre down corridors and through doors. She felt the outside warmth on her skin, then the hands picked her up bodily and threw her into the van. She fell on her face, lying on the floor of the van. Hands pushed her legs, moving her forward until her face hit something hard, then she heard the van doors slam shut. She heard the front door open, the seat creak, the door close.

"Get going," said Sheritr'a. "Temple of Mentju. Move!"

MacIntyre rolled over onto her back and sat up so she could breathe. The van rocked back and forth as it tore through the all-too-few streets to the Temple of Mentju. MacIntyre, sightless and disoriented, struggled to stay upright and lost the battle, rolling around on the floor. She pulled at the chains fastening her arms to her waist, to no avail. The van jerked to a stop and she rolled violently backwards, coming to rest against the back doors, which soon opened. She fell out backwards onto cold concrete. Hands pulled her up and shoved her toward the next stage of her life at the Temple of Mentju.

CHAPTER THIRTY-NINE
Shesmu Meets Seteh

"WE NEED OPTIONS," SAID KHENMES. The major, who we had propped against a wall, glared back at him and voiced angry sounds through her gag.

"How long do you think that lamp will last?" I asked Tahefnu.

"It's magic, it will stay on forever," replied Tahefnu. "Like the food and water." She hefted the half-full water bag draped across her shoulders with a strap.

"Oh, ha ha."

"We got bigger problems than a light bulb. Or food." said Khenmes.

"Nothing is more important than food," I said. A chef to the end.

"Reasonable people might disagree, Shes. Have you used one of these things?" asked Khenmes, pointing at the rifle I held.

"No."

"I'm sure Vasha here can give us a quick tutorial, if he wants to stay alive."

"Da," said Vasha. "I do."

"Well, then."

Vasha gave us details. "Vintovka Snayperskaya Spetsialnaya silenced sniper rifles, VSS, issued to Spetsnaz. 10-round magazine, SP5 bullets, can pierce any body armor those guys wear. Quiet. Effective 400 meters. This switch," he said, fingering his own rifle inside the trigger guard, "automatic mode, if need to kill herd of elephants."

I inspected my new weapon. "Safety?"

"Same switch. Safety, semi, full. Change magazine this way," said Vasha, popping out the magazine and putting it back in about a quarter of a second.

Khenmes gathered up the magazines from the floor. "How many magazines do you have, Vasha?"

Vasha checked. "Seven."

"There are ten here. Four rifles. Give me two, each of us will get four magazines."

"Nyet." Vasha smiled.

Khenmes said, "Share and share alike, man. 20 bullets ain't gonna make any difference to you."

Vasha relinquished the magazines, and Khenmes counted out four from his collection and gave them to me. He gave another four to Tahefnu, who took one rifle and looked it over, doubt obvious in her face.

"OK," said Khenmes. "No way we're gonna blast our way out of here with 170 bullets. I'd bet on more than 170 troops being out there."

I said, "They've got a strong negotiating position. They want the Russians and you, period. We can try…" I looked at the door to my father's tomb. "Khenmes, why haven't they broken into the tomb and gotten whatever you're hiding?"

"Not enough time, they've been busy stealing the gold from the other tombs since they took over from the Republican Guard. First thing I told them when they asked about the tomb, no gold. So they made it lower priority, brought me here, but didn't have time to break me. That's why they want me so bad now." He smiled. "It's not likely they're gonna blow everything up just to get us. Which opens the door, so to speak, to negotiating."

Opens the door. I looked at the tomb door again, the door that led to my father, or at least to his mummy. Every Remetj knows that survival in the afterlife requires a mummy. Was I Remetjy enough despite my new Miwuk identity to care that I'd finally found my father's mummy? That his name lived on, despite Khenmes's dark hints about him? And Heh didn't much approve of Akhen either. Maybe if I got out of this alive, I'd care. I cared most about staying alive and keeping everyone else alive. The dead could take care of themselves. My immediate worry was the hundreds of NATO troops outside that wanted revenge and whatever it was they wanted from the tomb.

I shook my head, put down my rifle, and picked up the walking stick with its dirty underwear.

I opened the chapel door a crack and waved the underwear again.

"OK," I heard a voice shout in English. "Come on out, unarmed."

I moved the door more and stepped out. It was late afternoon, and there was a slight breeze playing through the trees and bushes. The granite cliffs and blue sky were magnificent, the circling turkey vultures less so. The NATO and Russian bodies cluttered things up in the charming little clearing. A cloud of flies buzzed around the corpses. I closed the door and stepped forward.

"We want to negotiate terms," I called.

"You said that before. No conditions. You got two Russians in there and guns. Give us the Russians and the guns and Khenmes and we'll talk more. Who did you say you were?"

"A civilian, a chef in Menmenet. My name is Shesmu, look me up on the web."

The voice ignored this attempt at personal marketing.

"Do I sound like I give a shit, Shes-whatever? Get 'em out here. We're gonna intern everyone for the duration."

"Shesmu. Duration of what?"

"Never mind. Get them out here."

Other than throwing ourselves on their mercy, my bag was empty. I didn't even have any gold from the tomb to offer. I could cook them an excellent dinner if they supplied the food, but that was about it. I didn't think that would make it as a counteroffer. I could tell them this was the tomb of my father, but I had the idea that this information would not persuade them to let up on us; it would make everything worse.

What the fuck were these guys doing here, and why did they want my father's secrets so much? If I knew those secrets, I might bargain with them. I'd have to talk with Khenmes about that.

Another interesting thing: why was I not hopping up and down like a scared rabbit? I'm a cook, not a hostage negotiator, though I've had my brave moments. Where did that courage come from? Maybe Ma'at had my back, or maybe my Miwuk heritage had something to do with it.

I planted the walking stick with its white underwear in front of me and leaned on it and bargained for time. "OK, let me go back and convince those guys to give up. I understand your position, but they have issues, especially the Russians. Give me two hours to persuade them." Think of a number and double it. If we couldn't come up with something in an hour, we'd be dead. At least Major Suvorova would be easy to persuade, as long as she stayed tied up and gagged.

"You got 10 minutes."

I shook my head. "Give me an hour and a half. I need an hour and a half."

"An hour, Shit-mutt. Get your ass in there and get it done."

"Shesmu, Shin-ess-em-you. I'll do my best."

Back in the chapel, quiet reigned with Khenmes and Tahefnu sitting against one wall and Vasha on the opposite wall next to Major Suvorova. Everyone looked up at me in the dim lantern light as I entered and closed the door. The major's eyes were two bayonets ready to strike.

"We're in good shape," I reported. "We have an hour before they kill us."

"Great negotiating, Shesmu," said Tahefnu.

"I figure I'm lucky they didn't shoot me on the spot."

"What do they want us to do, Shes?" asked Khenmes.

"Surrender you and the Russians with no conditions."

"And what happens?"

"Internment for the duration."

"Duration of what?"

"They were reticent about that."

Khenmes shook his head. "We are it."

Confused, I asked, "What do you mean?"

"We're it. We're the last line of defense for the Republic, and Washeshu too."

There had to be an alternative to fighting our way out with the rifles. "We're not a useful fighting force, Khenmes."

Khenmes shrugged. "Yeah. Won't work, three guys and a surly woman with 170 bullets."

Vasha barked out a short laugh and closed his eyes.

"If you told me about my father, I'd be able to negotiate something."

Khenmes looked at me, then shook his head. "Wouldn't help, Shes. Sorry."

I'd always imagined until today that I'd open more restaurants and collect kudos for the rest of my long life in Menmenet. Dying of massive projectile trauma in my father's tomb had never been part of my plan. Not that there was any alternative. But I couldn't just give up. Time to consult?

"Tahefnu," I said. "Do you think you might consult Coyote?"

"He's not feeling very talkative," she replied. She got up and grabbed the walking stick leaning against the wall, white underwear attached. "You said you had this stick when you dreamed?" she asked. Back to the magic stick.

"Yes, Ma'at gave it to me, as a w'as scepter, a staff of dominion."

"It could help resolve things, its magic is powerful. If you hold it and pray, you will see a path."

"I've been holding it. And I don't want any more magic, any more dismemberment dreams. I have enough troubles."

"It's better than nothing." She offered the stick.

"It's not you getting dismembered and mummified alive and burned to a tiny crisp."

"True. But Hummingbird tells me it's the only path we have." She untied the useless, dirty underwear, tossed it into Vasha's lap, and held up the stick in front of me. I reached and took hold of it.

The blackness was absolute, I could see nothing. Then a light appeared in the distance and came closer and closer.

The light came from the cupped hands of a woman. She wore a linen dress, but her most prominent attribute was the head of a hummingbird. I looked again and recognized the body of Tahefnu. Her hands were bound and a long rope around her waist led off into the darkness behind her. She said nothing, but stood before me holding the light up. The hummingbird head fixed her nervous eyes on me.

The taut rope loosened, but the Hummingbird did not move. Into the light strode the god Mentju with his falcon's head and solar disk and plumes. He wasn't holding the rope; he held his khepesh sword. He arrayed himself beside the Hummingbird and fastened hungry falcon's eyes on me and hefted his sword.

The rope slackened more, and another god emerged into the little circle of light on the other side of the Hummingbird. I recognized the peculiar ears and snout of Seteh, who looked like no earthly creature. I realized this was the god I had seen in my earlier dream while burning to a crisp. Seteh held the Hummingbird's rope.

I looked around, hoping Ma'at would appear to rescue me. But Ma'at never came to the rescue, she only came when it was time for her to tell one the right path to follow.

A laugh came out of the air, and the Seteh head became the Coyote head. The Hummingbird's beak opened and closed with no sound.

"I suppose, Shesmu, that you believed you were hearing from your dead father through this empty shell of a bird, am I right?"

I could only nod, terrified.

"Do you realize who I am, little chef?"

I did. "Yes, Lord of Isfet, I recognize you now."

"And yet you persist in this blind search for a father you will never find. He is busy attending to the minor affairs to which his minor deity status binds him. And you persist in trying to live when you should die. And you persist in trying to serve the Lady Ma'at when you must serve me instead."

Mentju cackled and said, "Despite my teachings, you persist." He raised his sword and tested the blade with his thumb. The Hummingbird stepped backwards, as if to run away. Seteh drew the rope tight and put his arm around the woman's shoulders. "And this little one, she is not of our race or kind, but I can manipulate her with ease because she does not wish to be in her world. She has served me well." The god squeezed the woman, whose beak opened and closed again without a sound. Her tied hands still cupped the light that illuminated the falcon and coyote. The Coyote turned back into Seteh's head.

"Now you understandewith whom you are dealing. You must serve me."

"I may serve only Ma'at, Lord." And where did that come from? Why was I so damn noble suddenly? This was a cringe-and-bow situation, not a let's-all-be-noble-and-go-to-our-deaths situation. I'm a cook, not a hero, however courageous I might be.

"Ma'at? You know nothing. You have served me without knowing it for years, as had your father before you. Seduced by your w'abet of Ma'at, you think Ma'at powerful. That goddess will not aid you, as you cannot serve her ridiculous purposes, trapped as you are."

The damn thing was, it made sense. My life has been a life of isfet, not ma'at.

"What do you demand of me, Lord Seteh?" Not that I intended to comply.

"I expect you to do what the NATO commander has asked: give up Khenmes to his fate, then join with them in their journey into history."

"What will that history be, Lord?"

"America stretching from sea to sea, little chef. It is the fate of the world that it should be so. It is *my* time, the time of the world to experience its true destiny of chaos and power instead of the false promises of ma'at."

I felt the chill of truth. My thoughts flew to MacIntyre, alone and suffering in Menmenet, not knowing of this impending disaster for the Republic. But I must not yield.

"I may serve only Ma'at, Lord," I repeated.

"Then you, and your Hummingbird, and your ridiculous w'abet of Ma'at whom you love so much will die. So be it." The Lord of Isfet looked at Mentju, who hefted his sword.

I surged forward, but my feet stayed rooted in place. I could do nothing as the curved blade slashed through the neck of the Hummingbird, her head flying off in a spurt of blood. Then the sword swung toward me as the light died out of the Hummingbird's hands.

273

CHAPTER FORTY

MacIntyre Sacrifices Everything for Mentju

ORDINARILY, CHERYL MACINTYRE SLEPT WELL and did not dream. Lately, the dream thing had changed for the worse. You could blame Bastet and that damn tea for that, she thought to herself as she turned over with restless energy. But at least she had slept.

It is surprisingly difficult to sleep when shackled with chains and with a black bag over your head and the threat of imminent death looming. The long hours in which she had tried without success to get into enough of a comfortable position to doze off gave her time to reflect. She began with enjoyable fantasies about what she would do to all and sundry if she got her head out of the bag. These angry phantasms disappeared swiftly, replaced with more sober reflections on life and death—specifically, hers. The only question was what they would do to her before killing her. The eager gleam in Sheritr'a's eye dismayed her, and she did not look forward to seeing the hem-netjer-tepy of Mentju again. She found herself calm in the face of death and reflected on that for some little time. Perhaps her plight would be an effective way to get her to meditate and resolve her anger issues. Perhaps not.

Later, reflections stopped, and she simply existed in the blackness and discomfort and the effort to breathe. It was freezing, wherever in the Temple of Mentju she was, and it got colder.

She was still awake, but numb, when she heard the sounds of someone unlocking the door.

* * *

The light was harsh and blinding as the bag came off her head. MacIntyre sat up on the edge of the shelf that served as a bed in the small room and shook her head a little to clear away the cobwebs as her eyes got used to the light. Unfortunately, the first thing she saw was the face of the person who had removed the bag: Sheritr'a. Her expression had not changed, and MacIntyre still did not like it.

"Up."

"Give me a minute."

"Up!"

"Get fucked."

Sheritr'a turned to look behind her. "Get her up and take her."

Two soldiers came into the little room, grabbed MacIntyre by the arms, lifted her off her feet, and carried her out the door. Sheritr'a followed.

"OK, OK, I can walk," said MacIntyre. The soldiers dropped her to the floor on her feet. She stumbled, recovered, and stopped. Sheritr'a pushed her forward.

"Easy, easy, I'm going. Where to?"

Sheritr'a said nothing and pushed her forward again. She had to shuffle, as the ankle chains restricted her stride and her legs were still numb from the chilly night. The little group came to a side corridor, and the soldiers turned her into it. Elevators. She recognized the sub-basement; she was somewhere near where she had taken care of Hori's body. She'd made it to the dungeons after all. Sheritr'a pushed the button for the second floor. So they wouldn't visit the hem-netjer-tepy.

Sheritr'a said, as the door closed and the elevator started up, "We're going to meet with the Hem-Netjer-Tepy." MacIntyre looked over at her and saw a big grin aimed in her direction.

"Oh, good. Maybe I can hit him with a stick again."

The grin disappeared. "No, I don't think so. You'll be too busy dying."

"What, you mean he doesn't like being hit with a stick? From what I heard you say to him, I thought that was surely true, or I wouldn't have tried it. Or is it just you who likes it?"

"Such a clever spy you are, Cheryl. The trouble is, your mouth is far too big. May I call you Cheryl?" Sheritr'a was using her most silky toned voice.

"Sure," said MacIntyre, "if I can call you a lying bitch traitor and your boss a megalomaniacal rapist."

"Gag her. Here."

The soldier on her right took a piece of cloth from Sheritr'a's hand and used it to gag MacIntyre.

"We debated," said Sheritr'a, "whether to torture you to find out what you know. But it was a short debate, Cheryl. Because, Cheryl, it doesn't matter a damn what you know. The coup is ready, and you won't be able to do anything about it. And you won't care a bit, as you'll be dead, Cheryl."

MacIntyre rolled her eyes expressively in Sheritr'a's direction and shook her chains for emphasis. Sheritr'a's chins quivered as she contemplated with apparent pleasure the fate in store for her former employee.

The elevator door opened to the familiar sight of the second-floor elevator hall. The soldiers pushed MacIntyre out, and the little group marched around to the central auditorium where MacIntyre had first started working for the temple. Workers passing in the hall studiously ignored the gagged and shackled MacIntyre. Down the ramps past all the empty seats they shuffled, toward the central atrium. She saw Setehnekhet, in full regalia and an arm sling, waiting near the hetep of Mentju.

"Urr," she said through the gag. Sheritr'a ignored this insult and pushed her down into a chair near the hetep.

"Get the w'abu in and prepare this lovely woman," said Setehnekhet, smiling.

Sheritr'a used her phone, and a few minutes later, a door behind the hetep opened. Two w'abu of Mentju came through with a chest, which they set down next to MacIntyre. They looked nervously at the hem-netjer-tepy, who waved his good hand at the chest.

One w'ab said, "We'll need those chains removed to put on the regalia, Neb-Waset Setehnekhet."

"Very well." Setehnekhet looked around. "You two," he said, pointing to two soldiers, "get her up and hold her arms. Sheritr'a, you take off the chains. The ritual insists on an unconstrained, conscious sacrifice." He smiled again. "Leave the gag on, that won't be in the way," He giggled with the excitement, ruining his manly image for MacIntyre.

"Urr!" said MacIntyre again, with feeling. Again Sheritr'a ignored MacIntyre's insult as the soldiers picked her up, holding her feet off the ground. When Sheritr'a got close to her, MacIntyre kicked her feebly with her chained leg.

"If I may suggest, Neb-Waset Setehnekhet?" one of the w'abu asked, his impatience surfacing. He held up a hypodermic syringe.

"Do it," replied the hem-netjer-tepy.

The w'abu approached and, dodging a kick from the struggling MacIntyre, punched the needle into her arm and pushed the plunger. "Fifteen to thirty minutes, sir, to full sedation."

The soldiers sat MacIntyre back down in the chair and held her down.

"Well, Cheryl, we find ourselves in a very unpleasant situation," said Setehnekhet. "At least for you. I find it stimulating, stimulating indeed. I am sorry that you felt it necessary to do what you did, but the religious laws make the punishment very clear. It is unfortunate that your indomitable spirit requires chemical sedation, I would have preferred your full participation in the event. We'll go ahead with our military plans shortly, and we must have loose ends tidied away before that. A shame."

"Urr-wah!" said MacIntyre, forcefully.

"I daresay."

Setehnekhet and Sheritr'a seated themselves to wait and discussed their preparations for taking over the country. Lassitude overtook MacIntyre; she struggled, but that became harder and harder. Ten minutes later, she couldn't move a muscle, though she could hear and see. The best part, though, was that she no longer cared about anything. Listening to the two plotters, she didn't care about the NATO invasion, the internment camps, or the devious plots Setehnekhet wove to disperse and intern the NATO troops after they'd helped him into power, taking their military equipment and using it and the NATO hostages to shore up his new regime.

Sheritr'a approached MacIntyre, who smiled a sappy smile.

"I think we may proceed, Neb-Waset Setehnekhet." She removed the chains, and MacIntyre slumped in the chair, staring foolishly at the hetep altar. Setehnekhet approached and held up her head with a hand under her chin, looking into her eyes.

"Such a waste!" he said. "Mentju will not be denied, however." Sheritr'a smiled and tossed the chains to the floor, then removed the gag from MacIntyre's mouth.

The w'abu quickly removed all her clothes and stuffed her into a red ceremonial linen dress. MacIntyre dreamily wondered how it looked with her eye and hair color and whether she would take up the fashion later. They added a stunning necklace of multiple rows of lapis, turquoise, and carnelian beads. They fitted her feet with golden sandals that had covers that made her feet look like golden hooves. Then the w'abu reached into the chest and brought out a stiff, full-head mask made of plastic. It was the head of the Bakha bull, white with a black snout. The eyes were obsidian or something like it, and she worked out through her dreaminess that a person wearing the mask could see nothing, which struck her as very curious. The w'abu sprinkled some kind of water over the mask and mumbled over it. The last thing MacIntyre saw before the w'abu put the mask over her head was Setehnekhet carefully laying out the long, curved knife for a bull sacrifice on the hetep.

The mask covered her head down to her chin, and a thin Velcro strap across her chin secured the mask to her head. Curiously, the mask ended there rather than extending down past her throat. What an odd thing. She imagined what she looked like with the mask on; damn silly. Shesmu wouldn't like it much, he wasn't that much into costumes and things like that. Henutsenu would love it, though, especially with the bead necklace and the ridiculous sandals. Someone sprinkled water on her throat, then hands picked her up and carried her. They placed her on her back on a stone surface. She smiled and relaxed.

"Ready, Neb-Waset Setehnekhet." The disembodied voice came to her from a great distance.

The hem-netjer-tepy spoke a ritual in the formal language of the bull sacrifice ceremony, his voice loud and resonant. MacIntyre remembered from her earlier duties that this went on for quite a while. She really didn't know that language so well, so she got more comfortable and closed her eyes, which were useless to her now inside the dark mask. The hem-netjer-tepy droned on. After the long, cold, sleepless night, this was a welcome respite. She drifted off after a few minutes and fell into a deep sleep. She did not dream.

CHAPTER FORTY-ONE
Shesmu Calls Home

I CAME TO MY SENSES lying on the floor of the chapel, Khenmes leaning over me.

"Are you OK, Shes?" Khenmes asked.

I rubbed my aching head. "These dreams are killing me, Khenmes." I sat up and looked around. Tahefnu was lying next to me, completely out. At least her head was still on her shoulders. The walking stick lay next to her.

"How long was I out?" I asked.

Khenmes looked worried. "You just collapsed onto the floor five minutes ago, you and the woman. I didn't have time to catch you."

I reached over and took Tahefnu's hand. As I held it, she stirred and her eyes opened. She stared at the ceiling. Her hand gripped mine.

Without looking at me, she said, "Did we dream the same dream, Shesmu? Seteh and Hummingbird?"

"Yes, Tahefnu, we did."

"I'm sorry, Shesmu."

"I know."

"I've lost Hummingbird." Her eyes closed, and a tear escaped. "I thought I was a real shaman, but it was all fake," she said. "Seteh was in control. I did what he wanted, I assumed it was what Hummingbird wanted, what I wanted. I lied to you, Shesmu. I led you to your death."

"You did what you thought was right. And I'm not dead yet."

"It's not all right. It's all gone now. All gone. Seteh took it all away. And Mentju." Tears seeped from her closed eyes. "Not even our gods, your gods. How is that all right?"

"You can start fresh, Tahefnu. Be yourself, work with your father to do what needs doing."

"It's not for me, Shesmu. The spirit world is not a place I can live."

"Join the club, Tahefnu. At least we're alive in the mundane world."

"So you say. I'm barely alive."

"Same club."

"What am I going to tell Dad?"

"The truth."

"Can you imagine how tough that will be?" She looked at me with angry eyes.

"It's easier than figuring out what the truth is. You've done the heavy work."

Tahefnu sat up. "I'll go to Menmenet. I can't live here anymore."

Khenmes smiled. "I'd hold off on any decisions until we figure out how to survive the next several minutes."

"Oh. Yeah. NATO. Where are those rifles?" Tahefnu had recovered from her existential funk.

Khenmes said, "We have thirty-seven minutes to come up with a plan."

I asked, "How do you know how much time we have left? I'm clueless."

"The position of the sun."

I looked around at the dark chapel and its meagre little lantern.

"Right," I said.

"Tridtsat'-shyest', three-six," said Vasha. He held up his arm to show his watch, gleaming in the lamplight. It was digital, and it turned over to thirty-five as I stared at it. The bastard had set his stopwatch feature.

Vasha and Khenmes conferred in one corner while Tahefnu and I sat against a wall recovering after our dreams of Seteh. I hoped with my definitive rejection of that god that my visions were over, but that led me to think about the future. Whatever defensive strategy Khenmes came up with, it wasn't looking good.

I wasn't the type to relish dying in a blaze of military glory. My kind of heroism usually wound up with culinary awards, not bullets. But I had to confront the fact that I was not likely to survive any defensive encounter with the NATO troops arrayed against us. I spared a thought for my father and regretted I had never really known him.

The sight of Tahefnu suffering her loss reminded me about MacIntyre, an even deeper source of regret. I couldn't face death or years of internment without talking to her again. Between my phone running out of signal and charge and my life running out of time, I hadn't had the chance since I left Da'owaga'a. I took out my phone; dead as a doornail.

I said, "Vasha. Do you have a phone?"

Vasha looked up from his intense discussion with Khenmes. "Da."

"May I make one call on it?"

Vasha rolled his eyes but gave me his phone, ready to call. I estimated we now had about twenty minutes, and I thought I might as well give my loved one a call to say goodbye. At least she was safe, courtesy of Karkin. I regretted that I would probably never have the chance to thank him for everything he'd done for me, but nowhere near as much as I regretted not seeing MacIntyre again before my untimely demise.

Her phone rang and rang, then went through to voicemail. A second best to talking to my love but it would have to do.

"Hi, Cheryl, finally returning your calls, spotty coverage, no charge on the battery, and a tonne of disasters. I'm calling on somebody else's phone. I'm so sorry about everything. I've got to make this quick. I'm with some people, holed up in my father's tomb in Ta Sekhet in the mountains. I rescued Khenmes from a prison compound in the middle of the valley. About that: my father is a Miwuk, and so am I, at least half. Tahefnu, our Miwuk guide, is here too, and two Russian soldiers. Right now we have about a thousand NATO troops outside that are waiting to kill us or lock us up, our choice. We may surrender, but the situation is dire. Fuck, I hate this, I miss you. I miss your lips, I miss your attitude, I miss your love. Um. Maybe you could inform somebody about the NATO troops, figure out what's going on. If we survive and I can find you, let's not leave it this long again, OK? We can explore my new identity. Give my love to everyone you can think of, and take care of yourself, and if I don't make it, remember me, keep my name alive. I love—"

At that point, the voicemail cut out. She'd understand the last word, though.

"So sweet." Tahefnu smiled. I handed the phone back to Vasha. Tahefnu offered me the walking stick. I hesitated, then grabbed it. I waited; nothing. Seteh was done with me, and Tahefnu was just another beautiful maiden in distress, and this was just a well-made staff. I turned to the door to my father's mummy and raised the staff in what I hoped would not be a final salute; it made me sad to think I would never get to know more about him, the hero of the Secret War. Tahefnu touched my arm in understanding. I guess it was a Miwuk thing.

Khenmes and Vasha came over. Vasha's face had a sombre Russian look of resignation.

I asked, "What have you come up with? A brilliant plan to sneak through their ranks and make our way to safety?"

"Surrender." Khenmes didn't sound happy, probably because he knew that surrendering would put him right back into the hands of the people who wanted to extract information from him. "Carry out the major and give her to them."

Vasha nodded and looked even less happy, probably because the NATO folks were most unhappy with the Russian contingent and their assassination tactics. "Da, is only option. Every other option instant death. I want not to die just yet. I also want to keep testicles, but you can't have everything." He looked at the major, whose face expressed her deep desire to remove his testicles right there.

I nodded. The decision was no longer that hard for me. Tahefnu said in a subdued voice, "It's all we can do now. It's hopeless."

I re-tied the underwear to the walking stick. We piled the rifles, magazines, and packs at the side of the chapel. We had ten minutes left of the ultimatum, but there was no point in pushing it. Vasha sighed and stopped his timer. Khenmes and Vasha lifted the struggling major to carry her out, more angry noise coming through the gag. We were ready.

CHAPTER FORTY-TWO

MacIntyre Changes Careers

DREAMING OR NOT DREAMING? MACINTYRE could not quite decide but wasn't willing to open her eyes to find out. Her head hurt too much to move even her eyelids. She had a hazy memory, or was it a dream, about a bull mask and a bunch of traitors.

As she gradually came to, the images floating around in her brain coalesced into her sacrifice on the hetep of Mentju by a deranged, megalomaniacal rapist and his minions. Her eyes popped open, and she screamed, blinded by the bright lights.

"About time." The familiar disapproving voice produced a rush of adrenaline, and MacIntyre tried to sit up, only to have two powerful hands restrain her.

"Ow!" she exclaimed, raising both hands to her head and falling back to the pillow.

"Careful, MacIntyre. I think you need to stay put."

"You said that before, Mes," she replied, closing her eyes against the bright lights. She cracked one eyelid, letting her pupils contract at a more reasonable rate. Yep, it was Djehutymes, and there was Karkin, standing next to him, green army jacket and all. She was in a small bedroom just big enough for the bed and the two men who stood next to it.

"And was I right?"

Confronted with the choice of ripping into him or forgiving him, she said, "Of course you were right." She needed Mes to get her career back on track. "So, what happened?"

"Are you sure…?"

"Fuck's sake, Mes, talk to me. I'm lying here imagining all kinds of psychotic things. I need a dose of reality from a friend. Talk!"

"For once, MacIntyre, your psychotic imaginings and reality are probably one and the same."

"I was afraid of that."

"Yeah."

"Why am I not spouting blood all over the floor of the Temple of Mentju?"

"Imen-R'a."

MacIntyre opened the other eye and grimaced at the medja. "What the fuck does that mean?"

"It's a long story, MacIntyre. You need rest."

"Sure. Rest." She closed her eyes again. "Just tell me, it's not as though I'm going anywhere."

Djehutymes turned to Karkin. "Can you bring in those chairs from the other room?" Karkin silently brought two folding chairs. Djehutymes took on a martyred expression and sat down.

"Fuck. I must be getting old. I used to pound a beat for hours. Maybe my feet got too flat, then I got promoted."

"Mes...." MacIntyre's voice pleaded for information.

"OK. After you told me about Karkin, I figured I should talk to him. So I went looking. Hard guy to find, but I found him. But he was way down the peninsula, talking to some elders or shamans or something down there. No phone service. I drove down, and we compared notes. I still stink of sage and wood smoke. When I got back, the medja I'd put in charge of you told me that Mentju had you. It took most of the night to put together a team and figure out the legalities."

"Legalities?"

"You don't want to know. Trust me. Didn't matter, anyway."

"Why? What happened then?"

"Then we found out that the Temple of Imen-R'a had already intervened, first thing in the morning. Apparently a low-level functionary in the Temple of Mentju has a father high up in the religious hierarchy at Imen-R'a, and something he said made his dad suspicious."

"Fuck. Meryr'a again."

"Who?"

"Never mind. Keep going."

"So, they called in both their own security force and the Menmenet medjau tactical team. By the time Karkin and I arrived at the Temple of Mentju, they had it locked down. And there you were, wrapped in a blanket, dead to the world. Well, not dead, but out for the count. Cute outfit, by the way. Loved the mask. And the sandals." MacIntyre opened one eye to see her ex-boss callously grinning.

"Fuck."

"Yeah. Then one of Setehnekhet's people—a loud, angry, fat woman—"

"Sheritr'a."

"—got into it with the TAC team idnu. Pulled a gun. Before we knew it, Setehnekhet disappeared. They took her gun away and arrested her for attempted murder with special circumstances, the special being heresy. Apparently there are religious injunctions against human sacrifice."

"I hope it carries the death penalty."

"Funny, MacIntyre, hilarious."

She looked over at Karkin, both eyes open now. "And where the fuck were you? I called you ten times."

"Away."

No, she would not forgive Karkin. He wouldn't help with her career, she was sure.

"So, everything's good now, the bad guys are done?"

"Well, that's why we're here." Djehutymes looked down at his sandals.

"Where is 'here'?"

"Safe house," said Karkin.

MacIntyre had a sinking feeling. "So even Imen-R'a isn't enough to handle these guys?"

"Things are confused," said Djehutymes. "But when we left the temple, carrying you out, shots came from somewhere, I took one in my vest. We got out of there fast, Karkin brought us here."

MacIntyre looked at him with concern. "Are you OK?"

. He smiled and rubbed his chest. "Sore but alive."

She shook her head. "So they'll be after you now."

"We were…disguised. Masks and body armor. Amazing the stuff they have in the basement of the Temple of Ma'at. I'm OK, but I wanted to stick around here until you woke up."

Karkin spoke up. "Hekasepat."

MacIntyre looked at him. "What?"

Djehutymes pursed his lips. "Apparently the Hekasepat told the Temple of Imen-R'a, of which he's the titular head, to stand down. That's the confused part. It's clear that you need to keep your head down for a while, though. A lot of back and forth, according to Karkin's sources. Nobody knows what's going on or who is in charge now."

"Sucks," said Karkin.

MacIntyre was finally awake enough to figure out what her most pressing problem was. She had to pee, badly. She threw back the covers and levered herself out of the bed, which was when she found out she was naked except for the bead necklace.

After the embarrassed men left her to it, MacIntyre found only the red ritual-of-Mentju dress in a closet in the bedroom and put it on, much to her disgust. Worse, the bull-hoof sandals were the only footwear available. Djehutymes smiled, gave her a bag containing her personal items, and left, saying he had work to do. Karkin left as well but told her nothing.

The new safe house was a two-room apartment with a kitchenette and a bathroom. MacIntyre stood in the kitchen contemplating the fact that there was literally no food anywhere. She wandered back into the living room and picked up her phone from the small table there. She automatically checked for texts and voicemail. And there was one from Shesmu!

She pressed the play button and listened to the message. Voicemail cut him off, but the details of the message pounded into her aching brain and raised all kinds of alarm bells and thoughts. Monkey brain hell, she thought confusedly; what do I do now?

Karkin came through the front door without knocking, giving her overburdened heart another workout. She looked at him with wild eyes. "Where were you?"

"Arrangements." He scratched his chin.

"Fuck! You've got to listen to this message I got from Shes! I don't know what to do!" She handed him the phone and jabbed at the voicemail with a shaking finger.

He listened, grimaced, and gave the phone back to her. Saying nothing, he signalled her to follow him. They left the apartment and made their way down to the lower-level garage to Karkin's car. He refused to start the car until she had fastened her seat belt.

She peppered the Ramaytush with questions. "Where are we going? What about the coup? What about Setehnekhet? What about the Americans? What about Shes?" she ranted as they drove out of the garage. Karkin stamped on the accelerator.

"Why do I trust you? Why am I not out there making things happen? Does Mes know where we are? Where are we going? What about Shes? What about Ta Sekhet?"

The car zipped around several corners and drove south through the city along the bay-front boulevard down the peninsula. Karkin took the first exit to the airport, sped past five cargo warehouses, and drove up to a small back gate. He showed his identification at a guardhouse, then drove over to a very large chopper with three men standing by it, their coppery faces grim.

"Our ride," said Karkin. MacIntyre looked at the military attack chopper with disbelief. Karkin stopped the car just short of the little group and got out. MacIntyre scrambled out of the passenger seat and followed him, talking.

"What the hell are we doing? Who are these people? How did you get a chopper? Where are we going? What the fuck is happening, Karkin? Karkin? Karkin!"

Karkin briefly stopped to speak to one man standing by the chopper, then hopped into the hold. He turned and held out a hand. MacIntyre stopped talking and looked at him, grabbed the proffered hand, and jumped.

"They're Miwuk allies!" he shouted as the massive engines fired up. He headed off to talk to the pilot. After that, MacIntyre sat on a bench and nursed her headache as the noise and vibration of the giant beast dominated her being. The chopper rose and flew off eastward across the bay, gathering speed.

The chopper flew in a slow arc across the coastal hills and into the Central Valley, going ever eastward, R'a shining steadily behind them. MacIntyre stared at the snow-capped mountains of the Sen'aserqu range stretching across the eastern akhet. She felt the air heating up as they passed from the cool bay to the much warmer inland climate. The mountains hovered in the same place even though the land, farms, and rivers rushed by below her.

Karkin came over and held out his open hand with some pills. She took them from his hand and looked them over; aspirin. Two aspirin. She looked him in the eye while she threw them over her shoulder out the door. He shrugged. The chopper noise was far too loud for MacIntyre to tell him her thoughts properly.

An hour later, the chopper descended toward an airfield nestling up against the foothills of the mountains. MacIntyre had a vague notion that the Ta Sekhet Imenet Ma'at was up in the mountains ahead. There were several other choppers of varying types littering the little landing field. Military transport trucks with people loading things into them lined up along the side of the field. A limp Ta'an-Imenty Republic flag hung over the field, with only the wash from the chopper creating any breeze to make it flap. MacIntyre could see two military vehicles approaching. Karkin jumped down from the chopper, and MacIntyre followed.

"How's my hair, Karkin? Good enough to impress for success?" Karkin ignored this sally and walked toward the oncoming vehicles, armored cars of some sort. She made a rude noise with her lips, then followed him.

The soldiers that spilled out of the vehicles sported automatic rifles and pointed them in a direction that indicated they were not necessarily friendly. They wore Ta'an-Imenty desert uniforms. MacIntyre stopped and raised her hands, hair blowing everywhere in the chopper's wash, but Karkin just walked up to the officer in charge and spoke. The officer listened with a skeptical look that gradually changed to acceptance. MacIntyre moved toward them. The officer ordered his men to stand down, though he looked at MacIntyre with doubt in the set of his mouth and eyes.

"Who's she?"

"Menmenet medjau, seconded to me for this operation." Karkin looked at MacIntyre for confirmation.

"American?"

"Yep, that's me, Ms. Seconded American Medjat. I'm with him," she said with spirit, lowering her arms. "Want to see my medjat's badge?" The officer grinned, reassured by her sunny disposition, by her elegant red dress, by the silliness of her wind-blown hair and bull-hoof shoes, and not least because he had all the guns. His acceptance of her was good, since she still did not have her badge, just a can-do attitude.

Karkin and MacIntyre climbed into the back of the officer's vehicle. The line of vehicles set off toward a group of buildings at the edge of the airfield. The Miwuk chopper took off and flew away, due west into the setting sun. MacIntyre could see ranks of barracks behind the buildings, two lines of them stretching out to the south with a parade ground in the middle. Men in desert uniforms walked from building to building. The officer led Karkin and MacIntyre to an office in one building. The whole place looked like they'd put it together with a few screws and duct tape on a hot day a hundred years ago and had put it on the deferred-maintenance list immediately. A hand-lettered sign next to the door said "Imy-er-mesh'a Basa."

"This place gives me the willies," whispered MacIntyre to Karkin.

"Shut up," whispered Karkin.

MacIntyre grinned, slapped him hard on the back, and said, loudly, "Right, boss."

They went into the office. Behind an ancient desk with three legs and a block of wood holding it up sat an imposing man in a desert army uniform. As the little group entered his office, the man rose. His strong chin and nose, black hair sprinkled with gray, and massive black eyebrows projected a heavy aura of strength into the room. He must have been two meters tall.

"Karkin? I am Imy-er-mesh'a Basa, commander of this base. The Miwuk brigade command has informed me of the situation in brief, and we are mobilizing, but you owe me details. And who is this?" Basa eyed MacIntyre with disfavor.

Karkin said, "Hutyt-er-Semetyu Cheryl MacIntyre of the Menmenet medjau, Your Excellency. She can explain."

The Imy-er-mesh'a looked at MacIntyre with lifted eyebrows. "MacIntyre? European?"

"American, Your Excellency, but a citizen of the Ta'an-Imenty Republic."

"An American?" Basa looked at Karkin. "Why the fuck should I let her live, much less let her explain?" The Imy-er-mesh'a's massive black eyebrows contracted along with his mouth, giving him a fierce aspect. "The Americans and their NATO allies have taken my valley."

Karkin smiled. "Everyone has great faith in Hutyt MacIntyre's abilities and acumen, Your Excellency."

"Indeed. The hekasepat has great faith in me, too, and look where I am. Sitting in a century-old military ghost town in the middle of nowhere soaking in sweat and paying more attention to a bunch of indigenous traitors than to my designated commander." He waved a hand toward the window. "And now I find I must get my strategic intelligence from a blonde American woman wearing temple clothes and bull-hoof sandals."

Karkin turned to MacIntyre. "The imy-er-mesh'a, here, is the commander of the Ta'an-Imenty Republican Guard, usually stationed in Ta Sekhet and now at this base. He's out of sorts."

"Oh ho," said MacIntyre. "Suddenly my role in this becomes clear."

Imy-er-mesh'a Basa said, "So explain. Who are you? And why should I not have you buried in the desert up to your charming chin?" He looked her up and down with disdain, judging her by her elegant if disheveled red dress and high-fashion sandals.

"I'm a homicide semetyt, Your Excellency, though currently, ah, seconded from that position. I've been undercover in the Temple of Mentju, as you can see from my dress here. And sandals. No time to change." She summarized the situation for the imy-er-mesh'a, including the NATO troops in Ta Sekhet and in the south. Karkin listened and nodded approvingly. She did not go into details on her near sacrifice at the end, saying that a medjau team had extracted her from the temple and leaving it at that.

She finished up with a question. "And, Your Excellency, if you don't mind my asking, why are you here? Why are you not in Ta Sekhet, defending it?"

"A good question, Hutyt." The imy-er-mesh'a's did not smile. His eyebrows remained as thunderclouds in the akhet. "Two hours ago I would have said, 'orders.' After the communications from the Miwuks and your explanation, I can tell you that a NATO con man gulled me into abandoning my post. They had the right orders and the right uniforms to replace my men. National security troops, they said, from the temple, on special detail to protect the valley. They said they needed us for joint military exercises in the Central Valley. The only exercises here have been the daily workouts for my troops in the 40-degree heat. I even verified it with the hem-netjer-tepy's office, to make sure. But from your account of the conspiracy at the temple, and from my personal sources in Menmenet and elsewhere, that too was a con."

Basa gazed out the window at the parade ground, as soldiers crossed back and forth preparing for whatever fate they faced. From the set of his mouth and the continued thunderclouds in his expression, MacIntyre felt sure that Basa's opinion of Setehnekhet was about the same as hers. But he said nothing.

MacIntyre said, "Some people in Ta Sekhet, Your Excellency, urgently need our help. A man from Menmenet, a Russian, a Miwuk guide, and a Waashiw man. I can't tell you much about what they're doing there, but NATO wants them badly."

He looked her in the eye, his eyebrows lifting. "They would be the least of my concerns given the Justified Ones and their treasures. Civilians will have to take their chances. My mission is precise."

MacIntyre tried to put every gram of respect she had into her voice. "Yes, Your Excellency, I understand, but *our* mission is to extract them alive. And to be fair, the Justified Ones are dead. And they'll still be dead, whatever you do." Karkin smiled but said nothing.

"Noted. Next?"

Karkin spoke. "I need to consult with the Miwuk leadership to the north of the valley."

The big soldier grinned. "Do you mean Heh?"

"Yes, that's right. I don't know him, but the word is, he knows everything that's going on and can help us build a plan of attack."

"Fucking old hermit," said Basa with affection in his voice. "Making a nuisance of himself, as usual. Yes, he definitely knows everything that's going on, he's been in touch. I just didn't believe what he told me until you came. If any plan ever needed his shaman's magic, this one does. We don't have enough firepower to battle NATO on our own, but we'll get into position on the road to the valley entrance and wait. There's only the one road in. If NATO tries to break out, we'll stop them. We can take out a bridge or two, but that will just slow them down; we'll find ways to slow them down more. We'll send you up to Kikyapapli on a military transport chopper you can use for operations up there; it has secure-communications equipment you can use to keep us in the loop."

MacIntyre opened her mouth to make her case for rescuing Shesmu again, but Karkin took her arm and led her out of the Imy-er-mesh'a's office. "Relax," he said. "We'll find them."

MacIntyre acquired a used forest-green army uniform and combat boots from the base stores; a hairbrush, from a bemused idnut in a trade for the bead necklace; and a snazzy brown beret, a gift from Basa, who seemed taken with MacIntyre despite her American origins.

MacIntyre felt that the red ritual-of-Mentju dress and bull-hoof sandals had outlived their usefulness and sent the wrong message about her competence, so she burned them in a trash can behind a barracks. She then joined a complacent Karkin in a Republican Guard chopper, and in a few minutes they were on their way east to Kikyapapli.

Along with the beret, the imy-er-mesh'a provided her with a brevet rank of tjespedjut in the Republican Guard to give her a degree of military standing. This was at Karkin's request. She revised her earlier opinion that Karkin would not be helping her with her career as she adjusted the tilt of the beret in the fly-blown mirror in the women's bathroom. Maybe she'd forgive him after all. Wait and see. Five minutes into the air, she noticed that her headache was gone.

CHAPTER FORTY-THREE
Shesmu Imprisoned

THE PRISON COMPOUND THAT TAHEFNU and I had seen from the forest was even less attractive from the inside. It was temporary, a series of cages made of chain-link fencing with a metal roof over it. Each cage had a cot, a bucket, and a bottle of water. The only upside was the view of the massive granite cliffs and waterfalls. But even a great view gets old after a while, especially if you're cold and hungry.

The NATO troops had surrounded us after we came out of the tomb. Vasha, unsolicited, with me translating into English, advised them to leave the major tied up, and they did. They marched us down to the prison compound and put us into individual cages. They untied the major only when she was securely in her cage. They left five soldiers as guards, one for each of us.

One of the soldiers was the woman guard that we had tied up when we helped Khenmes escape. She had taken against us because of that, or maybe because of her friend, the other guard we had tied up. The Russians had cut off her friend's head. Her antagonism was understandable, but unfortunate. Right after we arrived, I saw her strip off the combat boots from Khenmes's feet after knocking him down with a blow from her rifle. At my shout, another guard hustled over and remonstrated with her. They withdrew and locked the cage with no more damage done. Khenmes got up and sat on his cot and held his head in his hands.

I was the only one of us that spoke English. They had me translate whenever they wanted one of us to do something complicated like hand out a bucket. Our lives were not complex. The American woman guard's nameplate said her name was Dunmore.

"Tell the Indian he gets dinner if he talks and starves if he don't."

I said politely, "We're all natives, Ms. Dunmore. Which one?"

"Fuck you. Him." She pointed to Khenmes. "And it's Specialist Dunmore to you, asshole."

I told Khenmes what Dunmore said. He smiled but said nothing. They came for him fifteen minutes later. They tied his hands behind his back and put a hood on him, then took him to their armored vehicle and drove away.

I tried to get Tahefnu to talk to get her mind off things, but she wasn't interested. Vasha, on the other side of her cage, was a little too far away to conduct any real conversation. He kept doing various exercises to keep himself busy. The major lay on her cot saying nothing whatever, ignoring everything. Lunch, such as it was, came and went. Dunmore spent a lot of time staring at Vasha and the major through the cage wire. They ignored her.

Khenmes came back late in the day, unconscious. Two soldiers carried him from the vehicle that brought him back. They dumped him on his cot. He lay face down, unmoving.

"Get anything from him?" asked Dunmore.

The two soldiers shrugged and got back into their vehicle, turned around, and drove off.

Dunmore stood looking in at Khenmes. "Betcha I could get him talking real quick," she muttered to herself.

"He's an old man," I ventured. She looked over at me with a fierce stare.

"You shut up, you. You pricks are lucky to be alive after what you did."

"I'm aware of that, Specialist Dunmore," I said in a calming voice. "But he's an old man, and I don't think he can take much of that kind of interrogation. And starving him isn't going to help any."

She spat at the ground and went back to staring at Khenmes. Another guard came and pulled her away, saying, "Come on, Beth. Let it go. They'll get theirs."

The baleful brown eyes staring back at me over her shoulder said they'd like that event to happen sooner rather than later.

Khenmes stirred and sat up, shaking his head.

"You OK, Khenmes?" I asked.

"Yeah. These guys aren't what I'd call experts, kept me down a little too long is all."

"Why not just tell them?"

He looked at me with a smile and crinkled his bloodshot eyes. "I figure it's one way to keep us all alive. Once they know what I know, they won't have much reason to do that, other than the threat of a war crime trial. You know?"

"All I know is that you're the only one who can tell me who my father was, what he did. It's going to be hard for that to happen if they kill you, even accidentally."

"Tuy knows, at least part of it."

"Even so," I replied. "I'd as soon have you around to do the telling." I didn't say what I felt: Khenmes meant more to me than my real father. I'd known him longer and I remembered everything he'd done for me as I grew up. I didn't want to lose him too, at least not before his time. I didn't say it, but he knew.

An hour later, Dunmore was back again, standing outside the major's cage this time, staring in at her.

"Why'd you do it, bitch?" Her voice was thick with anger. "Why'd you cut off their heads?"

The major got up and relieved herself into her bucket. This motivated Vasha to use his own bucket. This disrespect infuriated Dunmore even beyond her already high level of rage. She rattled her rifle barrel along the chain links of his cage. Startled, he turned, exposing himself to her, urine splashing out toward her. That put her over the top. She raised the rifle and flipped off the safety.

I threw myself against the cage, shouting at the top of my voice, and climbed up, distracting her. The barrel of the rifle swung around and pointed at me. I dropped off the cage fence to the floor and lay flat, hoping the shots would miss any vital parts. Before she had a chance to erupt, Dunmore's squaddies came running. She held the pose for ten seconds, all of us frozen in a little tableau of terror. Then she flipped the safety back on and lowered her rifle.

"What the hell's wrong with you!" screamed one of her squaddies, grabbing the weapon.

Tears streamed down her face. "They killed her. They fucked her up, stole her boots, then killed her and cut off her head! What the fuck do you think is wrong with me!? What's wrong with you!"

She was screaming by this time, letting off steam. I got up and brushed off some dirt as they led her away.

"Spaciba," said Vasha, his voice a little shaky. "I die for sure." He looked down and put himself back in his pants and zipped up. The major bared her teeth. She wasn't speaking to Vasha.

Dunmore did not reappear, and Khenmes got dinner after all.

CHAPTER FORTY-FOUR

MacIntyre Understands the True Value of Peyotl

THE CHOPPER SET DOWN IN a meadow near the river in Kikyapapli, near the roundhouse. A couple of Miwuk men approached as the chopper's blades powered down. Karkin exchanged a few words with them then came back to the chopper.

He said, "Heh's busy."

MacIntyre looked around in the deep twilight. "This place gives me the creeps. It looms."

"Daylight's better. Dinner's acorn mush."

"Wonderful. Always wondered what acorns tasted like, must be the squirrel in me."

"Might be a crawdad or two in the river."

The Miwuks showed their hospitality by bringing out a good deal of deer and elk meat, which they roasted over a fire. Karkin, using a little raw deer meat, was able to catch 23 crawdads, which he skewered and roasted himself. MacIntyre had to admit they were good, as Karkin insisted on her trying one. She liked the deer meat better, though. More substantial. The Republican Guard soldiers tore through it like starving coyotes. There was plenty of acorn mush to fill in the cracks.

MacIntyre stayed with the Republican Guard team in the building the Miwuks called the cookhouse. In the morning, she turned out to a packaged military meal of freeze-dried scrambled eggs and farro with Remetjy tea. Her new teammates told her that was standard fare for Remetjy forces in the field. As she ate, sitting on a bench outside the building, she watched the sunrise light up the cliffs, waterfalls, and river. She understood what Karkin had promised her the night before: Hetchetci was a wondrous and magical place. An hour or so after sunrise, Karkin came to get her, and they walked over to the roundhouse.

Heh sat in the middle of the building next to the remains of a fire. He rose to greet them, blinking and a little shaky. He smiled a broad smile.

"Not Hutyt MacIntyre?"

MacIntyre, surprised, said, "Cheryl MacIntyre, yes. Do I know you?"

"Shesmu's a good friend, Cheryl!" said the old man, embracing her. "And once my daughter left off trying to seduce him, he told us all about you."

MacIntyre faced a jumble of needs: to find out about Shesmu, to plan how to deal with NATO, and to find out more about Heh's daughter's seductive ways. Before she could articulate any of this, Karkin jumped in.

"Got anything?" he asked.

"Oh, yeah. Complicated plan, needs a lot of careful work to make it all happen. We've gotta get a few more people."

"Some Guard soldiers outside."

Heh smiled. "Damn, things are finally starting to go right. Hasn't been so good since my daughter left with Shesmu."

"Um. Where did they go?" MacIntyre found her voice.

Heh smiled at her. "After he figured out he needed to visit with the spirits of his ancestors, she decided she must guide him there."

"And where is 'there?'"

"The valley you call Ta Sekhet, over the hills that way," said the old man, pointing south. "A three-day hike. Nice place, even if the Remetjy spirits live there. That's what the plan is about, how to deal with the NATO folks taking it over."

She pulled out her phone. "The plan. You'd better hear this," she said. She played Shesmu's voicemail for the old man.

"Well, that's not good," he said. He thought for a little while, then said, "It makes sense though what the Bear told me to do. I couldn't figure out what he was talking about, seemed more complicated than necessary, but now I see. Hummingbird...." The old man's eyes looked into a distance none of the rest of the people in the room could see.

Karkin cleared his throat. Heh blinked and smiled. "Sorry, sometimes I get all wrapped up in my spirit world, especially after a session with the peyotl. At least I don't have too much of the shakes this time. Let's go over the plan."

MacIntyre, sensing all kinds of red flags waving in a very strong wind, asked, "What's peyotl? Who is the Bear? Why a hummingbird?"

Karkin covered his eyes with a hand.

Heh replied, "This is peyotl," holding out a hand with a couple of peyotl buttons. "A kind of cactus. It helps us shamans focus on the spirit world and see what we need to see. Bear is my spirit guide, the animal spirit that guides me through my visions and tells me what to do. Hummingbird is daughter's spirit guide. She's learning to be a shaman." Heh looked a little worried, but MacIntyre felt her own worries were more important.

"So, you're telling me that this plan is the result of an old man's drug-induced hallucinations about talking animals?" MacIntyre smiled cheerfully but didn't mean it.

"And birds. Yep, that's how it works. Don't worry, Cheryl, we'll get you back your boyfriend alive, daughter too." Heh grinned.

Karkin was nodding. MacIntyre rubbed a hand over her mouth to stop from saying something she'd regret. She adjusted her snazzy beret. She said to Karkin, "Can I talk with you a minute? Outside." She smiled at Heh. "We'll just be a minute, then we can hear the plan, OK?"

"Sure. We got the whole day to do it. Can't do anything until tonight anyway."

She grabbed Karkin's arm and pulled him outside the roundhouse.

She hissed, "You're not proposing to undertake a military operation created by a phantom bear talking to a drug-addled old man!"

"Yep."

"*Karkin.*"

"Easy. Heh's all right." Karkin looked up at the granite cliffs, mouth pursed, then looked at MacIntyre with sharp eyes. "He's connected."

"Connected? To what, spirit animals?" Her eyes were angry in the early morning light.

"Miwuks." Karkin paused and pursed his lips. MacIntyre waited until he finally delivered the goods, becoming voluble for once. "Look, you know that the Miwuks joined up with you Remetjet way back before the earthquake a hundred years ago. They had an understanding they'd have some political autonomy. *My* people didn't have that much choice, but there were a lot more Miwuks than Ramaytush, and that's the way it worked out. Now, Miwuks aren't more stupid than anybody else. They know about corrupt politicians and about Remetjy history. So, as a hypothetical situation, imagine that the Miwuks created a secret organization that operates throughout their territory in the Republic. Imagine that this organization gathers information and works with outside entities like my international security group to make sure nothing bad happens."

"Hypothetical?"

"Hypothetical. Heh's all right."

"So, you're telling me to sit down and shut up. Hypothetically."

Karkin nodded.

MacIntyre said, smiling, "I don't think I've ever heard you talk so much."

"Still haven't, I haven't been talking at all for the last five minutes. You've figured all this out on your own, maybe Ma'at told you. Keep it to yourself." Karkin's little mustache bristled with unexpressed emotion.

"Huh. All right, I'll listen, but if the thing is completely crazy, I'm not going along."

"Fair enough."

The pair went back into the roundhouse to find Heh sitting down again by the remains of the fire. He looked up at MacIntyre and shook his feathered headband. "Don't be nervous, Cheryl. Look, the whole peyotl vision thing is a lot like the dreams you had about Ma'at and Mentju and Seteh."

Startled, MacIntyre said, "How do you know about that?"

"Saw 'em in the spirit world, didn't know it was you until I saw you, though. Weird. Bad stuff for you, huh? That kind of thing can lead to PTSD, you know. Ma'at seems kind of tough to me, heartless. But if she's your goddess, she's your goddess, Cheryl. That Seteh, now, he's part Coyote, tricky sumbitch, you know? He's the random element in all this, the thing that could make it all go south in a minute. Bear can't see past him. Mentju seems a lot more straightforward but a little bloodthirsty. Sorry about the bull sacrifice thing, nasty. You oughta see somebody about possible PTSD, you know?"

MacIntyre turned to Karkin. "You told him."

Karkin said, "Nope."

Heh slapped his head, knocking the feather headdress he wore askew. "Sorry, doing it again. I must be getting senile, keep getting distracted. The spirit world is way too close to the real one here in Hetchetci. Kinda pulls me away from things in the physical world all the time."

MacIntyre thought the peyotl might have something to do with that. Given her own hallucinatory experiences with Ma'at, and given hypothetical secret organizations, it might be time to grasp the spiritual and let go of the physical. Hypothetically.

"Seize the god," the Remetjy proverb went, "and make the most of it." She had a god by the tail and was hanging on for dear life. PTSD wasn't in the same league. Her mind spun away to question how "spiritual" Heh's daughter's guidance of Shesmu was, and to ask where they were right now, and to imagine what they were doing. Spiritual, huh? She'd show him spiritual all right. Once she'd rescued him. If he was still alive. And once she'd gotten rid of Heh's daughter. Oh, and defeated NATO. And Setehnekhet. Definitely Setehnekhet. That had to come first.

It took three hours of Heh and Karkin arguing with MacIntyre to convince her that the plan had any chance of working. She refused to try the peyotl, much to Heh's chagrin. By mid-day, when they broke for lunch, their thoughts turned to practical details.

The biggest issue was the Republican Guard squad's mountaineering abilities. They weren't special forces troops. They spent all their days guarding tombs, mummies, and gold artifacts, which doesn't call for much action unless the mummies got active. According to the hutyt in charge of the squad, so far that hadn't happened. The squad had no experience on a mountain, despite having lived in a cliff-lined valley for years.

"When you got acorns, you make mush," said Heh.

MacIntyre rolled her eyes, but she'd make it work. It had to. If it didn't, they might as well cut each other's throats in a group sacrifice to Mentju. The bark-walled Miwuk roundhouse closed in on MacIntyre. She imagined the bark being on trees, and the trees weighing down on her. The ever-present aromas of wood fire and unfamiliar herbs, along with the queasy feeling she had about the plan and its peyotl-driven origins, made her nauseous.

She excused herself and went outside and wandered down to the river. She breathed the fresh air, felt the rushing water, and took in the massive mountain cliffs around her. What a place, she thought. She'd grown up exploring the Maine woodlands and islands, but that beauty paled compared to Hetchetci. Her city, Menmenet, was beautiful too, brown hills rising through fog, bay shining in the summer sun as the fog burned off. But nothing like this.

A swelling growl from down the valley intruded on her senses. She turned back toward the roundhouse and saw, coming up the road from the foothills, a line of pickup trucks. Shit, what now? She ran back to the roundhouse and breathlessly informed Karkin and Heh. They all scrambled outside to see what was what.

The line of trucks came to a halt next to the roundhouse. A small, shriveled, coppery-faced man alighted from the lead truck, helped down by a man in a combat military uniform. MacIntyre didn't know the symbol on his arm patch. The small man looked around, and his eyes lighted on Heh. He smiled, a big-toothed grin. He came right up to Heh, embraced him, and said something in a language MacIntyre did not understand. Heh smiled a huge smile as well and clapped the man on the back. He turned to MacIntyre.

"This here is the Waashiw demomili from Da'owaga'a. Big-time shaman. The boss doc. That man over there," he said, pointing to a man getting out of the second pickup in line, "is the sergeant who brought Shesmu here. These are Waashiw Rangers. Solves most of our problems." Heh introduced Karkin and MacIntyre to the Waashiw leaders.

There were thirty well-armed men in all in the trucks. Several of the men unloaded enough mountaineering equipment to start a climbing school and piled it up near the roundhouse. The sergeant said, grinning, "The boss doc wants it, he's got it, so we brought it."

Heh gathered the leaders in the roundhouse to work the Rangers into the plan. The enthusiastic demomili approved the plan, and the sergeant got a faraway look on his square, coppery face as he worked out the details. Over lunch, MacIntyre got acquainted with the sergeant, who was her kind of soldier. On finding out who she was, he grinned again and said, "Shesmu's got good taste in things besides Remetjy food!" He told her the story of the black site and Shesmu's unfortunate overconfidence in his rock climbing ability. After their joint laughter had subsided, she played him the voicemail. The sergeant's face showed determination as he absorbed the implications.

"We'll get him out, ma'am," he said. "And his friends. I like Shesmu, he's OK. Game for wahtever comes. Just overconfident. We'll get him out."

"Shes has always been lucky," replied MacIntyre. "This time he'll need luck."

The demomili came over and said something to the sergeant. He smiled.

"Boss doc says Shesmu plays with the gods, so he'll be fine," he said. "Boss doc ain't wrong much, you know? Especially about gods."

MacIntyre smiled. Maybe the plan stood a chance of working if the gods were on their side. She wondered which gods, and what those gods would extract in return.

CHAPTER FORTY-FIVE

Shesmu Gets a Gift From His Father

I AWOKE ON THE SECOND day in the prison compound to the sound of voices and rattling locks. I twisted around on my cot and saw several soldiers take Khenmes and Vasha out of their cages in ties and hoods. Tahefnu stood at the side of her cage, the one next to mine, looking at them, her eyes huge and her jaw clenched. I rolled out of my cot and stood up, but there was nothing I could do.

I spent the morning sitting on my cot, depressed into immobility. The sun was at its zenith, the heat intense, when Khenmes and Vasha returned. Soldiers carried them into their cages and dumped them on the dirt, then removed their ties and hoods.

Khenmes dragged himself up onto his cot and sat holding his head in his hands. I called to him, "What did they do? What did they ask? Khenmes?"

He looked over at me. "Same old shit. They want to learn what I know."

"I need to know it too, Khenmes," I said.

"No, you don't, Shes. You'd wind up like me, with a lot of water up your nose." He hawked and spat to illustrate.

"Vasha," I called. "What did they ask you?"

He coughed and spat off the edge of his cot. "All kinds bullshit. Why we come, why why why."

"What did you tell them?"

"Truth."

"Which was?"

"Killing soldiers."

"But why?"

He wiped his mouth with the back of his sleeve. "Because Major Suvorova order. Not believe me."

I didn't believe him either. It didn't matter, because we weren't going anywhere.

Dunmore had come back as a guard and walked over, rifle at her side. "Shut the fuck up, you shitheads! I don't want to hear any more of your goddam gibberish. If you wanna talk, talk to us and only to us. Get it?" All in furious American English. She banged on my cage with her hand to emphasize her request.

The major said something in Russian. Vasha grinned from his cot.

"What did you say?" asked Dunmore, turning toward her.

It turned out I was not the only one of us who spoke English. The major replied in that language, "I said your mother plays the balalaika in the brothel in which she raised and sold you to gypsy pimps."

I conveyed the gist of this to my fellows, and we fell silent.

Dunmore, whose face had turned an unhealthy shade of purple, walked over to a storage locker. She rummaged and brought out her prize: one of the Spetsnaz MPL-50 tools. She walked back to the major's cage. The major had advanced close to the cage and looked out at her, smiling.

Dunmore waved the tool, then banged it hard against the cage near the major's face. The major never moved. Dunmore shouted, "Is this what you used? To cut off their heads. Is this it?"

The major smiled. She drew a finger deliberately across her own throat. Then she spit.

"Matoskah!" called Dunmore. Another NATO soldier, this one a First Peoples man, came over.

"Cover me," said Dunmore.

"What—"

"I'm going in."

"Specialist, I don't—"

She swung around to him. "Get your ass over there by the cage gate and shut the fuck up! Goddam Indians. Goddamn Russians."

She marched over to the gate and unlocked it and swung it wide, then hefted the tool like the ax it was. The major walked toward her and Dunmore lifted the tool. The major stepped sideways in a blur of speed, punching Dunmore and grabbing the tool from her in one fluid motion. Dunmore fell backward. The other NATO soldier rushed in, raising his rifle, and the major swung the tool backhanded and took off his head while stepping out of the cage. Momentum carried the body into the cage where it fell over the scrambling Dunmore, spraying blood all over the cage and Dunmore. The major walked toward the locker. Dunmore was up, holding her rifle. As the major reached for the locker door handle, Dunmore screamed, "Freeze! Freeze!"

Major Suvorova turned and swung her arm up and threw the tool, her face a mask of hate. At the same time, Dunmore blasted a full magazine of automatic rifle bullets into the major's body. It spoiled the major's aim, and the tool hit the cage near Dunmore. The other guards came running. The major's body, slammed against the locker by the force of the bullets, collapsed on the ground in a bloody mess.

"Trying to escape," said Dunmore, lowering her rifle.

In late afternoon, Tahefnu woke up from a nap with a startled expression on her face. She rolled off her cot and walked around her cage.

I was lying on my cot, hands behind my head, thinking about death. I thought about my father and his death. I thought about the major and her death. I even thought about Tahefnu and her death. The last one would be my fault, as I'd gotten her into this.

"What's up, Tahefnu?" I asked in a quiet voice, walking over to her cage.

She came over to the side of the cage that separated us. She gazed in at me with her enormous eyes.

"It's Hummingbird," she said.

"What about Hummingbird?" I asked.

"She's here again, in me. She's scared to death, that's why she went away, and that's why she's waited so long to return to me."

"How do you feel?"

"Happy she's back, but…"

"Don't worry yourself about dying, we won't die."

"It's not that. She wants you."

"Tahefnu…."

"OK, I want you too, but this is business."

"Business. You mean, spirit business."

"Yep. Honest."

The guards sat out of easy earshot. Dunmore had disappeared after the incident with the major, as had the major's body and that of the soldier she'd decapitated. "What does Hummingbird want?"

She sat down and crossed her legs. "Sit," she said. I sat.

"Touch my finger." She stretched her forefinger through the cage. I reached up with mine and touched it, tip to tip.

My memory of earlier visions was of a frightening deep and icy blackness that made my bones ache. This blackness was warm and welcoming. My feet were on solid earth, and I could walk. I found one direction warmer and brighter, so I walked toward it. I saw a light growing larger and larger.

A man held the light in cupped hands so it shone up and illuminated his face. It was the Miwuk man I had seen in Kikyapapli in my vision. This time he didn't wear Miwuk shaman regalia, he wore regular Miwuk clothes. He wore the distant smile of a god. "Shesmu."

"Dad? Akhen?" I asked.

"Yes, Shesmu. This time, we can talk. The great god Seteh no longer interferes, he no longer cares whether you live or die. Before, he prevented me from speaking, he made himself Coyote. Now I may speak for myself."

"I was very sad when you died. So was Mom."

The ageless, smiling face did not change. He replied, "Gods have little sense of human suffering, Shesmu. I have been too long a god to concern myself with human emotions, and I have lost my heart to the judgment of Ma'at. My Miwuk side can guide you, but I cannot love, and I cannot atone for my life."

"Great."

"I come to show you your gift, Shesmu. You must understand who you are."

"I have no idea who I am!" I shouted this, though the sound vanished into the blackness without effect on my father. My anger came from a place I'd suppressed and from the knowledge I'd recently gained. The layers of emotional scabbing peeled off as I faced the father I had never known.

He said, "You are two halves of a whole. You are the joining of many colors of life, making a pattern of balance in the world."

I dismissed this as the usual Miwuk spiritual gibberish, which I suppose was not very filial of me. Not having had much experience with gods, or fathers, this was all new to me.

"Is this all part of the Miwuk spirit dance stuff? Because I don't need metaphors, I need factual information. I need a father. Why did you die? Why did you leave Mom and me? Why are you a god? Why am I here in this cage talking to you?"

"I am here for one purpose, Shesmu," said the god, looking at me without compassion. "To tell you what you must know to restore balance to the world. To counter Seteh and his utter chaos. To help those you love onto the right path.

You have heard the truth from a Miwuk spirit and a Remetjy god. Learn it, touch it, use it." With what little compassion remained from his human past, he explained, "I am a god, Shesmu, but 'Ammet has taken my heart. I cannot do more."

"Shesmu," said a woman's resonant voice behind me.

There stood Ma'at, wings furled in front of her and a determined look on her face. My father had vanished; only the blackness remained.

"Damn it!" I exclaimed, turning to Ma'at. "Bring him back!"

"No."

Ma'at shone with her own light, her long black hair shining with it. I figured that stamping my foot and insisting wasn't going to work. "What is this all about? Why are you here?"

"Balance, ma'at. I am here to make you understand what you must do."

"I'm standing in a cage, surrounded by people who want to kill me. I can't do a damn thing!"

"You always have dominion over yourself, Shesmu." Ma'at lifted the staff she held, a w'as scepter of dominion that all gods held. "Take it. Find your path. Find your father and yourself. You must choose and choose well. Take the path to restore my balance to the world, or take the path to the judgment of my feather in the Duat. Remember, my judgment may end in the devouring of your heart by 'Ammet. Or refuse the w'as scepter's dominion and face judgment now." The goddess held the staff out to me, her stare piercing my heart to its core, her eyes two flames of truth. I averted my gaze from those blazing eyes; truth can be very hard to accept.

I reached out and took the staff, and it was Heh's walking stick.

I felt the heat of the day and the brightness of R'a. I blinked; Tahefnu was sitting in front of me again, looking down.

"She's gone again. Hummingbird's gone. This time for good, at least that's what my heart says."

"I'm sorry."

"Don't be; it's my choice. I can't be a shaman, I can't live out my life in the old ways anymore. I must find a different path now." She wiped a tear away and tried to smile. She asked, "What happened, Shesmu? Why are you holding Dad's walking stick?"

Had the stick been with me in the cage? I couldn't remember. "I had a one-way conversation with my father the Miwuk spirit god. Then Ma'at helicoptered in to give me motherly advice. She gave me the stick. I can't make any sense out of it." At least my visit with my father hadn't crippled me as my other visions had.

"My dad always says the spirits can be difficult to understand, like mexcalli drunks on a week's bender. They sound like they're saying something profound, but the words don't make any sense." She grinned at me, her mood lightening. "But it usually means you've screwed something up. Otherwise you wouldn't be talking to the spirits. And you'd better hide that stick before the guards see you with it."

I hid the stick under the thin mattress on my cot. Dominion over myself. What I needed to do was to figure out who I was—and get out of this cage.

CHAPTER FORTY-SIX

MacIntyre to the Rescue

THE DEMOMILI, AS RANKING CIVILIAN leader, put MacIntyre in charge of operations as the ranking military officer. As the sergeant translated this with a smile, MacIntyre's queasiness increased.

"What the fuck. I'm a hutyt-er-semetyu, not a seasoned field marshal. I'm only a tjespedjut because Basa liked my bull-hoof shoes."

The demomili didn't wait for the sergeant to translate this insightful analysis of her capabilities. The sergeant smiled again and translated the demomili's decisive response. "Boss doc says you're it, so you're it. Don't worry, ma'am, gods say you'll do fine."

MacIntyre shook her head. She would seize the god and chalk it up to inspired leadership by the demomili. She was in the middle of events moving so fast that she didn't have time to doubt her ability to handle it all. But her career was on track now. Until she screwed up again. Compartmentalize, Cheryl, compartmentalize.

The Waashiw Rangers loaded the mountaineering equipment into the Republican Guard chopper. The sergeant put together a squad of four of his best mountain-trained men for the rescue operation. He added four more for the base team that would stay with the chopper and back them up. They armed themselves with both bows and assault rifles. MacIntyre took a rifle but refused a bow, saying that she'd just strangle herself with it. While Karkin and the demomili stayed behind to organize the second part of the operation, Heh came along on the chopper as navigator. The demomili said he was too old to be climbing mountains.

MacIntyre shouted to Heh as the pilot fired up the rotors, "I hope your navigation doesn't depend on peyotl or spirit bears."

Heh smiled and said, "I use the stars." As it was broad daylight, this did not reassure MacIntyre.

The chopper flew low over the forest toward the south. Heh guided the pilot to a burned-out meadow about five kilometers from the edge of the valley, and the chopper landed to disgorge the soldiers and equipment. Heh stayed with the pilot to await their return. MacIntyre and the Waashiw teams force-marched for an hour to the top of the huge granite cliff that dominated the middle of Ta Sekhet.

MacIntyre borrowed the sergeant's high-quality binoculars and lay prone at the top of the cliff. The panorama of the valley spread out below her. It took her breath away, both because of the beauty and because heights were not her thing. MacIntyre could control the tiny frogs jumping around in her stomach as long as she didn't look straight down. She scanned the various parts she could see of the valley and identified the main post toward the eastern part of the valley. There was nothing there that looked like a prison compound, only barracks and offices.

The sergeant said, "How about that structure down there by the river? What's that?"

MacIntyre focused the binocs on the sliver of shiny metal. She realized it was a galvanized roof that covered a fenced compound.

"I'll bet that's it," she said. She watched for a while and saw several guards patrolling outside the perimeter of the fence. A road stretched from the compound to the main post, crossing the river with a bridge. A vehicle crossed the bridge and drove down to the fence. Several men got out and extracted two other people from the back of the vehicle. Both prisoners had their hands tied behind them and wore black bags over their heads.

"Yep, that's it. Two prisoners delivered." The guards led the two prisoners inside the fence and under the roof. "Sergeant, how do we get past the guards?"

"The usual way, ma'am."

MacIntyre returned his binoculars. "We walk up and ask them nicely to give us their prisoners?"

"No, ma'am."

MacIntyre sighed and pushed away the decision. "We'll see on the ground."

The sergeant smiled. "I'll rappel down with the team, and you can coordinate the base team here while we're rappelling. Then you can get everyone back to the chopper to wait for us."

"Not a chance. I'm going down with you."

"You don't know what you're doing, ma'am. No offense."

"Never stopped me before. Just show me the ropes."

"And you don't like heights." Her body language must be an open book.

"I don't like *anything* that gets in my way, but I don't pay much attention to stuff like that either. I like you, Sergeant, and I'm paying attention to you. For now. Just show me the ropes," she repeated.

As they had plenty of ropes, and because it was easier than stopping MacIntyre from coming with the rescue team, they showed her the ropes, the mini-rappel racks, and the various knots she'd need to know. They rigged up an autoblock above the rack device on her climbing harness and showed her how to use it. The sergeant applied makeup to her face and gave her a thin, black balaclava to conceal her hair.

"It'll keep your hair out of the belay ropes, too, ma'am."

She was sure this look would not become fashionable in Menmenet, but it was right for the moment.

By the time the squad scouted the best descent routes, hammered in expansion bolts, set up anchoring systems, and figured out the equipment they'd need for the descent, it was dark. They all sat together and ate supper and got ready for action, as R'a disappeared in the western akhet.

The team went down the cliff in three stages, belaying MacIntyre through each stage. By the end of the third stage, MacIntyre dripped with sweat, even though the night had turned bitterly cold after sunset. She felt infinite relief as hands gripped her legs to lower her to the ground. The whole descent took about an hour and a half. The team removed their climbing harnesses and geared up for the rescue operation. They moved out toward the prison compound.

Two hours and a wet river fording later, MacIntyre lay prone again, this time under a bush about 100 meters away from the prison compound. Bright floodlights mounted on the perimeter fence lit the compound. The Rangers got as close as they could without the guards seeing them. The sergeant lay prone next to her, and they waited.

After another hour, the sergeant held up five fingers. He got five fingers in response from each of his team members. MacIntyre counted the five guards along with the sergeant, and no more guards appeared. The five were on patrol at different points outside the compound. Something moved in the compound. What the fuck? She could see, in the bright lights, that one prisoner, a blond man she didn't recognize, was doing pushups. Must be a Russian, she thought to herself, the one Shes had mentioned in his voicemail. The other prisoners huddled under blankets, and she couldn't make out which was which, but there were four of them, one fewer than Shes had said in his voicemail. Somebody missing? A guard stopped at the Russian, spat, and moved on.

The sergeant raised himself to a kneeling position and took up his bow, a complicated black thing with pulleys and sights. He signaled the question at MacIntyre: do they go ahead? She nodded. She wanted to avoid killing, but she had no choice, as there were too many guards and they were too vigilant and well armed.

The sergeant checked his watch and signaled a time to his team and sent them to their positions. He nocked a black arrow and waited, checking his watch. He pulled, aimed, and at a specific moment, released. The five guards collapsed all at once. One, a woman, crawled toward a dropped rifle. A dark figure shot out of the night, kneeled down with one knee on the back of the woman, and did something. The crawling woman jerked and stilled. None of the other guards stirred.

The other three Waashiw Rangers emerged from hiding. Nothing moved except the man doing pushups. He'd heard nothing and kept going until he sensed the soldiers moving. He bounced to his feet and came to the side of his cage. His fingers curled through the fence and gripped, but he stayed silent. The other prisoners didn't stir.

MacIntyre and the Rangers inspected the bodies lying outside the compound fence; all dead. The sergeant made a sign to the blond-haired man to stay silent. He got out a set of bolt cutters from his pack. In less than a minute, he was inside the perimeter. MacIntyre walked over to the compound, stepping over the body of the female guard and its pool of blood, and pushed through the cut in the fence. Besides the blond Russian, she saw a small indigenous woman, a large indigenous man, and what looked an awful lot like the back of Shesmu's head. She pointed at his cage with a jabbing finger, and the sergeant cut it open. She walked inside.

MacIntyre touched his shoulder. He jerked awake and peered up at her, eyes huge. She removed her balaclava and shook out her hair.

"Oh, fuck. Another dream," he mumbled.

"Not this time," she whispered, and grinned.

CHAPTER FORTY-SEVEN
MacIntyre Catches Up with Shesmu

THE RANGERS FOUND THE PRISONERS'S belongings in a storage locker. They also found three Russian VSS sniper rifles and ammunition for them. Shesmu explained that these came from the wiped-out Spetsnaz unit. Its only remaining member, Vasha, gazed wistfully at his rifle, but the sergeant decided against giving it to him for the present. Vasha accepted this with only a twitch of an objection.

Shes inspected the NATO bodies. He returned with a pair of boots for his friend Khenmes; he told MacIntyre they were from the dead female NATO guard, the only pair from the dead guards that would fit him. Shes looked ill, which she understood when she in turn checked out the NATO woman soldier's body. An arrow in the chest, throat cut, and a pool of blood spread around her head. The soldier's bare feet diminished her somehow. MacIntyre felt sick herself, despite her recent training in blood management at the Temple of Mentju and the many bloody crime scenes she'd investigated.

She asked, "What about the other Russian? You said there were two."

Shes grimaced and rubbed his forehead. "Don't worry about that one. She's… dead. Tell you about it later."

An hour later, MacIntyre stood on the trail about halfway up the cliff, looking at the huge waterfall.

"What a romantic place!" she exclaimed to Shes as they hugged each other. Heh's daughter glared at them, arms crossed.

Shes, aware of every emotional tic and nuance around him, moved uneasily in MacIntyre's embrace. He whispered in her ear, a smile in his voice. "Romance is relative, lover. We need to catch up, once we're back in the Miwuk village, OK?

I'll tell you all about Tahefnu and everything that's happened." She hugged him, then they released each other.

Heh's daughter lifted the corners of her mouth and said, "Sweet."

MacIntyre ratcheted up her instinctive response. "What was your name again?"

Tahefnu ignored this and asked the sergeant, "Where is this chopper?"

The sergeant pulled out his GPS and located the meadow about 5 kilometers away.

"As the crow flies, anyhow," he said.

"We're not crows," scoffed Tahefnu. "At least 8 or 9 kilometers from the top of the cliff. You go around that big peak there," she pointed, "then down a trail and across. I know that meadow, nice until all the surrounding trees burned down two years ago. Lightning."

"That's the place," agreed the sergeant.

Tahefnu said, "We should move on, those guys down in the valley are going to be coming after us. It's nearly daylight. Does anybody need more rest?" She regarded MacIntyre.

"No," said MacIntyre, "we're all rested up now, thanks. You?"

MacIntyre kept Shes and Khenmes company as they lagged behind on the tough hike up the cliff. They filled her in on the events in the tomb chapel and the prison compound. Khenmes remained reticent about his secrets. "There'll be a good time and place, but not here and now," he said. He was a tough old bird, his broad First Peoples' face stoic.

Shesmu asked him, "We're going to lose phone service soon. Do you want to call Tuy and let her know you're alive and well? She worries."

Khenmes mulled this over for a few minutes, then replied, "Shes, I'm gonna hold off. Wife's OK, she knows I'm as alive as I should be, spirits will tell her. She'll worry more if I tell her what's gonna happen. No guarantees over the next few days. Maybe I'll wait until I tell you what you need to know, then it'll be over for me and I can relax and wife can too. Not now."

Tahefnu set a fast pace up the last part of the cliff trail. MacIntyre had to rein her in from time to time when she and the Waashiw Rangers strayed too far ahead. MacIntyre reminded Tahefnu that she, MacIntyre, was in charge of the expedition. This assertion of dominant status in the baboon troop did not improve the relationship between the two women. Nor was it completely successful. The sergeant was inscrutable.

After a while, Tahefnu took pity on Shes's damaged ankle. MacIntyre acknowledged to herself that Tahefnu was the strongest hiker in the group. She was also the only one of them who knew where they were going. Even Khenmes the tough old bird sighed in relief at the rest stops. MacIntyre heard him mutter under his breath, "Surly." Tahefnu's mood improved with exercise, though she did not in MacIntyre's opinion show quite enough deference and respect to her leader.

MacIntyre said to Shes, "Is she humming, for God's sake?" He smiled and nodded, but put a finger to his lips, asking her to wait for an explanation. He would have much explaining to do.

Another couple of hours of hiking guided by Tahefnu took them around the big hill to the meadow, and there was the chopper. Heh jumped out and enfolded his daughter. MacIntyre went into a clinch with Shes. The impatient Waashiw sergeant broke it all up and made them all climb into the chopper.

"We got things to do, people, let's move," he complained.

The chopper flew into Kikyapapli in a few quick minutes and set down in the meadow next to the roundhouse. MacIntyre sighed as her feet hit the ground. The first part of Heh's operation done, she now faced the decision about the second part of the plan to defeat NATO. But first, the important task: getting Shes to explain himself.

CHAPTER FORTY-EIGHT

Shesmu Caters a Party

MY FEET HIT THE GROUND right behind MacIntyre, and Khenmes followed. The demomili was on hand to greet us, but most of his attention focused on Khenmes, his fellow countryman. The folds of his face settled into something like a grin as he found Khenmes hale and hearty.

Karkin and Heh jumped down and stood talking with MacIntyre, and the demomili joined them. The Waashiw rangers headed for the showers to wash the killing off, and Khenmes walked after them. Heh and Tahefnu walked off to their house to catch up.

As they all drifted away, I stood next to the chopper leaning on the walking stick. MacIntyre came over and hugged me.

I said, "Cheryl, why don't we take a walk, say up the river. Nice day, good company, and we have a shitload of things I need to work through."

She released me and stepped back. "How romantic! Do I get to have a say too, or is this a one-way thing?"

"We can do whatever you wish." I took in the set of her mouth and the look in her eye, as much as I could see of it through the black makeup she still wore. The military uniform suited both her and her mood: starched and cool. My own clothes were disheveled and sweat stained from my adventures.

"Cheryl, you have no idea how much I've missed you, or how much I have regretted leaving you mad at me. I'm sorry I couldn't respond to your voicemails, things spun out of control, you'll hear all about that. I love you more than I can say, but I need to talk."

MacIntyre retired to the cookhouse bathroom to wash off her makeup. She joined me with a smile. We hiked through the magnificent valley, up the river, telling our stories to each other. Told as a complete narrative, hers made a terrific thriller, all the way through rappelling down the granite cliff to rescue me.

I enjoy a thriller as much as the next man, but thoughts kept forcing themselves into my heart. This is MacIntyre raped. This is MacIntyre sacrificed on a hetep as a bull. This is MacIntyre tumbling down a cliff. The stuff of nightmares, but she escaped these fates.

I told her about everything: Tuy, the demomili, the visions, the black site, the Miwuks, Tahefnu and Hummingbird and her offer of marriage.

"If she tries seducing you again, let me know and I'll kill her," said MacIntyre.

"She won't, that's settled. But I'd be careful, she's not as easy to overcome as she looks."

"Neither am I." MacIntyre ambled along, looking at the whitewater in the river. "Sounds as though she's a powerful woman, though, and there aren't enough of those, Miwuk or Remetjy. So, OK—I'll befriend her rather than kill her."

I said, "Good. She's a little sister to me."

MacIntyre smiled her smallest smile. I continued with my story: Major Suvorova and the Spetsnaz, the tomb firefight, our surrender, the interrogations, Dunmore and the major.

She said, "There was a woman guard at the compound; she was the one that took an arrow but survived it. The one with her throat cut."

"Yes. That was Dunmore. She didn't like us very much, especially the major and Vasha, but Khenmes and Tahefnu took some heat from her as well." The nausea returned. Dunmore…was not a pretty memory for me. Nor was Major Suvorova.

"You have to be strong to be a woman in the Army," said MacIntyre. "Too bad for her: wrong place, wrong time, wrong mission. Powerful women; Americans have moved a long way in that direction. That Russian major was strong, and your friend Tahefnu is too."

I considered her and her own strength for a few minutes, then said, "Do you want to talk about the sacrifice? Wearing a bull suit." I didn't tell her I kept seeing Dunmore with her throat cut every time I thought about this almost-sacrifice.

MacIntyre raised her eyes to the mountains surrounding us. "It's hard to imagine all that now, looking at this scenery surrounding us, smelling the pine needles, listening to the rushing river water, walking hand-in-hand like lovers."

"Not *like* lovers."

We settled on a nice, mossy riverbank and managed not to slip into the river while catching up on our sex life. After, we turned around and drifted toward the roundhouse. The surrounding beauty silenced me for a while. A little breeze came up, cooling us after our exertions.

"How do you feel about being half Miwuk?" Her voice cut through my euphoria like a knife.

I could only reply with humor. "I have mixed feelings...."

"Ha, ha."

She deserved to know; it was a serious question. I told her about the Tahefnu-aided vision of my father I'd had in the prison compound. "My father the god said it's my gift to combine differences. My being half Remetj and half Miwuk is a part of that, it gives me access to both communities. I need to learn my new inheritance. I'll work on bringing the two cultures closer together. And...there's more, Khenmes knows it but won't tell me."

MacIntyre stayed quiet for a time, then said, "That leaves me out. Tahefnu has more influence with you than I do. Are you talking about bringing cultures together or people—like you and Tahefnu? Is that jealousy?"

"Don't be jealous. Besides, you're American."

"So what? Are *you* against Americans now?"

"No, and that's the point. I realized that you're part of my gift too, I can go beyond bringing Remetj and Miwuk together. If we get this NATO thing resolved, I'll start on bringing us all together."

"I can help with that." A long kiss followed. The euphoria resurfaced. We resumed our walk.

"I can't see how to do it, though," I said. "I don't know enough. What did my father do? How did he stop the Secret War with the Americans? Why is he a god? Why did he die when he did?"

"How will you figure all that out?" She was noncommittal.

"Only one way: I need to return to the tomb, with Khenmes, when he's in a more talkative mood."

"That might be difficult as long as NATO is there. They've got it in for you now."

"No shit."

"We have a plan."

"Thought you might. The sergeant had a look in his eye when he was talking about a conference later. And Heh had a sappy grin on his face, even given getting his daughter back."

"You'll love it. Ever heard of peyotl?"

I groaned. "We're fucked." In so many ways. I looked at MacIntyre with some horror. "Did you…?"

She shook her head. "Not a chance. But according to Heh's peyotl visions, Ta Sekhet ought to be in Remetjy hands in a day or two, so getting to your father's tomb ought to be possible, unless…."

"Unless what?"

"What side of the valley is it on?"

"South side, up from the prison compound, to the east."

"That should be OK, then."

"Part of the plan?"

"Yep, you'll see."

We arose and headed on. My euphoria dissipated with the thoughts about this plan and its inevitable dangers and horrors. Peyotl.

I said, "Cheryl, I have to tell you that your story…it gives me a huge, hollow feeling in my stomach, worrying about you. I'll have nightmares for weeks about bodies and bulls and rapists and cut throats. I did eat some peyotl. You should be in your normal job, running around catching murderers in perfect safety. Will that happen soon? Will this plan put you in even more danger?"

"I'll be a bystander for this part of it, now that you're here and not under threat," she replied.

I searched her face, which was not smiling but thoughtful. "But?"

"My job. I'm sure I can get the medjau to reinstate me when it's all over. My career is taking interesting turns lately."

"Tahefnu might help define that," I said, thinking about Hummingbird and peyotl.

"I can figure this out on my own," MacIntyre replied acerbically.

"Peyotl—"

"Heh tells me it can solve all my problems too. My American skull is too small to expand my brain that much, Shes. The fucking tea from Bastet—you remember I told you about that—that fucking tea nearly killed me. You're welcome to your visions, and I'm here with a shoulder to cry on. But fuck, I do not need any more visions of Ma'at or any of the other idiot gods."

"You're an American heathen."

"That's as may be. But it's a fact that I do not admire many of your gods."

"But you're a w'abet of Ma'at."

"And of Mentju, let's not forget Mentju. I won't forget Mentju in a hurry."

"But…"

"I'm not religious, despite it all. These gods are what we use to fool ourselves into doing what our subconscious brains expect us to do. My subconscious is fine with Ma'at, but it's my own sense of ma'at, not religious fervor."

"I understand." I twisted my mouth with the irony of it. "But me…"

She filled it in. "You *are* religious."

"Let's say more than I was. A lot more. I won't spend all my time in temples, but I'll pay more attention to what gods say to me. And magic sticks." I hefted the walking stick, which had gone quiet since we left Ta Sekhet behind.

"I can deal with that. As long as it isn't Mentju making love to me, OK?" She was again acerbic.

"Guaranteed."

"Well, then. I have to do something else, something more direct, something for the Republic, not for Ma'at or Menmenet. I haven't figured out what. But what I know is that I need to finish what I started. I need to end this coup. I need to stop the Americans and the Numunuu from taking over. I need to deal with Setehnekhet. The battle tomorrow will be a small part of that, but I can't back down now. And I'm sure my future will continue along that path."

"And that will return you to Menmenet and danger."

"Once we've dealt with NATO, yes. I'm sorry, Shes. Can you cope with all that worry about me? Because I need you around me to keep me alive."

"I'll cope. We've done well at keeping each other alive so far, I'll do whatever I can."

We approached the roundhouse and embraced and kissed; MacIntyre headed off to the showers, and I went looking for Tahefnu to see about lunch. It was all very well to talk the big talk, but people need to eat, and I could help with that.

As I approached Heh's small house, I heard a rumble. I saw a large chopper swoop down and drop soldiers onto the meadow. It departed in a hurry, and the soldiers advanced toward us.

The Waashiw Rangers and the Republican Guard squad scrambled out to confront the soldiers. Rifles pointed from both sides. Vasha jumped out and said something in Russian with his hands raised.

The soldiers lowered their weapons, and an officer stepped forward. Compared to Major Suvorova, whom I pictured as an athletic lioness, he was more of an angry rhinoceros. Vasha spoke with him for a while. Heh and Karkin walked over and joined them.

Tahefnu joined me. MacIntyre, Khenmes, and the demomili appeared from the cookhouse and came over. The demomili joined the group of conferees. We all watched as they conferred, then the officer embraced Vasha, slapped his back, and signaled to his soldiers. They slung their weapons over their backs and moved forward. The Waashiw did the same.

I told Tahefnu, "Looks like we'll have guests for dinner."

"The entire village is coming in tonight too," she nodded. "Gigantic party. Fire feast."

"Do we have enough food?"

Tahefnu complained, "For one dinner, yeah, but the freezer's gonna be empty after this gang of turkey vultures gets through." MacIntyre inserted herself between Tahefnu and me and put her arm around me.

Heh came over and said, "Never been this many people in the valley! Gonna be a sweet party." He rubbed his hands in anticipation.

"OK, Dad. Remember, we got things to do in the morning, OK? Not too much booze."

Heh clucked. "Always worrying, daughter. Even without Hummingbird. Now there was a worrier. Damn bird was a pest—no offense, daughter. Besides, we got to show these guys a quality time so they'll help us instead of sitting on their fat Russian butts." His face became thoughtful, gazing at the Russians. "My colleague the demomili has reservations, won't talk about them." The Russians set up their bivouac next to the roundhouse. The demomili's wrinkled face set in lines of grim disapproval. Heh shrugged.

Tahefnu looked over our unexpected guests. "Who are these guys, Dad?"

"Spetsnaz. That's a special—"

"I know who Spetsnaz are, Dad. That's where we picked up Vasha." She didn't care for the guests, her mouth mirroring the demomili's.

"OK, OK, daughter. They're on our side now."

"*You* say." She went into the house. MacIntyre disappeared with Karkin and the demomili for more planning sessions. Heh shrugged and followed his daughter.

Late in the afternoon, the sergeant detailed men to help with dinner. Tahefnu and I organized them into a kitchen team in the cookhouse. It turned out the walk-in freezer had plenty of meat. We built a fire trench and set up wooden roasting spits over it. Tahefnu supervised the roasting of the deer and elk. Heh and the Miwuks consulted, disappeared, then reappeared with several barrels of local brew in the bed of one of the Waashiw pickup trucks. Tahefnu rolled her eyes and said, "Hopeless." She set about cracking the elk carcasses with a cleaver.

I rummaged around in the pantries of Heh's house and the cookhouse and found enough ingredients to cook up an interesting set of dishes involving beans, herbs, spices, and rice. Heh took more Miwuks off toward the river and returned after a couple of hours with about thirty trout.

Tahefnu wondered aloud about the quantity of acorn mush to make. She wanted to put MacIntyre in charge of acorn mush. I demurred, understanding at a basic level that MacIntyre was not likely to offer the culinary expertise likely to create an appetizing dinner of acorn mush. I felt that she might react to the suggestion with scorn, but I didn't mention that to Tahefnu. "Useless," I heard Tahefnu mutter to herself. She had three of the Miwuk women do the job.

MacIntyre herself steered clear of dinner preparations. She donned her brown beret and spent the time getting to know the Russians. I glanced over to the group every so often. MacIntyre appeared very popular. Vasha translated.

Once the Miwuks breached the barrels, the party got going in earnest. After the partiers consumed most of the food, more barrels appeared. Everybody moved into the roundhouse to gather around the fire there. Tahefnu joined the Miwuks and Waashiw on one side of the fire, and the Russians gathered on the other side. MacIntyre left the Russians and came to sit with me alongside Heh and the Miwuks.

The Russians broke out what proved to be an unlimited supply of vodka. Prodded, Vasha stood up and related the story of Major Suvorova's mission. As the story wore on, Vasha took on more vodka and more pathos. The Russians moaned when he related the NATO ambush that killed Major Suvorova's team. They started shouting after Vasha told of the Major's valiant but tragic end at the hands of the NATO troops. The Spetsnaz officer stood up and shouted in Russian.

Heh, worried, leaned over me to speak to MacIntyre. "He says they will have their revenge for the deaths of their comrades. What do you think, Cheryl? Are these guys gonna screw up our plan?"

MacIntyre said, "They'll be OK, we won't need them until the mopping-up operations. Just to be safe, let's keep them in reserve, tell them we'll need them to back up the Republican Guard but then not use them. That should do it." She took a drink from her cup of brew. "What the hell is this stuff, anyway?"

Heh shook his head in doubt, then leaned over and spoke to the demomili in Waashiw. The demomili pursed his desiccated lips and nodded, gleaming eyes fixed on the Russians. He shrugged. Heh shrugged in response. Karkin pursed his lips.

Heh said, "Better party while you can, Shesmu. Tomorrow's gonna be a lot of work." To MacIntyre, he grinned and said, "Acorn beer. The best in the mountains. Old family recipe. Fresh brewed in oak barrels." MacIntyre shuddered and took another pull at her cup.

Tahefnu touched Heh's shoulder. "Bed time, Dad."

"Always worrying, daughter. All right, all right," he said, getting up as she remonstrated with him. He emptied his cup. "Sleep well, Shesmu, and you too, Cheryl." The two Miwuks walked away to their rest.

The party lasted another hour. The last of the Russians staggered off to their bivouac next to the Waashiw, who had staggered off fifteen minutes earlier. I took MacIntyre's hand and led her off to Heh's spare room, where we slept like the dead.

CHAPTER FORTY-NINE
MacIntyre Neutralizes NATO

Cheryl MacIntyre awoke from a deep, exhausted sleep, roused by a disturbance in the air. The noise of a large chopper taking off died away in the distance. Shesmu slept on, dead to the world. There was enough moonlight to see his face, peaceful and at rest. She'd seen the fear in his face when she woke him on his prison compound cot; that was gone. But he's lost weight. That Miwuk woman hasn't been feeding him properly. Acorn mush.

MacIntyre shook her head to remove this unwelcome distraction. She snuggled deeper in the soft bed and thought about the Waashiw Rangers and their mission. This plan roiled her emotions, and they weren't all that stable to begin with. Her usual work as a medjat kept people from killing other people, or at least punished them if they did. Now she'd approved an operation that might kill hundreds. Unsettling. Educational, though.

But everyone else was OK with it. Heh and Tahefnu, the subject-matter experts, would supervise the work. The subject, in this case, was the geology of the huge granite cliff she had rappelled down. Heh was more than a shaman, much more. Peyotl may have inspired the plan, but Heh didn't rely on mystical spirits or magic. He relied on science and engineering.

He'd expounded it two days earlier in the meeting in the roundhouse. The committee gathered around a small fire that Heh fed from time to time. He laid out his peyotl-driven thoughts and connected them to the real world while the team leaders listened.

"We're gonna bury these guys."

What MacIntyre took for a military pep talk statement turned out to be the physical reality, not an over-optimistic sound bite. She prepared to jump down Heh's throat when he got peyotl-silly. She never got the chance.

Heh explained, with photos, the geological formation of the granite cliff. MacIntyre, being a city girl, had considered cliffs as huge, solid rocks. Not even close to true. Heh showed them pictures of huge slabs of rock that hung on by just a few slim threads. A few small explosive charges placed where they would be most effective, and half of it would come down in less than a minute. If the NATO troops were under it, there wouldn't be any more threat from them. Heh followed up with pictures of rockfalls all over the valley that convinced everyone. The demomili smiled. MacIntyre remembered that the demomili had brought a ton of climbing gear and an experienced mountain team based on a hunch.

Heh pointed out that they'd need to rescue Shes and his daughter before the operation. This was the part of his peyotl vision he hadn't understood.

"Daughter knows that rock face well. With your guys *and* daughter, this'll be easy. Without daughter, wouldn't happen."

The Republican Guard squad leader leaned forward. "OK, say I buy all this bullshit, shaman. Our base, where the NATO troops barracked themselves, isn't under the cliff. We built it where rockfalls wouldn't be a problem."

"That's the rest of the plan, son. If you can't bring the mountain to NATO, bring NATO to the mountain. Your people got to get the NATO forces under the cliff, that's all."

MacIntyre jumped in. "We need Basa to fool NATO into moving into that specific location." She looked at the Guard leader. "Can we persuade him to do that?"

The Guard soldier mused on this for a while. He said, "The imy-er-mesh'a has no choice but to recover the valley, and he's an expert at battlefield tactics. So, yes, I think I can persuade him."

MacIntyre turned back to Heh. "And this plan came to you in a peyotl vision?"

Heh beamed. "Best way to sharpen the mind and show you the entire universe of possibilities."

"Yeah." MacIntyre herself thought the possibilities were damn limited. But she wasn't about to embrace peyotl with both arms to expand them. She considered the demomili's prescience along with Heh's vision. She looked at the demomili, whose stony, wrinkled face betrayed no thoughts. He nodded. That settled it. Go with the experts.

MacIntyre committed herself. "All right, let's do it."

Here goes nothing. Her first strategic decision in her new career, engineered by a peyotl dream, a wrinkled old man's hunch, a bunch of crazy soldiers, and a shaman's nod. Why not?

MacIntyre smiled at the memory of that planning session and at Shes's sleeping face. She put away her worries and cares, turned over, and went back to sleep. She dreamed of rappelling down endless cliffs of granite with Ma'at doing the fireman's belay for her.

Heh and Tahefnu roused the two sleepers. The chopper was back. The dream stuck in her mind this time, making her uneasy.

"We're ready," said Heh. The light of dawn crept into the bedroom as R'a whipped his chariot forward over the Hetchetci valley.

MacIntyre walked hand-in-hand with Shes toward the roundhouse. She considered the shadows under his eyes, his limp, and the walking stick he still used.

She asked, "Are you recovered enough to come with us, Shes? We'll be observers, but there's always the chance that we'll have to dive into the battle."

"I'm coming. How could I miss your debut as imy-er-mesh'a?" He smiled and squeezed her hand as they walked. "Wouldn't miss it."

MacIntyre smiled and shook her head. "Just a lowly tjespedjut with a snazzy brown beret." She let go of his hand and adjusted the article of clothing in question. Tahefnu still wore her climbing harness from her early morning cliff-face work planting demolition charges. She gave a slight snort behind them, which MacIntyre ignored. MacIntyre felt well disposed toward the diminutive woman. She got things done, despite being an annoying distraction. MacIntyre experienced the same female energy from Tahefnu she did with other tough women. But her instincts told her that Tahefnu was off limits. Shamans, hummingbirds, peyotl, and a male-oriented sexuality; too exotic for MacIntyre's prosaic tastes. As long as the woman kept her tentacles off Shes, things would be fine. Her thoughts moved to her lover, whose limits had shifted since the last time she'd seen him ruling over his kitchen with an iron will. Miwuk? Gods? A lot of adjusting to do. And the changes in her own life were challenging him, too.

R'a crept upwards over the hill, dew sparkling on the grass in the meadows surrounding them. The chopper sat ready to take them off to Ta Sekhet. The Waashiw force reposed around it after their early morning exertions on the cliff.

The demomili, seeing MacIntyre, spoke to the sergeant. He called to MacIntyre, "Ma'am, boss doc says, 'the spirits are jumpy.' He means that time is getting on, you know?"

"Time to get Imy-er-mesh'a Basa moving," said MacIntyre. The Guard squad leader grinned in anticipation and went off to get his team together. MacIntyre climbed into the chopper and consulted with the pilot. He gave her a headset and established a secure communication channel with the Guard command. MacIntyre reviewed her tutorial session the day before to make sure she remembered all the lingo. The Republican Guard call sign was RG, Romeo Golf. Her own sign was Ma'at, Mike. It was in a way hilarious that the phonetic alphabet the Guard used was the standard NATO alphabet with English terms. She smiled.

She began, "Romeo Golf Six, this is Mike One, over."

"Mike One, this is Romeo Golf Six, over."

"Ready to proceed with operation, over."

"Roger, proceed, over."

"Romeo Gold Six, this is Mike One, WILCO, out."

And so it begins. MacIntyre took off the headphones. She contemplated the surrounding beauty through the chopper canopy, then sighed and got up to take her place on the chopper bench. Her unease deepened.

The chopper, packed with Waashiw, Remetjy, and Russian soldiers, chuffed through the early morning air over the mountains between Hetchetci and Ta Sekhet. It set down in the same burned-out meadow as before, well away from the granite cliff. Everyone jumped out of the chopper and gathered together in teams as the pilot shut down the rotors. The Waashiw deployed to set up the detonating station within range of the cliff, radios tuned to a short-range channel the chopper pilot could use to communicate with them. Khenmes went with them, but the demomili remained behind.

MacIntyre looked around and found Karkin. "Karkin, can you translate for me with the Major?" They walked over to the Russian Spetsnaz squad.

"Major, I'd like you and your men to stay here until the Guard retreats and the cliff collapses, then we can see where you will be of most use. Is that satisfactory?"

The Russian major, who looked even uglier in the morning light, nodded, smiled with rotten teeth, and put his soldiers at ease near the chopper. His willingness to be out of the action for now erased some of the uneasiness in MacIntyre. The vodka-fueled revenge fantasies of the night before had stayed behind. All they'd brought was an arsenal of fancy rifles and a full set of hangovers.

She dismissed the demomili's concern over the Russians that was still clear in his expression. She regarded it as a Waashiw pessimism unwarranted by the facts on the ground. The small Republican Guard contingent sat nearby.

MacIntyre borrowed a pair of field glasses and a portable short-range radio from the chopper pilot. As she jumped down from the chopper, she saw Tahefnu waiting nearby.

MacIntyre asked, "Tahefnu, where would be a good place to check out the action? We can't do it from the cliff."

Tahefnu pointed up to the east. "There's a decent trail up to that peak, and the view is fabulous."

It was the peak they had come around the day before on their hike from the valley. Shes, Heh, and Karkin came, and Tahefnu led them up the trail to the peak. The demomili stayed behind, saying his peak-climbing days were over. They made quick time. They could hear the initial action starting far away below in the valley. There were small cracks and louder booms from grenades, rockets, or tanks attacking the bridges into the valley.

MacIntyre lay prone, inspecting the valley through the field glasses. Such beauty, about to become a killing ground. Couldn't be helped, she thought, but she imagined her goddess Ma'at having a twinge at the destruction to come. MacIntyre hoped that the Justified Ones in their valley tombs would lie undisturbed. That would be all she needed, a bunch of mummies wandering around out of control. She grinned at the thought.

Over the next three hours, they shared the field glasses and watched the NATO troops boil out of their camp to reinforce their fellows in the west part of the valley. The first Republican Guard tanks and armored carriers fought their way into the lower valley on the north side of the river, as planned, pushing back the NATO guards on the bridges. NATO forces from the base engaged them. The advance slowed but pushed up to the base of the enormous granite cliff, three tanks shielding the infantry that kept the NATO troops engaged. Basa deployed his troops well. He minimized his own casualties while keeping the NATO troops busy and drawing them into position. The NATO folks didn't seem to know much about Br'er Fox. And they weren't deploying anti-tank weapons, either. Much too sure of themselves.

MacIntyre's radio crackled. The chopper pilot's voice said, "Mike One, this is Mike Two, over."

"Mike Two, this is Mike One, over."

"From Romeo Golf Six, mission complete, over."

"Mike Two, this is Mike One, Roger, over."

"This is Mike Two, Out."

Time to decide. MacIntyre didn't hesitate.

"Break. Mike Three, this is Mike One, over."

"Mike One, this is Mike Three, over." It was the sergeant's voice.

"Mike Three, this is Mike One. Let her go, over."

"Mike Three, WILCO, over."

"Mike One, out."

They waited. Through the field glasses, MacIntyre saw the Republican Guard tanks, armored carriers, and infantry retreat at full speed. She heard what sounded like a series of firecrackers exploding in the distance, bang-bang-bang, all at once. Tahefnu pointed at a dust cloud that rose above the enormous cliff. The cloud got larger and larger, boiling up and obscuring the valley from their view. A colossal rumbling noise came to them from the depths of the cloud.

MacIntyre got up, the field glasses now useless. "I guess we should go back down to the chopper and fly everybody down there to help in the mopping up," she said. "There's going to be many people down there needing medical assistance."

They started down the steep path from the peak. Tahefnu stopped short and pointed. MacIntyre ran into her.

"What the hell?" said MacIntyre, in English. The chopper, their ride, shot forward toward the cliff and down past the expanding cloud of dust. She pressed the button on her radio.

"Mike Two, this is Mike One, over."

Nothing.

"Mike Two, this is Mike One, over."

More nothing.

"Something's wrong," Shes said.

"Well, ain't that fucking obvious!" snarled MacIntyre, again in English. She turned contrite. "Sorry, Shes." Her unease sharpened into worry.

Heh said, "Guess we'd better get down there and figure out what's going on."

MacIntyre gave him a sick look, then headed down the trail at a run, and the others followed at the various paces they could manage, Karkin right behind her. MacIntyre ran into the burned-out meadow where they had left the chopper. She found the pilot and the Republican Guard troops standing, disconsolate, in a small group gathered around the demomili.

"What the fuck is going on?" shouted MacIntyre in English, then repeated the question in more restrained Renkemet, as she approached at a dead run. She stopped in front of the pilot, breathing hard.

The pilot said, "It was the Russians, ma'am. We were all taken up with the explosion, and they were just there. Disarmed us all and made us lie down, then took off in the chopper. The entire squad of them."

The Russians. MacIntyre looked south at the expanding cloud of dust covering the now-vulnerable NATO troops. The sick feeling in her stomach intensified. Would the Russians leave? Take prisoners? Help the Republican Guard mop up? Her gut told her that wasn't likely; they'd do what they said they'd do: kill everyone in sight. Which was a war crime. On her watch.

"Fuck!" she screamed, throwing her snazzy brown beret on the ground and stomping on it. The demomili stood with folded arms, shaking his head in disconsolate sympathy.

Shesmu hobbled along with the help of the walking stick and came up to the little group. The Waashiw force returned a few minutes later from the south, and the demomili met them and filled them in. The sergeant came over to MacIntyre.

"Sorry about this, ma'am. What do we do now?"

MacIntyre picked up her beret, dusted it off, and arranged it on her head.

"How the fuck would I know, Sergeant? I'm a cleaning lady, not a soldier."

The sergeant called out to the Republican Guard squad, "Any of you guys have any long-range radio equipment?"

The men looked at one another, then shook their heads. The leader said, "We depended on the unit in the chopper to talk to base."

Khenmes came over, and MacIntyre gathered everyone together for a conference.

"We're stuck here unless the Imy-er-mesh'a figures out what's going on," said MacIntyre. She asked the pilot, "Will he see that the chopper isn't friendly?"

The pilot shook his head. "The Identification Friend or Foe interrogator is on," he said. "They'll regard the chopper as friendly until it fires on them. No missiles in that chopper, though."

"Yeah, well, they're not gonna do that," said Khenmes. "They're after scalps. NATO scalps."

MacIntyre opened and closed her mouth. "Real scalps?"

Khenmes half-smiled. "Naw. Figure of speech. They'll shoot 'em. Use the heavy machine guns in the chopper."

Shesmu limped over to MacIntyre and wrapped his arms around her from behind as she watched the dust cloud, which grew even larger. She remained immobile and silent.

He said, "Can we signal them? A mirror? Morse code or something?"

"Not through that cloud. Huh. It's impenetrable. Maybe they'll crash," she said, plaintive hope in her voice. He put his chin on her shoulder and nuzzled. She didn't move.

Tahefnu said, "We blew up the fast route. We'll have to take the long way. It's about 10 kilometers to the west valley floor. That's where the Guard will be."

The demomili said something to the sergeant, who turned to MacIntyre. "Ma'am, I don't know how to translate. Boss doc wants you to know…" The big man hesitated, then continued, "It's like the cliff falling, once it starts nothing's gonna stop it. Boss doc says Russians are like that, ma'am. Nothing you could do."

Heh nodded at this and said, "Wasn't in my vision, but he's right. Bear is definitely pissed. Ain't your fault, though."

MacIntyre stirred and said, eyes fierce and punching each English word into the ground, "Oh. My. God." She extracted herself from Shes's arms, faced the group, and took charge. "OK, everybody, listen up. I'm going down with Tahefnu as a guide. The rest of you stay here and wait—including Bear. The demomili is in charge here, since he's all read in about the Russians. I'll sent transport as soon as the Imy-er-mesh'a finishes chewing me out and demotes me to assistant cleaning lady, OK?"

Karkin stepped up and said, "I'm coming, need to talk to Basa."

MacIntyre looked at Tahefnu. "Think he can keep up?"

Tahefnu grinned. "Doubt it."

MacIntyre looked at Karkin, a smile spreading over her features, dissipating her rage. She said, distinctly, in English, "Last one there is a rotten egg." She and Tahefnu ran like hell down the trail. Karkin, caught flat-footed, dashed after them, leaving the rest of the group open-mouthed.

CHAPTER FIFTY

Shesmu Discovers the Truth

HEH OBSERVED, "THAT DAUGHTER OF mine, she's still got too much heat."

Sitting in a burned-out meadow for four hours with a bunch of anxious, unhappy soldiers waiting for rescue is not the way I would choose to spend a nice, sunny summer afternoon. I couldn't even pace nervously while I waited, because of my ankle. I mentioned this to Heh, as he appeared to be in a reflective mood. He suggested that Bear might help. Heh had no regalia nor a charming assistant, but the demomili offered his help in place of Tahefnu's. Experienced now with Bear's medical techniques, I asked a few questions about side effects of the treatment. Heh laughed and assured me the gods would leave us alone now. I said if they tried anything, I'd do something about it with the walking stick.

Heh assessed this statement with noncommittal silence. The demomili's wrinkles folded in what I took to be a smile. So, we moved ahead with the healing ceremony. A few of the Waashiw Rangers gathered around for moral support, though they didn't say whether it was support of me or Bear. The demomili settled on his haunches and chanted in Waashiw while Heh did the ceremony in Miwuk. Given my experience in mixing religions and gods, I imagined this might have a negative impact on treatment quality.

I drifted off to sleep after about ten minutes. I remember a dream about running in the woods after a large, black bear, but the impact was nowhere near the level of Mentju or Seteh. Peaceful, lots of fresh air and exercise. After I awoke, I walked around, and my ankle was a great deal better.

Heh said, "It will take another couple of treatments, Shes. Take it slow for a few days, OK?"

"Sure."

"And keep the stick. It's been through a lot with you, it will remind you of everything you've learned. And it will take the weight off that ankle."

"Sure."

I'd just as soon forget what I'd learned about body parts from the god Mentju. A good stick, even if it occasionally took over my life, was still a good stick. And my ankle hurt less. Whether or not Bear had something to do with it, I now had confidence in Miwuk medical technology. Khenmes slapped me on the back and congratulated me on my recovery.

I heard a whup-whup-whup sound. The soldiers around me instantly had their weapons in positions showing they were ready to use them.

Two choppers rose over the remains of the granite cliff and whupped toward us. Not the Russians, unless they'd procured another chopper.

The choppers set down in the meadow, and the first person to hit the ground as the rotors slowed and came to a stop was MacIntyre, in her brown beret. Tahefnu and Karkin followed, then two Republican Guard soldiers. The Rangers stood down.

MacIntyre came over to me, hugged me, and said, "Your ride's here."

After a long, thorough kiss and some hooting from the audience, I released MacIntyre. Her reappearance decided me on what I had to do.

"Cheryl, I need to get to my father's tomb, with Khenmes."

"You need to come home with me."

"No, I can't, Cheryl—unfinished business."

She looked me over with a critical eye. "I think that business will finish you off."

"Cheryl—"

She changed the subject. "I had a pleasant talk with Imy-er-mesh'a Basa. OK, well, the first part, maybe not so pleasant, but after he got over it, I explained the Russian problem to him. He sent in troops. They reported back. No survivors."

I gripped my stick tightly. "Sorry?"

She closed her eyes and said it again. "No survivors. The Russians killed anything that moved. Searchers report no sign of life at all. They're still looking."

I leaned on the stick. Yes, we had dropped a cliff on them. But we didn't hunt them down and shoot them in cold blood. I didn't need a vision of Ma'at to sense the pull of justice. The set of MacIntyre's jaw showed she didn't need a vision either. The day was suddenly colder than it had been, and I felt very tired.

A hand fell on my shoulder. I turned: Khenmes.

"Sorry, son. It happens." His eyes were sad.

I turned back to MacIntyre. "What did Basa say?"

"Say? I can't repeat it in mixed company."

I was silent for a few minutes, thinking. "We have to do something."

"No, Basa does. He's notified everybody he can think of about them."

"The Russians?"

"The Russians." She embraced me again. "In *his* chopper. Can you get rid of that stick for a minute?" she asked.

"Better not. It's all that's keeping me upright, except for you."

"I'm hoping I'm better than a stick."

"Some better, though it's a good stick." I leaned the stick against a nearby blackened stump and decided that MacIntyre was better than any stick. Way better. Magic or not.

Khenmes cleared his throat behind me and broke it up. "I think it's time we visited with your dad, Shes, now that NATO is gone. I could just tell you the stuff, but you won't believe it unless you read it for yourself." Karkin had joined Khenmes and nodded to reinforce his opinion. MacIntyre released me and glared at them.

The vision of my father as a god flashed through my mind. If I went to the tomb with Khenmes, perhaps he would reappear despite Ma'at's interference. He might tell me more about things I wanted to know about my childhood. And Khenmes was right, I needed to read the true history in the tomb to believe it; reality seemed very distant to me right then.

I picked up my stick and walked over to one of the choppers. The pilot stood near the front. His uniform told me he was an idnu in the Republican Guard.

I said, "We need to go down into the valley, to a tomb."

The idnu looked me up and down in my disheveled, worse-for-wear hunter's garb. The stick didn't impress him either. "My orders are to take you back to… whatever they call their village." He waved a hand at Heh and Tahefnu.

MacIntyre poked me in the back. I shot her a look, then said, "May I speak with your commander? Imy-er-mesh'a Basa?"

He looked over my shoulder and saw something in MacIntyre's face that impressed him more than my poor visage. "I guess so."

We climbed into the chopper and made our way into the cockpit. He spoke into the comm system, then offered me a set of headphones.

"This is Shesmu."

"Romeo Golf Twenty, this is Romeo Golf Six. You're not using protocol, over."

"All that 'over' stuff? Sorry, not my thing. I need to get to a tomb in the valley right away. Can I borrow your chopper for a little while? It's important."

"Idiot One, this is Romeo Golf Six. Negative, over. Fuck."

"I don't believe that's a protocol word."

"No shit. I'm so happy this is a secure channel." The imy-er-mesh'a's voice came through strongly, as did his displeasure.

"Look. I'm not asking a lot. I think I may be onto something about why NATO is here." I paused, then added, "Was here. It's Akhen's tomb. My father's tomb."

The silence dragged on for two minutes. Basa understood the importance of Akhen's tomb; he'd been around it long enough during his tour of duty in charge of Ta Sekhet. And now he knew I was Akhen's son.

The radio crackled. "Romeo Golf Twenty, this is Romeo Golf Six, over."

Twenty; that was the idnu's call number. I signaled him to get on. He took my headphones. "Romeo Golf Six, this is Romeo Golf Twenty, over." He looked at me as he listened and smiled grimly. "WILCO, out."

"OK," he said, "What the fuck, now I'm a fucking tour bus driver." He shook his head. "Get 'em on board." He added, as an afterthought, "Sir." He turned to the flight instrument panel to fire up the rotors.

My companions on the chopper ride were the pilot, two Republican Guard soldiers, MacIntyre, Khenmes, Karkin, and Tahefnu, who jumped on the chopper just before it took off.

"Got to come, Shesmu. If he's the bus driver, I'm the tour guide."

She waved out the chopper door to Heh, standing by the Waashiw sergeant. They both waved, then Heh held up a clenched hand, as though he were holding a stick. I raised my stick to salute. The pilot just leaned backward in his seat, pointed to a bench with a jabbing finger, and said, "Sit. Now." Tahefnu took the seat next to the pilot and donned headphones. And off we flew.

It took about five minutes to get to the clearing in front of my father's tomb. The NATO and Russian corpses were gone. The door to the chapel was wide open, the way we'd left it when we'd come out with the white underwear on the stick.

Khenmes looked over the tomb door at the far wall of the chapel. "Idnu, you got a tool kit?"

The pilot said, "Sure, old man. Whaddya need?"

"Pry bar."

The pilot fetched a pry bar. Khenmes took it and pried off two iron seals drilled into the stone of the chapel wall.

I'd been in enough tombs in Menmenet to know that we were on shaky ground with Inpu, the jackal god of the burial places. I suppose I ought to have cared more about the desecration of my father's tomb—but I didn't.

My stick was glowing. I lifted it.

"Does anybody else see this?"

"What?" said the pilot. He looked at the stick, but his eyes were shifting around nervously.

"The stick."

"What about it?"

Tahefnu smiled and nodded but said nothing. MacIntyre looked at me and the stick quizzically, shaking her head. Karkin cocked his head at me but said nothing.

I held the stick, my stomach queasy. "Wait. Give me a minute."

Khenmes leaned against the door and looked at me. The pilot said, with a sick expression on his face, "I don't know about this...."

I was about to desecrate my father's tomb. That was the worst interpretation. The stick glowed brighter. I had to decide.

The stick decided. My arm moved; the stick pointed toward the door. Power flowed through my arm. Did I believe the gods were leading me on, or was this a psychological manifestation of my obsession with my father? And which god? Was Seteh again taking a hand? I hoped I was not about to descend into another hellish daytime nightmare of gods and pain. Ma'at? Mentju? Another busybody god? The only god I was ready to see was my father. And where was Inpu in all this stress? The last time I'd dealt with Inpu, he'd mummified me alive, and everyone recognized the god of the necropolis took a dim view of tomb robbers. The stick answered in my mind, you have dominion here. Ma'at justifies you in what you do. You need to know. And you're ready.

I steeled myself and said, "Go ahead."

Khenmes said, "OK, then. I know the code, I set it when I closed this door, long ago." He entered a code on the big electronic lock set into the tomb door, and a loud snick came from it. Khenmes pushed with both hands; the door opened smoothly, but it was half a meter thick and made of solid granite.

We crowded into the space around the big, rectangular sarcophagus in the middle of the room. The atmosphere was stale, and Khenmes pushed the door wide to let in outside air from the chapel. Tahefnu brought out her light and played it over the sarcophagus. A generic representation of Akhen's smiling face stared up at us, cut into the solid granite sarcophagus. The inset obsidian eyes watched me intently, flashing in the light.

"We don't…." I fumbled for the words. "We don't need to open…."

Khenmes smiled. "We'll just explore the walls for now, Shes. No worries." He waved a hand at the walls with their hieroglyphs and carved images dimly visible in the meager light. Tahefnu came toward me with the light. MacIntyre stepped in front of her and looked her in the eye. Tahefnu grinned and handed the light to MacIntyre; the light shining up at MacIntyre's face made her appear demonic. They nodded to each other. MacIntyre turned to me and held the light high, shining against the wall where Khenmes pointed.

I checked out the hieroglyphs. They presented a long story in the ornate, archaic language we pay priests to write in tombs. I think it's because we believe the gods speak that language. I'm here to tell you it ain't so. Sure, they're on the formal side, but they get to the point expeditiously.

"It's the entire story of Akhen's life," said Khenmes. Karkin nodded.

I looked up and down the wall. "There's a book here. In small print."

Khenmes smiled, a touch grimly, and said, "Yep."

MacIntyre said, "Is there an executive summary somewhere?"

"Nope." Khenmes stepped in front of MacIntyre and took the light from her.

MacIntyre looked at Khenmes. "You won't tell us, will you? Or let us read it?"

"Only Shes. It's his father. And Karkin, he knows most of it. Need to know only."

"Look, old man…." The exasperated pilot was still nervous. I think the threat of Inpu's wrath weighed on him.

"Everybody else out. Now." Khenmes made a shooing motion with his hands.

"I got orders," said the pilot. "The Imy-er-mesh'a ordered that I stay with you at all times."

MacIntyre smiled her best superior-officer smile. "Let's go, Idnu. I know a stone wall when I see one. There's at least one too many stone walls in this tomb. We'll be just outside, so they won't be going anywhere from here." The pilot had to agree. There was only one door.

Tahefnu gave me an uncertain glance, but she followed MacIntyre and the pilot out. Khenmes closed the door until the edge was just beyond the doorframe so that those outside couldn't hear a thing. He reached and gathered me in to a hard embrace, father to son. "Time you learned this. Maybe you'll understand better. But it's complicated, some of it's hard to hear. You need to choose now: do we read the story? Do I fill in the blanks?"

My mouth felt parched. I looked up at an illustration of my father being given life by Aset, his tutelary goddess. Did I honestly want to learn what happened to him? I licked my dry lips and committed myself.

"Yes. I need to know."

I suppose I was searching for a connection to my father, to understand his life and why he left it, why the Republic made him a god. Khenmes had been right. I wasn't ready, before, to make the jump from needing a simple family connection to understanding my own role in the world. I didn't know enough.

"Over here," said Khenmes, pointing at one corner. We gathered around, and I read the archaic priest's language. It described my father's birth in a Central Valley Miwuk band, his tribal adventures and coming of age, and his boyhood loves and losses.

"Akhen told me once that he had an idyllic life in the Valley, so idyllic he couldn't stand it, so he left." Khenmes shook his head. "We both grew up poor in wealth and rich in family, him in the Valley, me at the lake, but we both needed more than that. Our paths were different before we met. He went to college, I married Tuy and worked odd jobs in Tzatlee Tosh, at the lake. Akhen showed up there one day, working on a paper on the Waashiw religion for his college."

"Paper? He was an academic?"

"Ethnologist, specialist in the western tribal peoples. We got friendly, and he started liking pine trees and mountain vistas and hunting deer more than Valley dirt and acorns. So, we bummed around together until we ran out of jobs and money. Never did finish that paper."

That part of the wall gave a more formal version that emphasized Akhen's knowledge and brilliance over the bumming around part. Obituaries always do that. Then things got serious. He married my mom and moved to Menmenet. First surprise: he joined the Temple of Mentju as a military intelligence expert on the tribes.

"Doesn't say so there, but I got him the job. I'd joined the Waashiw Rangers, and the army seconded me to Ta'an-Imenty because of rumors that the Paiutes were planning something nasty for both of our countries."

He stopped and pointed, and I read on. The light was not all that bright, and the glyphs flowed and moved as I tried to take in the history. I blinked my eyes to clear them, but it didn't help much. Every so often there was an illustrated scene of my father with various gods as he accomplished a major life milestone. Those images moved too, in the dim light. The stick I held glowed but cast no light; I held it up once or twice, but the glyphs and images twisted and shifted even more.

The story on the wall progressed through several top secret military intelligence gathering operations. My father worked his way up the chain of command. Khenmes gave me some anecdotes from the lives of the four friends: Akhen, Nebiunet, Khenmes, and Tuy.

Khenmes stopped me at one point and said, "Here's where it gets hard, boy. When Karkin showed up."

I looked at Karkin, and he looked back at me with a stony expression. "Secret War," he said.

Khenmes clucked. "Akhen disappeared one day. Your mom was frantic, we looked everywhere. Mentju wouldn't tell us anything. This guy," he said, slapping Karkin on the shoulder, "came by one night and told us what was happening."

"Broke protocol. Had to. Good friend." Karkin's dark eyes stared into mine.

Silence descended on the tomb. Khenmes looked at Karkin, Karkin looked at Khenmes.

"What happened?" I broke the deep silence.

The world shifted. I heard Khenmes's voice from far away saying, "We weren't there, Shes. It's on the wall. We never saw your dad again...." The small voice faded away to nothing.

I was again in a cave, but at the same time in the tomb surrounded by glyphs, moving, stretching, along the walls of the cave. There was light, this time from the stick in my hand. It had changed from Heh's walking stick into the w'as scepter, the staff of dominion Remetjy gods carry to show their power over the world. The curved top and forked tail of the scepter are the head and tail of Seteh, the god of power and chaos.

Into this light came a coyote, ambling along without a care in the world. He stopped and sat and looked at me, angling his head and panting as coyotes do.

"You're in Miwuk form now," I said, recognizing my father the god. He had appeared before in human form with a coyote head. Now, he was all Miwuk.

"Glad to know you worked it out in that cage, Shesmu."

"Friends helped."

"Yes, they did. Parts of a whole, balance in the world."

"You sounded very distant when you left."

"Yeah, well, that's the Remetjy god stuff. That part of me is off in the Sekhet-'Aru, working hard at nothing in the fields of reeds. I got other business, the Miwuk spirit part of me. You're it."

"I'm it what?"

"My business. I'll be going along with you from now on."

"Great. Fine. Finally, a connection to my father. Late, but better than never."

"I sense discontent."

I reassessed. "If you're here for good, we can talk later. I've got people waiting on me. What happened?"

"Yeah, that's why I'm here. To show you. You're ready."

"So, talk."

"I'll show. We have excellent technology here in the spirit world."

This next part was strange, like a full-immersion virtual reality show, flitting from image to image. The images were on the wall of the cave, like the images in the tomb, but holographic. You felt you were there, a fly on the wall. And you knew who the characters were, and you knew their back stories, and you knew something nasty was going to happen. I won't try to reproduce the total experience, it wouldn't come across. There are media people who would pay billions for this stuff. Anyway, highlights.

Richard B. Shane was Secretary of Defense of the United States. He had a round head, balding, stupid-looking wire-rim glasses, cynical smile that turned into a screaming raging grimace when he thought he would not get what he wanted. To-Pay Parker III was the Emperor of the Numunuu Empire, the country west of the Mississippi and east of Diné Bikéyah. They were together in a room in Washington. Shane had his sardonic grin on, and Parker a full First People's smile, while they agreed to split up the continent between them. The Americans would get land for expansion, the Numunuu Empire would get the oil and gas that extended from their borders to the Inuvik Republic. They saw no need to keep the people already living there around. They had plans on what to do with them: everyone from the Utes to the Anishinaabeg to the Siksikawa. Those genocidal plans were on paper on Shane's desk, and Parker had just signed off on them.

My spirit-god's voice said, "So, that's what I heard about, those plans. A little bird came and told me." I think he waxed metaphorical, but with spirits, you never could tell, might have been an actual bird. "So I flew off to talk to Parker."

"Where?"

"Numu City, capital of the Numunuu Empire. A big city on a river inland from the Aztec Gulf."

The picture changed. It showed Parker and my father walking along the river, talking. I heard Renkemet, but they were speaking the Numu language. It was a long conversation, but it came down to "What can we do to persuade you to stop?" and a one-word response: "Oil."

Switch to planes, trains, and automobiles all over the Plains Federation. My dad talking to landowners, oil men, gas men, chiefs, politicians. He was a brilliant talker, Dad was. He talked most all of them into making mineral rights leases available to Parker. And it was to Parker, personally.

"To-Pay got wealthy, after," said my spirit-god. "Didn't do him much good, died in the arms of a mistress at age 55. Heart gave out. Funny, didn't realize he had one. A heart, that is; everybody knew about the mistress. He did have quite a few cheerful kids, all that oil money flowing in. One of 'em is now chief, running with the Americans in NATO, pushing the current plans."

"Which are?"

He gave a coyote-laugh. "Not a chance, boy. Past is past, future is future. I'm past, you're future. Lord Seteh has spoken to you of the future, his vision of power. Sea to shining sea, remember?"

I kept the subject on my original concern. "What happened to you?"

"Hard stuff to hear. Sure?"

"Yeah, very sure."

A picture formed of my dad talking to Parker again, sitting cross-legged in Parker's Imperial office in Numu City. Parker slamming his hand on his leg, angry. Angry at the Miwuks. He called them obstructionists and traitors allied with the Remetjy colonizers. My dad asked what else Parker wanted. "Hostages," said Parker. "Five chiefs. Then we'll tell the U. S. to go to hell."

I watched as my Dad persuaded the Miwuk elders to select five of their number for hostages. He told them it was the only hope for survival if the Americans and Numunuu came calling. Eventually they agreed. The chiefs were on a plane to Numu City with my dad. They left the plane, and the Numunuu jailed them. Part of the deal was that my dad got the signed copy of the secret treaty and plans for genocide; I saw him take the papers from Parker at the handover ceremony in Numu City. The image changed to a split screen. I saw my dad getting on his plane to Menmenet and, at the same time, Parker giving the orders and his people torturing and executing the hostages.

"That was it. The rest is me dying. I never knew about the killings, and I never made it off the plane," said my coyote spirit-god.

"Poisoned," said Khenmes. I was back in the tomb, Tahefnu's light shining on the wall, leaning on my walking stick. "Hey, Shesmu, you're pretty quiet. You OK?"

"Yeah," I replied. I put a hand on the wall to steady myself. "Poisoned how?"

"Nobody knows," said Khenmes.

"The Numunuu Empire secret police do," said Karkin. "Sources."

"Anyway, the Temple of Mentju and the hekasepat declared your dad a state hero. They gave him a posthumous Golden Bee honor and built him a tomb in Ta Sekhet that no one could visit. Made him a god, then made everybody forget about him. We never did."

Should I? Forget him? Suppress my guilty spirit-god and exile Coyote to the Miwuk spirit world from which he came? I couldn't; he was my father, the only one I had. My life had become a series of never-ending atonements for my sins— my own and the ones I'd inherited.

I asked, "What happened to the original documents? The evidence my dad brought back?"

Karkin said nothing but looked at Khenmes, who said nothing and looked back at him.

Khenmes said, "Shes, you don't want to know. You don't want to have anything to do with that."

My heart thought differently. "If I can redress my father's mistake, I have to do it. I need the documents. Where are they?"

Khenmes came and embraced me. "You don't, Shes. You've done enough, you've been through too much."

"Yeah," I said into his strong shoulder, "as though you haven't, old man. The gods dream-dismembered me, but NATO kidnapped and waterboarded you. I need to know, Khenmes."

He let me go. Karkin said, "Tell him."

Khenmes shook his head, but it was with sorrow, not refusal, because he said, "In there." His hand was on the sarcophagus. "He had the papers on his body. The Ta'an-Imenty government took them and put them in the sarcophagus to make sure they stayed buried. That was the deal."

"Well, they've broken the deal." I looked at the sarcophagus, gripped the stick, and felt its approval. "Open it."

Khenmes nodded reluctantly and said, "I'll need help."

"More than the three of us?"

"Yes. The lid is solid granite. We put it on with a crane. Out there." He waved a hand at the tomb door.

"I'll get the help."

Karkin said, "Don't tell them. No need to know."

I got loud. "I'll tell them nothing except that we're robbing the tomb, OK? Does that work for you?" I shook my head at my outburst. "Sorry, Karkin. I'm unnerved by this." I walked outside.

"Can I get some help?" I shouted from the chapel door.

Everyone came over.

"What's wrong, Shes?" asked MacIntyre.

"We need to move the sarcophagus lid, and it's too heavy for the three of us, so we need all of you in there to help."

A beat passed, then the pilot blanched. "Lid? Take off the lid? What the fuck are you doing?" He looked around as though the minions of Inpu were coming for him.

I dredged up a reassuring smile. "On orders of Ma'at. Right, w'abet?" I asked, looking at MacIntyre for support.

She grinned. "Sure, orders of Ma'at."

The idnu stared at her. "Fuck Ma'at."

"Well, how about an order from your superior officer, then?"

"You? You're not an officer and you're not superior. The imy-er-mesh'a fired you."

"How about if I say please?"

The pilot said with force, "I'll wait in the chopper, OK? I'm out of this." He stalked off.

MacIntyre turned to the soldiers. "How about you guys? Scared of a jackal? Or are you up for a little tomb robbery?"

The pair looked at each other and nodded. "The only chance we'll ever have to do it, lady," grinned one. "Why not! Any gold?"

I gave him a look and shook my head. "Sorry, no."

MacIntyre, impatient, said, "Let's go."

We gathered everyone around the sarcophagus. Khenmes lifted the pry bar. "I'll lever up one end. When you lift it, I'll reach in and grab what I need, all right? So, get on two sides near this end, and when I pry up the end, lift it high so I can reach in."

I put one soldier on each side near the end, Karkin and I took the middle positions, and the two women were next to us. Khenmes levered with the pry bar, and we all heaved up. Khenmes shone the light into the sarcophagus and reached in and pulled out a roll of papers tied with a ribbon. I peeked in; I couldn't help it. I saw the inner coffin covered with hieroglyphs and an image of my father. Something was missing; the stick pulled. The Coyote wanted the power of the stick in the afterlife. I had to give it up.

On an impulse, I said, "Hold it up, I'm putting something in there!"

I let go of the lid, and Tahefnu next to me gasped but held it. I reached for the walking stick, which shone with bright light now, at least to me, and tossed it into the sarcophagus. A momentary flash of light burst in my eyes. That was my offering to my father, to replace the papers, to replace the weight of responsibility he had taken on and I had removed. I had nothing else to offer. And I didn't need Seteh's power weighing me down. I regretted giving up the stick, we'd been through a lot together.

I resumed my grip. Tahefnu shifted beside me as she got a better hold.

"OK, done."

Tahefnu grunted, "You…shouldn't have done that, Shesmu. You'll be sorry you gave up your power." Was she speaking from her loss of the Hummingbird?

"I already regret it, Tahefnu, but it feels right. Close it," I said. We lowered the lid back into place.

Khenmes looked at me and handed me the roll of papers. Tahefnu looked at me, her eyes glistening, shaking her head. MacIntyre came around the sarcophagus and hugged me. She whispered in my ear, "Not wise, but I'm proud of you, Shes. I love you. But I have questions, we've got to talk."

Khenmes said, "It's on you, now, son." In the light from the lamp, he looked much older, but a weight had gone from his face. He'd shed the burden he'd been carrying for a long time. "I think I'm ready to make that phone call now, to wife."

I said, "Let's get out of here. I need air."

We closed the tomb door, then the chapel door. I lent Khenmes my phone for his call to Tuy, which went very well. I took one last peek at the last resting place of my father's ka and followed the others back to the waiting chopper. The pilot fired up the rotors.

I climbed on board. Tahefnu turned her head to me from her seat next to the pilot.

"We're heading back to Dad's place, unless you have more graves to rob?"

"No, I'm set."

CHAPTER FIFTY-ONE

MacIntyre Gets the Full Story

SHESMU WALKED AWAY FROM THE chopper and stood, looking at the cliffs and waterfalls of Hetchetci. MacIntyre, who had her own problems to deal with, nevertheless felt compelled to help her lover deal with his.

The cloud of dust from the collapsing cliff in Ta Sekhet and the sound of angry chopper blades still filled MacIntyre's senses. She put it aside and said, "Whatever you learned in there must have been dramatic, Shes. You're changed."

Shes said, "I have to go with Khenmes to Da'owaga'a, to see Tuy and talk about my family with them. I need the full story. Then I'll be flying back to Menmenet from there. I'll call you."

"That's it? That's all you're going to tell me?"

He smiled and embraced her, saying into her ear, "It's all I have time for. The Rangers are packing up and leaving now. There's so much, so much more I'd like to do, to tell you. I'll need your help to deal with it. Just like you'll need mine to deal with your challenges."

He let go of her and extracted the roll of papers Khenmes had given him in his father's tomb from an interior pocket. "Keep these for me, keep them safe. Read them. This is the important part, I'll tell you about my father when we get together again. You'll need to know what's in these papers."

"You're willing to turn these over to an American?"

"You're not an American." He grinned. "Not anymore. Unofficially certified by me on close observation of your interaction with other Americans earlier today. They ought to confiscate your passport."

"Not funny," she said, and kissed him. "Not funny at all." Maybe one day she'd learn to laugh again. It might be awhile. Dark shapes of guilt twisted and ran through the clouds of dust that filled her.

Shes packed himself into the back seat of one of the pickup trucks between the demomili and Khenmes, and the line of trucks set off for the drive to Da'owaga'a. MacIntyre found herself enveloped in real dust. It gradually settled, leaving her looking again at the wonders of Hetchetci.

Heh and Tahefnu welcomed her into their house. Heh told her everything about Shesmu and his visions and about the Bear and the Coyote and how much he'd have liked to have had Shesmu as a son-in-law. Tahefnu squelched her father, then gave MacIntyre a lesson in making acorn mush the right way, the mountain way. She even took MacIntyre out back to the big rock with the holes in it and had her pound an unlikely number of acorns into dust. MacIntyre thought it was an excellent way to relieve stress but was ready to quit within two minutes. Tahefnu kept her at it.

"Making the mush the right way is what they teach us Miwuk girls will keep our Miwuk lovers happy," Tahefnu explained with a grin.

MacIntyre replied, "Now that I have a Miwuk lover, I guess I'd better pay more attention to these things." MacIntyre swore a solemn oath to herself never to allow an acorn to pass her lips again after that night. Ever. Miwuk lover or not.

The evening passed quickly as she answered Tahefnu's questions about Menmenet and read and re-read the Parker-Shane papers with their stunning revelations of American duplicity. The experts judged her acorn mush excellent, though she was sure they were just being kind. They tried to cheer her up when they noticed her sickened reactions as she read through the papers. Late in the evening, they bade her good night.

She couldn't sleep. Too much evil, too much killing. The coup still to deal with. And it was possible that acorn mush disagreed with her.

On the positive side, the Parker-Shane papers mitigated her own sense of responsibility for the Russian war crimes. War crimes were trending these days, so it wasn't her fault for the few she'd allowed to happen, right? Stay positive, Cheryl.

She walked out of the house and out into the meadow, under the vast sky teeming with stars, thinking about this, that, and the other thing. If half of what she read was true, it was obvious what her new career should be: chasing war criminals. Homicide was evil enough to have motivated her earlier career, but these crimes against humanity deserved everything she could throw at them as a detective. Between the Russians conducting secret missions to kill anything that moved and NATO planning genocide beyond anyone's wildest nightmares, she knew she'd have enough work to last the rest of her life. Head spinning with thoughts and plans, she sat in the meadow and contemplated the vastness of the sky and the mountains surrounding her and the smallness of the world beyond those mountains. After a while, tired and cold and depressed, she fell into bed and closed her eyes and slept and did not dream.

CHAPTER FIFTY-TWO
Shesmu Gets Spiritual Guidance

The demomili leaned his head against the truck's window and napped. Khenmes looked out the window on his side and thought unreadable thoughts. Sitting between them, I kept checking my phone in hope of a signal to call my myrmidons in Menmenet to see how my restaurant was faring. Nothing. After an hour, I dropped off to sleep myself.

I awoke to the touch of a hand on my chest. The demomili, awake and looking at me with beady black eyes, assessed the condition of my spirit with delicate, wrinkled fingers. He said a few words in Waashiw.

Khenmes translated, "Boss doc says that the spirit is still inside you, but quiet now, resting. Not busting out and making trouble all over the place."

"Tell the demomili the trouble is in those papers I left with my girlfriend." MacIntyre would know what to do. She always did. I'd never seen her so troubled, though. Trouble was everywhere.

Another lengthy response from the demomili made Khenmes smile. "Boss doc says that the papers are a fine thing, and so is your girlfriend, but it's other people that matter. Waashiw people, Remetjy people, Miwuk people, all people. Even American and Numunuu people. He says you understand what you need to do to bring people together, to stop them making trouble. Boss doc says you have to do it yourself, 'cause you gave up your power to your spirit god." He paused. "Boss doc, he really don't like trouble. Not a bit."

"Maybe I made a mistake, it felt like the right gesture to make to my father, to give him back the power he'd given me." I shook my head. "At least I still have my restaurants. I need to get back and get things in order there."

The demomili put his hand back on my chest and said something.

Khenmes translated again. "Boss doc says your cooking days are over. He says you'll understand it soon, as soon as you find your own power—papers, people, all of it. He said the spirit god within you can help, but only if you find what's good and right in that god." Khenmes scratched his cheek. "He said you got to trust the people around you, they'll help too."

Warmth suffused my chest from the shaman's hand, and I felt a surge in my heart. Not terrifying this time, more expanding and changing and redefining. I had responsibilities back in Menmenet, but after that...a blank slate, ready to write on. The weight of the responsibility my father had laid on my shoulders from beyond the Duat threatened to crush me. I honestly wasn't sure I was up to it. I had learned who I was, but now I had to decide who I wanted to be.

Khenmes scratched his neck and said, "Boy, you got a lot going on, Shes, and I'm some glad I'm not you. You better listen to the doc. He knows what he's talking about. And he really don't like trouble. Me: I'm retiring, gonna kick back for a while. Get back with wife. Forget about all this 'cause I'm turning it over to you. And to your girlfriend. And to your spirit god who shall henceforth remain nameless, now that we're back in a civilized country." The demomili withdrew his hand from my chest. Khenmes grinned as we headed north into the Washeshu night, not a water baby in sight.

The Rangers delivered us to Khenmes's house in Da'owaga'a late in the evening. The day had been hot. The heat lingered in the air with a piney, earthy taste that had Khenmes smiling as he opened the door of the pickup truck. He took a deep breath and let it out again, looking around.

At the sound of the truck, the porch light came on, and as we got out, I could see the front door open and Tuy appear. The demomili said something to Khenmes and slapped him on the back, then got back in the truck. We waved goodbye, and the truck drove off. We walked up the little path to the front door. A rushing Tuy met us half-way and threw her arms around Khenmes. After a few minutes, Tuy let go of her husband and embraced me. She expressed thanks for bringing back the old man and saving him from the water babies.

I disclaimed the honor. "Tuy, I'm not sure who saved whom from the water babies. And Khenmes gave me my father back." Tuy shot a glance at Khenmes at this revelation, but he shrugged and said nothing.

Arm in arm, the three of us walked back into the house. When Tuy got a look at me in the light, she exclaimed, "Shesmu, you're so thin! Those Miwuks, they been starving you!"

"We've been through a lot, Tuy. Not the Miwuks' fault."

"We've gotta celebrate with a dance, I'll call the demomili!" exclaimed Tuy.

Leave it to a Waashiw to organize a dance first thing.

Khenmes responded, "You don't have to, wife. Boss doc rode with us in the truck. Last thing he said to me just now was 'Big party, two days.' Nothing left for you to do, wife, except come to bed with me."

"I gotta get something for the boy to eat first, old man." And she did.

About 30 seconds into preparations, Khenmes, smelling home-cooked Waashiw food for the first time in a while, joined us.

"I got my fill of that Miwuk stuff, but your cooking smells so good, wife, can't resist a bite or two."

As we sat at the dinner table and consumed the meal, Khenmes and I gave Tuy the rough outlines of our adventures. Tuy's mouth reflected her inner thoughts; her chin tattoos rose and fell with her emotions. Khenmes glossed over the interrogation sessions he'd experienced. He also skipped Tahefnu and her doings. Same old Khenmes: compassion toward my conflicted and closely held feelings. Tuy would try to mother me out of it all, and Khenmes knew I would rather have water babies take me than have her mother me right now.

The opening of the sarcophagus of the as-yet-unnamed-individual-formerly-known-as-Akhen turned Tuy solemn. She looked at me with a compressed mouth and round eyes she struggled to keep from tearing up. She said, "Shes, your dad was a good man, for a Miwuk. He was! Even if he turned out to be Coyote, it wasn't his fault. Things pushed him into the middle of an impossible situation that needed Coyote's tricky nature. No man can be all good when the options are all bad."

The Coyote spirit within me made me queasy about this. I asked her, "Why all the mystery, why not tell me I was half Miwuk?"

Tuy looked sad. "It was your mom, Shes. She wanted you to grow up belonging in Menmenet, a Remetj through and through. She made us promise. I can't tell you how many times the old man and me talked about it. We always wanted to tell you who you really were, but we promised, and we don't break promises. You gotta run with it, change with it."

My father the Coyote, Khenmes, the demomili, Heh, Tahefnu, Karkin, and MacIntyre all wanted me to change my life. Tuy too.

"Do I have any say in this?" I wasn't sure I wanted that much change. I liked my life, liked my restaurants…loved my girlfriend, too. How much of that would remain after I changed?

Khenmes smiled, and Tuy said, "No choice at all."

She was right; I didn't have a choice. Did MacIntyre? I said, "My girlfriend Cheryl is a wonderful woman in an impossible situation, and I don't know what to do about it. She thinks she's responsible for the Russians and their crimes. I can't seem to help her shake her feelings of guilt."

"She sounds like a good person too, the warrior variety. We got a few of those around here too. High maintenance, but worth it. She'll straighten it out. Woman warriors rarely carry guilt a long way, but you have to be there for her. Warriors do best in teams, particularly woman warriors."

I reassured her. "Cheryl and I are going to be together for a long time. A very long time. If she doesn't wind up sacrificed on some hetep somewhere by diving headfirst into a disaster."

Khenmes said, "Your dad and I were warriors, awhile back. Together. Warriors…." He had a thoughtful look on his face.

"And you're retired now!" said Tuy.

"Yes I am, wife, yes I am." He smiled and took her hand and rubbed it. "But the boy here isn't, he's still got to figure out what to do with his life."

Tuy shook her head. "It won't be warrior stuff, he's not that kind of boy. He's got his girlfriend to handle that side of it." She looked me straight in the eye. "You got to atone for your dad, because he can't do it anymore himself, he's got other business in the spirit world. Your mom knew all about what he did, but she couldn't do anything about it back then. It wore her away until she died. She drew away from her in-laws because of what your dad did, didn't have any First Peoples' support other than us. You'll help her spirit rest easy when you atone for your dad's mistakes. And you gotta bring this girlfriend up here to meet me, real soon."

She looked at Khenmes, still holding her hand, and changed the subject. "Old man, if you think rubbing my hand is gonna make it for a big comeback, I got something to show you in the bedroom."

CHAPTER FIFTY-THREE

MacIntyre Hits the Wall

RISING LATER THAN SHE EXPECTED, MacIntyre found the house empty. Her somber mood had lifted in the night, dispersing enough of the doubts and dust to allow her to at least eat breakfast. She looked in the refrigerator. Leftover elk sausage, yes. Eggs. She could do something with eggs. Acorn mush from last night? Never. Toast, that wasn't too challenging.

Pleasantly full, she took a last walk down to the river before her transport to her new career arrived. She got as far as the roundhouse when Karkin accosted her from the entrance.

"Let's talk." He disappeared back into the roundhouse. MacIntyre followed him in, her early good feelings dissolving like morning fog on the meadow.

Heh stood in the center of the roundhouse poking a fire into life, and Karkin sat cross-legged in front of the it. MacIntyre dragged over a log and sat on that.

"What's up, Karkin?"

"Coup."

"What about it?"

"Menmenet's not safe for you."

"And what can we do to change that?"

"Not much."

Heh sat, the fire going nicely. "Now that's not true, Karkin, you need to lighten up on our friend here. She can get it done."

"Huh."

MacIntyre grinned. "Look how much I've done so far!"

"Huh!" Her achievements did not impress Karkin.

She said, "I need to get back to Menmenet to find a new job. If that means foiling the coup in progress, so be it. Job hunting is never a straightforward process."

Karkin got to his feet, but Heh put an arm out and sat him back down.

"No one leaves without a plan. What am I supposed to tell the council? They're waiting for a plan, or anyway something that they can chew into." Heh's face looked solemn in the firelight.

MacIntyre asked, "What council?"

Heh stared at her in silence.

"Need to know," said Karkin.

"We've had this conversation. Heh, what council? Karkin, is this the secret organization you told—"

Karkin's dark look stopped her before she revealed the full scope of his breach of ethnic secrecy.

Heh glanced at Karkin with a one-sided smile, then said, "Well now, it's not my secret."

"Come on, Heh. Give."

Heh sighed. "Council of Elders."

"And you're on it, right? One of the 'Elders'?"

"Naw, I'm not old enough to be on the council."

"Fuck me." MacIntyre visualized a group of toothless, acorn-mush-eating Miwuks. "Is this a secret Miwuk thing?"

"Naw, inter-tribal, from all over the Republic."

"And who is on it?"

"Can't tell you that." Heh's face turned stubborn.

"How are we supposed to come up with a plan that will please this group of elderly busybodies?"

Heh fumbled in a small pouch he had on his belt and withdrew three peyotl buttons. "Works every time," he said.

MacIntyre decided right away to exclude peyotl as a planning tool. Karkin grinned; this startled her, as it was the first time she had ever seen the man smile.

MacIntyre asked, "Do you know what's happening right now in Menmenet?"

"Imen-R'a on lockdown, Mentju garrisoning the palace, no NATO support, Setehnekhet busy at the Temple of Mentju working out an alternative plan for the hekasepat."

Heh said with admiration, "Wow. See now, Cheryl, ain't that everything in an acorn shell? Knew he could do it if he wanted to."

"Fuck me. How do you *get* all this, Karkin?"

"Sources. Basa, too," said Karkin. "But he can't leave Ta Sekhet, he's dealing with the NATO forces to the south."

"So, we've got to figure out a way to use a small force to immobilize the coup players and take back the city."

"See now," said Heh. "Once you get started, comes easy. Sure about the peyotl?" He again offered the buttons.

"Real sure," said MacIntyre.

"Too bad," said Heh, putting the buttons back in his little pouch. "Fun stuff."

MacIntyre wasn't having any. "Yeah. Sure. So how do we—"

"Bear." Heh smiled.

"I'm sorry?"

"My peyotl vision. I didn't think much of it at the time, just Bear complaining."

Karkin looked at Heh, raising an eyebrow.

MacIntyre rubbed her forehead, reflecting before speaking, but it did no good. "And what does Bear disapprove of?"

"Drinking. Too much beer, too many people drunk. I assumed he was complaining about the celebration we'd have here after the battle." Heh shook his head. "Nobody felt like it, everybody just wanted to go home."

"I sure as hell do, but I can't, because there's this coup…."

"Yeah. Well, I don't think the drunks I saw were here, I think they were in Menmenet. Tekh. I didn't realize it until now."

Karkin looked at the floor, then repeated the Remetjy word Heh had uttered, "Tekh."

Heh and MacIntyre looked at Karkin. The Remetjy word meant drunkenness but was also the name of a month in the old Remetjy calendar. It was the first month of the year, the month of the Inundation of the River. This month.

"So what?" asked MacIntyre.

"Heb-Tekh." Karkin closed his eyes.

"Oh. My. God." Illumination flooded MacIntyre's tired brain.

Heh smiled. "Somebody gonna fill me in?"

"What the fuck day is it? I've lost track." MacIntyre dug out her phone and opened her calendar app. She flipped around until she brought up the Remetjy religious calendar. "Yep. Today is 20 Tekh, the first day of the Festival of Drunkenness." She smiled. "Hut-Her's biggest festival in Menmenet. I'm sure they've been setting up the beer halls for the last week at the Temple of Hut-Her and all over the rest of the city."

"So the folks I saw in my vision were Remetjet, stupid drunk."

"I can't say, I don't know Bear that well, Heh," replied MacIntyre. "But the key thing is what happens tomorrow. Everybody drinks themselves stupid today. They go to bed to sleep it off. In the morning, the Temple of Hut-Her plays drums on their loudspeakers all over the city to wake everybody up. And I know for a fact that all the temple priests take part. The perfect opportunity."

"Hekasepat. Top down. Get it?"

She did. She saw it altogether, complete in all its parts. Take over the Palace of the Republic, isolate the hekasepat, deal with any Mentju troops likely to interfere. That done, convince the hekasepat to delegitimize both the coup and Setehnekhet through the Temple of Imen-R'a. Then deal with that son-of-a-bitch Setehnekhet, rapidly and efficiently and permanently, along with his local team of plotters. That would free her up to take on her new job of hunting down war criminals.

Too bad the Waashiw Rangers had left. "Damn, we'll need—"

"Troops. Heh?" Karkin looked at the old man.

"I'm sure the Council of Elders would be happy to round up a few warriors to help. Once they recognize we have a plan, that is. Have to go down to the foothills to check, though. Maybe you can get Basa to send one of those chopper things? Daughter took the truck."

MacIntyre heard, in the roundhouse's silence, a distant, throbbing roar.

"No need, our ride's here," she said. The dust in her mind settled as her path cleared.

Close to dawn on the morning after Heb-Tekh, two transport choppers gently settled in front of the Palace of the Republic. MacIntyre and Karkin jumped out of the Republican Guard chopper onto the Wesekhwat, the wide main street of the Tjesut. The street was empty of both people and traffic. The other chopper disgorged a K'ashaaya special forces team.

MacIntyre had put on her snazzy brown beret to look as military as possible, but she didn't impress the leader of the K'ashaaya team, Butakamen. She wore her dusty military uniform, no insignia. Karkin had on his green army jacket, now very much in need of a visit to the laundry.

"Civilians?" Butakamen asked, looking them up and down.

She replied, "Sure, why not? It's a civil problem. At least, so far. I just need you guys to back me up in case of trouble. We're here to negotiate, not to blow things up."

She carried her latest souvenir: a Russian VSS rifle that she'd kept from the raid in Ta Sekhet. Karkin's rifle was a fancy thing that MacIntyre concluded was some kind of Swiss innovation supplied by his secret organization.

Butakamen walked up to the gate of the Palace. A chain and padlock on the gate was the only barrier to entry; no guards visible. Butakamen made a hand signal, and one of his troops came up with a huge bolt-cutter and cut apart the chain. Butakamen swung the gate open.

"After you, ma'am," he said to MacIntyre.

The K'ashaaya set up an internment center in the chapel, putting several dozy guards and a janitor there for safe keeping. MacIntyre and Karkin had determined from the public schedule that the hekasepat would be in his office. He needed to be ready for the public awakening ceremony this morning. He'd conducted the Heb-Tekh ceremony in the chapel yesterday, then retired to his office to sleep it off with his admins. As the team entered the office suite, various admins huddled over their desks, either asleep or blearily gazing in surprise at the intruders. So far so good.

MacIntyre said, "Karkin, could you round these folks up and hold them in that conference room?"

Karkin motioned with his rifle. The few people awake rose to their feet and fled into the conference room. Karkin got the K'ashaaya to carry the others in.

MacIntyre walked over to the hekasepat's door and entered without knocking. She had no trouble finding Sebekemheb, she just followed the snores over to a large couch at the side of the room. MacIntyre smiled and set about waking him up.

"What...what's happening?" Sebekemheb tried what he thought was a brave smile, but the panic in his eyes when he saw an armed soldier belied it. MacIntyre was less than impressed. *He's got the looks of an actor but not the talent.*

Sebekemheb struggled up from the couch and sat upright. Holding his head in his hands, he said, "You're that American Set brought by that time. What the fuck are you doing here?"

She said, "I'm here with a message from your Republican Guard. Imy-er-mesh'a Basa has reestablished control of Ta Sekhet and put a stop to the NATO incursion. Second, I'm here to rescue you." She lifted the rifle. "From Setehnekhet and his coup."

"*Rescue…!*" Sebekemheb shrieked. "I don't need you to rescue me! Is this a coup? You're going to kill me!"

"Well, no, Seb. This is an anti-coup. See, we figured out what Setehnekhet was doing a few days ago, but shit happened and we wound up having to clean up the NATO mess in Ta Sekhet first." She hoped Sebekemheb wouldn't ask too many questions about that; not her finest hour. But that was far from his chief concern.

"Setehnekhet! He's the hem-netjer-tepy of Mentju! He's my principal military advisor!"

The hekasepat appeared to be very slow on the uptake today, even more than on a normal, sober day. MacIntyre leaned her rifle up against the big desk in the middle of the room and drew a chair over to the couch, then sat in it.

She said, "Seb. Shut up a minute and listen, OK? Setehnekhet conspired with NATO, and specifically the Americans, to take over the government here, keeping you on as a figurehead. You must have sussed that out by now."

"Set? Take over? But, no, he's…he said he was making changes, needed changes, in the organization of the government…." Sebekemheb trailed off as the reality hit him. "Conspired? With the Americans? NATO? In Ta Sekhet? I thought he was getting rid of the Americans!" His eyes got big. "*You're* an American!"

"It's complicated, Seb. First, he gets rid of them, then he invites them in, then he gets rid of them again. See? And don't worry about me, I'm loyal. I'm your best pal, take my word."

Sebekemheb shook his head, eyes round and mouth ajar. "I, that is, what?"

"Am I talking too fast for you, Seb? Setehnekhet is a traitor who wants to take over the government with the help of Americans he will then betray and kill. He wants total power here."

"Total…power?"

"Total. Power."

Maybe he'd grasp the situation better if she restated it in religious terms. Sebekemheb was, after all, the titular hem-netjer-tepy of Imen-R'a, the top priest in the Republic.

She said, "How about this? Ma'at figured out that Seteh corrupted Mentju. Then Seteh tried to create isfet beyond anything we've seen so far in this Republic."

Pseudo-mystical nonsense, but if Shes could make it convincing; why couldn't she?

"Seteh? Isfet?" Sebekemheb licked his lips. "I can't, what, gods? Those gods?"

"Those gods, Seb. Ma'at and Imen-R'a want this fixed right away, and you're the man to do it. With help from loyal troops. Loyal to you, that is. K'ashaaya. From the north." MacIntyre's impatience edged through her patient explanation.

"K'ash—what…what do I need to do?"

"You need to appoint a new hem-netjer-tepy of Mentju. You need to get orders out to your military units telling them to stand down and to take orders only from the new hem-netjer-tepy or you, personally. You need to get the Temple of Imen-R'a released from lockdown and get them engaged here. I know you can count on the Council of Elders to enforce the stand-down if you need to. After that, you need to sit here and do whatever you do until we need you to do whatever we'll need you to do."

"Council? What council?"

"Never you mind."

"You're sure Setehnekhet is doing all this evil stuff?"

"Sure. You have no idea how sure. Once we take over the Temple of Mentju, I'll be able to show you the plans."

"Are you going to kill him?"

"Not if we can help it. I don't enjoy killing. Ma'at doesn't enjoy killing. Much. But it's up to him, you know?"

Sebekemheb sat up straight on his couch. "I suppose it's all right." He rubbed his mouth and tried another brave smile, again failing. "Who should I get for hem-netjer-tepy?"

MacIntyre smiled. Now she was the king-maker, the power behind the throne of the gods.

"Seb. You are the hekasepat. You get to choose. Choose somebody loyal."

Sebekemheb was quiet, then said, "My next-in-line, the za-hekasepat?"

MacIntyre pursed her lips and said, "He's keeping the Temple of Imen-R'a in line."

Sebekemheb looked down, thought some more, and said, "Iyet, the hemet-netjer-tepy of Djehuty?"

MacIntyre smiled. "Your mistress? Not likely. And you know you can't trust a mistress. They want too much from you." He must be close to running out of people loyal to him. There couldn't be that many. Should she give him a hint?

"No, I suppose not." He thought some more, the strain showing on his knotted brow. Then he smiled. "I know; Basa! What about Basa?"

There we go. "Excellent choice, superb choice. Recall him from Ta Sekhet, he's there now cleaning things up."

Sebekemheb said, gathering his wits, his eyes meeting hers, "Who precisely are you and why are you doing this?"

"Seb, I'm your best pal right now."

"But—"

"Seb. I don't like murderers and war criminals, and I am damned if I will let them take over the country I've made my home. OK? We'll figure out who I am and what to do with me after it's all over. My immediate goals are to end this coup and to get Setehnekhet behind bars where he belongs. I need your help to do that. Will you help?"

Sebekemheb looked at her and nodded, but his worries showed. "I'll need my admins to get this done."

MacIntyre got up, picked up her rifle, and walked over to the open door to the office. "Karkin! Get 'em in here."

Karkin herded the admins out of the conference room where he'd been weaving the story for them and got them into the hekasepat's office. They were in various states of alertness but very, very quiet. At least they were all awake now.

"Everybody up to speed?" asked MacIntyre. The heads nodded, the faces shocked. "Great! OK, Seb, go to it. Karkin, you stay and supervise things. I need to get going with the K'ashaaya at the Temple of Mentju, before the drums start and wake everybody up. Seb, just tell Karkin what you need, he'll get it done. Are you going to be OK, Seb?"

"Compared to what?" asked the nettled but somewhat reassured leader of the Republic. He turned to Karkin. "Who the hell are *you?*"

Karkin shook his head. "Need to know," he said. MacIntyre laughed.

Butakamen, the K'ashaaya team leader, kneeled behind the colossal statue of Mentju in the park across from the Temple of Mentju.

"That's what we're supposed to take over?" he asked, eyebrows raised, his leathery copper face looking grim.

"That's it." MacIntyre was kneeling on the other side of the statue, staring hopelessly at the huge facade across the street. An idnu in the Republican Guard kneeled next to her.

Butakamen said, "Not a fucking chance."

"It is a fortress, isn't it? That's what Mentju is about."

The K'ashaaya sat back on his heels. "We need a better plan than 'storm the building.' You didn't tell me this was what you had in mind."

MacIntyre scoffed. "You guys are special forces, aren't you? Didn't they train you to do things like this?"

"No, they trained us *not* to do things like this." He smiled. "And 'they' are in there right now, we trained here. From my experience with Mentju, it's unlikely they've spent all of yesterday drinking themselves to sleep, like at the Palace."

MacIntyre smiled. "How about guile, then?"

"Or magic, take your pick. We don't have a shaman on the squad, though, so unless you got Remetjy god stuff going on that I don't know about, guile sounds good. Ma'am."

She straightened her brown beret with resolution, then pulled out her phone. She punched in a number.

"Yes, hello, could you connect me with Meryr'a in Security? We have a family emergency. Thanks!"

"Who the fuck is Meryr'a?" asked the K'ashaaya.

"Shut up." She waited. "Hi, Meryr'a, it's me. Oh good, you recognize my voice. No, no, don't hang up. Listen, I've got a minor problem I need you to help with." She listened to the phone, rolling her eyes. "Meryr'a, have I ever led you wrong? No, no, don't hang up. No, that's blown over long ago, we're fine now. Look, just help me, OK? I've lost my key and I need to get into the building to take care of some business with the Hem-Netjer-Tepy. Can you come to the side door near the delivery dock and let me in? It will just take you a few minutes, I won't keep you away from your work long." MacIntyre smiled. "OK, thanks. See you in a minute."

She put away the phone. "OK, come on, guys, around the back." She took off the beret and stuffed it into a pocket. She turned to the Republican Guard idnu. "You stay here, in reserve, Idnu. If the K'ashaaya need help, they'll signal, all right?" The idnu nodded.

The special forces team worked their way around the big temple. MacIntyre pointed to a small door next to the loading dock with large metal shutters rolled down over the openings. "Get on both sides of that door and stay quiet."

MacIntyre walked up to the door, handed her rifle to Butakamen, and waited. She heard noises and the metal door creaked open.

"Meryr'a, great to see you again! Thanks so much for helping me."

"What sort of uniform is that?"

"This? Not a uniform, it's a hunting suit. That's where I lost my key, hunting trip."

"I don't enjoy hunting."

"I don't give—I'm sorry to hear that, Meryr'a. It's an American thing. But thanks for letting me in, you have no idea how much I appreciate it."

"Sure." Meryr'a grinned. "My dad says to tell you, 'Well done.'"

MacIntyre blinked. "Your dad." The atch-netjer of Imen-R'a in charge of security, she remembered.

"Yeah, I just called him to ask what I should do, and he told me to let you and your friends in. Where are they, by the way?"

MacIntyre looked at her feet, then signaled Butakamen, who gathered up his men behind MacIntyre.

"Wow," said Meryr'a. "Looks like the Atchet-Netjer is going to have a fit. Can't wait! Well, come on." The gangly youth disappeared up the back stairwell, followed by MacIntyre and her team.

"Guile," said Butakamen as they climbed up to the fifth floor.

"Guile," she said, "works fine when you have someone guileless to work on. Having friends is even better. Now: rules of engagement—no killing, OK?" She waited until the K'ashaaya had acknowledged this reasonable request. MacIntyre looked hard at them, but their eyes were nowhere near as stony as the Russians' eyes had been. She retrieved the beret from her pocket and adjusted it.

The halls were empty. Regular employees had definitely partaken of the Festival. They turned a familiar corner, and MacIntyre stopped for thought. "Can you send two people down to the Records room to secure it? I don't want any evidence destroyed. I'll need it to show the hekasepat. And remember, no killing! Please."

The K'ashaaya consulted, and two soldiers got directions from MacIntyre and went off on their mission. The team then deployed around the door to the hem-netjer-tepy's office. MacIntyre opened the door, and they all rushed in, surprising the assistants in the room. The K'ashaaya had them facing the wall in short order.

"Butakamen, you'll need to take care of the Security Department, however many of them are still awake, and any remaining guards. The Atchet-netjer of Security, Sheritr'a, is one of the coup leaders. She's going to be awake for sure, don't underestimate her. Get the Republican Guard troops from the park to help."

MacIntyre approached the hem-netjer-tepy's door and knocked. She was sure Setehnekhet would be his usual bright and chipper self, given his discipline.

"Enter."

She did. Setehnekhet, stone-faced, rose from his desk.

"What is this?" He smiled his grimmest smile. "Come back to finish our little ritual? I'm afraid I don't have the time today."

MacIntyre hefted her VSS sniper rifle, which was surprisingly lightweight. "I'm sure you'll make the time for me, Set." She swung the rifle up and let off a round, the dull thud of the noise-suppressed shot punctuating her request. The plaster head of Mentju behind the hem-netjer-tepy exploded.

"Gun on the floor, please." MacIntyre pointed with the rifle barrel. Setehnekhet unsnapped his sidearm, checked the safety, and tossed it to the floor. It fell with a flat clunk on the carpet. MacIntyre kicked it off to the side of the room. "It's over, Set."

The hem-netjer-tepy cracked his knuckles. "You are very capable, Cheryl, though you may be unaware of the danger you have put yourself in. Don't you see that it might be wise to understand the full scope of what you're interfering with? And how the gods will react? Mentju, for one, does not take kindly to disloyalty in its w'abut." He waved a hand at the now-headless statue of his god.

"Set, that crap may work for the uninitiated, but I'm fully initiated now. As for understanding the full scope, I may have a better idea of it than you, given the secrets I've learned. We've put a stop to the NATO incursion and mobilized most of the armed forces against you. You haven't spoken with Seb yet today, have you? Don't bother, he won't be taking your calls. I'm thinking Mentju won't be taking your calls either."

"I underestimated you, Cheryl—your resilience, your vigor. But there is still time. I will forgive your assault on me and work with you to share power. Think, Cheryl. You do not understand what the Americans, your fellow countrymen, plan to do."

"I know precisely what they're planning: genocide. And I know that you're planning to preempt them on it by doing it to them first. And don't talk to me about assault, you fucking rapist. It makes me want to shoot you where you stand." She raised the barrel of the VSS a little to emphasize this last point.

"I did underestimate you, Cheryl." He smiled with his down-turned mouth. "You realize that if I do not take power, the Americans will surely roll right over our poor little Republic with its dim hekasepat and complacent populace. There is still time; I will share power. This," he smiled wider, "is a concession to your obvious ability and strength, Cheryl. I am not used to women with such strength. I can learn; we can share genuine power here."

"The only power you'll be sharing, Set, will come from the electric light in your cell."

"Uncompromising, that's what you are, Cheryl. Relentless."

MacIntyre smiled. "Time to go, Set." She motioned with the rifle.

Setehnekhet came around the desk. MacIntyre backed away, holding the rifle at port, and nodded toward the door. Setehnekhet walked past her, then stumbled slightly. Before she could react, the knife he had drawn from his boot was flying toward her. It landed with a solid thunk in her right thigh. She tried to raise the rifle but fell over as her leg buckled beneath her. Setehnekhet wasted little time. He ran to the back of the office and behind the statue of Mentju, then disappeared.

MacIntyre heard sounds from the outer office. "Butakamen!" screamed MacIntyre. The K'ashaaya ran in and saw her on the floor. She jabbed a pointing finger. "Setehnekhet! Behind the statue!"

Butakamen ran over to the statue and yelled, "There's a secret door open here, I'll follow him!" Then he disappeared after his prey.

MacIntyre struggled onto one knee and gripped her VSS, the excitement of the hunt briefly fortifying her until she realized that her leg wouldn't support her. For a hunter, the chase was everything. For her the chase was over, with no dinner at the end of it all, and she was so hungry for a pound of Setehnekhet's flesh. But being the hunter was still better than being the hunted, even if the hunted got away. Always another day, another hunt. The situation here, though, was not under control.

MacIntyre contemplated the knife sticking out of her thigh. Half-in, four-inches of blade showing, she saw it had no handle, just a small tang. Some kind of ballistic knife blade, fired from its handle. Normal time resumed as the adrenaline subsided. She became aware that there had been a good deal of noise from the outer office for the last few minutes. She pivoted around on her knee to cover the office door with the VSS.

Two K'ashaaya ran in and helped MacIntyre to her feet and out to the outer office. One body on the floor, a fat woman who wouldn't be hooding anybody ever again. Sheritr'a had gone to the Duat.

"Sorry, ma'am, she came in shooting. Had to take her out."

"Fine," she said. "Just fine. Infirmary, third floor. Now."

The soldier said, "Yes ma'am," and signaled two other soldiers to pick up the corpse.

"Not her, fuckhead. Me."

CHAPTER FIFTY-FOUR

Shesmu Comes Home

THE PARTY AT TZATLEE TOSH started mid-morning. There was an overflow crowd of everyone Khenmes had ever known. They took turns dancing in the hall and partying in the sacred grove outside. At mid-day some of the men dug a barbecue pit and set up for a big feast. The demomili was everywhere, orchestrating things and looking on with a dour satisfaction. I caught his eye as he stared at me with a concentrated look that I had no idea how to interpret.

I took a break from the party and gazed out at the evil little island in the middle of Tzatlee Tosh. The water was still and deep blue in the day's heat, and the water babies slept soundly on this day of joy. My phone rang.

"Shesmu here."

"She's in the hospital. Knife. Leg. She's OK." It was Karkin.

"How's she taking it?"

"Not a fucking nursemaid," he complained. I could only imagine the nightmare that an immobilized MacIntyre would be for the not-very-sympathetic Ramaytush. Whatever his debt to me, some things were too much.

I allowed, "No, you're not. Can you wait a day? Big party here."

"No. Things to do."

"Mmph. OK, I'll see what I can arrange for a flight."

Karkin hung up.

I manipulated the phone awhile, got lucky, and took the last seat on a flight to Menmenet that left in four hours. I stood, phone in hand, weighing the idea of calling MacIntyre right then. On the positive side, I loved her and wanted to be with her to help and wanted to tell her that. On the negative side, her mood would be beyond foul. She'd tell me I should already be there and to take it and put it where it hurts. I decided to surprise her, and I put the phone away.

I found Tuy and Khenmes in the dance hall and told them about the development. Khenmes offered to drive me to the airport, but the demomili popped up and spoke to him.

Khenmes told me, "Boss doc says it's my party, I can't leave or the spirits will get on my case. They're not water babies, you know, but still." More talk from the demomili. "Boss doc says he'll drive you."

"Very kind," I bowed to the demomili. I wondered how I could, without offense, avoid being driven along dirt roads by a half-blind, 125-year-old man guided by angry, party-deprived spirits. But it turned out not to be a problem. He had a driver and a nice black SUV with plenty of refreshments in the back, as befitted a major player in the government.

I got a big hug from a tearful Tuy and a bigger hug from Khenmes. I told them I'd visit again soon.

The demomili and I communicated through the driver. The demomili told me he was sure MacIntyre would soon recover from her slight wound. He told me it was unfortunate that the hem-netjer-tepy of Mentju had escaped, but she would soon recover from that failure as well. All this impressed me, since as far as I was aware no one had told him anything about her. He discovered more about it from his spirits than I did from my local informant on the scene, Karkin.

I thanked him for the ride to the airport. He grinned, and the driver interpreted, telling me that the demomili wanted to make sure I got on the plane with my spirit-god. He didn't say why, but I remembered that he really didn't like trouble, and I don't think he was that fond of Miwuk spirit-gods either.

My spirit-god whispered in my internal ear that, as of now, trouble was my business.

CHAPTER FIFTY-FIVE

MacIntyre and Shesmu See the Doctor

"I SURE WISH YOU HADN'T thrown away that walking stick, Shes, I'm going to need it," groused MacIntyre, lying in her hospital bed. In a word, her mood was foul. The K'ashaaya team leader Butakamen, Karkin, and her boyfriend Shesmu sat around the bed keeping her company.

Shes had arrived on a plane from Da'owaga'a and had come directly to the hospital. He still wore the fetid hunting suit he'd worn the last time she saw him, she could smell it. He hadn't even gone home to change before coming to see her, so touching. But that small emotion vanished under the weight of her pain and anxiety to be up and doing. Also, he smelled of a rank combination of wood smoke, pine sap, sweat, and the undefinable, squalid aroma of a man who has spent too much time by himself. A few days in civilization had sensitized her to this, as she hadn't noticed the same smells while they were in the mountains. Now, they made her nose itch.

"How are you feeling, Cheryl?" asked Shes.

"Nice of you to ask, Shesmu, I am feeling fine. Just fine." She put a good deal of bitterness and anger into her eyes and tone to convey her disgust at her immobile, painful state. The high degree of imbecility in the people surrounding her offended her even more. "Hunky-dory," she added in English to nail it down.

"You don't look it," said Karkin.

"Shut up, Karkin." Funny; she usually wanted him to talk more.

Butakamen tried to change the subject back to the reason for the meeting. "The latest information is that Setehnekhet has surfaced requesting asylum at the United States Embassy."

"Fine. Just fine," repeated MacIntyre. "How the hell could you not catch him? You were 15 seconds behind him."

"A minute is as good as a mile," replied Butakamen, undisturbed by her tantrum. "That place was a fucking maze, and I was the fucking mouse. I'm lucky I made it out without starving to death."

MacIntyre grunted and shifted her leg. "Unh! That fucking doctor says I can go home soon. Here's what I want to do. I want to take a special forces unit—a *Remetjy* special forces unit—and take the embassy. After that, we can do what we need to do with them both. Or we could blow it up. What do you think?"

The three men exchanged glances. Karkin took up the challenge. "International law. Prison for life."

Another joke fallen flat.

"Well, hell. I can't just lie here and watch the gangrene set in." She winced with the pain. It was remarkable how much pain there was in a knife wound *after* the fucking doctor got through with it. On the whole, she preferred walking around with a knife in her leg.

Shes tried soothing her. "It's not that bad, Cheryl, twenty stitches and a course of antibiotics. A flesh wound. The knife wasn't even poisoned."

"You say. It's not your fucking leg. I say it hurts like hell, and I want to move."

Butakamen stood. "I got to get back to Fort Rus, the council says the Russians are restless up north. Have you guys got this?"

Shes stood and bowed. "Yeah, she'll come around."

MacIntyre groaned and adjusted her leg again. But she said, "Thanks, Butakamen. It's been a pleasure working with you. Unlike these idiots."

"Right. I'm off, then." Butakamen walked out. Shes resumed his seat.

MacIntyre asked, "OK, Karkin. If I can't blow up the embassy, what *can* I do?"

Karkin said, "Negotiate." Shes nodded.

"Negotiate what?"

Shes replied, "I don't know, talk with them and see whether you can get some justice." He was persuasive rather than insistent, which she appreciated.

"OK, I'll get down to the Embassy as soon as they let me out of here and negotiate." With a large stick.

"I didn't mean you, personally," said Shes.

"Why not me, personally?" asked MacIntyre.

Shes's face got the look that a boyfriend gets when he needs to tell unpleasant, very personal truths to his girlfriend. "You're...not the best at negotiation, Cheryl. You're more, like, rip their lungs out and stomp on them."

"I don't need to be diplomatic here."

"Somebody does," said Karkin.

"Shut up, Karkin."

Shes continued, "Also, between John Smith and Setehnekhet, you have the two people who would most like to see you dead and dismembered. It's not smart to walk into the U. S. Embassy alone."

"You think I can't handle them?" MacIntyre smiled a dangerous smile.

"I have enough unpleasant visual memories," replied Shes.

"Prison for *life*. Professional negotiator," recommended Karkin. "Temple of Djehuty. Diplomats. Know what they're doing."

"Cheryl, please. Don't even think about doing this yourself. For me. For all of us. Let a professional do it." Shes's face was serious, and he put a hand over hers. She gripped it.

"OK, OK. A pro. Djehuty—another fucking god and more priests involved. Maybe this pro diplomat can do something about the Russians, too. No harm in asking. I need to get out of here. Where the hell's that fucking doctor? Hand me that phone!"

CHAPTER FIFTY-SIX

Shesmu Cleans Up His Life

MacIntyre, having called for the fucking doctor, lay back in the bed.

"Things to do," said Karkin. He got up and left. MacIntyre stared after him with blazing eyes.

I smiled and said, "He's not the best nursemaid."

She said in a hot voice, "I don't need *Karkin* as a nursemaid. You either." She closed her eyes.

"I know. I'm not a nursemaid, I'm the guy who's going to take you home and put you to bed. Once the doctor says it's OK."

She opened her eyes and glared at me but said nothing.

At that point, the door opened to admit a harried Remetj in a white lab coat. His face expressed his wish for a quiet life. He smiled a doctor's cheerful smile and said, "Well, Cheryl, how are we feeling today?"

"Like getting out of here, Doc. Now."

"Let's just..." The doctor pulled down the sheet and probed a nasty set of sutures on MacIntyre's leg.

"Ahh! Jeez! Oh my fucking....!" Her eyes popped wide, and she tried to sit up, nearly making it before falling back in bed.

"Looks nice, very nice, Cheryl. No sign of infection, nice tight sutures—"

"I swear if I could get out of this bed and stay out of jail, I'd wrap your testicles around your neck and choke you to death." MacIntyre struggled to sit up, and the doctor put his probing fingers back on the sutures. She collapsed backwards onto the bed, swearing.

"Now, Cheryl, we talked before about medication for that pain."

"No fucking way, you drug pusher."

"And you are…?" The doctor addressed me, a question in his eye.

"Shesmu. She's…my girlfriend."

"Ah. Good. I think she needs support."

"I don't fucking need any support, I need to get out of here!" said MacIntyre, pounding on the bed with a clenched fist. "Jesus, the pain!" In English. The doctor probed some more.

"Now, Cheryl," he said, in his most soothing and patronizing voice, "calm down, calm down; it would be better—the medication—"

"Just sign the fucking form, you son of a bitch," said MacIntyre, voice quieting but still intense.

I tugged on the doctor's sleeve and took him outside the room, followed by several English imprecations that we both ignored.

"Is she always like this?" asked the doctor.

"Only when somebody's telling her what she can't do," I replied, smiling. "So, Doc, what happens if she goes home and gets looked after so she doesn't get gangrene and lose the leg?"

"She'll be fine. To be frank, I've kept her here because of her psychological state. The wound is sensitive to touch, but there's no sign of any underlying problem with infection or torn muscles. She ought not to be out and about with that level of pain and anger. She won't take the painkiller medications I prescribe. I understand she's been through several seriously traumatic experiences, and I want to observe her for signs of PTSD. The anger indicates—"

"She's seen some dreadful things, me too. But do you want to go through the next few days undergoing the trauma of dealing with her? You'll have PTSD yourself. You'll need the medication too. Why not let me do it? I've plumbed the depths of PTSD myself and can give her advice."

The doctor, expression alternating between harried and the smile that doctors get when you try out gallows humor on them, said, "Wait here."

He disappeared around a corner. Two minutes later, a nurse appeared. I followed her into MacIntyre's room.

"Hello, Cheryl," she smiled.

"Oh my God, another one."

"Doctor says you can leave."

MacIntyre sat up in bed and threw off the covers.

"Wait, just a minute!" The nurse raised a hand. "Instructions."

MacIntyre fixed her eye on the nurse and said, "I'm listening."

"You must get a walker or crutches at the medical supply, and you'll need to come back to get the sutures removed in ten days."

"Promise me," I said. The nurse looked at me quizzically, but I knew that MacIntyre would try to take the stitches out herself.

"OK, OK."

"And you may experience pain—"

"May, shit. Every time that fucking doctor comes in here, I experience pain!"

"Yes, well, that may continue for a while, Cheryl, the nerves—"

"Can I go now?"

"Here is a painkiller that should help. Only one every 6 hours, please. There's enough in this bottle for a week, come back for a prescription if you need more. It's addictive, Cheryl, so please be careful. No alcohol. And you need to rest for several days in bed." The nurse handed MacIntyre a pill bottle.

"Can I go now?"

The nurse looked at me with a superior smile. "Are you…?"

"Yep. Chief crutch."

"Oh, fuck you, Shes." MacIntyre eased out of the bed.

The nurse just kept smiling, and I imagined I could see the desire in her eyes for us to leave as quickly as possible. She got MacIntyre's clothes out of a drawer and laid them neatly on the bed. Professional.

MacIntyre stripped off her hospital garb so fast the nurse had no time to even gasp and push me out the door. I smiled and stepped over and held things. The last bit was her beret. I held it out, and she looked at me with a concentrated look, then took it and adjusted it.

The nurse helped MacIntyre into a wheelchair. With a stop at the hospital's medical supply for crutches, she wheeled MacIntyre out to the front of the hospital. She seemed happy to see us off. I got the same feeling from the nurse I had received from the demomili on leaving Washeshu, and the nurse didn't even know I had a spirit-god.

As the rideshare took us the short distance to her apartment, MacIntyre held up the bottle to the light and looked at the pills.

"You should take one now," I said.

"I am not putting anything in my body that will in any way get me closer to the gods. Any gods," she replied. "Fuck, that hurts." She put the bottle in a pocket.

I got her up to her apartment and onto her couch, then sat next to her.

"Shes, thank you so much for everything, getting me here, and…everything. But—"

"You need alone time."

"Fucking right, I do. Sorry."

"No, I understand." I made to embrace her, and she recoiled, palms up in the air, pushing me away before I got close.

"Shes—sorry, you smell like a dead animal." She winced. "And I hurt. A lot."

I didn't take this personally, mainly because I did smell like a dead animal. The man next to me on the plane from Da'owaga'a had been vocal about it, but we came to terms after I explained my predicament; it was a short flight, and the man was Waashiw and knew the demomili. His exact words were, "Boss doc says you gotta do it, you gotta do it. Have a nice day, asshole."

I shifted further away from my girlfriend. I said, "I need to ask you something, then I'll go home and shower, OK?"

"What?"

"The Russians—how do I convince you it wasn't your fault, what they did?"

She smiled and pointed at her kitchen table. I got up and went over, and I found the Parker-Shane papers spread out.

MacIntyre said, "I read them again once I got back here, just before heading out for my visit to the Palace of the Republic. To refresh my mind on the details, so I could convince the hekasepat to change sides."

"And I assume you succeeded?"

"Didn't even need the details. You can take them and make good use of them."

"Sure." I gathered the papers up and tied them with the ribbon. "But about the Russians?"

"Yeah. Well, after reading the papers, I think it's a matter of scale. And I didn't have any way to know what they would do."

"I should have seen what would happen with them, given my interaction with the major."

"Right now, I'm concentrating on Setehnekhet. I'll get onto the Temple of Djehuty tomorrow and we'll see what happens with the United States Embassy. After we get that bastard taken care of, we can worry about the Russians and NATO and the war crimes. So, what are you going to do?"

"Go to the restaurant to salvage what's left. I have an idea that I can use the restaurant to encourage the hekasepat. Long story, won't bother you with it right now."

"OK. Call me? After a shower. And new clothes."

I nodded, and my spirit-god and I left her to her diplomatic tasks.

I stood in front of the Wenmyt, having alighted from the rideshare. The driver had made me sit in the back seat once he got a whiff. He drove off like a rocket, tires squealing.

The restaurant had just opened for early dinner, and a few people headed in, avoiding me with annoyed looks. I expected somebody to tell me to get a job. Maybe I should. Everybody was telling me that these days. I walked around to the back entrance rather than annoy the patrons further.

"Hey, you can't come in—" The cook froze as his gaze rose from my disgusting clothes to my face. "Chef?"

At this, Khay turned around and rushed over. About to hug me, he caught a whiff and stopped cold. "Fucking Hut-Her, chef! What happened?"

"I'd like to say, Khay, that I've been on a two-week-long bender, but I haven't. How's things?"

The cooks gathered around. The doors to the dining room opened and Webkhet stuck her head in, radar clearly alert to the change in atmosphere. She said only one word: "Dinner."

The cooks scattered back to their stations and resumed their activities.

"It's going great, chef!" said Khay, grinning widely. "Webkhet and I—"

"Let's go out back, Khay, don't want to get in the way. We need to talk before dinner gets going, it's important."

Now, there's two things a celebrity chef, such as myself, never wants to hear: that a restaurant reviewer has eaten through a whole meal undetected, and that nobody has noticed that the chef is not in the kitchen. I explained this to Khay, to bring him up to speed.

"Sorry chef, very sorry, won't happen again."

"I know it won't, Khay, because I'm making you chef."

"I—what?"

"Tell me you're ready."

"I'm ready, chef. For what?"

"For anything, Khay. That's what being chef is all about."

"Why? Why now?"

"It would appear that the gods have elevated me above my chef's pay grade, so I can't run the kitchen anymore. I mean, smell me. Is this the boss you want in your kitchen? Hence, you."

Khay was silent while he absorbed this, then said, "OK, chef. Whatever you say. Gods. Um. Does Webkhet know about this? See, we've, kind of, that is, sort of...."

"Spit it out, Khay."

"We're getting married."

"Fuck me. I go away for a few days and the entire world goes crazy."

"It's—"

"No; just kidding. I'm happy for both of you. You will be a husband and wife team, running my restaurant together. Khay, if you're ready for marriage, you're ready to run the kitchen."

"OK, chef."

"And stop calling me chef."

"OK, chef." He grinned. "Are you gonna come in to work with us in that?" He pointed at my chest.

"I've got to get home and shower. I just got off the plane, why I'm wearing this and stinking. And I won't be coming back to work with you, as much as I want to."

"OK, chef."

"Khay, stop calling me chef. Get Webkhet out here."

He did. My business manager looked me up and down and said, "No hug, chef."

"Don't call me chef, Webkhet. I need a favor."

"Shoot, chef."

"I'll need the dining room tomorrow night. All of it."

Webkhet blanched but was game. "For what?"

"A dinner for the hekasepat."

"A..." Her mouth was open, but no sound emerged.

"I'll explain later, but right now I need you to round up a guest list of the most important citizens in Menmenet and invite them to the dinner. The haty'a and so on. It's a comp, I'll pay for everything out of the marketing budget, and if that's not enough, just send me the bill. You might drop a note to the papers, and invite that society columnist, might as well get some press. Make sure you mention that it's my party. I've got to go now, dinner's up, but I'll be back tomorrow dressed up in my formal dinner outfit, OK? I expect you all to treat me as a god."

"Of course, chef! The hekasepat...doesn't he have his own formal dining room? In the palace?"

"Yeah, but the palace is a little disorganized, I understand. Don't you read the papers? It's going to take hard work to get it back into shape. But it's important the hekasepat be out and about showing the face and palling around with me."

Webkhet gave me a knowing look. 'You're not coming back. As chef."

"No, Khay will explain. New job."

"How about the embassies?" she asked, already focused on the task at hand.

"Skip those. Remetjet only. White shendyt, it's formal-formal. Oh, and skip the high-priced wines, please. None of 'em will notice."

She gazed at me with a smile. "Welcome back, chef."

CHAPTER FIFTY-SEVEN
MacIntyre Loses a Battle

TWO DAYS LATER, MACINTYRE PACED back and forth behind the armored vehicles lining the little street next to the United States Embassy in Menmenet, limping and cursing every so often because of the still-painful wound in her leg.

Shes had convinced the hekasepat to declare John Smith, the American Consul General, persona non grata. MacIntyre wanted to be inside at the table helping him with his flight schedule out of the country. She wanted to be talking the American Ambassador into surrendering his surprise guest, the ex-hem-netjer-tepy of Mentju, to her tender mercies.

But she had to admit that Shes was right about her diplomatic skills. She'd have to work on those skills and on her impulsiveness when she got a little spare time. It could only help her new career.

What the hell was taking so long? She paced.

Shes's persuasion worked like magic on the hekasepat's compliance with their demands. She'd joked it was magic coming from his new spirit god. He'd said it more likely stemmed from a very nice formal dinner at his new restaurant, with the social elite of Menmenet celebrating the hekasepat's timely decision to nix the coup in the bud. He said it also had something to do with the hekasepat's recent acquaintance with the Parker-Shane papers.

MacIntyre paced back, stopped, and looked at the embassy gate for the hundredth time. The U. S. marines on guard stared stonily back at her. She saw some movement, and the Remetjy negotiator emerged. He had that odd look on his face that diplomats get when they've made a deal with some objectionable dictator that would save the world but would sorely compromise justice and truth. MacIntyre knew she was projecting again.

"Well?" asked MacIntyre.

"A bit public, isn't it, Tjespedjut MacIntosh?"

"MacIntyre. I'm not an apple. And I'm not a tjespedjut anymore."

"Courtesy title. Sorry." Courteous, maybe; not sorry.

"Just give me the deal."

"It's in the best interests of all concerned—"

"Do I have to pull a gun?"

The negotiator smiled, on-off, and sighed. "The Americans granted him asylum. They're refusing to surrender him to our custody or to extradite him. He and the Consul General fly back to Washington this afternoon, and there's nothing we can do about it."

MacIntyre wanted to stomp on her brown beret again, but she had decided after the last time that, like slamming hands on tables, the aftereffects were not useful. And she'd just had it cleaned. This was not an auspicious start to her new job, whatever it might be.

"So, that's it? We just let the son-of-a-bitch go?"

"I'm afraid so."

"What about the Russians?"

"Nobody cares."

"What?"

"Nobody cares about the Russians. That's our problem, they say."

"But they're the ones whose troops the Russians slaughtered."

"Most of the neutralized NATO troops were Lakota, and the Americans don't seem terribly worked up about it." The man's smooth tones implied that he wasn't terribly worked up about it either.

MacIntyre smiled grimly. "We'll have to see about that." She'd let go of her feelings about Setehnekhet's escaping her, but she would be damned if she'd let the Russians get away with murder. She'd talk with Shes about the Lakota and what they might think about it all. Especially once they had the Parker-Shane papers.

The Remetjy diplomat smiled politely, bowed, and walked away, formal white shendyt gleaming in the noon-day sun. She breathed deeply, calming her tangled emotions.

Later that day, the black United States Embassy limo with its Stars and Stripes fluttering above the fender eased out of the embassy gate. She locked eyes with

Setehnekhet as the car slid by her and the watching Remetjy troops. The tinted windows of the car could not obscure the smile of disdain on his face. The car went on its way to the Menmenet airport, leaving her with an itch she could not scratch.

CHAPTER FIFTY-EIGHT

MacIntyre and Shesmu Shift Careers

I'D SPENT TWO DAYS CLEANING up the shreds of my former life, getting my three restaurants set up to work without my involvement. I learned two things from the experience, one about restaurants and one about myself.

It turns out that, once you create a restaurant, hire good people, and train them to do what needs to be done, you can leave them to it. The key is having somebody in charge of the kitchen who knows how to make things move and somebody managing the entire operation who knows how to make customers happy.

Even after my experiences in the mountains, even after learning I was part Miwuk, I had this image of myself as a dynamic and innovative chef in the mold of the great French and Remetjy chefs of the past. Over the last two days, I learned that while I am very good at hiring the right people and creating a vision for them, I'm very bad at leaving them to it.

Sebek, Qenna, and Khay were those people: the chefs at the Neferti, the Per'ankh, and the Wenmyt. I called them together because I had to confront my conflicted feelings about my entire *career* as a chef, and I had to do it with them. My restaurants minted money, my chefs did a fine job with them. I wanted to cook, to experiment, to push the boundaries of cuisine. But my journey into the mountains had changed me. I had a spirit-god to deal with now, and he did not care a thing about food.

I poured each of the chefs a glass of 1989 Chateau Petrus from a bottle I'd brought up from the Per'ankh cellar. I wanted a serious atmosphere for this meeting. Petrus is not a celebratory wine like champagne; it's a wine for serious people doing serious thinking about serious work.

"See, Shes, it's just your vision now," said Sebek. "We do all the work." He swirled the Petrus, inhaled, then sipped.

"Vision and money," said Qenna, always the practical one. "But yes, we do all the work."

Khay, the newest member of this small band of brothers, just smiled and said, "Leave it to us, chef." He glanced at Qenna and deferred sipping his Petrus until he saw Qenna do it. Qenna, trained in France, had the most discipline of the three. But he was a touch rigid in his thinking sometimes, both qualities being hallmarks of his French training.

Every bone, ligament, and tendon in my body strained at this consensus. But I wasn't the same person anymore, I had changed since opening night at the Wenmyt. I taken on a spirit-god. I'd changed the very nature of who I was as a man. Had I matured, internalized the message that life was meant to be lived and so on? No—I'd found a father, taken on a spirit-god who was too insistent to ignore. I would no doubt mature in time, like a fine, young, deep-red wine constrained by a barrel and pounded into submission by time and oak tannins. Like the Petrus, in fact. And unlike the bottle I saw in front of me, I wasn't ready to drink yet.

Sebek asked, "Do you think you'll build out an empire of high-end restaurants?"

I grinned. Sebek, my best and oldest friend, knew his limitations. He was a chef, not an empire builder. Henutsenu was the empire builder.

I said, "I could, but I don't think my spirit-god would approve." I was putting this out there for the first time, to gauge their reaction. I sipped the Petrus and rolled it around in my mouth and waited. The complexity of the wine reflected the complexity of my feelings well.

Sebek was the first to react. "Spirit-god?" I could see him actually biting his tongue. Annoyed, Qenna said, "You've *finally* understood the gods." Qenna had always been serious and reserved. He took up his glass, toasted my newfound faith, and sipped. Khay, the new boy on the block, said nothing, but his eyes were alive and interested, and he quickly sipped his own Petrus.

I explained my adventures and my newfound belief in the gods in a few well-chosen words.

"Miwuk? You're Miwuk?" Sebek, no longer biting his tongue, was incredulous. "All these years we've known each other and just now you find out you're Miwuk?"

"Yeah, it's been an interesting couple of weeks, Sebek. And, Qenna, I don't know whether my spirit-god is Remetjy or Miwuk."

"It does not matter, Shesmu," replied Qenna, dark face serious. "Gods are gods. The essential thing is to realize you are not in control, the gods are."

"So," said Sebek, fighting back, "you're saying we should pray for success instead of working for it?"

"I'm saying that if you have faith in the gods, and you follow the path of Ma'at, you will have a better chance at succeeding in this world and the next," replied Qenna evenly. "Working is part of that, no?"

I had followed the path of Ma'at myself down the rabbit hole, and I thought this noble conclusion was overstated. But I didn't want to ruin the moment for Qenna.

I said, "At any rate, the deal I made with my spirit-god is to use my new knowledge of myself to bring people together. My god is most concerned about people at the continental level, not restaurant customers. I can't decide. I love cooking, running a restaurant, but I need to do something for the world beyond thrilling rich people's taste buds."

Sebek laughed and said, "That's what's keeping us going, love of work and love of money, Shes. Rich people's taste buds are all that's between us and homelessness." Qenna gave him a dark look and sipped his wine. Khay wisely said nothing.

"You're not helping, Sebek," I said.

"Shes—we can handle this. I'm not saying I'm delirious with joy that you need to move on, but we can do it. Right? Am I right?" Sebek looked at his fellow chefs.

Khay nodded, Qenna pursed his lips. Qenna said, "Without the gods, you would not have realized ma'at, you would not understand the path you must tread, Shes. The gods have redirected your heart, and you must follow that path now. You have no choice. Neither do we."

"Of course I have a choice," I responded with heat. "So do you, Qenna." Why was I even here in this room if I had no choice?

"Perhaps in terms of this life, we do; but not if you consider the Judgment of Ma'at. You must weigh your choice and think about the Duat as you do that.

This is a moral choice, not a practical one. I see no alternative for myself or the Per'ankh. Stay out of my kitchen."

Qenna's quiet voice filled my heart, the spirit-god reinforcing his sermon. I looked at the other two chefs. Neither looked convinced by Qenna's sentiments about Ma'at, but each brought his own ambition to bear and agreed with his choice: I should leave them to it and get on with whatever my spirit-god required of me. A hard thing to do, but I had to do it.

I raised my glass. "Well then, to the outstanding success of our kitchens!" We toasted with the last sips of Petrus.

As the last rich, thorny complexity scratched its way down my throat, my phone rang; it was MacIntyre, who was more complex than the Petrus. I'd called her the day before, and she'd suggested talking things out over dinner or something.

"Hi," I said.

"Hi yourself. I just watched Setehnekhet drive away to the airport, and I need serious companionship to get the taste out of my mouth."

"Your apartment?"

"I'm tired of my apartment, let's meet at your place. Um, hold on, call I have to take."

I held on, grimacing at the knowing smiles of my three subordinates.

"Shes?"

"Still here."

"We need to get to the Temple of Mentju to meet with Basa. Neb-Waset Basa, that is."

"Why 'we'?"

"He wants to talk to you, something to do with the Miwuks in the mountains."

"Right now?"

"2 p.m. I'll meet you in front at the steps." Her voice sounded a bit grim; considering her history with the place, I wasn't surprised.

MacIntyre waited impatiently for Shesmu at the base of the great flight of stairs that led to the Temple of Mentju. He wasn't late, she just wanted to get on with it. The place made her itch.

There had been something in Basa's voice on the phone that gave her hope for recourse to her utter failure to capture and imprison that son-of-a-bitch Setehnekhet. She very much wanted to find out what it was. Maybe invade

America, take Washington D. C., and burn down the White House, as the British did in 1814. On the other hand, Basa could have the same idea that Setehnekhet had had at the beginning of all this pain: to get rid of her as the American encumbrance she was. She needed to get her head clear, deal with Basa, then get on with whatever remained of her life.

Shesmu turned the corner at the end of the block, walking fast.

"It's great to get fresh air," he said, coming up to her and hugging her. "I miss the mountains."

"You can pretend you're hiking up a mountain here," said MacIntyre. They walked up the stairs, then whisked up to the fifth floor by elevator. This was the first time she'd visited the temple since leaving with a knife in her thigh. She limped along next to Shes, pointing out the big door to the office of the hem-netjer-tepy of Mentju.

"You going to be all right?" he said, looking at her grim face with concern.

"As long as you're there to keep me from falling over, yes. And I want to see if they've repaired that enormous statue I shot up," she said. She hoped that was enough of an answer, because she couldn't say whether she was going to be all right.

Neb-Waset Basa, the hem-netjer-tepy of Mentju, rose to greet the pair when the assistant showed them into his office. MacIntyre, limping forward to bow, noticed that they had indeed repaired the statue. Basa wore the ceremonial robes of the hem-netjer-tepy with more authority than had Setehnekhet. She could swear that Basa was at least a foot taller than she remembered him. She imagined the malevolent, onyx eyes of the statue of Mentju staring down at her, but on a second glance, determined they were just rocks.

"And Shesmu, the son of Akhen, Justified," said Basa. Akhen may have passed the test of Ma'at on his way through the Duat, but the gods had been overly lenient to justify him.

Shes bowed. "A great man, my lord. I hope to achieve half as much as he." MacIntyre smiled to herself; the right half is what he meant.

"Excellent dinner the other night at your restaurant. Sit, sit," said the hem-netjer-tepy, indicating the chairs while taking a seat on the new couch. The furniture was new and functional, not the antique lion-paw chairs she'd seen before. MacIntyre looked up and found Basa and Shes looking at her.

She straightened up in her chair and hurriedly found something to ask. "A total remodel, my lord?"

"Yes, quite. The furniture I inherited was not practical. We will auction it off, I'm sure it will help our budget for years." His voice was dry. He did not mention the bill for the statue repair. MacIntyre imagined it would just about match her bill for leg repair.

The three people sat in silence for a minute, then Basa cleared his throat.

"I asked you here today for two different things, one personal and one at the hekasepat's request. Cheryl. We've worked on an operation together. Impressive results."

MacIntyre heard his sardonic tone with dismay. "Again, I apologize, Neb-Waset Basa. I should have—"

"No need, Cheryl. Shit happens. What's impressive is how well you *make* shit happen. You're superb at it."

"Erm…"

"Am I correct, Shesmu?"

"You can't expect me to answer that, my lord," responded Shes, with a diplomatic smile.

"No, I suppose not. So, let me explain. We have this department here. Security."

She perked up. "Yes, my lord. I am familiar with it."

"Yes; I've read the files."

"Oh. I apol—"

The hem-netjer-tepy held up a hand to stop her. "Despite this, you have the potential to do things the right way, the *Mentju* way, if you will. Now, I've spent a good deal of time with Idnu-er-Semetyu Djehutymes of the Menmenet Medjau, getting his impressions of you."

MacIntyre's heart sank. This reference stuff was the pits. At least it wasn't Sheritr'a, her last boss. Sheritr'a's only regret at losing her as an employee had been that it wasn't by her bloody demise.

Basa smoothly continued, "So, you make shit happen. Djehutymes was quite complimentary of your detective skills, Cheryl, quite complimentary. I will set aside the other aspects of your performance that he brought up." Basa smiled, to MacIntyre's mind a little grimly. "What I need is a load of shit removed from the Security department. I think you're the person to do it."

MacIntyre smiled for the first time since she'd entered the temple. It looked as though the job interview had taken a positive turn. "Happy to oblige, my lord. Do I use the dungeons in the basement or just have 'em all thrown down the front stairs to the street?"

"I don't care."

MacIntyre's smile grew broader. "Well then. Pay?"

"We'll defer that discussion. A trial, a minor task to complete. Then we can negotiate a *reasonable* compensation package as well as the set of duties suited to your personality and skill set. And you're initiated as a w'abet of Mentju?"

"Yes, my lord." She dredged in her pocket and came up with her bull pin.

Basa smiled, then looked more closely at the pin. "Ah. We've wondered where that went to. That's the hem-netjer-tepy's pin." He reached a finger out and touched Setehnekhet's old pin, a more ornate version of the pin still in MacIntyre's pocket.

MacIntyre mentally slapped herself for forgetting she'd had both pins in her pocket. "My lord, I apologize, it's a long story—"

"One that I do not care to hear." He smiled. "It may please you to know that my predecessor, for unaccountable reasons, did not keep files on his…personal interactions with his employees. You may keep that pin; as you can see, I have a new one. What I would like you to do is to go ahead with the qualifying steps for promotion to hem-netjer."

Nonplussed, she said, "I…don't know that I have oracular powers, my lord." She would not tell him she didn't believe in the gods. Her record on discerning the future wouldn't bear much scrutiny either. But she wanted the job. Hem-Netjer—wasn't Hori a hem-netjer? Karkin had said being a hem-netjer was an asset for a spy. Perhaps it would be an asset for hunting war criminals as well?

"Being a hem-netjer enhances your status in the Republic, Cheryl. I think you underestimate yourself. With the right training and initiation into the mysteries of Mentju, you would be an excellent hem-netjer. And, as a hem-netjer, you would wield considerable power in your position."

Status and craft wrapped up in one package. Why not? What was an oracle other than somebody who figured things out quickly? She could do that.

"Very well, my lord, I'll give it my best shot."

"Bigger pay package too, especially if you are Atchet-Netjer of Security."

"I'll be a hem-netjer within a month."

Basa smiled and nodded. "I guessed as much. Now, you, Shesmu."

"My lord?"

"The hekasepat found your savoir faire at the dinner you gave impressive. I did too."

"Thank you, my lord."

"Never ate anything quite like that during my stint in the Guard." Basa grimaced. "Acorns. You'd think the fucking Miwuks would develop a taste bud or two in a thousand years. Sorry, no offense."

Shes smiled again. "None taken, my lord. My people but not my cuisine."

Well, there. Basa was a man she knew she could work for.

"At any rate, the hekasepat wants you as his special envoy to the First Peoples, both internal and external. I have to say I was dubious about this, about the need for it. Until the papers."

"Ah. You've seen those."

"The hekasepat gave them to me to read, yes. I understand they come from the internal coffin of your father, from his tomb."

MacIntyre froze and wanted to scream at Shesmu: this is the imy-er-mesh'a in charge of executing tomb robbers in Ta Sekhet! She limited herself to clearing her throat.

Shesmu licked his lips. "Yes, my lord, sorry, my lord, there were gods involved."

"It came up in the anointing ceremony as I spoke with the god." Basa looked up at the dark statue above them. "He harbors no ill will toward you, Shesmu. In fact, he acknowledged a mistake or two in his association with…other gods. He feels that it may be time to take a softer approach, less use of the stick and more of the carrot, on the First Peoples."

"I am happy to hear that, Neb-Waset Basa. Truly. While I do not worship Mentju, I value his contribution to the pantheon."

Basa said, "Please go see the hekasepat and work out the position with him." He turned to his desk and took up a paper roll. "Here are the papers; I've had copies made for our archives." He handed the Parker-Shane papers to Shes.

"Very well, my lord, happy to be of service."

"Indeed. And Heh sends his regards. You come highly recommended." Basa paused. "Heh also asked me to tell you to check up on his daughter, she's on her way here. And he wants his truck back."

MacIntyre kept smiling, but she knew she'd have to cope with that too. High status might give you leverage over war criminals, but not over boyfriends, *Miwuk* boyfriends getting in touch with their newly discovered roots.

MacIntyre made a hurried set of decisions the next morning about her clothes. It was the first day of her new career as a manager. She gave a fleeting thought to body armor but decided on standard Remetjy business attire: white with gold edges and not too revealing, with working sandals. Just on the off chance that things might get ugly, she added her favorite accessory, the collapsible baton, in the small of her back under her jacket. She'd acquired a practical-looking metal support stick to help her walk. She smiled. Two sticks ought to do it, if somebody got obstreperous.

She'd made several calls the night before, to Basa for a Republican Guard squad to handle security and to Djehutymes for his participation. And to Karkin. She had to be at the temple early to set things up. She hurried from her apartment to the temple, walking rather than dealing with the traffic, even though she now had an atchet-netjer's parking space in the temple garage.

The requested Republican Guard squad showed up right after she got to the temple. She stationed them around the big office to ensure that no stressed employees misbehaved. MacIntyre sat at her new desk on the atchet-netjer's podium in the Security Department, scanning the personnel list she'd put together. The personnel themselves filtered in over the next half hour, gathering in small groups as they waited for the ax to fall. Imenka arrived at 8:45, dressed immaculately and bearing a self-satisfied expression on his face. MacIntyre got up and met him before he could sit down.

"Imenka, I'm so happy to see you again. Let's talk. Don't worry, you're safe from serious bodily harm." She smiled as she hefted her metal support stick.

He smiled. "Anything that happens to me, happens to you, 'Atchet-Netjer.'" He's thinking blackmail, he's thinking he's the power behind the throne now because he knows too much. She smiled.

"Let's talk in the conference room." She led him over and went in.

Idnu Djehutymes, sitting at the conference table, looked up.

"This is the traitor?" he asked.

"Imenka, yes."

"And who might you be?" asked Imenka.

"Idnu Djehutymes, Menmenet medjau. You're under arrest." The Idnu flipped his credentials at the traitor.

"For what, might I ask?" The smooth security man sat in a chair opposite the Idnu.

Djehutymes pushed across MacIntyre's picture of the very dead Hori, throat cut, in the chair, blood all over the place. The call to Karkin was to ask him to deliver Hori's frozen body to the Menmenet morgue at the Temple of Sekhmet-Hut-Her for the pathologist to autopsy. He also delivered Hori's thumb drive with the complete documentation of the coup plans to Djehutymes.

The idnu said, "We have recovered this man's body and the physical evidence about his death collected by Atchet-Netjer MacIntyre at the time. Your confession will doubtless be useful in the trial. As will the intelligence he gave to Atchet-Netjer MacIntyre."

MacIntyre smiled sweetly. "And I have that confession recorded. Oh, and don't forget, Mes, my testimony about Imenka's covert meeting with the American Consul General John Smith, a dangerous spy." She sat down next to Djehutymes. "We're combing the records now for evidence of links with the Americans."

"You won't find anything; there is nothing to find," said Imenka.

Djehutymes smiled. "I wouldn't rely on secret channels. The Temple of Imen-R'a tells me they have an interesting set of software tools for tracking things like that. Who knew? The temple often does not share information that they ought to share. That may change, now. I'm sure much of that material will interest the Sepat Prosecution Service."

Djehutymes arose and signaled to two uniformed medjau sitting in the back of the room. "Cuff him." He then assisted by helping to drag Imenka out of the chair as he resisted.

"You're going to regret this, bitch!" Imenka shouted. "There are things you don't know, hidden people who will make sure you're dead. They'll get you when you least expect it! And they're not Americans."

MacIntyre walked over and opened the conference room door. "Time to leave, asshole. Hey, Mes—add threatening a sepat officer performing her duties to the charges," said MacIntyre. "And resisting arrest. Can you club him a bit just for that? I'd do it but I've got more important things to do."

They took Imenka out through the silent groups of security officers, a sea of blank faces watching the medjau march Imenka out of the office.

MacIntyre got the list from her desk. She walked up and down the desks, tagged various people and had them escorted out by the Guard soldiers. About half the employees remained. Was there time for team building? Did she know anything about team building? No, and no. Better just do it.

"Listen up, people," said MacIntyre, speaking from the podium in her loudest voice. "Things are changing here, and you'll need to face up to it or get out. You can all take the rest of the day off to think about it. Department meeting, all hands, 9 a.m. tomorrow." She paused, then said, "Meryr'a, conference room, now." The gangly youth disconsolately walked to the conference room, where MacIntyre joined him.

"Thanks, Meryr'a, for letting me in; and thank your father for me," she said.

"I guess that was the first time I've been useful."

She grinned. "True. I can't keep you on here, Meryr'a, you're too damn dumb for security work."

He hung his head.

"But I can get you a nice restaurant job."

He looked up at her with surprise. "Restaurant? Cooking?"

"Well. More like dishwashing, but you can work your way up. What do you think?"

"I like to cook."

"Well, then." She punched Sebek's number into her phone. "Hey, Sebek. I've got a boy here who needs a job, entry level. Can you use him? It's that, or he starves to death, and it's my fault." She listened to his hurried acquiescence and said, "Great! I'll send him over."

She explained to Meryr'a about the Neferti and Sebek and Henutsenu and Shesmu. She sent him off with instructions to go to the back door and ask for Henutsenu, the manager. "I'm sure you'll be happier there than sitting here pushing around two-year-old garbage paper," she said, as she showed him the door. "At least they have fresh garbage." She called Henutsenu and explained what was coming. Henutsenu said she'd watch over the boy. It might work out.

"A little more ma'at in the world," said MacIntyre out loud to the empty room. She checked over her list once more to make sure she'd fired everybody who deserved it, crossing out Meryr'a's name. She sat alone in the big office for the rest of the day and into the evening and worked on proposals for what to do about the Russian war criminals.

CHAPTER FIFTY-NINE

Shesmu Has Trouble at Home

I TOOK THE AFTERNOON OFF and took my Remetjy acacia bow, a childhood gift from my father, to the archery range at the Didiresy Open Space. My spirit-god helped me with my woefully out-of-practice archery skills and was happy to do it.

In the early evening I headed home up Dju-Keta, the hill in the northeast corner of Menmenet. A warren of steep and twisty streets took me to my street, a narrow affair with blank-walled houses, a classic Remetjy neighborhood, secretive and circumscribed by hidden lives, silent.

But tonight was different. The action focused on a house across the street from mine, medjau coming and going from the open front door. Tonight, blue lights flashed, and the street was full of medjau cars and officers milling around like angry ants from a disturbed anthill. One ant in uniform stopped my car with a hand.

"Residents only, sir," he said through the window.

"That's my house there," I replied, pointing. He turned his head.

"Idnu! Here's the guy you were looking for!"

A man standing near one car turned. It was Djehutymes, MacIntyre's old boss. I pulled over and parked.

Djehutymes came over and said, "Shesmu. We looked for you at your house, no one there."

"Just getting back from a long day. What's going on?"

"Murder." This was not a surprise, since Djehutymes was on the homicide squad.

I asked with trepidation, "Anyone I know?"

"Let's find out, why don't we." He stared at me longer than necessary, then turned and walked. I followed him to the house across from mine. A man lay flat on his back in the hallway, his head a bloody mess from a gunshot wound to the forehead. Two medjau in protective suits examined the body.

"Do you know this man?" asked Djehutymes.

"He's my neighbor who lives alone in this house. I've seen him, but I didn't know him well. Robbery?"

Djehutymes stared hard at me again. He said, "No." He pointed up the stairs, then followed me up. The houses in this neighborhood had roof decks in the old Remetjy style. Great views of the bay and its islands.

Today, I had eyes only for the second body, lying sprawled out near the front parapet of the house. Black clothes with black gloves and a black balaclava mask over his head. The mask appeared to be wet. On closer inspection, this body too had a massive head wound. There was a rifle with a scope and a noise suppressor several feet from the body. Medjau in protective clothing were closing up cases.

"You done?" asked Djehutymes.

"Yep, all done, Idnu. He's still warm, dead only an hour or two. Same as the guy downstairs. Bullet came from below, went through the eye, and exited at the top of the skull in the back, 9mm." He held up a small plastic bag with a misshapen hunk of metal. "Found this over by the parapet on the other side, spent."

Djehutymes leaned down and pulled up the man's mask. The face was European, what was left of it. One very dead blue eye, half closed, next to a hole where the bullet had entered. My stomach twisted.

"Know him?"

I shook my head. "Nope. Was that rifle the murder weapon?"

Djehutymes stared at me some more, saying nothing, then walked over to the parapet near where the body lay. He looked over. I joined him. We looked straight down at my front door. The Coyote stirred in my heart.

Djehutymes said, "We need to talk, Shesmu."

"A cup of tea?" I waved a hand at my kitchen counter. I've always found a cup of Remetjy tea good at settling my nerves.

"No, thanks." Djehutymes pulled a chair out from my kitchen table and sat.

"I'll make one for myself, I'm beat."

Without acknowledging my subtle try at friendly conversation, Djehutymes launched into his primary concern. "Why do you suppose somebody shot a foreign assassin in a place overlooking your house, Shesmu?"

I put the tea things together, boiling water, measuring Remetjy tea, heating my cup.

"You're not saying anything, Shesmu."

"I'm thinking. Who called the medjau?"

"Anonymous caller, didn't give a name. Foreign."

"Um. You know—"

"I know everything." He sat, hands folded in front of him on the table, staring at me.

"I have a friend who does know everything," I said. Karkin had sources far exceeding anything the Menmenet medjau could command. "I'd say some players in this game have decided I'm a liability." And I needed to do something about that; I just wasn't sure what.

Djehutymes smiled. His face wasn't used to it. "Shesmu, you've been a liability of one kind or another since I've known you. What do you think makes you a liability someone wants to dispose of with a bullet?"

"Sir!" A voice from the hall outside the kitchen came.

"What is it?"

"I found a gun, sir!"

"Bring it here, watch for fingerprints."

A medja came into the kitchen, wearing evidence gloves. He carried my souvenir of Ta Sekhet: the Russian VSS Vintorez sniper rifle I had acquired from the late Major Suvorova. I'd last seen it in Kikyapapli; I'd left it in Heh's house. I deduced Karkin; he must have brought the rifle back with him and put it in my garage.

"What the hell is that?" asked Djehutymes, rising from the table.

I sipped my tea. "A sniper rifle."

"What do you use it for? Shooting rabbits or whatever it is you serve in your fancy restaurants?"

I ignored his sarcasm. "No, I used it for protection, as you must be aware, since you know everything. Surplus from a Russian Spetsnaz team wiped out in Ta Sekhet by the NATO troops. MacIntyre has one too. Souvenirs of our vacation in the mountains. I left that in Kikyapapli; Karkin must have brought it down to Menmenet for me and put it in my garage without my knowing."

He closed his eyes. "Great. A souvenir. Karkin. Well. That simplifies things, doesn't it?" He opened his eyes to glare at me. He shifted the glare to the medja with the rifle. "Ammunition?"

The medja holding the gun said, "Yes, sir. Lots. Right with the gun. Right on a shelf in the garage. Sir, this uses the same caliber bullet that took out the guy on the roof. The gun he had was an American MK-17 sniper rifle. It shoots a 7.62, this shoots a 9 millimeter round. The neighbor was shot with a 7.62, the sniper with a 9. Not fired recently but he could have cleaned it."

Djehutymes looked at the rifle, then at the floor, then at me. "Would you care to explain, Shesmu? Where were you two hours ago?"

"Nothing to explain." I took another sip of tea. "I was out shooting at the archery range."

"Anybody you know see you?"

"Nobody else there today."

Djehutymes stared at me with a moody expression. "Shesmu, I've wanted to put you in jail for as long as I've known you. I've got you cold for possession of an illegal firearm and criminal storage of a firearm. I have every reason to suspect you of murder. Tell me why I shouldn't arrest you."

"I didn't do it." Even I heard the clichéd response of the guilty murderer in that attempt to justify myself.

"Cuff him." Djehutymes recited the ritual Warnings of Ma'at.

That ruined the rest of my evening. The night and next morning, too. They didn't even let me finish my tea.

"Rise and shine, my man! There's a gorgeous woman who wants to talk to you."

I opened my eyes to the same jail cell I'd closed them on last night. The cot I occupied was a board hanging from the wall; the blanket was indescribable. I had gotten two hours of sleep. I sat up and rubbed my eyes.

The jailer took me to an interview room. The chair there was as uncomfortable as the bed had been. As my brain slowly awoke, I remembered why I was there. Murder.

The door opened, and there was MacIntyre with a sunny smile.

"I always thought I'd be coming here to see you one of these days, Shes," she said.

"They—"

"I know everything."

"People keep saying that to me, and it isn't so!"

"I'm not 'people,' am I?"

As there was no suitable answer to that question, I didn't answer. I think my sense of humor had gone somewhere else when they'd locked the cell door on me the night before.

MacIntyre sat in the chair across the small table from me and folded her hands on the table.

"The good news is that I'm getting you out of here."

"Oh, good. How?"

"Mes isn't charging you with murder, and I got a hem-netjer of Ma'at to release you on your own recognizance on the firearms charges. They confiscated the rifle, though, for now. You'll get it back, I'll see to that."

"Thanks for that. Why not murder?"

"Not enough evidence. The bullet was too beat up for any ballistics tests. There was nothing to show your rifle had been fired in a long time. The gunpowder residue test they did on you last night came back negative. I pointed out to Mes that he had no evidence to hold you. Also, I vouched for you, Basa vouched for you, and even the hekasepat vouched for you. The consensus is that you wouldn't hurt a fly."

"That's all they know. What else have you found out?"

"The dead man was American. He had a special-issue MK-17 sniper rifle that's only used by United States Special Operations troops, and his clothes were all American. Mes asked me if I'd killed the guy." She rolled her eyes. "As if I'd kill somebody just because he wanted to kill you! Not worth the eternal damnation of Ma'at, take my word." I'd call her grin impish if my mood had been better.

"I'm so happy that you have your priorities straight. Now can we get out of here? I have bedbugs."

"You can't get bedbugs in this jail, they douse it in gallons of disinfectant and poison every morning."

"I'm being allegorical. I have things to do."

"You're being crabby, which I suppose is allegorical too. Unless…"

"No," I said, "No crabs either. Can we leave?"

"Let me ask." She got up, knocked on the door, and had a brief conversation with somebody outside.

She stuck her head back in and said, "Let's go home."

"Cheryl, hold up a minute. I'm not sure I should go home. That's where somebody tried to kill me. I can see where the Americans might try again. Maybe I ought to just stay here, bedbugs and all."

"I've taken measures. My security people are checking out the neighborhood. If you want real safety, I can transfer you to the dungeons in the basement of the Temple of Mentju—absolutely safe there, at least from Americans."

A girlfriend with security people and dungeons; what more could a man want?

"Let's go home," I said.

An hour later, after getting the all-clear from her people, MacIntyre and I arrived at my house in her little red car. Crime-scene tape cordoned off my neighbor's house. MacIntyre's people, in the guise of a large, bald man with a permanent squint of suspicion, got out of a large, black car parked across my driveway.

"Ma'am, two guys just showed up and walked into Shesmu's house. A local and a European. I stopped them, and the local said to tell you it was Karkin. He had a key."

"Yeah," said MacIntyre. "I'm sure he's not here to finish the job on Shesmu."

"I guess, ma'am. The other guy looked dangerous. Big, and the wrong kind of haircut, if you know what I mean."

"I'll risk it. I have a stick." She gave him a smile, hefting her metal stick.

The security man shrugged and said, "Your funeral, ma'am!"

"His," she replied, pointing at me.

We found Karkin sitting at my kitchen table with a disheveled and bearded Vasha, the lone Spetsnaz survivor of my adventures in Ta Sekhet.

"Prastiti, Shesmu!" The Russian got up and hugged me.

"Don't I get a hug?" asked MacIntyre.

"Nyet, too scary." He hugged her despite his trepidation. He stood back and looked at her. "You got problem with leg?"

"Fuck me," said MacIntyre, wincing.

"Nyet, too scary."

Karkin said, "I brought Vasha along to tell you things."

Vasha said, "Da, I want to defect."

"Defect?" I asked blankly.

"Da," said Vasha. "Defect. Is right word, nyet? I start my new career now."

"You don't defect to do that, you immigrate."

"I defect. I know too much."

"Really," I said. Seemed unlikely to me.

"They want to kill you, Shesmu." Vasha had a very earnest look on his face.

"I surmised that, Vasha. Who, exactly?"

"Amerikantsi."

"Americans. So, the guy across the street?"

"Americanski Ranger, pro assassin. He had MK-17 with sniper scope."

"And how do you know this?"

"I kill him for you."

"Ah." I pulled a chair up to my table and sat down, folding my hands.

Vasha continued, "That's why I defect. And other things."

"Ah," said MacIntyre, pulling up another chair.

Finding these responses too mild, Vasha shouted, "Fuck your mother! They try to kill you, Shesmu! I defect now?"

"Quiet, you'll disturb the neighbors." The ones that were still alive.

Exasperated, Vasha pressed his lips together. Karkin sat like a stone; nothing unusual there.

"Where's the gun you used?" asked MacIntyre.

"Bottom of the bay. Don't need anymore, because I defect."

I asked, "Vasha, why did this American gentlemen have it in for me?"

"No clue, I see him kill neighbor and figure it not be good thing to allow keep doing that."

MacIntyre cut in. "So, you just happened by?"

"Waiting for Shesmu. He said he help me out when I come to Menmenet to be with sister. So I come to defect."

"With your sniper rifle?" I asked.

"Da, no big deal. Lucky, too, huh?"

"Yeah. Sure. Lucky."

"Took rifle down to bay, tossed it, then back to wait for you, Shesmu. You help me defect. Her too. Cold fucking night. Can I defect now?"

Karkin spoke up. "Heard about the security check. Saw him, got him to come here." I wondered how Karkin had "got" Vasha to come, but he was a wonder for getting things done. I'd take up the subject of how he got a key to my house, too. And a talk about putting illegal guns in my garage.

MacIntyre looked thoughtful. "You heard about the security check. Hmm. Never mind; you know everything. I get it." MacIntyre's eyes narrowed. I suspected she was thinking about security leaks and international spies. I'd always enjoyed her stories of catching murderers; the spy stories were something to look forward to, if her new focus on security didn't shut her up entirely. Unlikely.

The Americans had an interest in getting rid of me because of what I'd discovered. Or it could have been the New York Times restaurant critic, angry at a dreadful dinner at the Wenmyt. Sure.

I said, "I suspect the Americans think that by doing away with me they can prevent my publication of the Parker-Shane papers. I have to get that done, fast. Once it's out, they'll back off—at least I hope they will. Maybe Karkin can help me with a publishing deal."

Karkin scratched his chin. Which I took to mean he'd happily take me on as a client.

MacIntyre groaned. "Now you're off saving the world from America. We were just getting back to normal! I haven't even slept over."

"What about my defect?" asked Vasha, feeling left out.

"I can help with that," said MacIntyre. "You're under arrest."

Vasha got to his feet. "Comrades tell me you got new job. Arresting defectors?"

"Among other, less exciting tasks, yes." She tapped the bull pin over her breast. "Warrant of Mentju. Let's get you to a nice safe house somewhere. Unless you'd prefer the dungeons at the Temple of Mentju?"

"I like sound of 'safe,' try that. Bomba!" Vasha grinned, teeth bright in the black beard.

At our bemused expressions, Karkin said, "Means 'amazing.'"

"Da. I defect now?" Vasha's sense of urgency at the very least equaled my own.

CHAPTER SIXTY

Shesmu Confronts Seteh One Last Time

MACINTYRE HADN'T COME PREPARED TO arrest people, so she told Vasha that she'd kill him with a stick if he tried to escape. He smiled. To be frank, he did not understand what he was dealing with. I think it was only him not wanting to escape that kept him alive. She led him out to her little red car; unofficial, but it would get the job done.

"Need to do some stuff," said Karkin, walking outside with us. I expected him to blink out like a god and appear somewhere useful in the world. But he just walked down the street and got into his clunker car and drove off.

As MacIntyre stuffed the largish Vasha into her little red car, a pickup truck drove up. The door opened, and out popped Tahefnu. She reached into the back of the truck and extracted a pack and a cloth bag full of something.

"Hi, Shesmu! I'm here!"

"I see that," I said.

"Take my bag?"

"Um."

"What the hell are you doing here?" asked MacIntyre, leaving Vasha in her little red car to deal with this latest emergency. Her body language suggested ramped-up energy levels.

"I want to defect!" shouted Vasha.

"Shut the fuck up!" yelled MacIntyre over her shoulder. The neighbors would surely have words with me; at least, the ones that were still alive.

Tahefnu looked from me to MacIntyre and back.

"You said I could come anytime, Shesmu!"

"Some times are better than others, Tahefnu," I responded. "But OK. Is that Heh's truck? He wants it back. Do you need a place to stay?" I reached for her bag.

MacIntyre strode past me and took Tahefnu's bag out of my hand. "You're staying at my place, Tahefnu. Put this stuff back in the truck. Let's go, I'm in a hurry." She handed the bag back to Tahefnu.

Vasha stepped over the side of MacIntyre's convertible without opening the door and walked over to the truck and hugged Tahefnu. Old acquaintances. He said, "I ride with her? She not scary like you, Cheryl."

"Vasha. Get in my car now, or I'll beat you to death. You're under arrest." She grabbed his arm and pulled him over to her car.

"But Cheryl," said the big Russian, looking over his shoulder, "she's—"

"Get in the car!"

I intervened. "I'd better ride with Tahefnu, in case she falls behind." Both Tahefnu and MacIntyre looked at me scornfully. I closed my front door and got into the truck. It was safer than standing in the street, where I was vulnerable to attack from two sides.

MacIntyre's adrenaline kicked in, and she took command. "Fucking circus. It's complicated, but we can do this. I'll take Vasha to the temple and hand him off to my folks there to get him into a safe house. We'll go on to my place and get Tahefnu settled, then we'll come back here. We can get some 'quality' time in before you leave for wherever you need to go, Shes." She turned to Tahefnu. "You follow me in your truck. I'll go slow."

MacIntyre's slow is not your average driver's, particularly once her action level elevates to high. Tahefnu kept up, barely. Her driving skills were fine, but she didn't appear to know basic urban things like what the little lines in the middle of the road were for. Or that other drivers weren't obliged to get out of her way.

MacIntyre stopped first at the Temple of Mentju to drop off Vasha. She parked in the hem-netjer-tepy's spot in front, and Tahefnu double-parked beside her car. MacIntyre and Vasha walked up the stairs to the temple, where MacIntyre would sort him with her security people. Five minutes later, a security guard emerged from a side door, did a double-take at us, and ambled over. He rapped on Tahefnu's window. She cranked it down with a hand crank.

"Sorry, ma'am, you can't park here."

"I'm waiting for someone."

The security guard shook his head. "Can't do it. The Hem-Netjer-Tepy—" His gaze fell on MacIntyre's little red car. "What the fuck is that?"

I leaned over. "It'll just be a minute, she's coming right back."

The guard walked around the red car, shaking his head. As he pulled out a radio from his pocket, MacIntyre came striding back down the stairs. The guard froze.

MacIntyre, seeing the guard blocking her path to the door of her car, smiled a tight, frosty little smile and motioned him away.

"Thanks for watching the car for me." She waved to the guard, and we all drove off.

MacIntyre led Tahefnu to her parking place in her apartment building's garage, then parked her own car on the street. We gathered at the front door of the apartment house. I handed Tahefnu her bag, which I'd taken from the back of the truck.

"My backpack! It's still in the truck," said Tahefnu.

MacIntyre said, "I'll get it. I need something from the garage, too." MacIntyre handed her two keys off her key ring. "Outer door, inner door. Apartment 36. Why don't you let yourself in and make yourself comfortable? Shes, could you give me a hand?"

Tahefnu took her bag and lugged it up the stairs to the apartment house door and entered. We walked back into the garage. MacIntyre lifted out the backpack.

"What do you need help with?" I asked.

"Life. Lookit. I know you and this woman share your brand new ethnicity, a bunch of intimate bonding experiences, and a mutual attraction. I understand. I get it. Stay away from her or I'll break both your legs." She smiled.

There was only one answer. I stepped over to her, wrapped my arms around her, and kissed her.

MacIntyre rated this response as acceptable. After a while, she broke the embrace and said, "More like it. Come on." I took Tahefnu's backpack, and we walked up the stairs to her apartment. The door stood open.

I walked into the living room. Tahefnu lay in a heap on the floor, her bag's contents scattered around her.

"Cheryl!" I exclaimed, dropping the backpack. MacIntyre was right behind me and saw the Miwuk woman over my shoulder.

"Don't touch her, Shes."

"Now's not the time—"

"No, I mean it, I've seen a case like this before, it's a nerve agent. You touch her, you'll be just like her. And don't touch the front door, that's likely where they put the stuff." She pushed buttons on her phone.

"Will the medjau—"

"I'm calling my people, they'll know how to cope with this."

She spoke with someone and told them her suspicions and said to bring a hazmat team.

She disconnected and turned to me. "He says we should get out and stay out until the team says it's OK. Come on."

"But we can't just leave—" I turned again to Tahefnu, silent on the floor.

MacIntyre grabbed my arm, and I stumbled out of the apartment with her pulling me. We waited on the outside steps, and in two minutes a large van screeched to a stop in front of us. People in white suits and all-covering helmets jumped out of the back.

"Third floor back, door's open," said MacIntyre to the man in front. An ambulance pulled up behind the van and two paramedics in protective suits rushed in after the hazmat team. Ten minutes later they brought Tahefnu out on a stretcher. The lead paramedic told MacIntyre, "We injected atropine, but she's going to need a lot of medical attention. How secure does this need to be, Atchet-Netjer MacIntyre?"

"Security level 3. Take her to the Temple of Mentju infirmary and post guards. No names, no logging, no visitors until I get there. She doesn't exist. This wasn't meant for her, but I want her protected round the clock. I'll be there directly." The paramedics loaded poor Tahefnu into the ambulance and drove off with no siren.

A hazmat team member, a woman, emerged and said, "Definitely on the door, ma'am. It's going to take a few days to decontaminate everything. This fits the pattern of a Russian assassination, ma'am. I think you should take measures."

I looked at MacIntyre's grim face. A nerve agent on her door. A Russian assassination try. It looked very much as though the Russians did not want MacIntyre to last long in her new job.

"I'm damned if I'm going to spend any more time in a lousy safe house eating chips for dinner because of a Russian apparatchik afraid of a war crimes charge. Not going to happen. I've got a job to do," she complained.

I offered an alternative. "Stay at my place, it's only under assault by American snipers. The Russians like me. I'm breaking up NATO for them."

"Shesmu, my darling Miwuk," she murmured, stroking my cheek. "I think we're in this together for now. Neither of us can go home."

"If I can't go home, then I want to go help Tahefnu. Maybe there's something I can do. Even spiritually."

MacIntyre shook her head. "What a job. At least the pay is better."

I sat by Tahefnu's bedside, watching her small breasts rise and fall. She was comatose, tubes in her nose and arm and other places. A soft beeping from the surrounding instruments showed her heart was still working, and the doctor had assured me that her brain looked fine. We'd have to wait and see what damage there was. So I waited.

The infirmary at the Temple of Mentju, a secure facility, was very basic. The infirmarian had to bring in a desk chair from a nearby office for me. Glaring lights bounced off the bright white walls, making my head hurt.

The door opened, and Heh walked in, carrying a paper bag, followed by the Waashiw demomili. I rose to greet them.

"How did you find out?" I asked, embracing Heh, then bowing to the demomili. "How did you get in here?"

"Just knew. Got a ride on a motorcycle up to Da'owaga'a, flew here as quick as I could. Daughter's still got my truck, you know. The demomili here insisted on coming too. Then we snuck in, used a little magic and indirection."

The demomili said something in Waashiw. Heh smiled. "He says daughter is too important to everything to ignore."

He walked over to the bed and smoothed the back of his hand across his daughter's brow.

"She don't look too good."

"It's a nerve agent, probably Russian. Meant for MacIntyre. It knocks you down and kills you, but we got her treated in time to keep her alive. She's still in a coma. I'm sorry, Heh."

He turned to me and embraced me. "You're a good man, Shesmu. Would have made a great son-in-law." He looked at the demomili. "Better get to it."

"Get to what?" I asked.

"Healing ceremony. Why we're here. Why you're here."

I had thought myself done with shamanistic rituals. "Um. I don't think—"

"Shesmu, you have strong spiritual power. You're close to daughter, too, powerful bond there. She needs you." Heh hesitated, then continued. "You got a chance to square things up, too."

"Things?"

Heh looked uncomfortable. "You know, with Akhen and the Miwuks and all. I can't say more."

But I got it. This was an opportunity to atone for my father's betrayal of his people—my people—so many years ago. I owed Tahefnu all the help I could give, and I owed our people even more.

The temple infirmarian walked in and blanched. "Who the hell are all these people?"

"Father, friend," I said, pointing. "Patient." I again grasped Tahefnu's hand.

"Get them out of here."

"Nope. We're going to heal her with a shaman's ceremony."

"What the fuck! Get them out of my infirmary! I'll call the guards!"

"Call Atchet-Netjer MacIntyre."

He pursed his lips as though he'd bitten into a lemon and left the room. Soon MacIntyre came in with him, pretending to listen to his expostulations.

"What's up?" she asked, eying the demomili in particular. His wrinkles folded at her.

"Healing ceremony," I said. "You remember Heh and the demomili. We're going to fix her."

"Sure. A healing ceremony. Shamans. Why not? What a job." She turned to the infirmarian. "What's your name again?"

"Nakhy, ma'am."

"Well, Nakhy, you have the choice of learning some new medical techniques or taking a brief break while these gentlemen perform their medical ministrations."

"They're fucking shamans!"

"What can I say, when you're right, you're right. So—watch, or leave?"

"I'll stay with the patient, then. This is so wrong!"

MacIntyre turned back to me. "You got this? Because I'm right in the middle of explaining to Djehutymes about our defector and his preemptive killing and how it's a Security matter now and we can't let the medjau have him, and it's not going well. Also, Vasha has some interesting details about GRU agents he saw in his brief sojourn in Russkaya Amerika last week. Something about how they were setting up a trip to Menmenet to 'handle things.' So, I'm somewhat busy right now."

"I got it. But can you stay and help? Tahefnu could use the female support."

MacIntyre looked at the still form on the bed and smiled. "Sure, if the medical professionals here are amenable."

Heh grinned and nodded, then unpacked his paper bag, which held his ceremonial regalia and a small drum. He laid the regalia out on the bed, handed the drum to the demomili, and started taking off his pants. The infirmarian looked up at the ceiling in disgust. MacIntyre smiled.

The demomili said something. Heh looked up from his regalia.

"Got to get my friend here a chair. He says he's too old to dance around for hours."

I gave him mine. I kneeled next to the sickbed and resigned myself to what might come.

I stood on a trail in a dark wood, the leaves rustling in a light wind. I saw a large black bear on the trail with a small, red bird sitting on his shoulder. A coyote sat next to the bear on the trail, watching me.

"Who's the bird?" I asked the Bear.

"Red Crossbill. He's a solid spirit, ancient, loves pine nuts."

"And him? An uninvited guest?" The Coyote cocked his head and lolled his tongue but said nothing.

Bear said, "No cause to be like that, Shesmu. The Coyote is a useful god, just sometimes you need to be careful around him, you know?"

I stared at the Coyote. "So we're Miwuk now?"

"Always were, son," said the Coyote. I realized he was speaking Miwuk, and I understood him.

"Better get to it," said Bear, turning and heading up the trail. The Coyote trotted after him and I followed.

After a time, we came to a clearing in the forest. I stepped forward to enter the clearing.

"Watch it!" said Bear.

I looked down. At my feet was a hummingbird lying on the trail, its eyes closed. Red Crossbill flipped down and came to rest next to the little bird and nudged her with his crossed bill. Nothing.

I leaned down and scooped up the Hummingbird in both hands.

"You must carry her, son," said the Coyote. "We can't." He held up a paw.

"She don't look too good to me," said the Bear, peering at the little Hummingbird.

"We need to get to the cave," said the Coyote.

I looked around at the forest. "There's no cave," I said. Red Crossbill flew off, and the world turned dark.

I was standing in the dark. The Hummingbird was warm and soft but unmoving in my hands.

"Let me get the stick," said the Coyote from somewhere. A light appeared, coming around a bend and lighting up a tunnel. I looked down: a dirt floor. We were in a cave.

"This way," said the Bear from behind me. I looked back; Red Crossbill was sitting on Bear's shoulder again. The Coyote padded by me carrying Heh's walking stick in his mouth. The stick glowed like a torch.

Bear said, "Keep up, now, Shesmu. It's all about you and the Hummingbird, not us." The Coyote trotted. I lengthened my stride to keep up.

The tunnel opened out into an enormous cavern. There was a deep red glow in the middle. It looked like a magma pool, bubbling with red heat, but the temperature was cool. The light breeze still blew behind our backs.

Seteh, in his part-human form, sat on a rock next to the pool. His square ears stood erect over his odd animal's head as he stared at us.

"Lord Seteh," said the Coyote in greeting. The Bear rumbled, not quite a growl but sounding as though a growl might escape if he let it. Red Crossbill clicked his beak and chirped.

"I don't like birds," said Seteh. "And I don't like coyotes."

"No cause to hurt them, just because you don't like them," said the Bear in a deep voice.

"I don't like bears, either. You have no say here, fellow," said Seteh, his hands motionless on his thighs, palms down. His voice was dismissive.

"I do," said Coyote, mumbling through the stick. "And my son does."

"He abandoned his power, he has nothing."

The Coyote padded over to me and offered the stick.

"I can't hold it while I'm holding the Hummingbird," I said.

"Sure you can, son," mumbled the Coyote around the stick in his mouth. "If you're careful."

I eased the unmoving Hummingbird into my left hand. I reached for the stick.

"Don't do that!" thundered Seteh. "I will not permit it!"

"You have no say here, fellow," said Coyote, no longer mumbling as I grasped the stick in my right hand. It became a w'as scepter, a staff of dominion, and I planted the forked base in the earth beneath my feet. Its light entered me, filling me with strength, the strength I'd need to confront my enemy.

The light breeze strengthened on the back of my neck. I turned my head to look behind me. There was Ma'at, wings spread, feather erect over her head, her austere face expressionless. She nodded. A large bald eagle flew in past her and alighted on my shoulder, talons gripping ever so lightly.

"Sorry I'm late, Ma'at had to figure out how to get me here," said Bald Eagle. She had a pleasant voice and brilliant blue eyes. "Nice stick," she said, blinking at my w'as scepter.

Coyote said, "Bald eagle, excellent choice. Means a lot to me."

Bald Eagle fixed one blue eye on him. "Where I come from, bald eagles are power. Just right for this exploit."

I turned back to face Seteh, still seated on his rock. He glared at me.

"We need to talk," I said.

"Which part of you needs to talk?" asked Seteh.

"I am not made up of parts, I am a man." Where was I getting this stuff? Ma'at putting words in my mouth, I daresay. But it worked. Seteh wasn't tossing me into the fire pit or pulling a khepesh sword or calling in deity reinforcements.

Bear and Coyote closed in, Bear on my right, Coyote on my left. Red Cross-bill hovered above, wings beating in the wind. Bald Eagle tightened her grip on my shoulder. The flesh of Ma'at pressed against my back, her truth bracing me from behind.

I insisted, "You must heal this Hummingbird, Lord Seteh. You must undo the damage you have done. We can protect ourselves, she cannot. Your chaos, your isfet, cannot justify damage to the innocent."

"No one in the world is innocent, Shesmu," said Seteh, with a disdain I could feel in my bones. "No one. Living in the world takes your innocence from you."

"Let me put it another way." I raised the w'as scepter and thrust it at the sitting god. He moved his head out of the way of the crook at the top of the scepter.

"You have power, Shesmu, but you are not strong enough to wield it," grinned Seteh, the jackal-like mouth showing teeth around its lolling tongue.

"Not by myself. But I'm not by myself, am I?"

I stepped forward, and the Bear, Red Crossbill, Bald Eagle, and the Coyote moved with me. The winds of Ma'at howled past me toward the Lord of Isfet. I stepped nearer and nearer to the god, scepter held vertically in my right hand, Hummingbird in the other.

Bald Eagle rose and alighted on top of the scepter, gripping it with her talons, eyes fierce. She said, "We, too, have much to talk about, Lord Seteh!" The voice was no longer nice but harsh and guttural. "Now, with Mentju tamed, we can deal with one another directly instead of through Russian and NATO proxies."

Seteh growled, "I do not deal with underlings of any sort. I see your mistress behind you, but she is powerless to intervene."

"There you are mistaken, Lord of Isfet." The booming voice behind us flowed past as the wind howled even more fiercely. Ma'at's wings beat relentlessly, and the scepter in my hand grew warm and bright with its blinding internal light. "Your power is strong, but your resolution is weak, Lord Seteh. Let us see what we can do."

Bald Eagle looked at my companions with one yellow eye. "Are you gentlemen ready?" At their nods, the eagle expanded her wings and slowly rose from the scepter, an impressive sight. Red Crossbill joined the eagle, sharp bill snapping. Bear growled and trotted forward, and Coyote joined him, squealing as only coyotes can squeal.

The fight began with a rush. Bald Eagle flew right at Seteh's head. Red Crossbill crossed his bill on the god's right hand. Bear and Coyote rushed the god, Bear reaching for his thorax, Coyote snapping at his left leg. I advanced with my scepter in front of me, heat flowing from it toward the god of isfet.

Seteh tried to shake the crossbill off his hand, but the bird maintained his forceful grip. Bald Eagle's beak snapped at Seteh's neck from behind. Bear's arms closed around the god and shook him. Coyote's teeth chewed and snapped at the god's leg. With a roar, Seteh rose from his rock and twisted about, slapping at the spirits assailing him on all sides. I continued to advance, the heat of the scepter flowing toward him. Sweat dripped from the god in the heat of my scepter. I had not been aware that gods could sweat.

"Enough!" shouted the god.

"Do you yield yourself to me, Lord Seteh?" boomed Ma'at from behind me. "It will only get worse for you. Stop while you are still whole. Remember your nephew Wesir, and do not let his fate be yours, torn to pieces and scattered over the desert. Heal the bird, Lord of Isfet!"

Bald Eagle had made little progress on the god's neck, powerful as she was. She beat at his head with her wings, then grabbed his large, square ears with her talons. Her grip was fierce and twisting.

Lord Seteh had had enough. "Oh, very well. I yield this time, Lady. But the cycle of time will turn toward me again. Now call off your pests!"

The small bird in my hand awoke, shook herself, and jumped from my hand with a buzz. She flew at Seteh, making him duck, then shot off into the darkness of the cavern. Seteh laughed, then hurled a few choice oaths at Bald Eagle, who gave his ears an extra squeeze before she let go and flew away.

Coyote sat and panted, gazing at the departing eagle, and said, "That one's a keeper, son."

* * *

I rested my head on Tahefnu's hand, Seteh's laugh and curses echoing in my heart. The hand was upturned, the fingertips unmoving. I focused on a callous on the palm, possibly something she got from crushing acorns all her short life.

The demomili stopped his drumming, and Heh stood beside me, feathered headdress bristling. I felt hot in the little room. The hand moved. I raised my head; her eyes were open, blinking.

The infirmarian, shocked, ran out of the room. A little while later, the doctor stormed into the room, ready to assert his authority. But by that time Tahefnu was sitting up in bed, pale and shaking, no longer comatose. I held one hand, her father held the other. MacIntyre leaned against the wall by the door, tired but smiling.

The demomili sat in his chair, drum at his feet, his wrinkled, tattooed face grinning that foolish grin that older people get when things finally come right in the world.

CHAPTER SIXTY-ONE

MacIntyre Walks the Path of Ma'at

MacIntyre sat at her desk, surveying her new domain. Atchet-Netjer of Security at the Temple of Mentju. No more trudging around crime scenes looking at blood spatter patterns. No more enduring criticism from the higher ups over unconventional detective methods. All she had to worry about was GRU assassins, murderous defectors, and angry medjau. And political intrigue in the Palace of the Republic, of course. Nothing personal there. Now, personal—personal was a boyfriend who—

Shesmu walked into her department with a smile on his face. He crossed the room and came up to her desk on the little podium. She hadn't seen him since Tahefnu had left the infirmary with her father and the demomili to go back to Kikyapapli to recover. Her feelings were mixed; she liked the Miwuk woman for herself, but she was glad to see her influence on Shesmu removed to a long-distance relationship. Shesmu, invited for lunch, seemed happy enough, though he kept insisting on talking over the dream she'd had while dozing off in the infirmary. A dream about bears and coyotes that she was more than willing to forget.

The interoffice phone on her desk rang. They still used wired lines in the building. They told her it was something to do with secure communications and hacking. Nobody could tell her exactly. This worried her, since she was in charge of security. Work to do there.

"MacIntyre," she said into the phone.

"Atchet-Netjer MacIntyre, Huty R'amesse down in the Secure Interrogation Facility. Agents just delivered two GRU men apprehended trying to leave the country. They tested positive for the same nerve agent found on your apartment door. They're putting up a fuss claiming diplomatic immunity. In loud Russian."

"OK, I'll come down. Get the Russian boy up here."

She hung up the phone, her mood much improved. "Want to help me torture some GRU men?" she asked Shes. "They're down in the basement dungeons waiting for me."

"No, I don't approve of torture, even of Russians. I wasn't aware this temple had dungeons. Are they at least humane dungeons? Anyway, I'll be busy: Karkin called and wants me to approve a leak. I just came to tell you I can't do lunch today."

"More security breaches for me to worry over?"

He smiled. "No, on that website run out of Switzerland that specializes in leaked government documents, the Intelleaks site. Karkin has them excited by dangling the juicy bits from the plans. Especially the bits about the genocidal plans for the Plains Federation. Once they're out on the web, NATO will break apart for sure. Karkin's organization has some subterranean interest in the site, they use it to promote world peace through forced transparency. I'm off to Kitchigami, the capital of the Plains Federation, to start things moving with the Anishinaabeg."

"Good to know," mused MacIntyre, filing the leak trajectory away in her brain under a red label designated "SECURITY BREACHES" in large glyphs. Shes might not consider it a problem, but she certainly did. This brain-file was getting rather full, in fact. "The dungeons—they're not actually dungeons, you know, we call them the Secure Interrogation Facility, much nicer. I've had them repainted. Oh, did I tell you I have a new assistant to replace Imenka?"

She pointed to the door across the room. Vasha had entered, wearing new Remetjy business clothes that fit him very well and a sanctimonious look that did not. He walked up to the podium and looked up at them. He'd gotten a haircut and trim, too.

"Reporting for duty, ma'am," he said, saluting.

"We don't salute here, Vasha. I need your translation services downstairs, two GRU types. Ready for that?"

Vasha grinned. "Could be I even know these peoples. Da. And if so, I use electrical equipment?"

MacIntyre arose from her chair. "I fear, Vasha, that you are sadly behind the times." She smiled. "We Remetjy interrogators no longer use such crude implements. We just hit them with hard questions and storyboard them until they break."

She put an arm around Vasha's broad and well-clothed shoulders, turned him around, and pushed him toward the door.

"Trying him out to see whether he's a security risk. See you," she said to Shesmu.

Vasha looked back and waved. "Scary."

A week later, MacIntyre and Shesmu walked into the outer office of the hekasepat in the Palace of the Republic five minutes early for their appointment. MacIntyre noticed the admins looked like they wanted to hide under their desks when they saw her. More PTSD.

Shesmu had just returned from the capital of the Plains Federation and his meeting with the Federation's chief executive, the Ogimaa. The newspapers had been awash with reporting and analysis of the Intelleaks website revelations. Repercussions from the leaks cascaded like the huge waterfalls in Ta Sekhet, crashing and foaming and dissolving whatever stood in their path.

Hem-Netjer-Tepy Basa arrived on time—to the second—and strode past them as they rose, meeting the hekasepat at his office door. Basa had been training the hekasepat in military precision and exact timing, and it was working. MacIntyre and Shesmu followed Basa into the inner sanctum. Setehnekhet may have been an on-time guy, but Basa took it to a whole new level. Logistics and attention to detail, that's what it was all about.

Sebekemheb gestured them to the couch and chairs and sat in a chair with a high back and ornate, lion-pawed legs. A throne. Relaxed and jovial, he welcomed them to his office. He had no idea how close he'd come to handing his throne over to a grasping autocrat.

Basa said, "Atchet-Netjer MacIntyre has an update on the Russian GRU agents, Seb. Atchet-Netjer?"

MacIntyre smiled. "My people caught the two agents at the Menmenet airport just as they were boarding an Aeroflot plane for Novoarchangelsk, Seb. The Aeroflot people weren't happy, but we extracted them and took them to the Temple of Mentju for gentle interrogation. After two days of questioning and sleep deprivation, they broke and confessed to the nerve agent attack on my apartment that severely injured Shesmu's Miwuk friend. We've bound them over for trial. The Temple of Djehuty sent a stiff letter of protest to the Russkaya Amerika government, but they tell me they expect only denials." Of course, the trial would have to wait until the agents got some rest. Ma'at required defendants under the Rule of Ma'at to be responsive to questions during the testimonial phase of the trial, and they needed their beauty rest.

Basa said, "Djehuty has started proceedings in the International Criminal Court on the war crimes the Russians committed in Ta Sekhet. That will be harder for them to ignore, although that was the Russian Federation, not Russkaya Amerika. The folks in Novoarchangelsk still dance to Moskva's tune. NATO claimed they knew nothing about the force in Ta Sekhet, but once Shesmu's documents leaked, their credibility score went into negative numbers."

Shesmu said, "The Ogimaa wasn't thrilled to see me. By the time we'd finished, he'd clarified that he grasped the nuances of American thinking about First Peoples. He was most pissed off about the Lakota deaths in Ta Sekhet. He believes the Americans and Numunuu would have hit a stone wall if they'd moved on the genocide. I had a hard time convincing him that American and Numunuu interests acting together would have pushed his people up to the Arctic Circle as a refuge, but I finally did it. I mentioned nuclear weapons and Japan." He smiled. "Being part Miwuk makes it easier to convince people like the Ogimaa. It took little effort to persuade the Ogimaa that NATO was no longer workable. I checked in with the Temple of Djehuty, and they tell me most countries now realize that NATO is finished."

Basa said, "We got confirmation yesterday the Plains Federation, Canada, and Nunavut have formally withdrawn from the NATO alliance, leaving the Numunuu Empire and the United States. The Canadians and Russians proposed a set of sanctions at the U.N. to censure the United States and the Numunuu Empire, but it won't go anywhere. The Americans imposed financial sanctions on the Anishinaabeg and the other First Peoples countries because of their agreement to the Canadian proposal. The Ogimaa told me he's not that concerned about the sanctions, given the Federation supplies most of the oil to the United States."

The hekasepat had his own concerns. "The Americans put sanctions on us, too, Basa. This is going to hurt our exports to America a great deal, you know. Farm goods from the Central Valley. None of my farms will make a profit this year. We may have to let the crops rot in the fields."

MacIntyre and Shesmu stirred, but Basa with a look put them back in their seats with mouths closed.

"You realize, Seb," said Basa, "that if none of this had happened, your farm would be an internment camp. We'd be rotting there instead of your vegetables."

CHAPTER SIXTY-TWO

Shesmu Gets a Cooking Lesson

I heard a key turn in the front door. I smiled and continued chopping onions for dinner since the only people that had keys other than me were MacIntyre, various gods, and every spy in Menmenet. Roast duck, one of her favorite dishes, was nearly ready to come out of the oven. The onions were for an appetizer I'd invented involving a sauté of local greens with bits of Remetjy sausage.

Two arms reached around my middle and hugged.

"You feel like the goddess Ma'at when you do that," I said. I laid the knife on the chopping board and turned and kissed my visitor. No, not a spy. Not Ma'at, either.

MacIntyre, released, went to the counter and deposited a bottle of 15-year-old local Primitivo. This was a wonderfully dense and dark red wine that she'd learned to adore in the last couple of years under my tutelage. It was much smoother and more celebratory than the Petrus and far less expensive. She sat at my kitchen table, where I'd set up two place settings. Using her Harvard-acquired skills of opening wine bottles, she deftly unscrewed the cap and poured herself a glass.

"Want one?" she asked.

"Sure. It'll be perfect with the dinner tonight."

"What are you magicking up?"

"Acorn mush with sage and onions. I had this idea…." I kept talking, but the words disappeared somewhere in the air between me and MacIntyre.

She was silent, eyes on the wine. She swirled her glass, took a long, slow, sensual inward breath of the smooth aromas, sipped, tasted, swallowed, and put the glass on the table. She reached behind her and extracted her collapsible baton and put it beside the glass. I raised my eyebrows.

She asked, looking me in the eye, "Am I going to have to use this?" But she smiled when she said it.

I reached and took the baton and expanded it, balanced it in guard position. A nice stick. I said, "You know, I've had pretty good luck with sticks lately. You too." I collapsed the baton and put it back on the table. "Not an acorn in the house."

I opened the oven and tested the duck; perfect. I took it out and put in on a cutting board. The wonderful roasted aromas filled the room. I felt two arms encircle me again, and I turned into them for what turned into an extended, very romantic moment.

"What do you think," I said into her hair. "Marriage and kids? Are you ready for that?" In the back of my mind, I heard the distant howl of a coyote.

"I am ready for anything."

Glossary

Note that Renkemet forms the plural by adding the suffix "u" or "ut" to a male or female noun, respectively.

akhet	the horizon, out of and into which R'a rises and sets, symbolizing death and rebirth; a place of great magic
'Ammet	the Eater of Hearts, a goddess who devours the heart of a dead man when the heart, weighed against the feather of Ma'at, came up short
'ankhu djet	alive forever, a blessing
'Aapep	giant serpent god embodying the concept of isfet (chaos); Greek Apophis
Aset	powerful protective goddess; Greek Isis
Anishinaabeg	a First People's group inhabiting the northern plains of North America; also called Ojibwe and Algonquin
atch-netjer atchet-netjer	Superintendent for the god, a formal Temple staff rank for the supervisor for a department (male and female forms)
ba	the aspect of a person representing the soul or spiritual force
Bastet	powerful cat goddess
b'stra	quickly (Russian)
Da'owaga'a	Lake Tahoe
demomili	Waashiw, shaman
deben	unit of money, about 3 to the USD
Didiresy Open Space	a Menmenet city park in the south-central part of Menmenet; site of the city archery range and many other recreational opportunities

djar-netjer, djaret-netjer	adjutant to the god, a formal Temple staff rank, assistant to the hem-netjer-tepy of the Temple (male and female forms)
Djehuty	ibis-headed god of wisdom, husband of Ma'at ; patron god of scribes and accountants; Greek Thoth/Hermes
Dju-Keta	"The Wrinkled Hill", a hill in the northeast corner of Menmenet
druzya	friends (Russian)
Duat	the path leading to the judgment of Inpu and Ma'at in the underworld
dushki	duckies (familiar Russian)
Gewe	Waashiw, Coyote (god)
haty'a	mayor of a city
Heb-Tekh	The Festival of Drunkenness, a festival run by the Temple of Hut-Her celebrating R'a's getting Sekhmet to drunk to kill everything that moved in a revengeful frenzy. Everybody gets drunk on red beer symbolizing blood, then sleeps it off. The next day, the Temple of Hut-Her awakens everyone by playing drums. The Menmenet equivalent of Oktoberfest or Saint Patrick's Day.
Hekata'an	Ruler of the West, an epithet of the Hekasepat of the Republic
hekasepat, hekausepat	head of state (singular and plural forms)
hem-netjer, hemu-netjer	priest, prophet (singular and plural forms)
hem-netjer-tepy, hemet-netjer-tepy	high priest or priestess, the priest in charge of a temple (male and female forms)
heryhebu	lector-priest, judge
herypedjut	captain, military rank above idnu
hetep	an altar for making sacrifices or offerings to a god
Hut-Her	powerful fertility goddess, patron goddess of diplomats; Greek Hathor
huty-netjer, hutyt-netjer	sergeant-priest, a supervisor of w'abu (male and female forms)

huty-er-semetyu, hutyt-er-semetyu	detective-sergeant (male and female forms)
idnu	lieutenant, a military or police rank
Imen	the great god of Waset, the Hidden One; Greek Amun
Imen-R'a	the great syncretic sun god of the Remetjy Empire, its state god
imy-er-mesh'a	General, a military rank
Inpu	jackal god of the necropolis; Greek Anubis
isfet	chaos; imbalance or wrongness in the universe; opposed to ma'at
jireugi	a punch in Tae Kwon Do (Korean); pronounced jai-ryu-gai
K'ahshaaya	the indigenous people living on the border between Russkaya Amerika and the Ta'an-Imenty Republic, with branches on both sides of the border in Fort Ross and the city of K'ahshaaya
Kemet	an ancient country and empire in North Africa; Greek Egypt
khepesh	a curved sword; emblem of state power
Kitchigami	capital city of the Plains Federation; also the name of the adjoining lake in the middle of North America
Ma'at	goddess of justice and truth, sister of R'a, wife of Djehuty
ma'at	justice, truth, the right way
medja, medjat	police officer (male, female)
medjau	police, cops
Menmenet	capital of Ta'an-Imenty Republic, city on Menmenet Bay; the word itself means "cattle" or "earthquake"
Mennefer	The capital of the Remetjy Empire; Greek Memphis, in Egypt
Mentju	falcon-headed god of just war and military power; Greek Montu/Ares; also represented as a powerful bull
mexcalli	Aztec liquor made from the agave plant

Miwuk	a constellation of indigenous peoples in the Ta'an-Imenty Republic ranging from Coast to Valley to Mountain groups
molli	a range of sauces from the Aztec Republic, usually made from dried chile pepper puree and other signature ingredients like tomato and mimosa
Nebethut	powerful protective goddess, sister of Aset, wife of Seteh; Greek Nepthys
nesubit	the chosen or "throne" name of a political leader or pera'a
Numunuu	a First People's group inhabiting the south-central areas of North America; Spanish-influenced name "Comanche"; pronounced Nuh-muh-nuh-uh; main tribe of the Numunuu Empire
Ogimaa	the hereditary head of state of the Plains Federation and the Anishinaabeg
pera'a	emperor, "Pharaoh"
peyotl	an Aztec medicine, hallucinogenic, used in spiritual rituals; buttons from a cactus that grows in the Aztec Republic
prigotovitsya	get ready! (Russian)
privyet	hello (Russian)
R'a	the great sun god; Greek Re
Ramaytush	the indigenous people of Menmenet, part of the Ohlone or Costanoan group of indigenes
remetj	a man of Kemet
remetjet	a woman of Kemet; people of Kemet (collective noun)
remetjy	of or relating to Kemet
Renkemet	the language of Kemet
sehy, sehyt	counselor, attorney (male, female forms)
Sekhet-'Aru	Field of Reeds; paradise, where the justified dead enjoy their afterlife after passing the test of Inpu and Ma'at in the Duat
semety, semetyt, semetyu	detective (male, female, plural forms)

senet	an ancient board game of strategy
sepat	state; nation
Seteh	god of the desert and chaos (isfet); Greek Seth
shendyt	a linen wrapping around the waist; a belted kilt
Siksikawa	a First Peoples tribe, the most northern of the Plains Federation states; translates to Black-Foot
spaciba	thank you (Russian)
Ta'an-Imenty Republic	a republic on the west coast of North America; formerly part of the Empire of Kemet; capital Menmenet
tavarishch	comrade; Russian term for "mate"
tjespedjut	colonel or commander, a military rank above herypedjut
Tjesut	"The Heights," neighborhood in the north-central section of Menmenet, location of the Palace of the Republic and many palaces and mansions with magnificent views of Menmenet Bay
Tzatlee Tosh	Emerald Bay in Lake Tahoe
Waashiw	the indigenous people to the east of the Ta'an-Imenty Republic in their own country of Washeshu; the language of that people
Washeshu	the country bordering the Ta'an-Imenty Republic to the east, populated by the indigenous Waashiw people among others; capital Da'owaga'a
w'ab, w'abet, w'abu	a working priest (male, female, and plural forms)
we'muhu	Waashiw waterbaby
Wennefer Street	"Uncovering of Beauty," a street in Menmenet on Tjesut
werkhet	master status at Remetjy stick-fighting
Wesekhwat	"Broad Way,"the wide main street running along the Tjesut from Wennefer Street; location of the Palace of the Republic
yob tvayu mat'	fuck your mother (Russian), expletive expression

za-hekasepat	"son of the hekasepat", first in line to replace the hekasepat
za-r'a	Son of R'a, the "birth name" of a political leader or pera'a
zatknut'cya	put a sock in it (shut up) (Russian)

Wiki North America

North America is a continent entirely within the Northern Hemisphere and almost all within the Western Hemisphere; some also consider it to be a northern subcontinent of the Americas. It is bordered to the north by the Arctic Ocean, to the east by the Atlantic Ocean, to the west and south by the Pacific Ocean, and to the southeast by South America and the Caribbean Sea.

North America covers an area of about 24,709,000 square kilometers (9,540,000 square miles), about 16.5% of the earth's land area and about 4.8% of its total surface. North America is the third largest continent by area, following Asia and Africa, and the fourth by population after Asia, Africa, and Europe. In 2013, its population was estimated at nearly 350 million people in 25 independent states, or about 6.2% of the world's population, if nearby islands (most notably the Caribbean) are included.

North America was reached by its first human populations during the last glacial period, via crossing the Bering land bridge approximately 40,000 to 17,000 years ago. The so-called Paleo-Indian period is taken to have lasted until about 10,000 years ago (the beginning of the Archaic or Meso-Indian period). The Classic stage spans roughly the 6th to 13th centuries. The Pre-Meryimen era ended in 1453, with the first landing of Meryimen za-Djehutymes in the Caribbean and the beginning of the transatlantic migrations—the arrival of European and Remetjy settlers during the Age of Discovery and the Early Modern period. Colonization occurred by Britain, France, Kemet, and Russia, leading to the modern countries of the United States of America, Canada, the Ta'an-Imenty Republic, and Russkaya America (France was forced out of Quebec by Britain). The Consolidation period shortly after the Civil War in the United States resulted in the various indigenous peoples' countries, armed and encouraged by Kemet and Russia as a buffer against the Americans. The North American Treaty

Alliance (NATO) formed after World War II includes Canada, the United States, Nunavut, the Plains Federation, and the Numunuu Empire. Present-day cultural and ethnic patterns reflect interactions between Remetjy and European colonists, indigenous peoples, African slaves, and their descendants.

The countries of North America divide into 6 main regions:

- East: United States of America and Canada
- West: Ta'an-Imenty Republic, Washeshu, Modoc
- North: Russkaya America, the Inuvik Republic, and Nunavut
- South: Aztec Republic, Diné Bikéyah, Anasazi Confederation, the Numunuu Empire
- Central: Plains Federation
- Island: the various countries of the Caribbean

Owing to the diverse population and colonization of the Americas, North Americans speak a large variety of languages, and their cultures are extraordinarily heterogeneous.

Wiki Mentju

Mentju is the embodiment of the conquering vitality of the per-a'a. A solar deity, Mentju emerged as a state god in the reign of Tepya Mentjuhetep of Waset, circa 2055 BCE, the first per-a'a of the reunified Kemet after the first Time of Troubles. Mentju's primary temple is in the city of Iuny, and the city of Waset reveres him as well.

Role and characteristics

A very ancient god, Mentju was originally a manifestation of R'a, the sun god, and as such often appeared as the syncretic god Mentju-R'a. Tepya Mentjuhetep, being a warrior per-a'a, adopted this warrior god in his birth name, "Mentju is Content." Mentju attacked the enemies of Ma'at (that is, of the truth, of the cosmic order) while inspiring, at the same time, glorious warlike exploits.

Worship

Because of the association of raging bulls with strength and war, Mentju manifests as a white, black-snouted bull named Bakha: a living bull revered in Iuny. This special sacred bull has hundreds of servants and ceremonial rituals today in that city. During the reign of Userma'atr'a Setepenr'a R'amessu the Great, during the creation of the Great Empire of Kemet, the per-a'a venerated Mentju as his personal god, giving thanks for the victories in the many battles of his long reign and building a temple to him in the great temple complex of Ipetsut across the river from Waset. The Greeks worshipped Mentju as their god Ares and Mentju-R'a as Apollo, and the Romans worshipped him as their god Mars. As the Great Empire evolved into the modern Second Imenite Empire, the god Imen-R'a replaced Mentju as the state deity, relegating Mentju to the responsibilities of war and defense.

Iconography

Scribes and artists depict Mentju as a falcon- or bull-headed man with his head surmounted by the solar disk and two plumes: the falcon as a symbol of sky, the bull as a symbol of strength and war, the solar disk as a symbol of R'a. In artistic representations, he can also wield various weapons such as a curved khepesh sword, a spear, bow and arrows, or knives: such a military iconography was widespread in the Great Empire.

Wiki Seteh

Seteh is a major deity in the Remetjy pantheon. Originally the god of the desert and still worshipped in desert communities throughout the countries of the Second Empire, Seteh came to represent the forces of chaos, disruption, trickery, and confusion (isfet), often interpreted as wrong-doing and opposed to ma'at. As a solar deity, Seteh stands in the bow of the barque of R'a with a spear to repel 'Aapep, the cosmic serpent.

Role and characteristics

Seteh appeared with the first gods of prehistoric Kemet. As civilization emerged out of the desert, Remetjy venerated Seteh as they venerated the desert from which they came. Over the years, Seteh came and went as a major god as one pera'a or another venerated him as a source of strength and power.

The myth of the conflict of Heru, the tutelary deity of Kemet, and Seteh appears in many early tombs of the kings of Kemet. Embroidered over the years, it is the story of disputed kingship. Seteh fights, kills, and dismembers his brother Wesir. Aset, Wesir's sister and wife, then reassembles him and posthumously has his son, Heru. Heru then fights and defeats Seteh, losing the Eye of Heru in the process. Some texts have Heru retaliating by stealing Seteh's testicles. Wesir leaves the world to become Lord of Silence and the judge of the dead on their way to the afterlife. Heru became the symbol of the kingship of Kemet and the nation's tutelary deity.

Worship

The cult center for Seteh is the city of Nubet in Upper Egypt. During the First Imenite Empire, the capital Pi-Ramessesu became a cult center as well during the reign of Pera'a Menma'atr'a Setehy, a strong proponent of the god. Most modern Remetjy countries no longer worship Seteh, and the Temple of Seteh, even if it exists, no longer plays a role in government after suppression of the cult of Seteh by the Temple of Imen-R'a four centuries ago following the attempted assassination of pera'a Setepensetehakhenr'a Ramessesu by the priests of Seteh in Pi-Ramessesu.

Iconography

Scribes and artists depict Seteh as a man with the head of a mythical animal with a long, curved head; tall, square-shaped ears; and a long tail. At the time of the suppression of the cult, a decree specified a representation as a donkey with a knife in its head, but within two generations Seteh resumed his normal representation.

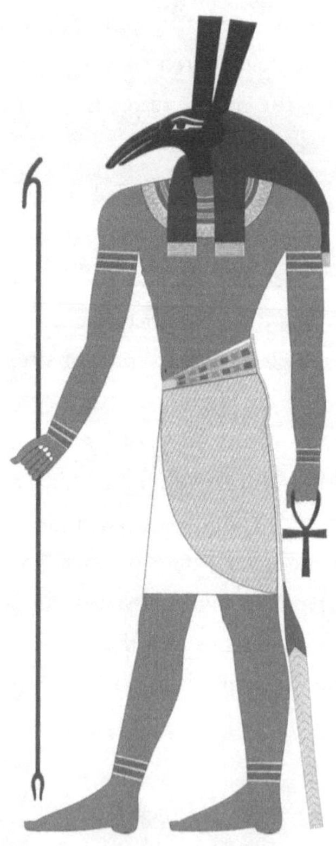

Wiki Ma'at

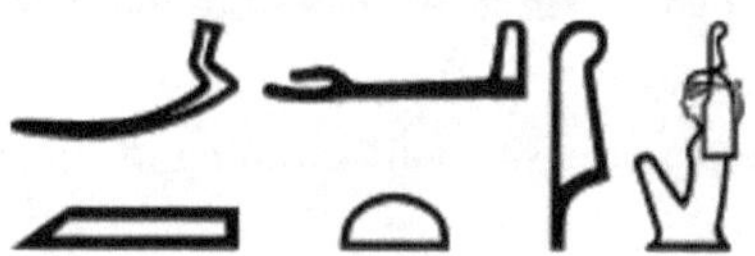

Ma'at is the embodiment of the concepts of truth, justice, and order. She is the daughter of R'a and thus the sister of the reigning pera'a, who has it as his duty to maintain order in the lands he rules.

Role and characteristics

Ma'at has two roles: as the daughter of R'a, she represents order in the universe and the continual fight against isfet, or chaos (personified by Seteh); and as the goddess of judgment, she works with Wesir, the lord of the Duat, to judge the dead on their path through the Duat in the ritual ceremony of the Weighing of the Heart. In the Book of Going Forth By Day, Ma'at weighs the heart of the dead person against the feather of ma'at; if the heart is lighter than the feather, the dead person becomes akh, justified, and passes into the Sekhet-'Aru, but if it is heavier, Ma'at feeds the dead person to 'Amut, the crocodile goddess called the Devourer of the Dead. Most who deal with the goddess on a regular basis say that she has very little sense of humor.

Worship

Ma'at had no temples until after the War of Liberation fought by Iahmes against the Hyksos invaders. As time went on and systems of justice developed as part of the Empire's bureaucratic division of labor, the Temple of Ma'at became the center of justice, containing the police services and the legal court system. Various warrants and other characteristics of formal legal relationships carry a reference to the goddess, such as the Force of Ma'at (arrest warrant) and the Warning of Ma'at (the ritual language that tells a criminal his rights in the courts). Many police are also w'abu (working priests) of Ma'at, and all judges are heryhebu (lector-priests) of Ma'at. The Hem-Netjer-Tepy of the Temple of Ma'at oversees the entire system of justice in a jurisdiction (similar to a district attorney or attorney general or chief justice in the American system of government). The Hem-Netjer-Tepy of Ma'at gives a small figure of the goddess to a ruler or top executive of government when they take the oath of office.

Iconography

Scribes and artists depict Ma'at as an anthropomorphic goddess wearing a feather and arm and leg bracelets. The goddess often has great wings along her arms; scholars disagree over the symbolic meaning of these wings but agree they imply an increased power in the fight for order.

Acknowledgements

I would like to express my unending love and gratitude to my sister, Colonel Grace Edinboro, retired, for her support and advice on the military aspects of the book. I absolve her of responsibility for the strategic and tactical mistakes my characters have made; they're on their own.

I want to thank my two writing groups—a mystery fiction group and a speculative fiction group—for their insightful and very useful comments on the book. The Mechanics' Institute of San Francisco supports both groups and provides an incredible library and environment for writers of all ages and stripes and I am very grateful for its continued existence as an oasis of calm in the middle of the chaotic city of Menmenet.

My wife and illustrator, Mary L. Swanson, gets my thanks both for her art and for her support for the long periods of taking up space in our home.

Thanks to Wikipedia for the following pages:

https://en.wikipedia.org/wiki/North_America

The illustrations of the gods come from the relevant Wikipedia pages and are all licensed:

Jeff Dahl, CC BY-SA 4.0 https://creativecommons.org/licenses/by-sa/4.0, via Wikimedia Commons

Thank You

Thanks for reading *The Bull of Mentju.*
If you liked the book, please leave a review on the web site through which you bought it.

Sign up to our mailing list for notifications and get a free ebook!

https://www.poesys.com